SCYPHOZOA

A NOVEL

TYLER GEIS

SLIDE OIL
PRESS

Slide Oil Press

Copyright © 2024 by Tyler Geis

"In a Bed of Wildflowers" copyright © 2024 by Tyler Geis

Trade paperback edition June 2024

Interior design by Tyler Geis

Manufactured in the United States of America

ISBN 979-8-9902625-2-2 (paperback)

ISBN 979-8-9902625-1-5 (ebook)

For John G. Geis
1940 – 2023
Love you forever, Papa.

SCYPHOZOA

OVERTURE

The pinks and oranges of early sunset shone through the shedding branches of the lone oak tree, cascading rays of light upon the two lovers in the autumnal bed of fallen leaves below.

Kyrie gripped Asher's arm as he leaned in for another kiss. He felt the fibers of Asher's muscular bicep, strung tightly against the bone like finely tuned guitar strings. Between the subtle moans emanating from their joining of lips, birds chirped for miles, singing songs without lyrics, harmonizing with the subtle bass of the lake water and the rhythmic rustling of tree branches and crushed fall leaves.

He felt for his face, caressing the stubble Asher recently grew during the past week on tour. The short hairs gave Kyrie a rough yet comforting feeling. Like newly manufactured Velcro that sticks just right. He cupped Asher's cheek in his palm, pressing deep to lock their lips. He leaned in, shifting his arm from its grasp on Asher's bicep to the center of his chest, where the beating of his heart thumped under the rippling pectorals concealed by a tight gray crewneck sweater.

They had sat under the oak tree beside a glistening lake for hours before this moment, talking about love, death, and everything in between.

"What's your home life like?" asked Kyrie.

"Don't have much of a home life anymore, since we've been touring for so long," Asher replied.

"That's very nomadic of you."

Asher had laughed, a shy chuckle that was unbefitting of someone with his gargantuan level of confidence in himself. "You enjoying your time on tour?" Asher continued after stifling this break of character.

"Oh, the band's great," Kyrie responded with a pause, "but you're the highlight."

"Well, I'd hope so. I *am* the lead, after all."

"Don't be such a bitch! I'm trying to flirt, dammit."

Kyrie hadn't meant to say that, as his infatuation with Asher Gaumont had been a deeply repressed attraction since he saw Scyphozoa live in the closest city to his hometown two years ago. It had been a night of lust and sweat, a tinge of horniness blossoming in the vape fumes above the venue. Asher, much skinnier back then, still commanded the attention of the audience like no other performer Kyrie had ever seen. More so than the other ravers around him, Kyrie had fallen completely and utterly in love with the beanpole white boy at the mic. To seal the deal, during their cover of Queen's (or Smile's, depending on the pretentiousness of the person you talk to) "Doing Alright," Asher had winked at Kyrie as he sung.

The butterflies had sprung right then and there, filling every crevice of his stomach with the tickling sensation of first love. He was starstruck, in awe. But why feelings for him, of all people? What would Dad think? And don't get him started on the Jesus-infused tirade his mother would provide if she knew.

Even after joining the band that same night—in a backstage conversation that culminated in his first stint with marijuana—Kyrie knew in his heart and soul that those feelings he felt for Asher needed to stay buried, at least until after his parents helped him pay off his tuition.

But that wasn't an issue for Kyrie anymore. He had dropped out of college three weeks later, much to the dismay of the old Madre and Padre back home. Maybe that's what he felt now: Free. Free from the shackles of

American education, free from the fear of using that marketing degree to sit in a cubicle until he got fat, retired, and moved to Florida. Free from the weight of parental disapproval. He had already dropped everything to be Scyphozoa's trombonist; what else did he have left to lose?

Asher was speechless, and if there was one thing to know about Asher, he *never* kept his mouth shut. His eyes widened slightly, revealing those beautiful blue irises centered with a soft brown hue that burned in the late evening sun. The awkwardness in the air was so thick you could swim in it. Kyrie, in only a moment's notice, felt his world crumbling around him. He was a knight on a battlefield, the last of his troop left, surrounded by the enemy hordes. As a last battle cry, Kyrie softly whimpered, "I'm sorry."

He lowered his head into his chest, embarrassed. Tears welled in his eyes. A single drop fell when he felt the gentle caress of a palm against his cheek. Asher thumbed the tear from Kyrie's face and began to lift his head to meet his.

They stared at one another for what seemed like an eternity. Floating in the vastness of the space between them. A vacuum of reassurance. No matter how much Kyrie wished to look away, he couldn't. Asher smirked with a huff. "What?" Kyrie asked.

"Don't be sorry, Ky."

Another tear streamed down his face, a catalyst for another loving thumb-rub from Asher.

"Kyrie, listen. There's nothing to be sorry about. You are loved; we all love you. Some more than others, but… You get what I'm saying?"

Kyrie could do nothing but either nod or shake his head; all the words he wanted to say were jammed in his throat.

He nodded.

"We're a goddamn indie rock band for Christ's sake," Asher said. His hand jolted for a moment as he said this, and his face became marked with signs of discomfort.

"Are you okay?" Kyrie asked.

"Yeah," Asher reassured. "Just a headache."

They stared at each other for another impossible eternity, when finally, Asher said, "Let's give you what you want."

He leaned in, to which Kyrie pushed back.

"But is it what *you* want?"

With that priceless smile of his, Asher said, "You don't know how long I've wanted this."

They sat under the lone oak tree, in a passionate entwining of lips and bodies, welcoming the glow of a setting autumn sun with the renewed vigor only a first kiss could provide. Just as the sun lowered itself behind the endless trees, Asher pulled away and jolted upright. Kyrie, stunned, began to think of all the things he had possibly done wrong. *Did I bite his lip too hard? God, I hope I didn't make him bleed.*

"Let's go for a swim," Asher said.

Relieved and hopelessly infatuated, Kyrie stood up from the bed of leaves. As he brushed stray leaves from his clothes, Asher had already stripped naked and beckoned Kyrie to join him on the lake shoreline. Too besotted to be shocked, Kyrie took the situation as it was and removed his clothes as well.

The ground shifted from soil to sand as he approached the water, twinkling with the day's last bits of sunshine. The sand sifted through his bare toes. Asher waded a few yards out in the open water, his member laying to the left across his thigh. Kyrie slowed, studying Asher's body. Every nook and cranny. Every crevice. Every muscle body protruding over bone, under a thin sheet of skin. That skinny lead singer with the baggy shirt and greasy, long hair was no more. What Kyrie saw laid sprawled naked on the cusp of the water was a god amongst men; a walking-and-talking Greek statue.

Kyrie slipped into the chilled water. His skin erupted in goose bumps as the lake consumed his body up to the neck. Asher heard Kyrie's teeth chatter and swam over to him. In the last few seconds of daylight, he wrapped his toned arms around Kyrie, burying him in his warmth. Asher kissed his neck from behind. Warm breaths ran in tandem with each passionate peck.

Kyrie leaned his head back, resting on Asher's shoulder, and gazed at the night's first stars, ready to watch those blossoming lovers from light-years away. He turned, still within Asher's grasp, and rested his hands upon his chest. They locked lips the best they could in the slowly rippling water.

4

Kyrie never wanted this to end. He wanted nothing more than to stay in this freezing autumn lake, held tight by this man, making love in the blooming night. Away from the lights of the cities, the bustling streets. Floating through the endless and beautiful sky with no one but himself and Asher Gaumont.

Eventually, the warmth between them faded with the billowing current of the water. One last burning kiss sealed the night. "Thank you," Kyrie whimpered. He couldn't tell if the liquid running down his cheek was lake water or tears. His shoulder-length hair stuck to the back of his neck and tickled his spine. Chills slithered like a garden snake through his nerves.

Asher, silent, gently grasped Kyrie's hand from beneath the water and led him back to the shore, into the shivering night. The beads of water on their skin became frigid in an instant as their wet feet met the sand, then the dirt, then the grass and leaves.

They struggled back into their clothes, fighting against both the cold and the water that hadn't finished drying in the still air. They gathered the rest of their things; an acoustic guitar and speaker that went unused. They had sat in silence with the ambience of early fall, encompassed by the miles of red and orange trees on all sides.

This silence continued all the way from the alcove to the cabin half a mile away. The sun was gone; their only way of seeing the path ahead being the faint glow of moonlight.

They made it back to the cabin, Adam and Evelyn greeted them, smoking a bowl on the porch, illuminated by the yellowed porch light swarming with moths. "Must've been one hell of a shit," Adam said to Asher as he handed the bong to Evelyn. "You left around six and now it's sundown."

"You really think the 'I need to take a shit' thing was true?" Evelyn jabbed with smoke seeping from her mouth and nose. "Sure, the toilet isn't working inside, but who takes a fuckin' guitar with them while they shit in the woods?"

Kyrie had no idea what they were talking about, but yet again, he had wandered out to shit in the woods right after dinner, and that was around half past five. Adam beckoned Evelyn to give him back the bong, which still held a bit of smoke in its tubing. Being the bass guitarist, his outstretched hand notably stood as still as a rock at the bottom of the ocean.

Evelyn rolled her eyes. "Evie, you better gimme that shit before it burns out," Adam said. "Paid good money for that bud."

"Okay, addict," she responded.

Kyrie couldn't help but chuckle at this exchange. There was something so *them* about the words they used, the way they spoke, the slight twang every time either of them said a word with the letter A. The twins were inseparable, to a fault. They were in the same traveling band, but they despised each other. The only things that could bring them together were their music and their weed.

"Well, for your information," Asher said, "I was just making an excuse to check up on the runt here."

"Runt?" Kyrie asked, slightly hurt.

"Well, I mean. You'd already been out for like thirty minutes by the time I went out."

"But *he* didn't take a speaker with him," Evelyn said.

"What're you getting at?" Asher asked.

Evelyn glanced at Kyrie, locked eyes. She quickly shifted her gaze back to Asher, as if she had just read Kyrie's mind and knew everything: the lakeside talk, the lake itself, the kiss, and the next kiss, and the next, the next, the next. "Nothing," she said, leaning back in the rickety wooden chair. "Why're you getting so defensive, Ash?"

"I'm not."

"Uh huh… right," she snarked.

Both Evelyn and Adam had that knack for crawling underneath a person's skin. They likely didn't even do this on purpose; it simply came with the two-for-one package. They even managed to pick at Asher from time to time, which was no small feat. The years had been kind to him, but he grew tougher with every passing day. Yet, those two managed the impossible day after day by making him squirm. He let out a short breath and stomped into the cabin, closing the door behind him with a sharp slam.

Kyrie stood motionless on the first step leading to the porch. Crickets chirped in the distance, accompanied by the moths fluttering inside the one lightbulb outside the cabin. "Sorry, Ky," Evelyn said.

"For what?"

"Ruining it."

"What? What did you ruin?"

"Well," Adam said, coughing smoke, "your night, obviously."

"Don't be a dick, Adam," said Evelyn.

"You're thinking exactly what I'm thinking, though, Evie."

"I know."

"So how was it?"

How was it?

Kyrie was instantly taken aback. "How was what?"

"The sex."

"Oh," Kyrie laughed. "We didn't... well. Well yeah, no. We didn't, like, *fuck* fuck, but..."

Evelyn slipped a twenty-dollar bill from her wallet, ashamed, and handed it to Adam, who seemed to have been waiting for this news all day, if the sly smile scraping his cheeks was any sign of it. "Told you Ash was too pussy take it that far."

"Shut the fuck up."

"Did you two... bet on us?"

They lurched forward in their chairs and giggled like a group of little schoolgirls passing by a conventionally attractive man in a nineties rom-com. Through their fits of laughter, Adam managed to say, "Evie said you two were gonna full-on fuck out in those woods, but I said, 'No fuckin' way Ash wants to do that with all those bugs out there.'"

Their laughter was so contagious that Kyrie felt a smile crease its way through his blushing cheeks. "You two are complete dicks."

"We know," they giggled in horrifying unison.

Kyrie took a few steps toward the front door before stopping, pondering, and tapping Evelyn on the shoulder. "What's up?" she asked.

He leaned in and whispered, "We skinny-dipped in the lake and his dick touched my ass, so you should honestly get half your money back."

As he went inside the cabin and shut the door behind him, Kyrie heard Evelyn squeal with glee, to which Adam started hurling expletives in retaliation. All the lights were off, so Kyrie took out his phone and shone the flashlight instead of being a complete idiot, stumbling around in the dark, and fumbling for a light switch. *My glasses, I can't see without my glasses*, he thought, amusedly.

The air was thick and infested with dust. Motes swished past his face, hanging static in the space. The cabin's decrepit aura gave a notion of abandonment, like no one had set foot in the space for decades. Yet, that's the paradox of dust. Dust is the byproduct of humanity; minuscule motes flaking off the skin that's in a perpetual state of dying. But people see dust as a sign of nothingness; untouched space. There is no dust without the people, and there are no people without their dust.

Kyrie walked past the kitchen toward the staircase leading to the second-floor loft. The hallway seemed to grow smaller and smaller with every step he took. His steps dampened, decreasing from stark vibrations to low hums. There was nothing to fear, but he felt his heart run a marathon in his chest. His breaths shortened to quick bursts.

Something rough brushed his arm.

He turned with a jolt and blinded Jessica with his flashlight.

"Kyrie, what the hell?" she yelped, shielding her eyes.

"'What the hell?' You're the one trying to Jason Voorhees me!"

He lowered the phone to cast a dim glow in the hallway instead of a nuclear blast. "First of all," she said, "Jason wouldn't sneak up on you. That's more of a Michael Myers thing."

"Oh, that's so smart of you."

"Not my fault you're an idiot."

"Ouch," he said, feigning hurt on his face.

"Anyway, I needed to talk to you about something."

"Could you have done that in a less creepy way? Where the hell did you even come from, anyway?"

"I was in the kitchen."

"In the dark?"

"Yeah."

"Why?"

"Forget it." She shook her head, waving her billowing red hair in a cascade of scorching flames. "I need you to know something, because I know you're trying to go upstairs, and I know he's up there."

"Well, yeah. Ash seemed pretty mad. Just wanted to check up on him," Kyrie said.

"Yes, that's amazing and awesome and so cool of you. But please don't go up there right now."

"Why?"

"You know how he gets. Especially with Marty up there."

Marty, his neurons seethed. No one in the band was fond of him. In most cases, people would say, "Oh, it's nothing that *he* did! I just don't like his vibe." But in this special case, the members of Scyphozoa despised Marty because of every action he took. Suckling the bronze tit of Asher Gaumont, as Adam and Evelyn Stone said incessantly: most of the time while Marty was within earshot.

But when *wasn't* Marty within earshot? He was the local snitch prowling about the band, and nothing more. He couldn't play an instrument, he couldn't sing for shit, and—*Lord help him*—he couldn't perform; not to mention that meager height of sixty-two inches. The mic stand always towered over him.

"Right," Kyrie said, "*Marty.*"

"But seriously. *Don't* go up there."

"I'll take my chances."

"You're fucking stupid…" Pause. "And horny."

Kyrie wasn't exactly sure how to take this. He wondered if it was seriously *that* obvious he'd been fawning over Asher since he joined the band two years before. As his right foot planted itself firmly on the first step, he said, "I may be both those things, but I'm also caring."

"That's just 'stupid' and 'horny' with different seasoning."

"Like your white ass would know anything about seasoning," he scoffed.

Jessica spouted an exaggerated gasp—placing her hand upon the cusp of her bosom, clutching imaginary pearls—and rebutted, "Get back to me when you start putting something other than Tajín on your food."

Another step, despite Jessica's odd warning.

"Don't disrespect my heritage, Jess."

Another floorboard creaked.

"Like you haven't done that enough," she said.

"Oooo! That hurt," he acted as he grabbed for his chest, faking a fit of cardiac arrest.

Jess apologized, not with words, but with her eyes. With the way she scrunched her nose into a button. The faint freckles that dotted her cheeks creased into each other as she sent her telepathic *sorry*. She turned away from the staircase looking defeated. Kyrie assumed it was because of the playful word spar. As she walked down the hallway and toward the front door, he redirected his flashlight to the top of the stairs.

He ascended the steps one creak at a time, reaching the top with as much noise as possible, despite his every attempt at the contrary. The doors were shut up there, but one stood out from the others: A door at the end of the hall, ringed with the faint glow of light from the other side. It was foreboding, ominous. Like a not-too-subtle doorway to Hell. Or an obvious trap room in a horror movie. Like those characters in those movies, he would open the door and never see daylight again. *No*, Kyrie thought, *Jessica's petty. I just need to check on him.*

Blinded by lust, Kyrie knocked on the door and entered without an answer.

And despite his every attempt at the contrary, he never saw daylight again.

So it is written.

MOVEMENT I

DOING ALRIGHT

CHAPTER I

1

She broke up with me the day after my birthday.

I don't blame her in the slightest; it had been coming for a long time. I'd been wondering for the past few months when the spark finally died out. When it failed to ignite the flame that was supposed to carry us through university life like a phoenix spreading its fiery wings and taking flight. Maybe it was over the summer, when we'd been doing the long-distance thing for over a month because she lived in Florence, Kentucky and I lived in Chicago. We'd done it before, and I was sure we could do it again. Had she met someone new during that time? Did they offer more to her than I ever could? Or maybe her friends were drunk one night at the beginning of the semester and all redownloaded Tinder or Bumble or whatever the fuck. Maybe she saw a total stud on there and swiped right. But would she willingly do that? Cheat, I mean.

Even now, through the pain of losing her, I cannot bring myself to accuse her of such a thing. But humans work in mysterious ways, and infidelity is one of mankind's biggest riddles. It's like a virus that everyone is susceptible to, whether they like it or not. Our collective fear is that there is someone out there who is better suited for our partner than us. And it's true! We passed eight billion people on this world, and a billion is a lot larger than most will have you to believe. Within the next decade, it will be nine billion. That's an extra billion people we have to fend off to keep our sense of normalcy. To keep your status as two pieces locked together on the world's largest jigsaw puzzle.

But that was that. I'm glad she had the power to trudge through my twenty-first birthday, despite that nagging feeling scratching at the back of her head screaming, "END IT! END IT NOW! YOU KNOW YOU WANT TO!" What's more impressive was her willpower against the rum and cokes that night, too. How many times did that voice plead with her to do the deed in that bar? Countless times, most likely. "Alcohol is the ultimate spiller or beans," as my mother always says. And I will always believe her, because my father was an expert in that field. And she was always his prime test subject.

We had entered a place downtown called Toss & RUMble (cute, I know) around ten o'clock that night. It was an early November night, which meant climate change wasn't going to allow me to wear shorts or—God forbid—a short-sleeved shirt. So, naturally, I wore a short-sleeved Hawaiian shirt and pink khaki shorts. I knew enough alcohol in my system would warm me up, since I had three other semesters' worth of experience drinking underage under my belt. It's college in the United States! We all do it! Ship me off to war, that's fine. But a beer or two? Oh, no no no. Gotta wait three more years for that, stupid.

Funnily enough, I didn't have just a beer or two at the RUMble. With my newfound sense of liberation from the shackles of *interesting* national laws, I found myself downing three Jell-O shots, two rum and cokes, an unopened beer I found in the disgusting men's restroom, and half my girlfriend's Bud Light seltzer. Don't ask me the flavor on that one, because I was too far gone at that point to remember.

But what I *did* remember was clear as day: a laminated schedule of bands performing at the RUMble within the next month, sitting right at the edge of the bar. It immediately yanked my soul out of its drunken stupor, planting me back on my feet in the land of the sober. Lots of local bands I had never heard perform but was *very* aware of. Us & You, Dumpster Cat,

Topsoil, Jack-Off Lantern. My finger perused the list until it hit the absolute jackpot: Scyphozoa.

"Holy fuck," I whispered, drunkenly slurring through the *L* in *holy*.

I snatched up the schedule and stumbled over to my girlfriend and Todd, who were on a far wall away from the main crowd. Interrupting whatever conversation they were attempting to have underneath the loudest speakers known to man, I lifted the sheet and pointed clumsily at the topic of interest.

"Scyphozoa!" I slurred.

My girlfriend had been getting scarily good at smiling without her eyes, and the smile she pulled off then had to be her best performance yet. How did I not know what was to come? Well, I guess I knew, as the warning signs were all there. The standoffishness of her. The pleading of me.

Unlike her, my roommate Todd grew wide-eyed and started bouncing like a goddamn basketball. Scyphozoa isn't just any indie rock group; they are *the* indie rock group. They have a trombonist for Christ's sake! What other rock band has a trombone, and a prominent one, too? No one, that's who.

I switched my degree from Psychology to Music Performance the year before at the beginning of that fall semester. Trombone in hand, I left that metaphorical psychiatric chair and stepped out into the spotlight, and all because of Scyphozoa. Well, there hadn't been much of a spotlight; only piles of music theory and history homework and a trombone instructor who would rather fuck the girls in our studio than teach me how to play overtones. But I'm doing what high school me wanted to do from the beginning, despite my mother's dismay. She only wants the best for me, which probably only means she wants me to make money. Can't do that with a Fine Arts degree in 2023, that's for sure.

Todd and I jumped around each other locking hands like two planets orbiting a star while tripping on LSD tabs. He was as big a fan of Scyphozoa as I was, maybe a little bit more.

"Holy fuck, man!" he yelled.

"That's what I said!"

My girlfriend rolled her eyes and crossed her arms over her chest. Even her willpower against the alcohol couldn't hide that disapproving stare. "You two are complete fucking nerds!" she said.

"You just don't understand them like we do!" Todd said.

"You're right! I don't! Because I'm normal."

"How was the Eras Tour movie, by the way?" I jabbed.

"Oh, shut the hell up, Joel."

She had said that with such a clarity of anger that was commonplace between us at that point. The drinks were getting to her. The cracks were showing, but she never faltered that night. Bless her heart and bless mine the next morning. I needed all the prayers I could get.

The next morning was headlined by a raging headache and chapped lips. I didn't remember leaving the bar, but I remembered the strobe lights, the fog machines, the blasting music, the bodies grinding against each other with love and lust and hatred and longing as they danced the night away. And I remembered the event schedule as my face hovered over the toilet bowl and saw the remains of whatever I ate last night.

My birthday landed on the first Friday of November, luckily for my bowels. There's nothing quite like the feeling of knowing you have absolutely nothing to do on Hangover Day. Just drink some water, watch a movie with your TV dimmed to its lowest brightness setting, and you'll be all good by five in the evening.

So, five o'clock came, as it does every day. I heard a knock on the door to my apartment. Todd was nowhere to be seen most of the day, and I assumed he had gone home to a different building with another college girl with another set of boobs that he was so fond of and stayed the night there. I trudged to the door with nothing but a T-shirt and underwear clad to my body, thinking it would be Todd on the other side. But it wasn't.

It was her.

"Oh!" I said. A little too loud, in fact. The nausea was gone, but the headache still thumped away like a bass drum mallet inside my skull. "Hey, Roselle."

"Don't use my government name," she said, letting herself in.

As I closed the door I said, "Sorry, Rose. Did you get home safe last night?"

"You called me an Uber, remember?"

She plopped down on the couch and kept her eyes fixed on the carpet, avoiding me as if I were the most horrific thing she had ever shared a room with. Like I was a devil she didn't want to make a deal with.

"I'll be honest, I don't remember. But I'm glad you got home safe, babe."

"Don't."

There was that anger again. The type that was a signature play in our relationship for months at that point. "Is there something wrong?" I asked.

She paused for a moment. Her left leg sporadically thumped on the carpet, to which she smoothed her hand over it. It stopped, but only for a little while. "You know there's something wrong, Joel. There's always been something wrong."

As much as I knew this had been a long time coming, I still tried to avoid talking about it. I studied her, memorizing every detail of her before the inevitable came and I couldn't bear to look at her anymore. The wavy auburn hair, the short lashes, the perked and full lips, the short button nose that twitched every so often. She looked amazing in that button-up top that day. The light green complimented her hair and hazel eyes beautifully. We had fallen in love after she spilled her coffee on my laptop during a developmental psychology lecture. With anyone else, I would've been furious. But she was so kind, so innocent. A ray of sunshine sitting right next to me in a lecture hall I absolutely did not want to be a part of. The laptop survived, but apparently, we weren't going to make it. *I'm sorry for your loss.*

I inched toward the couch, to which she scooted over by a whole cushion. I sat down and knew deep in my heart that there was no comfort in this interaction. What was I supposed to do? I couldn't wrap my arm around her and give her the old *everything's going to be okay* shtick. Consolation was a huge no-no now. We had to figure this out together, only from opposite corners of the world.

"Explain it to me, then," I managed to say.

Roselle broke the bond between her eyes and the floor and stared directly into my soul. There was fire in her pupils, smoke in her irises. "What is there to explain?" she said.

"Well, you came all the way to my place. I would assume you had something to s—"

A tidal wave of disgust adorned her features. That shut me up real quick. "I *came* here to break up with you," she said. "Nothing more, nothing less. We're done."

My throat tightened at those last two words. A lump wavered somewhere in there as tears welled in my eyes. Not enough to spill over onto my cheeks, but enough to make the dimly lit room go foggy. Her eyes, however. Her eyes were as dry as the Sahara. She had prepared for this, with no more tears left to cry. This was certainly a long time coming, but I had forgotten to do the homework until the day of.

"Goodbye, Joel. I hope you find love."

I hoped she would, too. But that thought stayed in my head as she rose from the couch and exited my apartment for the last time. As the door slammed behind her, a gust of autumn breeze swept into the space. The last fading remnants of her perfume wafted into my nose. I savored that smell.

I savored every particle until it diluted into the air.

I finally wept when her essence escaped my life forever.

2

Sunday rolled around just as most Sundays tend to do. There's always that hollow dread of knowing you must pull yourself up by your bootstraps tomorrow or you'll get swept up in the action. However, I spent this particular Sunday in bed, in a pool of tears.

Metaphorically speaking, obviously. But that's what it felt like. Maybe not even a pool, but an ocean. A sea of tears that I found myself drowning in. Air was nothing but a foreign concept to me. That Sunday was a day for suffocating under the pressure of a newly single life. Roselle was out of the picture, so who next? I immediately hated myself for thinking about a rebound so soon after a breakup, but if whatever deity in the sky didn't want humans to have rebounds, then why did it make the deal so damn enticing?

There are so many people out there. Why not just go for it? We are born, we fuck, and we die, as none of the old sayings go.

I choked those feelings out of my head the instant it became too much to bear. They would still linger, sure, but I just needed to relax a bit. The thunderclouds of depression were seeping into my apartment, and I needed to be as levelheaded as possible when the storm came.

Todd checked in twice that day: Once in the morning with a complementary cup of peach tea, and once in the evening before he was ready to do a third night of barhopping. I was still in my T-shirt and underwear from the day before, and thankfully hidden under my bedsheets when he barged in that second time. "You sure you're doing okay, bud?" he asked for the fifth time that day, with the tone of someone who was expecting to actually get a different answer this time.

"No, man," I repeated.

He huffed and said, "You gotta pull yourself together, Joel. This isn't healthy for you."

"Yeah, no shit," I said, turning my back toward him.

He must have stood there for eons. I wanted him to leave so bad that I must've frozen time on accident. Silly me.

"You're going out to the bars with me tonight," he said.

I turned back toward him and scowled.

"Now why the fuck would I want to do that?" I asked.

"I think it'd be good for you."

"So, you say you want *me* to be healthy, but my liver is fair game to get royally screwed over?"

"Yes."

There was no convincing Todd that you didn't want to drink with him, so I did exactly what the clouds of depression were fending off against and slipped out of bed. Todd looked down at my underwear and back up again.

"You might wanna put that thing away before we go."

3

I had put that thing away with a nice pair of khaki slacks and covered the days-old T-shirt with a flannel button-down. I pulled the red and black sleeves up to the base of my forearms, making sure my tattoo was peeking through.

I used to read a lot before college. Incessantly so. Like, there wouldn't be a single month that went by without me having shoved at least three or four books into my brain. I was very fond of Stephen King; still am. So much so that my favorite novel is *The Stand*, that ginormous tome about the virus-induced post-apocalypse and the fight between good and evil. And sitting on the inside of my forearm, there—wallowing in permanence—is the cover design for the first edition hardcover of that book. Does it mean anything to me? Does it hold sentimental value, as most permanent body ink should? No. I'm a creature of habit, and my habit is to do dumb shit for no discernible reason. People may get tattoos of their late grandmother's birthday, or maybe a paw print of a long-lost childhood dog. But for me, I just want things that look cool, and this tattoo is no exception. Much like my ink philosophy, the cover image makes no sense in the context of the story within the pages, but it looks sick as shit. A man in robes fending off against a beaked demon wielding a scythe, set against the backdrop of a vast and empty desert. It may mean nothing to me, as it did with the book it was printed with, but it's cool. And isn't that all that matters in life?

Anything I could do to garner some attention at those bars was fair game. Clean (enough) outfit, good hair, clear-rimmed glasses that seemed to be in this season, a tattoo with a design so obscure people just *have* to ask. I was lonely; that shroud of being single blanketed over me with every step I took down the streets of Sanduhr with Todd by my side. Human interaction was at the top of my list of needs. So, when we hit the first bar, obviously the bouncer accused my ID of being a fake.

"Come on man," Todd pleaded. "He turned 21 two days ago! His birthday's right there!"

He pointed to my birthday as if the bouncer hadn't already seen it. The bouncer, who looked like a jacked Munchkin compared to Todd's tall and lanky frame, simply stood there with my very real ID in his grasp. He scowled at Todd, held the ID up to the nearest lamppost, and handed it back to me, still with that scowl adorning his face. "You really think this shit's gonna work on me, kid?"

"Uh… no?" I said, totally confused. "What 'shit?'"

"Don't play dumb."

Confusion was slowly, but surely, turning into anger. Was this bouncer having a bad day, too? Probably not, because look at the size of this lad! If he put me in a headlock, his biceps would probably turn my skull into a mess of strawberry jam and bone shards. At least that would have helped to escape my misery.

"I'm sorry, sir," I said. "But I'm being *so* honest when I say this: That's my *real* ID, and I was literally in this bar two nights ago… on my birthday. Which is on the card."

"I've been in this business for years, kid. I've seen every trick in the book. And I know your skinny ass isn't trying to pull one of 'em."

"Skinny?"

While he may have been right somewhat, my knuckles still went white with fury as I thought about everything I could possibly do to him. These thoughts were obviously not rational at all, but please don't fuck with a college student who just got out of a relationship. Hell hath no fury for those who are caught disrespecting the disrespected.

Todd noticed the wave of anger cascading over me, grabbed my arm, and turned me around. "We can go to RUMble some other time, man," he said. "It's not worth getting your ass kicked here."

"Would you two stop making out and hurry the hell up!" someone shouted from the back of the line the bouncer created.

"Get a room, fags!" another shrill voice rang.

While I didn't think RUMble was a good enough bar to warrant yelling slurs at someone holding up the line, my rage got the best of me. I turned back around, snatched my ID from the dumbass bouncer, and stormed through the packed line. I don't remember if Todd followed me through the crowd, and I hope he didn't. I scoured the line, listening for anyone who had the same voice as the slur-hurler.

Who I found may have been them, may not have been, but they were laughing. And I didn't want to see joy on anyone. If I couldn't be happy, why should they be happy? The world was dark and gray and full of nothing but unfairness and grief. I grabbed the skinny boy with curly hair shoved into a too-tight baseball cap. His laughter died as I planted my fist directly onto his cheek. "Who's a fag now, bitch!" I screamed, standing proud over his fallen form.

His friends—who must've been in the same fraternity, since they all looked and dressed the same—shouted in terror, recomposed, and locked their newfound anger onto me. In any other situation, I would've cowered in fear. But not then. I was a raging ball of fire ready to decimate anything in my path. I raised my aching fists, inviting them to try their best. One of them swung first, clapping me square in the cheek. I saw stars for a faint moment, snapped out of that cartoonish daze, and blocked the next punch.

We tussled in that line for ages, going at each other like gladiators in the ring trying not to die at the blade of a lesser man. Blood and spit began to dot the pavement below blow after blow. My arms ached, but the sheer adrenaline kept me in the ring. The other people surrounding us made no attempt to separate us. The ones in front of us in line squished toward the bouncer, while the ones behind left the line altogether and searched for a different bar. Lord knows Sanduhr had a surplus of those.

One guy choked himself on the line divider as he plummeted to the ground. I don't think I even hit him; he just kinda did that on his own. Another lost a tooth, which flew from his mouth and embedded itself in the mouth of the other lookalike next to him. The original kid, the one who finally decided to get up after receiving my first blow, posted up and invited me to try and beat him. I wanted to take this offer and run with it, even as he said, "I knew a fag like you would throw a punch that shitty. Try again, fucker."

I tightened my knuckles once more, bone against bone. But just before I could land a hopeful final blow, two arms wrapped around my torso and locked my own arms in place at my sides. I squirmed like a school of fish caught in one of those comically large fishing nets. "Let me go!" I yelled at the mystery assailant, pounding on their forearms with my open palms.

They pulled me out of the line, away from the chaos, and dragged me kicking and thrashing like a child not getting the chocolate they wanted at Walmart. Across the street, in a dark alley decorated with mist and smoke and rot, they threw me onto the ground. I landed on my hands and knees. My vision faded from a deep, blaring red back to the normal colors of the world. My breathing slowed from its locomotive chugging to its typical, low pace. I watched as a drop of spit unspooled from my open mouth and onto the wet pavement below. It was tinged pink with my split lip's blood. I put a finger to my mouth and studied it, seeing the blood pooling in the trenches of my fingerprints.

Everything tasted and smelled of rusting metal, like your hands after holding some pocket change for a little too long. I collapsed onto my elbows and rolled onto my back, staring at the dead, light-polluted sky. Void of stars.

Todd slowly bent over me, snapping his fingers inches from the tip of my nose. "Hey," he said. "What the hell, man."

I decided to lay still and not respond. Why would I? I was hopeless, anyway.

"Don't ignore me, Joel."

I didn't even blink; only stared at the vast, smoggy sky between the two rooftops.

"I can't leave you here. Come on."

He slipped his arms under mine and hoisted me up on my feet. I stumbled as if my legs forgot how gravity worked. There was a low thumping pain in my ankle, possibly from a sprain. Definitely over-exerted myself with that gaggle of frat bros. I didn't know I had it in me to start a fight like that. It was as if someone else took over my body, like I was a puppet controlled by another person's hand.

"Let's just go to a pub. Maybe the bars weren't such a great idea," Todd said.

No kidding.

4

We sat side by side on rickety stools at O'Sullivan's: One of many Irish pubs dotted around Sanduhr that gave the city an interesting case of green chicken pox.

"Seriously, man," Todd said over a glass of Guinness. "Why'd you do that? You're lucky no one called the cops."

"I don't know," I said. I stirred my Amaretto Sour with my

bloodstained finger. The ice tinkled against the glass as I mixed the liqueur and lemon juice. A whirlpool formed, sucking the ice down under, only for the rocks to reappear and repeat the cycle once more.

A subtle jazz tune rang through the speakers. Saxophones guided the way while trombones glided atop the melody. The bass was weighty and the piano added ornaments wherever necessary. The tempo was slow, calming. A stark contrast from whatever the hell happened thirty minutes before.

Eventually, I downed another drink, then another. For a moment, the world revolved around me, spinning at intervals unfamiliar to the human psyche. Brain fog was exactly what I needed in that moment, so I seized it one drop at a time.

"I know you're hurting, and I understand your pain," he said. "I've been through it before. But you need to focus on yourself now. Do what you love, and learn to love without someone else to attach that love to, you know?"

"I guess," I responded, not really listening.

"I'm worried about you."

"Thanks."

"I mean it, dude."

He put an arm around my shoulders, swaying me back and forth like a mother comforting her crying infant. "We've known each other for almost three years now. I'd hate to see you go down a path you can't get out of."

"I'll be fine."

"Well, you're not exactly helping your case on that one."

I stirred another Amaretto with my finger, now dissolved with any dried blood. It was all back into the drinks and into my system. Back to the mothership. "Promise me you'll work on yourself," he said.

"I'll try," I said.

"No." He turned me in the swivel stool, so my face met his. "Don't *try*... Do... You're better than this."

"I just don't know anymore."

"You know," Todd sipped more of the Guinness he surprisingly hadn't finished yet, "you've always been too hard on yourself."

"Performance majors do that."

"But you weren't a performance major in the beginning. Even when you were in psych you were such a perfectionist. Always thinking things were your fault."

"It's hard to not think that when things usually *are* my fault."

"Shut the hell up, man."

I gulped that sweet liqueur down as if my life depended on it.

"You got your vape on you?" I asked to avoid talking about this.

"No," he lied.

"I know you have it."

"I'll give it to you, but only if you absolutely *promise* you will stay healthy; keep up with yourself. I don't wanna come back to the apartment on some random Wednesday and see you lying on the floor with an empty bottle of pills in your hand."

I hadn't thought of suicide since the breakup, but the prospects of simply going to sleep forever seemed too good to pass up, now that Todd mentioned it. But I shook the thought from my drunken mind. Zoloft and alcohol aren't a good mix, anyway.

The jazz faded out and was replaced with a song I found all too familiar. Through the haze of O'Sullivan's, I recognized the tune immediately, and so did Todd. His face lit up, basked in the shine of a lightbulb that seemed to go off in his head. "You know what?"

"What?" I asked.

"Scyphozoa."

"What are you talking about?"

"Well." He leaned toward me, raising a limp hand as if he were about to propose the greatest trade deal in the history of late-stage capitalism. "I heard that Scyphozoa's trombone player quit a month ago. Just… out of nowhere. And they're looking for a new one."

I laughed for the first time in days. "There's no way you're suggesting what I think you're suggesting," I said.

"Yup."

As much as I didn't want to admit it in that pub, the prospect of joining my favorite band was so enticing.

"But, there's no way… right?" I asked.

"There's always a way."

"But school!" My brain was spewing excuses against one of my dreams. My heart tried to fight against these pessimistic thoughts as hard as it could.

"Fuck school! Music is what you live and *breathe* on," Todd said.

"They'll probably find someone before I even get the chance."

"They don't even have auditions on their website. My theory, and get this, is that they're touring right now to find new potential recruits," he reasoned.

"My mom would be so pissed."

"Fuck her, too! Well, don't *actually* fuck her... you get what I mean."

As he ramped up his drinking—graduating from sips to hardy Irish gulps—the idea of rising to the ranks of Asher Gaumont and his gang shifted from pipe dream status to something with a little more reality backing it up. As their most popular song "Frictional Fiction" hummed on the overhead speakers, this dangerous idea manifested itself as not just an idea, but a goal. As the event schedule at Toss & RUMble said: They would be in Sanduhr, Massachusetts on November 24th. Day after Thanksgiving, be damned. I would hitchhike my way back from Chicago if it meant forgetting about this mess. The breakup, the fight, the bleeding knuckles, the path down a road I wasn't willing to take.

In nineteen days, I would be front and center in the pit of the hackjob RUMble venue. With my trombone case in hand, I would find a way—*any* way—to convince the band to take me under their wing. Anything to escape the weight crushing my world.

The journey was set, my destination imminent.

CHAPTER II

1

I woke up the next morning with a more subdued hangover than expected. I had downed more sours than I could remember, and I woke up the morning after feeling like a new man. I even made it through an entire date with my toilet without thinking about Roselle! Unfortunately, I fell victim to that pitfall while taking a shower right after, but progress is progress.

I cried over a bowl of Reese's Puffs. A few tears dropped into the bowl as I ate, making the usually sweet and salty cereal a little saltier than I would've liked. I checked my phone's calendar to see if I missed any assignments that may have been due while my blood stream was dense with liver toxins. Nothing, thankfully, but I did have a music history assignment due by noon. "Ancient Instruments Worksheet" as the online page called it. Most of the instruments weren't as ancient as the word *ancient* would have most to believe; bagpipes, recorder, hurdy-gurdy, all the basics.

The best thing about switching majors now was that I didn't have psychology classes with Roselle. A week before, I would have loved to sit next to her in a social or child psychology lecture, but now, the winds had shifted. I thanked the academic gods for this small, but appreciated, fate. Unfortunately, however, that meant I had to subject myself to music classes

I couldn't give two shits about. A small price to pay to not be reminded of Rose's existence.

I went through my first day of school as a newly single man as well as expected; only with a few pit stops to empty public restrooms so I could sob into various toilet bowls. Everything reminded me of her because everything *was* her. There's a lamppost a block from the School of Music under which we shared our first kiss, in the dewy mist of late spring. I walked past that light every morning, still smelling her sweet perfume as if she were infused into the post itself. If, God forbid, I needed to mail a letter to my mom for some reason, I couldn't write the return address. Todd and I lived on Rose Lane, another cruel joke from the clammy hands of fate.

Even the restroom I occupied now—one right at the entrance of the dining hall closest to my apartment—reminded me of her. She was inescapable! Because, like a goddamned shapeshifter, a girl walked into that gender neutral bathroom with the same turquoise Scrunchie Rose wore to keep her soft, silky brown hair out of her beautiful, hazel eyes that gleamed like blazing suns in the night sky. I was washing my hands as this mystery woman entered the restroom, and she stood at the sink to my right, tightening her Scrunchie and poking at a small skin blemish an inch or so below her left eye. A blue eye, thank fuck. I don't know how many more reminders it would've taken to force myself into a swirly in the stall behind me.

I quickly rinsed my hands and dried them off; left the mystery girl in the restroom with no intention to ever see her again. Another tear welled in my eye, dripping subtly down my cheek as I entered the dining hall.

Cameron was sitting at a booth halfway into the large dining space. Accompanying him were Jasmine, Alvaro, and Fran, all sitting at that booth as if they were attending an important council meeting; arms crossed, contemplative faces, not a smile between them. I sat at the end of the booth's bench with the worry of a man second guessing his suicide attempt when the pills had already gone down the hatch. They were trying their best to pretend they hadn't noticed me sit there, but they knew. They knew so much more than they let on.

2

"You're gonna be okay, Joel."

It could have been Cameron who said that, or maybe Al. No, it was definitely Fran… but maybe it was Jasmine? To be honest, I'm not too sure. Everything they said in those first five minutes blended; each one of them repeating the same reassurances but with slightly different variations. There comes a point in the aftermath of a breakup where all the words you hear turn into a hodgepodge of meaninglessness. Like eating a bowl of chowder or stew while sitting in a pitch-dark room. That could be a carrot I just ate, but who am I to judge?

"Guys," I said, "I'm gonna be fine. Don't worry about me; we've got a lot more things to worry about. Have you guys finished Dr. Porter's assignment yet?"

"The one due in an hour? I'd hope so," Cameron said.

"I'm sure you could get an extension if you lie hard enough," Alvaro mumbled as he shoveled potato soup into his mouth. This warranted a kick under the table from Jasmine, who obviously wasn't taking any bullshit today, as she usually did.

"No, I don't need an extension. Was just wondering," I said.

My backpack clung to my shoulders, pressed against the back of the bench and pushing me toward the abyss past the edge of the seat, under the table. Cameron noticed this and asked, "You not staying long?"

"Oh," I said as I struggled to put the backpack under the table between my feet, "no I just kinda forgot it was there."

He looked worried, even after telling me to not do the exact same thing.

"Hey," Fran said, placing her hand on my shoulder, "we're here for you if you need anything."

Then the confusion finally set in: How did they know about the breakup? I hadn't told them, as I had basically sworn off talking to anyone over the weekend. Depression can be a roadblock on the highway toward social interaction. It's just the natural course taken of feeling alone in this beautiful, terrifying world. You kind of bring that pain unto yourself, like a cruel form of self-punishment.

"Thanks, Fran."

The rest of this brief interlude at the lunch table was marred with more interjections of apologies that held no merit. Sorry for what? You didn't know, you *shouldn't* know. But yet again, news travels fast in the School of Music. The culture inside that building is akin to that of a small Midwestern town. Everyone knows each other, and everyone feels entitled to be in on everyone else's business, no matter how personal. It comes with the close quarters, the isolation from the rest of the world outside those walls.

We walked from the dining hall toward the School of Music, each of us with earbuds dangling from our phones and music playing at the lowest volume in case we wanted to chat during the walk over. We didn't talk, only trekked in silence. The quiet music and the cool breeze of early November accompanied our journey. Nothing more, nothing less.

3

A whole lot of nothing occurred for the rest of that Monday. Class, class, dinner, more class, ensemble rehearsal, the moonlit walk home, the staying in bed scrolling endlessly through Twitter, or whatever they were calling it nowadays.

Lots of drab comments that meant nothing in the grand scheme of things, but the scrolling was so damn addicting. Millions of people spewing their thoughts, shouting into the void, hoping someone notices them and clicks an arbitrary heart below their words. I found myself contributing to the monotonous cycle a little more than I'd like to admit, because at least it took my mind off things, no matter how brief.

Todd barged into my room at around eleven that night, disrupting the dark cave I had built for myself as the door to the living room flew open. Shielding my eyes from this sign of humanity outside my door, I asked, "Knock next time?"

"For you? No," he responded.

"What do you want?"

I was getting that sinking feeling of déjà vu, harkening back to last night when he did this same thing and convinced me to go out and drown myself in Amaretto sours.

"Just checking in," he said.

"I'm fine."

"No, you're not."

"Then why did you ask?"

My eyes found themselves shifting between a random Twitter post and the ominous Todd-shaped silhouette in my doorway. "Because I wanted to see if you still remembered our conversation from last night," he said.

"I remember."

"So, what are you doing here?"

"Excuse me?"

"I said, '*What* are you doing *here*?'"

I was dumbfounded, for sure, but deep down I knew what he was trying to get at. "Resting," I said like a smartass.

"You can't rest after a breakup, Joel. Get up."

"What?"

He bomb-rushed me, and I mean BOMB. RUSHED. I saw my life flash before my eyes. He was like a high school's top football brute charging at me: a meek computer geek with tape on his glasses, a pimple on his brow, and nothing to live for. He tackled me like that imaginary football player, too; scooped me up from under my covers and strained with all his might to lift me out of bed.

"Dude, fucking stop!" I shouted.

"No, man!" he grunted. "How are you gonna get into Scyphozoa when you aren't practicing?"

"That's what this is about?" I asked as if I didn't already know.

We tussled and walloped some more until Todd eventually overwhelmed my defenses and basically threw me onto the carpeted floor below. I must've looked like a baby straight out of the womb, laying on that floor in nothing but my underwear. Just put a thumb in my mouth and the resemblance would have been uncanny.

"What the fuck?" I said, cradling my head in my hand as I feebly rose from the carpet. I thought the fall had shot my frontal lobe straight to the back of my skull. My temples ached.

"Didn't mean to get that rough, I'm sorry." Another apology on a day filled to the brim with them. Empty promises of forgiveness on my part.

I attempted to slip back under the covers, to which Todd grabbed my arm and made the unsaid promise to never let go; at least, until he got what he wanted.

"Go practice, Joel," Todd said bluntly.

"Why?"

"If you wanna get into that band, you gotta give them your all."

"My all? Yeah, you're right. *My* all. Are you sure this is what *I* want? Or is it something *you* want? To be able to say your roommate is in your favorite band?"

He took a step back, shocked by my defiance. "No… no, no. Of course not, man. I just… what we said last night. I thought it was something that could… you know… get your mind off things."

"What if I don't want to 'get my mind off of things?' Did you think about that?"

"Well, you never gave me the cha—"

"And I was drunk!" I interrupted. "You really think I would agree to shit like that when I'm *not* tipsy off my ass?"

"You didn't even drink that much."

"Maybe to you! Always out, every goddamn night. Bringing home one girl after another. Your tolerance is probably so high that it'd take you fifteen shots to even get a fucking buzz!"

There were many unspoken rules in our apartment, but one of the rules at the top of that stone tablet was *Thou shalt not speak about Todd's love life.* Or, in all honesty, lack thereof. After I spilled everything in a strange fit of rage, fueled by my pain of Roselle deciding I wasn't worth her time, Todd looked hurt. Like a dog getting reprimanded for stealing a sock from the laundry hamper. A silence brewed between us, him standing there with defeat stricken across his face and me standing there in my underwear. Only the glow of the single lamp in the living room illuminated my bedroom, setting the tone for whatever this was becoming. Something somber, something toxic. I couldn't let this silence continue. Not for another second. Because with each passing moment, our years-long bond was fraying like an old rope hanging from a single thread. "I'm sorry," I said into the vast ravine between us. Another apology to add to the day's count, but I hoped this one was genuine enough to slice through the thick air separating us.

"I know," Todd responded, his eyes glued to the floor.

Rose had done the same thing when she walked up here a few days before; to tell me off and burn the bridge we had built together. Her eyes had stayed fixed on the floor, avoiding the confrontation. People are funny like that. If you can't see it, it isn't real.

Todd broke his gaze from the carpet and glanced up at me.

"I mean it," I begged. "I just... I just haven't been in the right mind."

"Right," he said with a sternness I wasn't familiar with.

More silence, then I said, "You wanna go out again, don't you?"

A smile crept onto his face, and he glanced back up again.

"Yeah," he said.

"Not for yourself?"

"Not for myself. I care about you, man."

He took a step toward me and beckoned me to dap him up. I pushed that aside and went in for a hug instead.

4

Not a single drop of alcohol met my lips that night. Barring the fact it was a Monday night, I wanted to stay sober while I repaired my friendship with Todd.

This wasn't some story about two dudes being best friends since elementary school and going to the same college because they were *that* strong of BFFs. It was more the story of two down-on-their-luck eighteen-year-olds getting randomly assigned as roommates their freshman year. Classic undergraduate story of fate and fortune, so on and so on. COVID was an absolute bitch that first year, as many around campus were still hesitant to get vaccinated. Masks were still prevalent in the fall of 2021, making the social scene of Sanduhr University essentially nonexistent. But we had each other, me and Todd. And we had been inseparable since.

But there comes a time when friendships start to wither and rot, as they did when we entered our junior year. Fall of 2023 brought new formulas to the equation. My first full year as a music performance major, his first year as a Tinder fanatic. I was always in the practice room; he was always at the bars. We barely talked despite living together in the same two-bedroom apartment. I had simply been too busy with my education, while he had been too busy working on his social game. I don't blame him; he always complained about how unpopular he was in high school, and for good reason. He was a good-looking kid back in those days, and much better looking than some of the people deemed "popular" in his school that he showed me pictures of from time to time.

Todd was a man of strong features: Chiseled jaw, light stubble, a perfect nose, and a body that wasn't bodybuilder-strong, but defined enough that people would turn their heads in public to catch a glimpse if he wore a shirt one size too small. And don't get me started on the strawberry blonde hair. I have seen way too many Tinder users fawning over that shit, jealous as I am with my curly, dirty-blonde hair.

We sat at the same two stools in O'Sullivan's from the night before, him sipping on another Guinness while I sat and watched, attempting to make conversation in any way possible. A futile effort, especially after our little spat, but at least I tried.

"How's life been, Todd?" I asked.

How original, Joel. You're a natural.

"You know, just the same old, same old," he said.

Another sip passed his lips as the highlights of a football game from a few hours before blared on the TV above the racks of half-empty bottles. I saw myself in the mirror backing these shelves, not liking the reflection staring back at me. God, I was a mess. My hair was lopsided, such is the curse of having those oh-so coveted curly locks while also wanting to lay on your side in bed. The bags under my eyes stretched in lavender streaks down to my cheekbones, granting me a gaunt look not unlike your typical undead assailant. My face was in the early stages of a tectonic shift, as evidenced by the mountain range of pimples forming on my forehead and cheeks.

"But, honestly," Todd said, pulling me out of my self-loathing daze, "I haven't felt better. I met this girl a few weeks back, and I think we might really work."

I knew it would be wrong of me to look shocked at this revelation, so I offered that signature Joel Auguste smirk that gets the Todds of this world swooning.

"You didn't tell me about that!" I spoke. "Who is it?"

His expression shifted from pure bliss to caution. He attempted to hide it with a smile and a chuckle, saying, "Oh, she goes to some community college in Barnstable on the Cape, so. I'm sure you'll see her sometime, but she's really busy with work and all that."

"You're seriously not giving me the 'You wouldn't know her, she doesn't go here' thing, right?"

Another sip of Guinness, then: "Well, it's true."

"I don't doubt it. You got a pic of her? I'm curious."

That cautious look glossed over his face again like a windshield wiper set to its highest setting. "You know? No, I don't! Because *this*," he turned his palm over the bar and made circular motions with his arm like he was attempting the world's most lackluster arcade crane impression, "Why we're here? It's about *you*. So, let's move this away from me. I'm sure you'll meet her someday. If I manage to keep a woman for that long, anyway."

I laughed. Not a roaring bellow, but a calm and short exhale through the nose. "So, what now?" I asked.

"You know what."

A song I was vaguely familiar with—"How Long" by Tove Lo, I guessed—snuck into the O'Sullivan's Monday night playlist. It was nearly empty in the pub, save for the bartender, an older couple shuffling near the nonfunctional jukebox, and these two goons sitting at the bar talking about women.

"Todd," I reasoned, "there's no way."

"There is."

"I just... I can't. Can I?"

"Joel, you are literally one of the best musicians I've ever heard. That little recital you had last semester? Like, come on! Don't be so hard on yourself."

"It's a little hard to not be."

"And I get that. I really do."

I wasn't sure if he truly did. Having your entire college degree depend on your ability as a musician isn't all it's cracked up to be. The tireless nights spent practicing measures at a time, the perfection needed, the stress of a looming performance. It all becomes too much at a certain point, and I hated every second of it. But I would've rather been doing that than sitting in lectures about neurons and schizophrenia and the Oedipus complex, snoring over my school-provided iPad with an Apple Pencil between my teeth. For the business major Todd was, I couldn't imagine he would be stressed about anything to that magnitude.

"There's just so much that could go wrong with that… you know," I said. "Trying to shoot for the top when you're at rock bottom."

Todd sighed and gulped the rest of his beer. Setting the mug, lined with foam, onto the counter, he rose from his stool and beckoned me to join him. "I'm glad you didn't drink tonight, because you've got work to do."

5

A common feeling amongst the recently broken up with is an aching numbness. A sort of hollowness within one's soul that allows you to go with the flow, but nothing more.

Todd led me from O'Sullivan's—which was no short walk from campus—to the School of Music building. I was surprised he even knew where it was, as he didn't have his maps app on his phone pulled up for easy directions. I avoided small talk on the way by sticking my earbuds in and listening to whatever my music streaming app decided I might like: Nothing But Thieves, Cream, The Police, Royal Blood. It was eerily warm on this Monday night, much to my pleasure as I was wearing a Sanduhr University hoodie and basketball shorts in the early weeks of November.

It was late, so the front door was locked. I swiped my student ID card and let myself and Todd in. Only a few lights were on in the building, illuminating the hallways and maroon lockers lining the walls with a dimness reminiscent of early morning on the new horizon. The fluorescents hummed with a low buzz, something that went unnoticed during the normal hustle and bustle of the school day; with all the chatter and footsteps amongst the other unfortunate souls with music degrees to fulfill.

I maneuvered the floors and halls down to the first floor, stopping at the locker containing my concert tenor, jazz tenor, and bass trombones. I spun the lock combination, failed it the first time, mumbled *shit* under my breath, spun it again with extra care, and let the lock snap open. I grabbed my tenor, to which Todd offered to carry it, and to which I denied his humble request. I slammed the locker shut because who was going to tell me no? The cockroach that lurks in practice room 217? Better yet, it'd be a good idea to avoid that room just in case that fucker was creeping around for a late-night snack.

I went upstairs, Todd trailing behind me like a dog begging for a milk-bone. The halls were just as foreboding at night as they were during the day with more people populating the area. As with many Fine Arts programs in the country, the atmosphere in that building was not as happy-go-lucky as non-music majors would have you to believe.

I wished that singular cockroach didn't inhabit room 217, since it was widely agreed upon that was the best practice room in the building despite the glaring pest issue. Unfortunately, we went into the room across the hall—room 218—which would have to do.

Like every practice room, there was a piano, its bench, a foldout chair, music stand, and beige walls adorned with grey noise-canceling pads. The quality of each piece of equipment varied from room to room, as room 217 was the top of the batch in that regard. But I always enjoyed the humble nature of the quaint, smaller room across the hall. Good to build yourself from humble beginnings so your Wikipedia page is a lot more interesting later.

I unloaded my tenor from its case, assembling the slide with the bell, placing the mouthpiece on the other hole in the slide, releasing any unwanted spit and other condensation with the spit valve. I tuned as Todd got as comfortable as he could on a piano bench. He laid flat on his back while I pulled some illegally printed Scyphozoa sheet music from a zippered pocket on my trombone case. I slipped the trombone part for "Frictional Fiction" to the front of the stack. I pursued the intricate rhythms and challenging technical work as Todd said, "Well, go ahead."

"If you want me to do this, you gotta be less of a dick about it."

"We went over this: *I* don't want you to do this. *You* want to do this." He sat up from his severely uncomfortable position, opting to lean his elbows on the piano behind him instead, accidentally playing some rather disgusting (not in a jazzy way) chords in the process. "You *need* to do this."

I was still hesitant with this whole pipedream we had manifested the night before. Why couldn't I take up a different hobby to mitigate all five stages of grief in one fell swoop? Maybe I could've spent my time writing a novel, working out, or even fucking crocheting, I don't know. Give me your best suggestions for useless hobbies because God knows I need one nowadays.

But I agreed with him at the time, despite my hesitance. Scyphozoa, man! The Big Scyph! I had all their records on vinyl, and Todd even had some unreleased songs on custom printed ten-inch records. Who could pass up the opportunity of a lifetime? To travel the country and create music with a band you've idolized for years? In the back of my mind, like a barricade being torn down by thousands of rabid fans, the opportunity was too sweet to pass up. Even depression couldn't contain the swarm of something as exciting as that.

"Play," Todd commanded.

And I did, one note at a time.

CHAPTER III

1

The few weeks leading up to November 24th were full of nothing but practice and practice and even more practice.

This persistence was time-consuming to a fault, as I began slacking in my academic endeavors. Going to classes became a chore: coursework wasn't a thought that crossed my mind. Social activities? Forget about it. The only activity I needed was between me, my trombone, and Scyphozoa. I practiced the transcribed parts to "Frictional Fiction," "Past Tense," and "Drive," among others. The group started off with covers of other, more popular songs to get their name out there, and I practiced those trombone parts as well. Everything I could find online became part of my repertoire, entering the library of my mind and seeping into my muscle memory. Every note, every slide position; the tempos, the dynamics, the accents, accidentals, ornamentations, key changes. Sometimes, a string of overtones would be written on the page, those sly little shits. Must've been that Kyrie Castillo's doing; their trombonist who quit out of nowhere. Sucked for him, I guessed, but good for me. Because now there was an open window of opportunity, but it was on the third floor of a locked house, and I forgot to bring my ladder.

The few times the presence of others graced me in this span of time were either late at night while Todd was in and out, or in the School of Music when I had to pass people to get to the coveted practice room before someone else took it. Room 217 was always occupied during the day, but that cockroach could keep it; room 218 was where it was at.

One of these fateful encounters happened a week after the Monday night Todd incident. I ran into Jasmine on my way to room 218, to which she stopped me and asked, "Where have you been? You haven't been to theory in a week."

Yes, I hadn't. It was a miracle that I hadn't started skipping Dr. Leo's class sooner in the semester. What with her stupid tirades that went on and on and on, never having anything to do with chords or scales or whatever else; having everything to do with not so subtly trashing her cheating husband.

"I've been busy," I said.

It wasn't a complete lie, since I had tunnel vision set on one thing and one thing only, which didn't include utilizing my tuition for all its worth.

"With what?" Jasmine asked, sensing the bullshit.

"I've been practicing."

"*For* what? Didn't you already get your recital done?"

"Yeah."

"So, what is it? What could be *so* important that you need to skip all your classes for it?"

"Do you have to ask so many questions, Jaz?"

"Yes! Because I'm worried about you! We're *all* worried about you. And you not going to class and ignoring all our texts isn't helping whatever case you're trying to build for yourself."

We had stood in the hallway for too long. Within the conga lines of students passing between classes, Cameron peaked his head through the shifting crowd.

"Joel! Oh my God, there you are!" he yelled.

He shuffled over to us, adding, "Are you doing alright, man? I haven't heard from you since last Monday."

Jasmine rolled those gorgeous almond eyes of hers.

"I was *just* asking him the same thing," she said, feigning intrigue.

"Guys," I said. "I'm fine. Please don't worry about me. There are a lot more important things to be concerned about."

"Yeah, but I'd be more concerned with you winding up dead one morning."

"Jasmine!" Cameron exclaimed.

"What? Is that not a valid concern?" Jasmine rebounded.

"I mean, it definitely is, but you don't want to plant that in his head. Especially with what he's going through."

"But he should know about how much we care about him."

"Maybe that's not the right way of doing that."

"What do you know?"

There was a fight brewing between those two; the strong and snarky Asian violinist and the gawky white-boy trumpeter. If I didn't intervene, it would get ugly really quick, but it seemed that they had essentially forgotten I was there as the conversation grew more and more malignant. I took the opportunity to slowly inch away from them, yet as soon as my back was turned, I felt a hand grip my arm with the firmness of a zip tie.

"Joel!" Jasmine yelled.

Some passing heads turned in our direction. A glare from him, a stare from her, a jeer here, an exhale from the nose there. All familiar yet anonymous faces. I barely got to know anyone who frequented those halls, but I knew their faces. Every single one of them. They were all like that one extra in any cheap 2000s movie that kept ruining scene continuity by showing up in the background all the time.

"Don't you dare try to leave," Jasmine continued.

"Fine," I huffed.

She pulled me back toward Cameron, who stood fearfully as still as a statue.

"Seriously, why don't we take you to class?" Jasmine asked. "Where's your backpack?"

"I didn't need it," I said.

"But you have class."

"I'm aware."

"Don't be a dick."

"I'm not."

"Sure."

She became so angry I could almost see an atomic bomb detonating in her eyes. If I didn't do something to defuse the situation, we would've had a real death, destroyer of worlds on our hands. I decided to tell her the truth.

"Scyphozoa's gonna be in town toward the end of the month," I carefully said, stepping on hot coals. "Their trombonist quit, and they apparently have an opening. I want to fill that spot before anyone else does."

Jasmine's eyes widened. Not with shock and awe, but with resent and overwhelming disappointment. A hydraulic press of dismay that crushed me into the world's goriest pancake.

"You can't be serious," she said.

"I am."

"I think that's really cool, actually," Cameron said to remind us he was still two feet away.

Jasmine swiveled and locked her gaze onto him, providing a gnarly death stare that shut him up immediately. If that wasn't enough, she added onto the total shutdown by saying, "Don't encourage him!"

"But didn't you just tell him to kill himself?"

"No! Of course not!"

She turned back to me and continued: "So, you're telling me Roselle broke up with you, you got super fucking sad, and decided to join a band—which, mind you, isn't a guaranteed gig—instead of finishing the degree you are actively in debt for?"

"Yeah, basically," I responded.

"You're insane."

"Being insane is better than being nothing at all."

"Oh, so not only are you insane, but you're also hopeless. Is that what you're saying?"

"Not really, no."

The density of students in the hallway slowly but surely dissipated as our one-sided argument pushed onward. Cameron continued to stand just out of focus, staring with watchful eyes at this train wreck he simply couldn't look away from.

Instead of egging it on any further, Jasmine checked her watch, gave a heavy sigh tinged with annoyance, and left, fusing with the train of nameless students as she trekked to her next class. Cameron merely stood in the same place she left him, watching blankly as she fled the scene. His bottom lip trembled; his eyes glazed over with a thin film of tears.

"Cam?" I asked. "Are *you* alright?"

"Not really," he said with a vibrato common in most tearful statements.

I stepped toward him and locked him in a tight embrace. His arms stayed locked at his sides for a while, but he eventually bent his elbows and reciprocated the hug. He buried his head, wet with tears, into my shoulder as I watched each passerby give us uneasy stares, some giggles, and a whole lot of empty sympathy.

"I don't want to lose you, man," he sobbed, his voice muffled by my sweatshirt.

I rubbed his back with the palm of my hand, wordlessly reassuring him that I would be fine; great, even. Especially if I could leave all the school stuff behind and perform across the country instead. But now I was worried, go figure, despite abhorring the worry being thrown my way in the last week.

"Cam," I said. "I'm going to be alright; you know me. But I need to ask you something."

We mutually released our squeeze on each other. Cameron stepped back, wiped his nose with the back of his hand, and shakily asked, "What's up?"

"If I manage to join this band, and have to drop out, promise me *you* will be okay."

He sniffled, then said, "Yeah. I'll be okay. For you."

Reflections and remembrances of Todd from a week before.

"You can't just be okay for me, okay?" I said. "You're your own person, and a great one at that. Don't let anyone tear you down, especially Jasmine when it's her time of the month, alright? You're better than that, and probably one of the best people to ever grace this shithole building. Even for a trumpet player."

Cameron grinned at that; not a wide grimace, but a softened twinkle still imbued with an underlying sadness.

I continued: "Now, I'm gonna go practice. Tell Dr. Porter I'm in the third-floor bathroom puking my brains out or something."

"Alright, Joel. I know you'll make it out there. Knock them dead."

He said that last bit with so much confidence, I could already see the strobe lights and hear the amps. The people dancing, drunk and high out of their minds. Smoke filling the venue, a beautiful mix of fog machines and cigarettes. I brought him in for another hug—shorter this time—and then he was on his way.

Cameron Wright was going places, I was sure. But he needed to make it to music history class for now.

Godspeed, soldier.

2

I blocked Jasmine on every social media imaginable after that hallway spat. And to be absolutely sure I wouldn't flake on this endeavor; I blocked her school email as well. Just as a precaution, obviously. *That'll send a message at least*, I thought.

I didn't hear from her again before the fateful night of November 24th. I made sure to maneuver the halls of the School of Music as sneakily as possible, avoiding being seen during the passing periods. Room 218 was always available, because why wouldn't it be? I played and performed and felt the music rattle in my bones. Every note eventually sang with the resonance of an overweight opera singer after their thirtieth water bottle of the day.

Days passed; my nerves softened. Muscle memory engrained itself into my body, making sure I would never forget the key change in "Drive." That piece-of-shit key change. I saw Todd a few more times, obviously. He began going out less and less as the days went by, and the Xs on my calendar slowly crept toward the big **SCYPHOZOA** printed in sloppy handwriting on the 24th. He was saving his energy for the big night; him drinking until his liver gave out while his favorite band played over the loudspeakers in

Toss & RUMble. Asher Gaumont and Jessica Fitzgerald and Evelyn and Adam Stone. All of them working in unison to create beautiful, earth-shattering music, even with their trombonist absent.

And I would be there.

I would be there to swoop in and save them all.

To fill the void left by Kyrie Castillo.

Because without a trombone, Scyphozoa wouldn't be Scyphozoa, and I needed Scyphozoa in my life. Lots of people needed them, and I was the only one who could keep them alive and thriving. Roselle be damned, Sanduhr be damned, everyone and everything be damned. I needed to live, to be free. College wasn't for me, none of this was for me. But performing? Traveling across the country? Being free of the restraints binding me to my sad life in academia? That was an offer I could never pass up.

Todd was right; I needed to have a factory reset of sorts. To forget about everything so I wouldn't go down a path I'd rather not trudge down. What waited for me at the end of that trail likely involved a rope hanging from a ceiling fan, or an empty bottle of pills at my bedside, or slashes down my arms while lying in a tub.

So, I practiced. Practiced again, practiced some more, practiced a bit here and there with an extra helping of more practice. I became music incarnate in those few weeks.

Nothing could stop me.

CHAPTER IV

1

"You can't bring that in here, kid."

Just my luck that the bouncer checking IDs on the night of November 24th happened to be the same brawny jerk who wouldn't let me in the weekend Roselle broke up with me. Specifically, the night I got into a fight with a bunch of other jerks who called me a slur that was only half true when thrown my direction. "Can't I stick this in a private room or something?" I asked, gesturing toward the trombone case securely held in my grasp.

"Oh, sure," the bouncer said with biting sarcasm. "I'd just have to melt it down to make sure there's no explosives in there. Can't have a Manchester Arena incident at some random bar in Massachusetts now, can we?"

That bouncer had obviously done his homework on tragic incidents, and I couldn't imagine how he'd react if a different college student walked by and made a passing joke about September 11th. I slouched my shoulders slightly, attempting to look more desperate than I was letting on. "Sir," I pled, "this is *really* important. The band playing tonight requested I came and played with them."

A bold-faced lie, I know, but in this hour of desperation I needed to pull any bunny out of my magic hat that could possibly persuade that prick to let me in.

"If that were the case, I would've been told in advance," he said. "But, oh no! It seems that no one told me anything about anyone guest performing tonight! Sorry, bud. If you want to get in, show me your ID and leave the case out here."

"No way, man!" I shouted. "That's bullshit!"

"It's just the rules."

Tears glossed over my eyes. The world blurred around me, turning into a soupy mess of smoke and neon lights. I groaned and left the line, my trombone in tow, my face a toxic mess of tears and white-hot rage.

2

Todd had already made his way inside, clad in a Scyphozoa shirt he bought on Etsy from a random guy in Sacramento, a highlighter orange bandana tightly bound around his forehead. He made life seem so easy, the way he strolled his handsome ass past the bouncer and up the steps and through the doors of Toss & RUMble. I had watched him go with that confidence imbued in his stride and thought wrongly that his strong poise could be applied to myself, too.

I sat in the alleyway next to the bar, my back against the brick wall and my butt sat on the damp, uneven pavement below. I breathed in through my nose, out through my mouth. Breaths that were shaky and wavering like a Slinky during an earthquake. They went in and out in short unsupported bursts, blockaded by the clots of anger within me. I was pissed, sure, but *who wouldn't be?* I thought.

The hands of fate were actively striving to bar me from seizing the moment. Those greasy, slimy hands that craved nothing but my downfall. They slipped their fingers into every crevice of my life, manipulating my every action and reaction to keep me complacent. I was more than a broke college student with a useless degree path, a slim picking of friends, a dead drunkard of a father, and a mother who was an agent of those hands of fate. She always called from our home miles away in Chicago, a minuscule apartment in the city's pulmonary artery. Without fail, she would make sure everything was to her liking in Sanduhr: The classes, the dining halls, the apartment, the downtown crime, and sometimes her son occasionally, but rarely.

Julie Auguste never had a great childhood, especially since the last few years of her teenage life were headlined by my father grooming her until she was old enough to legally marry; he was twenty-one when they met, she was fifteen. Barely out of a training bra, and he was still trying to get into her pants. And eventually, he did. That son of a bitch. Had poor Julie pop out my older sister, Bethany, at the ripe age of eighteen. She wasn't even ninth months into being a legal adult, much to the alarm of my grandparents on both sides of the family.

They had their spats, and by "spats" I mean my father would wail on her while she took each blow helplessly; the intensity of each hit depending on his blood/alcohol level on any given day. It was a miracle, as the doctor had put it, that I was even born. "All that physical and mental trauma must have done *something* to the baby," he had said when he saw the bruises my mother brandished like tiger stripes. Some on her face, some on her arms, many more around the bulge of her stomach that once housed little fetus Joel Auguste.

Some would think she would have healed from all that pain and suffering once my father decided to drunkenly ram his pickup truck into an electrical pole, but no. She decided to take all the trauma she absorbed from him—one lash at a time over decades—and hurl them back at me as if she were the Death Star's laser cannon and I was poor little Alderaan. My sister went completely unscathed from my mother's wrath, as she was older than me and escaped the potential scrutiny by becoming a measly therapist after her college tenure.

My mother never approved of anything I did: The school I chose, the degree I switched to, the friends I made, the relationships I formed. But in my fit of contempt and anguish, sitting in that dark and dreary alleyway, I decided to pull out my phone and give her a call.

It took her five rings to pick up on the other end.

"Hello?"

"Hey, Mom," I said, my voice still wobbling with overwhelming grief and resentment.

"It's so late, Joel. Why're you calling?"

"I don't know. I just needed someone to talk to. Thought a mother such as yourself would be a good option." I didn't believe that, as per the slight snark drilling its way through my tone.

"Are you okay?"

I paused. Each second went by slowly and painfully; the passage of time trudging along like a turtle with severe arthritis.

"No," I said.

Now it was her turn to pause. She'd never been good at having the hard conversations with me. She wasn't a boy, after all. My mother would always have those girl talks with Bethany—the talks of boys she found cute, professors she found abhorrent, movies she liked, books she didn't—but always avoided talking to me about anything personal, shallow, and everything in between. When my father died, she stopped talking to me altogether. Unless I said or did something she didn't agree with, which, I guess, was all the time. No conversations between us, just one-sided scoldings that went nowhere.

"What do you mean 'no?'" she asked.

An ambulance screamed by on the street; the siren's pitch rising and falling as it passed the alleyway and the line of people clamoring to see Scyphozoa in the bar next door. "Where are you?"

"At a bar," I said.

"Doesn't sound like you're at a bar. Were those sirens?"

"Yes."

"You're not doing any drugs?"

"No," I said, the molly in my pocket saying otherwise.

"Then why did you call? I'm trying to sleep."

My face grew hot with disappointment, both in her and in myself. As much as I resented the lack of affection she showed me in my twenty-one years of life, I also resented myself for crawling back to her like a lost bear cub looking for his mama on a stormy winter night. She wasn't even distraught that I opted to skip Thanksgiving in Chicago the day before. "Why wouldn't I call, Mom? Obviously, I'm not doing well! Show a little care once in a while, and maybe I'd try to come home more often."

"That's no way to talk to your mother."

"You barely talk to me, so what's the matter? Show some compassion, man."

"Don't call me that."

"I'm dropping out."

That... oh, wow. That spewed out of me so unexpectedly that I slapped my gaping mouth with the velocity of a jet engine. Had I really been thinking that? Did I just tell my *mother* that? I mean, I had been thinking about the idea of dropping school for a while at that point, but was I ready to commit to that idea so fully? So confidently?

Was I sure?

Yeah, I think I was.

"No, you fucking aren't," my mother spat into the receiver.

"I'm joining a band tonight and they're going to sign me on. I won't have time for school anymore, since they tour a lot and are making new music all the time. That's why I called, I'm pretty sure. To make sure you were the first person. The first person to know that your little fuck-up of a son is going on to do greater things than you ever could."

"What about your debt, Joel? You won't be able to pay that off without a degree and a *stable* job! You must be taking *something* right now because this is just outrageous!"

"I'm completely sober, Mom. My mind's made up. Maybe I'll come visit when the tour bus stops by Chicago."

I hung up before she had the opportunity to respond. After I clicked that red button on my screen, I saw my notifications slide into view. Mostly text messages from Todd wondering where I was, wondering if he should come out and persuade the bouncer to let me and my trombone in with that flawless Todd charm. I scrolled for a bit, saw Roselle had texted me, and heard a tinny sound clatter in the distance before I could make the mistake of responding to her.

I turned off my phone, shoved it into my pocket, and stared into the misty abyss where that noise ceaselessly echoed from.

Nothing but darkness down that path.

3

My shoes scraped across the rough pavement as I rose from my stoop. I planted my hand on the wall behind me for balance, having not realized I'd sat on the ground so long my feet were in a frenzy of pins and needles. They picked and prodded from under my skin. I almost lost my balance when I heard the sound again.

I checked the outside world behind me; the cars whizzing by, the people chattering in line, the music easing in and out of earshot when the doors of RUMble opened and closed. Signs of life, for sure. I wasn't dreaming; I knew that. But this alleyway seemed a lot darker than I had remembered from ten minutes before.

The further the walls extended from the road behind me, the denser the shadows became, swallowing all the light in their wake.

I picked up my trombone case, felt its weight. It kept me grounded while the sudden fear coursing through my veins took hold. Despite the coolness of late fall, I broke out in a cold sweat. Beads of perspiration welled in my pores, drowning me in a fit of sheer terror, creating an ocean of horrifying possibilities. Questions swam through my mind; Who was down there? *What* was down there? Could I see them? Could they see me? Please don't see me; I'm not here. I can leave right now, mister, if you so please. Anything for you, but just let me live. I have a concert to attend.

But, for reasons I couldn't explain, I stayed with my feet planted in the spot I rose from, unmoving. I was a statue and whatever was at the end of that alley was a sledgehammer. I dared not take a step forward, a step backward. The inexplicable being lurking in the dark of night would likely lurch from the shadows at any sigh of movement. Even a bead of sweat falling from my brow would set it off.

Clink.

My heart sunk into my stomach; the air in my lungs had a mass exodus of sorts. Breathless, I stared with falcon eyes into the void, attempting to discern any reflections of lamplight beyond the veil.

Clink. Gurgle. Gurgle?

Where did that come from? The addition of a second strange noise to the mix must have lifted the hex put on me, as my left foot decided to move without thinking of doing so. I stepped on those persistent pins and needles toward the source of the noises. One step at a time. Left, right, left, right like the world's slowest marching band. Tooting my horn as I paraded toward certain danger.

Gurgle. Clink. Gurgle.

A primal curiosity overcame me. Most of the thoughts that bogged me down in the past weeks left my mind like the air rushing from my lungs. My waning friendship with Todd, my distaste with Jasmine, my breakup with Roselle, the empty apologies thrown my way, poor old Cameron Wright. The only remnant of brain activity that remained was the unbearable weight of my mother, and the potential evil lying in wait just beyond the cusp of late November moonlight.

A light fog rolled in. Steam from the rooftops descended into the alleyway in a haze. The bass from the speakers inside RUMble shook the brick wall to my left. A rhythmic heartbeat thumped from the bar. It beat in sync with the heart in my own chest, each contraction pounding at my ribs with an increasing tempo. Faster and faster as I approached the darkness before me.

Clink.

Is this what I wanted?

Gurgle.

To wander into the vast unknown?

Clink.

To let the monsters skulking within grab ahold of me?

Gurgle.

To allow them to rip me limb for limb?

Clink.

That intrusive idea didn't seem all that terrible. Sure, it would turn out to be a gory mess, but at least I would be free. And that's all we want, right? To free ourselves from the sorrow and agony and wretchedness of life. By any means necessary. Even if that meant meeting my fate with the shadow demons in the alley next to Sanduhr's most popular Friday night spot.

Then, like the sun peeking from behind the horizon on a warm summer morning, I spotted a small flame in the darkness.

It tore the fabric of the pitch black with its blazing tendrils. My heartbeat slowed to an ordinary pace. I began to feel like a kid on Christmas morning. That strange joy and nostalgia, all bundled up with a decorative bow on top.

And what to my wondering eyes should appear, but two identical blondes smiling ear to ear. A bong passed between the two, its bowl piece clinking in the downstream while water gurgled in the wide chamber at its base.

Evelyn Stone glanced up and beamed at me with pink-tinged eyes.

"Hello," we said to one another.

Completely in sync.

4

"Whatcha got there?" Adam Stone asked, a puff of smoke billowing from his mouth and nostrils.

I was completely awestruck; unable to let any words pass my lips after the short greeting Evelyn and I shared. I looked down at the trombone case, remembering *(oh yeah)* it was there.

"Shut the *fuck* up," Evelyn said with exasperation.

The rusty stool she sat on creaked as she leaned forward. Her robust forearms, likely toned from years of drumming, planted themselves firmly onto her thighs as she seemingly peered into my soul. She glared at me with curious intent, but with an aura of already knowing the answers to the questions racing through her head.

"You're trying to join the band, aren't you?" Evelyn asked.

Flabbergasted, I ignored the obvious warning signs I gave in terms of that fact.

"Well," Adam chimed in, "come on, man. Let's hear the pitch."

He set the bong on the pavement, leaning toward me with the same air of interest that Evelyn offered. Their blue eyes shot through the dark like laser beams decimating my brains, or a lighthouse shining its rays through dense sea fog. Their facial features were nearly identical, save for the differences in jaw structure that came packaged with the two opposite genders. Where I felt a sense of dread from Evelyn's gaze, I felt warmth in Adam's, despite the eyes cut from the same cloth. That seemed to be my ticket to enter the conversation.

"I've been a fan for years, and I heard that your trombonist quit a little while back. I thought if I—"

"No, no, no," Evelyn interrupted. "Not a *sales* pitch. Play."

My heart, which had just recovered from sinking into my stomach a few minutes before, dropped down to the same spot again. A lump manifested in my throat. The most I could muster was a frantic nod.

Evelyn Stone motioned toward my trombone case. I set it on the ground, bent down and released the latches securing my horn inside its cage. I assembled the parts one after another in quick succession. I allowed no room for errors in that process, including the warmup process; lips slurs in first position, followed by glissandos up and down the partials. *WAAAaaaaaAAAH, WAAAaaaaaAAAH.*

The Stone twins giggled at the conclusion of my rapid warmup. Adam noticed the look of embarrassment on my face and reassured me, "We're not laughing at you, I promise. It's just that Kyrie had the same little routine before he performed."

That was a relief, at the very least. I permitted a modest grin to ornament my lips.

"What should I play?"

"Whatever feels right," they said in unison.

I was terrified of the two of them; more in a fear of God way than a fear of nuclear annihilation way, but the point still stood. *Whatever feels right* was not the response I wanted. Actually, it was the *exact* response I didn't want. I thought about what I could blast through my trombone's bell. But that was a big deal; the first notes any member of Scyphozoa would hear me play. My choice had to be something technically challenging yet pleasing enough to the ear to warrant a good response from both Evelyn and Adam. I searched the darkest dungeons of my brain to figure out which part of any of their songs would most likely persuade them. *That's right!* I thought. *I should probably play a section from a song* they *wrote.*

And what better song to play than "Drive," a song the twins cowrote with the intention of creating the most mind-boggling, insane rock song heard this side of the galaxy? I pressed the mouthpiece to my lips, emptied the spit valve, and tapped my foot with the song's tempo in mind. One measure of prep, and then another, and soon I wailed the bridge of "Drive" on that trombone.

The bridge was infamous for its overindulgent length, spanning around two minutes as it had the sole responsibility of switching the key from A flat minor to the E flat major scale the end of the song sat upon.

By the halfway mark—the exact spot where the key shifted—my right arm began to show early signs of cramping up. My elbow joint cracked every time I slid the slide down from a higher position to a lower one. I fought through the menacing weight of slowly approaching joint pain. Sweat pooled in my brows and pits. My lips were on fire, chapped beyond belief in that malevolent combination of chilled weather and moving partials with intense speed on a brass instrument.

But I finished against all odds. I had done it; I played my heart out in front of members of Scyphozoa. Maybe I could've died happy right then and there.

If only.

I jolted the mouthpiece away from my lips as if I had just kissed a hot stove. Heavy breathing ensued. Short but weighty bursts of breath charging from my lungs as I regained a sense of place. The alleyway blurred for a split second; came back into focus.

I saw their faces, those two mirror images of each other. Mouths open and eyes widened. I had done it. All those days wasted in room 218 didn't feel like such a waste in that pocket of time. That moment of euphoria still haunts me to this day. Adam raised his arms slowly, his hands as straight as ends of boat oars. He began a slow clap, a clap that echoed through the brick walls bordering us from Toss & RUMble and the abandoned building next to it. Evelyn did the same after a few short seconds, even rising from her creaky stool as if giving me a stand ovation at a film festival.

"That," she said, "was fucking amazing!"

Adam rose to his feet, adding, "Where the hell did you learn to play like that, man?"

I wanted to spew paragraphs of Joel Auguste lore their way, to tell my entire life story from birth until now, but settled for a shrug of the shoulders instead. In show business, you gotta learn to keep it humble.

"Ahhh, we got a bragger over here," Adam remarked to Evelyn.

"Ash is gonna love him."

5

For reasons beyond simple explanation, I had completely negated the fact that if my plan of personal redemption worked, I would have to meet Asher Gaumont. "How would you like to play tonight?" Evelyn asked as she shuffled me toward the side door of Toss & RUMble.

"Didn't I just do that?" I asked in return.

"No, silly. *Play.* As in: *play* with the band tonight," Adam said from behind, carrying my empty trombone case in one hand and the bong in his other.

I'd been so stupid in that instant that I failed to recall why I was at RUMble in the first place. Of course, I knew what they meant, subconsciously at the very least. But the puzzle pieces were falling into place and the big picture was taking shape. This was monumental. Had I actually done it? This could've been a dream. Besides, neither of them even knew my name.

"What's your name, by the way?" Evelyn asked as she propped the door open.

"Joel Auguste."

Well, that cleared the air faster than I expected. Almost as if she knew I was wondering when the question would arise.

"That's a rockstar name if I've ever heard one, right Adam?"

"Right on," Adam responded.

The music booming from inside the bar drowned out their voices. As the back door squealed open, a rush of humidity radiated from inside. That distinct musk of dense sweat filled the air and warmed my body as we entered the backstage area. We continued forth, stepping in time with the rave occurring further into the building. As Adam shut the door behind us, the ambience of the outside world faded, and the bright neon of the club washed over me.

6

I saw Asher Gaumont in person for the first time through a mirror, his back faced toward me.

He was a hunk of a man; I couldn't deny that fact. With those broad shoulders and thick arms and a neck that was so meaty and raw you could almost see it throbbing with the weight of those muscles. His hair was cut short, fading at the sides into a light stubble that complimented his strong features quite astonishingly. His eyes were closed; his head tilted downward as he slouched in his chair. He wasn't sleeping, I was sure of it, because through the buzz of college town nightlife, I could hear him humming a tune to himself. It was low and raspy, but I could discern the song as their early cover of "Doing Alright."

"Ash?" Evelyn asked, knocking on the door. "We have a visitor."

I watched as his head rose, those neck muscles contracting under the weight. His eyes opened, but he didn't swivel the chair toward us. He glanced at my reflection, just as I'd been staring at his. That reflective barrier separated our beings. His eyes scanned my figure up and down. Blue oceans centered with chocolate brown. I thought of a joke involving a child swimming in a clean pool that was about to not be as clean anymore but disregarded it out of respect for the living indie rock legend sitting mere feet away.

Asher let out a contemptuous grunt and finally decided it was the right time to face me without the help of the mirror in front of him. He pulled a cigarette from his shirt pocket and pointed the filter at me. "Want one?" he asked, his voice gruff from years of strained singing.

Despite my crippling nicotine addiction, my allegiance was with the strawberry banana flavored vapes of the twenty-first century. But a cigarette was a cigarette, and it was offered to me by Asher Gaumont. I couldn't help feeling that this was a test. Some sort of weird pact I agreed to. As the last few weeks had me to believe, I was desperate for this, so I took the cigarette from his fingers and leaned in to catch the flame of his lighter.

I lit up, breathing in the aroma of burning newspaper. A taste of mint graced my tongue as I pulled the cigarette from my mouth, let the smoke sit in my lungs, and blew. Smoke filled the air. My brain went fuzzy, and my legs turned to jelly. For an uninterrupted eternity, I felt nothing but an indescribable buzz. I forgot about everything that dragged me down. Those aching emotions that tried to bury me six feet under dissipated with every subsequent drag off the cigarette.

Asher lit up with me, almost like a sort of ritual.

I had no idea what was in that cigarette. I still don't know, but it wasn't just the usual tobacco, nicotine, and menthol. Yet, I was fueled with desperation and a drive to succeed. I was right there at the finish line, and I needed to sprint to beat out the rest of the runners. Laced cigarette or no laced cigarette, performing that night was all I could possibly think of.

I didn't meet any of the other band members until it was showtime. The world whizzed by in a brightly colored blur as I stumbled onto the stage, trombone in hand. A short man—or a tall boy, but who could really say?—whose name might have been Marty helped hook a mic up to the bell of my horn. He said something completely inaudible against the cheering fans. Maybe something about what the microphone was supposed to do? Couldn't tell you.

But those fans, all cheering for Scyphozoa. I had no idea there were so many clamoring fans in little old Sanduhr, Massachusetts. They hooted and hollered until their throats could only let out harsh rasps. Shrill screams cut through the dense air, thick with sweat, like a blazing knife through butter. Those voices—masculine, feminine, and everything in between—mixed together in a hodgepodge of sheer excitement. I didn't know what to make of it all, but I knew in my heart that it was what I was destined to do. As far as my mind could see, empty of rational thought, I was the center of the universe. Floating within the vast nothingness of space, the actors of this grand opera orbiting my soul.

Evelyn adjusted the drum set to her liking; Adam tuned his bass guitar to the best of his ability against the blaring nightlife just past the edge of the makeshift stage. Then there was a girl, a girl so oddly familiar. I knew her from pictures and videos, but I couldn't place her name for the life of me. That flaming red hair beamed through the night and shook me to my core.

Jessica Fitzgerald.

That was her, in all her fiery glory.

In my drugged stupor, I began to stroll over her way. But before I could embarrass myself as she tuned her guitar and made sure her rickety keyboard worked; Asher Gaumont stepped out from behind the curtain.

An eruption of shouts ensued. Men cried; women screamed. The power that man had over a crowd was unlike anything I had ever seen.

And with a swipe of his hand, the crowd went silent.

Into the microphone, against the stillness and sudden tranquility in the bar, Asher purred to the crowd, "Let's bring you back to life."

7

The room erupted in cheers and applause. Unintelligible responses echoed, bouncing from wall to wall in a garbled wave of sound.

I flinched as the short man I presumed to be called Marty stuck an earpiece in my ear without so much as a warning. Asher removed the mic from its stand, carrying the cord in tow as he sauntered back and forth across the limited space the stage afforded him. A spotlight shone on him, following in a beam of artificial light. It harshly contrasted with the blues and purples common in Toss & RUMble, cutting into the night. Shining brightly on the real star of the show; surely not me, but Asher Gaumont.

He waved his arms, those limbs bulging from his tight shirtsleeves, to hype the crowd. He lurched to the left; the people followed suit. He bent to the right; they did the same. It reminded me of the university's marching band's drum major, standing at the front of the group in the football field stands, pretending to be riding a rollercoaster while all the other band members mimicked her movements. This tsunami of people in RUMble waded in cascades of indigo and glitter and spilled drinks. Liquor and beer sloshing through the air from open cups and bottles, spilling to the floor in a cacophony of alcohol.

With the crowd properly warmed up, Asher turned and nodded to the rest of the band and me. He mouthed the word *Drive*, and I immediately smiled. I disregarded the fact that playing the bridge earlier almost ripped my arm in two at the elbow; I was ready.

The grimness that had adorned Asher's face in the mirror back in the ragtag dressing room was completely gone, lost to time. He grinned and nodded once in my direction. *Show me what you got*, he must've thought.

He meekly counted off a tempo, wiggling his arm in a haphazard conductor's move. *1, 2… 1, 2, 3, 4.* Then we were off.

Jessica strummed a meaty chord, accompanied by Evelyn going hog wild on the set. Adam's bass thumped with the tempo, easing us into the hell that would be this seven-minute rock opus. The crowd went into a frenzy; the spotlights zipped through the people, illuminating the patrons in zigzags of light. It reminded me of a game I used to play with the family cat, Dante, years before. I would take that orange cat into my closet, shut off the lights, and shine a flashlight. He would pounce from corner to corner as I flicked the light every which way. Some of those people were like Dante, but none as close as Todd, who I spotted around three rows of patrons deep into the sea of bodies.

His eyes fluttered in spasms, both in shock and awe. He was watching his favorite band perform live mere feet from him, and his roommate was in the group itself. He yelped louder, raising his voice above the crowd. As Asher began to sing the first lines of the ballad portion of "Drive" (*There's a mountain between us, agents of Judas*), Todd roared at the top of his lungs. I couldn't read his lips, but there was certainly an "O" sound in there. Joel, maybe?

It was my time to shine. The guitars faded, Asher's voice dwindles, and then it was just me on my trombone and Evelyn Stone wailing away on the drums. Thank God the band didn't play "Drive" in a different key than I practiced on. I played the first long tone and was instantly surprised by the sound emitting from the horn's bell. It wasn't brassy in the slightest; just metallic, grating, and perfect for rock. Whatever the mic attached to my bell was connected to, it was distorting my sound so perfectly that I resonated with near-perfect accuracy to the studio recording of the song. Instead of the typical *wah wahs* that instrument was known for, I produced some of the most intense bass sounds heard in the Western Hemisphere that night.

I played, my arm aching instantaneously with the midpoint of the bridge section. I pushed through the stabbing pains, pretending my arm wasn't about to be removed from its goddamn socket. I tuned out the crowd, focused on the music. I squinted my eyes, concentrated on my pitch and performer's stance. I needed to look proud and confident. A band like Scyphozoa wouldn't want a weak member dragging them down. They were climbing up the charts and didn't need a ball and chain such as myself to make the journey more difficult. I played and played and played until my chops were ready to burst. My lips felt limp and dead underneath the mouthpiece, but I continued. Every neuron in my brain focused on the task before me: Finish the song or die trying.

I chose life.

8

The song ended in rapturous applause. Whoops from frat bros close to the entrance directly across from the stage, screams from the sorority sisters down in front, reaching past the bulky shoulders of security guards to get a sensory taste of Asher.

I still couldn't believe what was happening was real. I kicked myself in the ankle to test the theory. I felt a throbbing sensation down there. *I'm here*, I thought. *This is now.*

Asher took a bow and gestured toward me on his way back up. Not a drop of sweat graced his skin. He was as dry as the bottom of my grand-mother's water well on the hottest day of summer. "And let's give a big round of applause to the real star of tonight's show: Sanduhr's own... Joel Auguste!" he shouted in the mic.

Cheers, for me. All for me.

My mind was foggy from whatever was in that cigarette, but I managed to get enough juice for a tear to roll down my cheek. I waved to the crowd, who disappeared from my view as the main spotlight shone directly into my face. I didn't mind the temporary blindness. I could still hear them, and they loved me. That was enough.

"This next one," Asher introduced. "Is for all the lonely people out there. Here's the Beatles on 'Eleanor Rigby.'"

That was a lesser lauded cover of theirs from the earlier days of indie stardom. In fact, one of their least popular songs in terms of times streamed on Spotify and the likes. But of course, I knew my part anyway; I didn't ditch school and any hope for a social life without memorizing Scyphozoa's entire discography note for note. The modulator attached to my horn played a normal brassy sound this time, but added chordal tones over or under my played note based on where in the song we were. Very complicated live sound design, but the result was absolutely fantastic. Asher sang the melody; Evelyn sang the harmony when the time arose. Playing something as mellowed as "Eleanor Rigby" after the musical hellfire that was "Drive" was cause for some major whiplash, but the audience loved it all the same. That was the power of music. It binds us in song, hand in hand, carrying us through our separate ways as one conjoined unit.

The song ended as they all did: with laudation and acclamation in the form of ecstatic cheers. We played more songs, naturally. It was a damn concert, after all. The cycle of performance and congratulations continued until the setlist reached its conclusion.

There was one song that was notably absent from the schedule until the very end. I knew it, the crowd knew it, even some of the bartenders off to the sides knew it.

Fric-tion. Fic-tion.
Fric-tion. Fic-tion.
Fric-tion. Fic-tion.

The audience started in a low murmur. They crescendoed to a

monumental chant. They stomped their feet into the floor with every syllable. Asher took a massive swig of a plastic water bottle and threw the rest
of its contents into the crowd. The weird thing about American society is
that in any other situation, it would be seen in the same vein as terrorism.
But since it was an idol people adored, this aqua-based attack was welcomed. Famous people get a free pass on stuff like that, and that's how
having any level of celebrity status is. Instead of throwing insults and curses
his way, the crowd cheered louder. Most of the girls and some of the gays
reached levels of horniness unheard of in college town Massachusetts.

"We got one more song for you, Sanduhr."

Bloodcurdling screams burst from the audience like a dormant volcano
not liking the way a nearby village was looking at it. Explosions of shouts blew
toward the stage. The *Fric-tion. Fic-tion.* chant continued underneath the eruption.

"This is…" Asher paused. "'Frictional Fiction.'"

A love song disguised as a pseudo-Metallica rock tune began as the
drums slapped, the bass guitar thumped, and the keyboard carried the song
on its back. Asher borrowed Jessica's electric guitar and strummed the hints
of a melody that would arrive soon enough.

Fans had debated the meaning of that specific song for years. On the
surface, the lyrics were narrated by a lonely man lamenting over a rocky
relationship.

> *You're a fire in the Ozarks,*
> *always burning with those sly remarks.*
> *You hated me and my bottle of Jack,*
> *So why'd you keep coming back?*

But in my mind, I found it to be the opposite. Maybe it was about a
person trying to separate themselves from a toxic lover; one that won't stop
making the subject of that story feel like they were the issue. The meaning
stuck with me in the weeks after Roselle climbed the stairs to my apartment
and rid herself of me. I couldn't be mad at her, but I just wished she would
stop reminding me of her existence without doing anything. That was all
on me, her manifesting into my mind at every slight inconvenience.

This time, however, she wasn't just in my head. She was in the crowd. Watching me, arms crossed the same way they had been when she sat on my couch, staring at the floor, not looking me in the eye. Telling me that I wasn't worth it. Strobe lights illuminated her face milliseconds at a time, but she was there. I was sure of it. As I played my part in "Frictional Fiction," I glimpsed her slipping through the crowd, her eyes (oh, those beautiful hazel eyes) locked on an unknown target. She hovered from the sixth messy row of people, to the fifth, then the fourth, and then she stopped.

The band grew louder in unison as the song reached its emotional peak.

> *Oh, this frictional fiction,*
> *How I wish you could be real.*
> *How I wish we could be here,*
> *In the friction of it all.*

The volume peaked on the last *real*. And with that dynamic marking at the top of the mountain, Roselle tapped Todd on the shoulder, he turned to her, brought her in for a hug… and they kissed.

Fuck this place.

CHAPTER V

1

All the legal documents were signed and filed by noon the following day.

I had the rest of the weekend to pack my bags and hit the road with Scyphozoa. I didn't see Todd for all of Saturday and most of that Sunday, much to no one's surprise. That little cunt could sleep with everyone on campus if it meant I didn't have to see him again. I said my goodbyes to Cameron, Alvaro, Fran. Not Jasmine, as we were still on bad terms from that little spat. My landlord dropped my lease after I made it clear I wasn't a student at Sanduhr anymore. "No non-student residents in the building," as per that stringent document. The complex was so close to campus that having non-residents would pose a threat to student safety, so I took that small warning with open arms. Another shackle tying me to that place was unlocked.

I packed all my belongings into a set of four backpacks and a large suitcase. I preferred to live light while at school. Less things to take home during the long holidays where it was morally the right thing to go back home and spend time with family. Or whatever family I truly had left back in northern Illinois.

The Scyphozoa tour bus was parked outside my apartment in the middle of the road. Red and yellow, the band's signature colors, adorned the bus's metallic sheen. Not a gross yellow, but a more subdued dandelion yellow. More pleasing to the eye, but the bus still would have looked like an eyesore on the highway. Cars probably got into accidents with how eye-catching it was. It was meticulously clean. People I had seen wandering campus—those familiar faces, but unfamiliar people—stood around the bus. They had looks of awe and wonder stricken across their faces, wondering why the hell this monolith of a bus was parked on *that* street of all the streets it could've been parked on.

I heard a knock on my door, walked over through the apartment with only enough stuff for one person to be living there now, unlocked the deadbolt and opened the door. It was Jessica Fitzgerald standing on the other side, her orange hair blazing under the fluorescent lights just as it did in the strobe lights of Toss & RUMble. Her freckles popped in the dim glow, punctuating her features against the gloominess of the hallway outside my door. "Hey, Joel," she said.

There was a hint of unease in her tone. She didn't want to be the one they sent to fetch me, but the others on the bus must've been too high or wasted or both to do that honor. She raised her arm to me, her hand outstretched. As we clasped hands and shook, Jessica said, "I'm sorry I didn't introduce myself sooner. It's been a crazy weekend."

"Yeah, you're telling me," I said.

We released our grip on each other. I slipped my hands into my pockets while she let hers fall gracefully to her sides.

"Well, they sent me up to ask if you needed any help getting your stuff down to the bus. Do you need any help or are you good?" she asked.

"I mean, I wouldn't be opposed to some help."

That must have humored her a bit, as shown by the smile that scrunched her nose and loosened her nerves.

"Did you want to come in?" I asked.

She nodded.

2

"It's not unlike them to just grab a random guy like you off the street and have them play in the band for a tour cycle," Jessica said. "It's happened before, and it'll certainly happen after they're done with you."

"Done with me?"

"Yeah, *done* with you. Could I get a water?" She paused with a look of confusion contorting her features. "If you have water."

"Yes, I have water, Jessica."

"Call me Jess. Please."

"Alright. You want bottled or tap?"

"Bottled for sure."

Jess sat on the exact couch cushion Roselle had sat upon the day after my birthday. The divot created under her weight could still be seen, going unnoticed by Jess, who asked, "This isn't *your* couch, right?"

"No. It came with the place."

"Figures. I can feel the springs poking my ass."

"Probably because it's old."

"Probably because it's old," she repeated as I handed her an unopened water bottle. She nodded as a sign of thanks and untwisted the cap. Thin plastic cracked with each twist until there was a sudden, satisfying *pop*. She guzzled half the bottle's contents and sealed it back up, resting it on the carpet at her feet. She wouldn't let that bottle leave her sight, as if she were worried it would sprout legs and run away before she could finish her business with it.

"So, what did you mean by 'done with me?'" I asked.

She looked as if she'd forgotten what we had been talking about not even a minute before. Then the memory flooded back into her system. She met my eyes.

"Exactly what you think I meant," she said.

"I'm not following."

She groaned, took another sip of water, and set it back into its resting spot, eyes glued to its transparent sheen. "There's a lot they want me to say, a lot they don't," she said. "But what I *can* say is that this industry is malicious. Ruthless. The system will eat you up and shit you out without a second thought. I'm happy for you, I really am. And I hope you stay. But with the way this band works, you'll be gone by next summer. Guaranteed."

"I appreciate the confidence."

"Don't be snarky with me. Just trying to soften the blow before the inevitable happens. I don't want to see anyone else get hurt. Not after Kyrie."

"Kyrie? What about him."

"Can I smoke in here?"

"Technically no, but I don't live here anymore. So... I don't see the issue."

"Perfect."

She whipped a pack of cigarettes from her pocket, selected one, and propped the filter in her mouth all in one autonomous motion: With the finesse of an expert in the field of smoking tar. As she took a long drag, I repeated, "What about Kyrie?"

"There's not a lot I can say on that."

"That sounds like bullshit."

"It's complicated."

"I got all the time in the world. Indulge me."

Another pull off the cigarette sent her head back in a euphoric daze. Her eyes rolled into her sockets as the couch cushion encumbered her skull. She looked as if she were fighting the urge to say more on the subject, like the words were there, swimming in her throat, but simply couldn't escape her mouth.

"It's just too much," Jess said after a short while, taking another drag. "Forget I mentioned him."

"How am I supposed to forget if it might affect me directly? What happened to him? Why did he leave Scyphozoa?"

"It's more a matter of *how* he left, not *why* he left. I know why he left, everyone does. He was too good for us. I took no offense to it, obviously. I recognized talent when I saw it, and Kyrie definitely had us beat in the talent department. Asher saw that, too. The way Kyrie played, the way he blossomed from some nobody into a massive black hole, swallowing up all the stars around him. Even Asher. And, in Asher's own little selfish opinion, he didn't need someone overshadowing him. So, Kyrie left. It was mutual, from what I heard. Or, at least, I hope that was the case. Because Kyrie was so sweet and kind. He deserved nothing more than the spotlight, and I was happy for him. Sad to see him go, obviously, but I'm glad he gets to go on and serve a better purpose than Scyphozoa granted him."

A tear welled in her eye, but her face didn't register sadness. Her bottom lip didn't tremble, her eyebrows didn't curve upward, her mouth didn't morph into a frown. A look of contempt complimented her features. But that tear, the gloss of liquid glazed across there, added an artificial look to those eyes, like both were suddenly replaced with glass eyes from a pawn shop. Undoubtedly real, but unnatural, nonetheless.

Her fingers holding the cigarette began to tremble; a clump of ash fell from the burning white tip. I didn't bother picking up that little charcoal bit. For all I know, it could still be imbued into the carpet. That little burning coal simmering in those carpet fibers. If a cigarette burns in an apartment and only I notice, did it actually burn?

"Well, I'm glad he's doing alright. You were worrying me a bit," I said, wincing at my use of *worry*.

Jess noticed, and asked, "Are you okay?"

"Yeah, I'm okay."

She lifted the remnants of her cigarette to me.

"Want a hit?" she asked.

I plucked it from her grasp, held it between two fingers, and breathed in. The same sensation from Friday night filled my nerves with a familiar yet distant bliss. It wasn't tobacco, but it was doing wonders for my psyche regardless.

Jess rose from the couch, smoothed her jeans with the palms of her hands, and sighed. "Let's get these bags to the bus."

"Agreed," I said.

I took another drag, staring around my apartment like a sitcom character leaving the soundstage during the series finale. The popcorn ceiling, the cracking hardwood floors, the bathroom tile. The refrigerator whose freezer door would never fully close regardless of how much food was in there. The heater hummed incessantly from the furnace closet next to the bathroom. The singular light fixture planted above the living room couch. Jessica hauled two of my backpacks out the door as I wandered into my bedroom. The mattress was barren, stripped of its sheets. Those beige walls wouldn't bother me anymore with their lack of life, their lack of spunk and punctuality. There were some things I would miss about college life, but none that could anchor me to Sanduhr. I had no deep love for that place. I picked the campus from my pool of college applications, not because of its graduation rate (which I was *not* helping to raise) or its academics or the area or any of that, but because it was the furthest from home. A fifteen-hour drive from here to there, there to here. Enough time to believably make excuses not to visit home.

Oh, I just have so much homework, Mom.

Oh, I can't afford a plane ticket.

I could probably afford a plane ticket with that sweet Scyphozoa salary, but would I pay for one anyway? Only the gods could decide, and I hoped they were on sabbatical.

I slugged the other two backpacks onto my shoulders, one in front and one in back. I looked ready for combat as I dragged the suitcase out of the apartment, locked the deadbolt, and slid my key under the door.

3

I couldn't take two steps out the front door before something went wrong. Todd stood there, disgustingly handsome as ever. I wondered for a split second why he was here but remembered (*OF COURSE! DUH! SILLY FUCKING ME!*) that he lived here. I rolled the suitcase past him without so much as a glance. We brushed shoulders. A light breeze hit my face, soothing my boiling anger. He hadn't even done anything in those few seconds we crossed paths, but I wanted nothing more than to beat him into a fine paste on the pavement.

"Hey!" Todd shouted.

I halted. My suitcase stopped skidding its wheels, desperately in need of some oil in their system, on the rough asphalt. I contemplated whether I should turn around, to give him the satisfaction of grabbing my attention. *I'm better than this*, I thought. Apparently not, however, as I turned around and leaned against the suitcase. The wind picked up a bit, howling softly between the two of us. In the distance, sirens wailed; car horns beeped. Sounds of the city, that bygone dwarf planet across the galaxy.

"What?" I sternly asked, hoping for something superficial to come of the question.

"I wanted to apologize."

"Right," I agreed with the air of disagreement.

"I'm serious, Joel."

"I know."

"Then why are you acting like this?"

Put a gun to my head and pull the trigger, why don't you? I thought.

"Why am *I* acting like this?" I blurted, abandoning the small talk shtick. "What the hell is *this*? Mad? Yeah, I'm mad. Of course, I'm mad! I'm fucking pissed, dude."

We stood six feet apart, reminding me of the COVID years. We may have been a person's length between each other, but we were worlds apart in my eyes. Not even in the same universe. His neurons were firing in completely different directions than mine. He may have thought the situation was going one way, but I saw the whole picture. Roselle had left me for him, plain and simple. They were chatting it up at the bars the night of my birthday, at a time in which it was obvious she was ready to move on from me. I still respect her decision to leave me; I would've done the same if I were in her situation. But to leave me and start presumably sleeping with my roommate? Oh, hell fucking no. There was no way to forgive a betrayal such as that.

"I understand that. I really do…" he lied.

"Do you? I don't think you do."

"Will you just give me a chance to explain?"

"Should I, Todd? Should I?"

I stood stupidly on the sidewalk, looking like a turtle standing on its back legs with how crammed the two backpacks on my shoulders were. Their weight bore down on me. I broke out in a thin sweat despite the coolness of that November morning. It was almost noon, the shadows of midday shining down and granting an eeriness to the situation at hand. Shadows raced down our bodies in harsh streaks, catching on the wrinkles of our sweatshirts, spotting us like cows on the pasture.

"I know you're angry, okay? I'm not saying you shouldn't be." He raised his hands methodically as if I were a rabid dog he needed to fend off.

"Then what, Todd?" I asked. "Why're you even talking to me right now?"

I straightened myself, releasing my lean against the suitcase and uncurling my spine. I stood as tall as my scoliosis would allow.

"Because you're my friend."

"Please," I scoffed. "A 'friend' wouldn't do what you did. How long had you two been seeing each other, huh? Were you two fucking in the other room while I was sleeping? Is that why she would never fuck me?"

"No, no. Nothing like that."

"Then what?"

"We just… we just started talking one day after one of her classes. I was at one of the dining halls. Paddy's, I think. She came up next to me at the table I was at and just started talking. I knew it was wrong at the time, and I still feel that way now."

"Then why did you egg yourself on? How long ago was this?"

"Beginning of September."

Beginning of September… oh, wow. That really solidified everything for me; the loose ends strengthened and lifted everything into perspective. They had basically started dating the moment she seemed to have lost interest in me, if there was even interest to begin with. As much as I wanted— knew I *should*—blame her for this fit of infidelity, my heart wouldn't budge. We had been through so much together. Hard times and good times. Arguments over our postgraduate plans; a candlelit dinner for our one-year anniversary. I couldn't throw that sort of ill will her way.

But I could certainly throw everything I had at Todd, the two-faced shit.

"So, you two have been seeing each other for almost *three months*?" I asked through gritted teeth.

"I guess so."

"And you didn't think to mention that to me?"

"I love her, man."

I clenched my fists, the knuckles almost bursting from their fleshy prison. I slung the two backpacks to the ground with the force of a power-lifter throwing a barbell after a skin-splitting set. Todd backed up, understanding that the situation had gone from tense to explosive. "Sorry," he reasserted, "I didn't mean to say that. That was wrong."

"You're right," I agreed, taking a step toward him.

Then another, and another.

"Joel," Todd said, his voice wavering, "don't start something you don't wanna finish."

I said nothing, only feeling rage and sorrow and an overwhelming pain in my heart. My pulse skyrocketed; I felt my jugular vein throb under my skin. I was inches away from him, close enough to feel his quick and sharp breaths on my face.

"Have fun being on the banned list, you bitch."

The first punch sent my right hand into shock with profuse pain. The second punch split his lip; the third broke my nose.

4

Splatters of rich, dark blood stained the sidewalk; a mix of my and his, but mostly mine.

A Nile River's worth of blood streamed from my nose as we tumbled to the ground. The meaty punches from minutes before were reduced to limp slapping as both of our energy levels sharply decreased. Everything smelled and tasted like metal. My second fistfight in one month and the taste of blood still shocked me.

I saw stars as an open palm struck my temple. Todd stuck me in a headlock, taking a few cheap blows to my stomach as I tried to slap him off me. Through the haze of violence, I spotted the bus door opening, along with a crowd of random Sanduhrites packing around us like moths to a flame. Most had their phones whipped out and ready, some with their flashes on despite the sun hanging high and bright in the sky.

Through the sea of bystanders, a figure clad in all black clothing emerged, shoving one of them so hard their phone slipped from their hand and shattered on the asphalt. They inserted themself into the scuffle, trying with all their strength to pry us two idiots apart.

I had managed to break one of my arms free from Todd's chokehold. I strained my vision to feel the ground for any substantial shards of glass. I felt a rather long piece prick my outstretched finger, to which I grasped the entire goddamn thing and swung it blindly behind me.

Todd loosened his grip and fell backward, taking me with him. He lay on his back, fumbling at the sizable gash on his forearm. It gushed blood in a red stream, adding to the splatters of my own on the ground below. I struggled to flip onto my stomach, succeeded, and planked over Todd with one hand placed firmly on the ground beside his head, the other raising the same glass shard, stained pink with blood, above his head.

The crowd of Scyphozoa fans screamed in panic and terror but did nothing. Only watched, go figure. But that mysterious figure from before, who must have fallen in the other direction after I had slashed Todd, went in for a second round. Just as I tensed my grip on the glass, sliced my palm, and readied myself to dig the tip into Todd's exposed neck, the figure wrapped their arms around my torso and sent me flying back.

5

Some *oooos* and *ahhhs* from the crowd, some weighty sobs from Todd, and me panting like a dog after a long day of squirrel chasing, laying on the stomach of whoever saved Todd from certain death at the hands of a broken iPhone screen. They pushed against me and sent me rolling off their body. With a short thump of my head against the concrete, I snapped out of whatever sort of rage had overtaken me. I could almost feel my pupils shrinking as I regained my sense of self.

"You've gotta be fucking kidding me," the figure said as they rose from the ground and shuffled back toward the bus. "Another goddamn wildcard."

I caught a glimpse of them as they climbed the steps: A bulky man with the darkest skin I'd ever seen in my extremely white life. I didn't recognize him as a member of the band, so my only assumption at the time was that he was the ordained Scyphozoa bus driver. As the crowd disappeared, each member walking off one by one, the band emerged from the bus.

Evelyn looked ecstatic, like she bet on the underdog at an MMA fight and somehow won. Adam looked high as shit, which wasn't a surprise based on my short interactions with him thus far. Jess looked horrified, and Asher looked... well, he didn't really look *anything*. He simply stared at the bloody mess before him, studying the details. Then there was Marty. I feel bad for saying he was short, but that's all he was to me at the time. Just a short little guy who seemed to follow Asher with an invisible leash around his neck. He looked mortified, even more so than Jess.

"What the *hell* happened?" he asked in a voice shriller than I expected for someone of his stature.

I got up on my feet as best as my wobbly knees could allow.

"Just some personal stuff," I said. "Nothing serious."

"Nothing serious? Do you know how bad this will look for us when those videos are posted on the Internet?"

Marty spoke with such an enormous amount of awkwardness that his speech sounded AI-generated.

"I'm sorry," I said, speaking slowly, but surely, through coagulated blood soaking above my lip and into my teeth.

"That was fucking *sick*!" Evelyn yelled.

Marty glared at her, to which she didn't falter in her enthusiasm.

"Someone should call him an ambulance. Hopefully the videos prove self-defense, since no one started recording until after you started this whole mess," Asher spoke, directly his attention to me.

I nodded, grabbed my things, and loaded the bags under the bus where Jess had placed my other two backpacks.

And that is how I started my tenure with Scyphozoa.

With a broken nose and no shortage of determination to leave that place behind.

MOVEMENT II

STONE COLD CRAZY

CHAPTER VI

1

I saw my first dead body in Charlotte.

It was in the early stages of decomposition. Pale skin wrapped around a lifeless husk, completely alabaster in the absence of blood coursing through its veins. Dried spittle crusted in a ring around their mouth, like that ring of gunk you would see around the inside of a tub that had seen better days. Surely that corpse had seen better days as well, or... I hoped so.

The body was sprawled in a dark alley, leaning against a bright blue dumpster with their arms outstretched and limp. I checked their pulse in a spur of desperation. No one wants to see a dead body, let alone their *first* dead body. I hadn't even seen my father laying in his casket before we put him in the ground. His body was so brutally disfigured after the crash that the embalmers had to resort to asking the funeral home for a closed casket ceremony.

But unfortunately for me, the corpse slumped before me in that dank and grimy North Carolina alleyway was, indeed, a corpse. No pulse to be felt, no more life to experience. Dead.

I'd never felt anything so creepily frigid as the skin on that body. I immediately pulled my fingers back into a closed fist. My nails grazed past the scar that had formed over the laceration sustained by that piece of shattered smartphone screen. It had crusted over one of my palm prints almost perfectly.

I spotted two empty syringes and a dirty spoon lying next to one of the corpse's open hands. Maybe they didn't have those better days I had imagined for them. A shame, really. I imagined the living version of that body in many occupations. A doctor, a dentist, a business manager, a CEO, anything. Maybe they could have come home to their loving husband, wife, partner in crime, whoever. Maybe they had children, or a dog, a cat. Hell, even a goldfish. But any of those possibilities went up in smoke when they drove that first needle into their arm, and the second one shortly after.

I imagined what they must've seen when they died. Was it just like flicking a TV off, a life consumed eternally in darkness? Was there actually a light at the end of a long tunnel, like those stories the church preached? Were they happy? Was there a long-lost loved one waiting for them at the pearly gates?

Were there pearly gates?

Is there fire in hell?

2

I neglected to mention the body to anyone, opting instead to let them stumble upon it during their own after-show endeavors. The look on Marty's face would be priceless in its own ironically morbid way, but he barely went outside as it was. The odds of him walking into any dark alley, let alone one containing the remains of a heroin addict, were next to none. Unless, however, Asher went down that alleyway, to which Marty would undoubtedly follow him without a second thought.

Marty was, against all odds, the most interesting person associated with Scyphozoa. He wasn't exceptional at anything. He couldn't play an instrument, or work on sound equipment, or even work a smartphone well enough to manage a social media presence for the band. All he was good at was putting in earpieces before shows and eavesdropping. He had a habit of sneaking behind you when Asher was busy doing something that didn't involve him. He had eyes like a hawk and ears like a bat.

He was the local gossip among the group, airing our secrets to each other as if they were front page headlines on a national newspaper. I knew about Jessica's relationship issues and Adam's crippling porn addiction and Evelyn's furry phase back in high school. The only person who left the gossip train unscathed was Asher, for reasons obvious to anyone with a functioning brain.

Marty was infatuated with Asher, and no one could tell whether or not Asher was fond of him in return. Asher always had that mysterious aura about him, never letting anyone know what was going on in that mind of his. Even Evelyn, who had a knack for reading people based solely on the way they looked, never had a clue what Asher was thinking.

So, when I entered the hotel in Charlotte, I immediately spotted Marty standing on guard outside the men's restroom in the main lobby. At least he had the curtesy to leave Asher alone while he was taking a dump. I sauntered my way over to him, pocketing my vape into my pocket. Marty wasn't a huge fan of me smoking, specifically. Just another weird quirk from a weird… man? Boy? I had no idea how old he was, in all honesty. He looked both twelve and forty-two, like merging two separate pictures of a father and son together into one photo.

"Hello, Joel," he said without so much as catching a glimpse of me.

"Hello?" I confusedly said.

"What were you doing out alone before the show?"

"Just getting some fresh air."

"Right, of course."

A freakish smile appeared on his face. His eyes were locked on the men's restroom door; his cheeks creased in fleshy folds. "You know," he continued, "it's not safe for someone of your status to be wandering the streets so late in the evening."

"Yeah," I said, "but air is air, and this hotel smells like mothballs and pot."

He broke his gaze with the bathroom door and stared directly at me in one swift movement. I jolted back in shock, not expecting such quick speed from the little runt. His greasy black hair tumbled over his forehead manically. "It would be wise for you to not leave the property without supervision," Marty growled.

The hotel lobby's gloom grew thick with this outburst. The forest-green furniture and the hum of a nearby ice machine grew more sinister with his increasingly intense plight.

"You need to chill, man. I'm sorry," I consoled.

"I am *chill*," he spat, as if that word wasn't in his lexicon. "What would Asher think? With you going out all by your lonesome? It would worry him sick if he knew."

"You're saying that like he doesn't know I take walks sometimes."

"Well, if he knows about that, he certainly has not told me anything of the sort."

"Everyone knows, man."

"How do *I* not know?"

That question felt more contemplative than aggressive. Marty seemed genuinely curious as to how I managed to have a before-show ritual that everyone knew about except him. He, with his unfortunate omnipotence, was utterly baffled by that revelation. He swiped a lock of oiled hair back onto the top of his head; hair so black you'd mistake it for oil slick.

"Let us let bygones be bygones," he segued, looking defeated. Marty offered his hand for a shake, to which I hesitated. His fingers were coated in whatever pomade or actual grease he used in his hair. I opted not to escalate the situation, and shook his hand, an artificial smile on my face.

Right on cue, Asher exited the restroom, patting his damp hands on his pant legs. He was glowing as ever, almost like he got some work done on his face; a nose job, cheek fillers, face lift, forehead reduction, you name it. But there was no way you would spot Asher Gaumont in any doctor's office, let alone a plastic surgeon's. Every day that passed was another in which Asher woke up a changed man, constantly improving like a machine that never goes a day without being well-oiled. "Hey, Joel," he said in that gruff voice that never translated to the higher pitch he used while performing.

I waved with my shiny pomade hand. No matter how close the two of us got during my time with Scyphozoa, I never got used to being in the presence of someone I had looked up to for years. I was in a constant state of awe when I was around him. I idolized that man from the moment I listened to "Wrong Place, Right Time." And here I was, working with him and the whole gang. I found myself speechless around him, even after three weeks of traveling with the group.

"Do you mind if I have a chat with you?" Asher asked me, brushing past a progressively pissed Marty.

"I don't mind, no," I said.

"Perfect."

He patted me on the shoulder, and we headed toward the elevator. I glanced over my shoulder. Marty stood in the same spot I found him in, staring with dead eyes as Asher and I left the lobby. He did not blink; he didn't even seem to breathe. Just stared, as if he witnessed the atrocities of both World Wars all in the blink of an eye.

3

I sat on the couch in Asher's suite, my hands clasped in my lap as I waited intently for whatever he was about to say.

It was the night of December 22nd, only a few days before Christmas Day reared its nostalgia-tinged head. I thought of the body in the alley as the snow began to fall outside the fourth-floor window. I pictured the lifeless husk being caked in white flakes; its eyelashes glittered with that wintery dust. No way for them to wipe the snow from their face.

Asher sat down next to me, both his arms lying atop the vertical cushions, one reclined behind my back. I felt his forearm rub past the nape of my neck, a chill running up my spine. "You weren't planning on doing anything else before the performance, were you?" he asked.

"Not particularly," I responded.

"Great!" He paused for a moment, and settled in. "I just wanted to see how you were doing with all this. It must be such a big change for you."

"I've honestly never felt better," I said.

"That's good to hear. We haven't been able to chat one-on-one since you joined, I feel."

I pondered on that sentiment and realized that—yeah—we never talked about anything ever. For us both being in such a tight-knit group, it was surprising to say the least. "Yeah, I noticed that, too," I said.

"So, I thought it'd be good if we got to know each other a little better before the show tonight. Especially with all the time we gotta kill."

"Okay, shoot."

"What?" I was shocked by how surprised he was.

"Ask me anything. I'm an open book," I lied.

The truth was I didn't want to air out my dirty laundry with everyone, let alone Asher. I was thankful when he asked, "How was school before you dropped out?"

"It was fine, I guess. Just not for me."

"I get that. I was the same way. College dropout with dreams bigger than the campus he was on. Bigger than the professors and doctors and all of them."

"What was your major?" I asked.

"Oh, I don't remember… Wait, I do. I think I was a double major in botany and philosophy."

"No music?"

"Kubrick didn't need to go to film school to direct *Barry Lyndon*."

"You seem like the type to watch *Barry Lyndon*."

"I have no idea what you mean by that, but I'm going to assume it was a compliment."

I found myself laughing at that, because of course I knew about that movie; I'd even watched it before when I went down the Stanley Kubrick pipeline after watching *The Shining* for the first time. Definitely not the best movie, but I appreciate it for its merits like any normal person should.

"What's so funny?" he asked.

"Nothing, man. Cheer up a bit. You got the personality of a rock sometimes. Loosen up. Live life."

He smirked at that last statement, nothing else. "Oh, you aren't the person to talk to me about living life. I've lived my life more fully than anyone else, I'm sure of it."

"Sometimes you don't seem like it."

"There's a lot you don't know."

"Apparently."

He slouched a tad bit further onto the couch and sighed. "So why did you want to join Scyphozoa?" he asked.

A tough question to be sure. The original seed that planted the idea in my mind was Todd at O'Sullivan's during one of the worst weekends of my life. I chose to not disclose all my personal drama, opting for a bit of a white lie with nuggets of truth sprinkled throughout. Nothing I couldn't double down on in the future if the question popped up again, for consistency's sake.

"I've always been a fan," I explained, "I even have all the vinyl, including some unreleased ones on custom printed records. It was just a huge combination of being such a big fan and being bored with the road my life was taking. I didn't like college; I switched my major from psychology to music performance before taking this gig. The classes, the instructors, the overall vibe weren't for me. So, one day I went to a bar and saw you guys were performing there in a few weeks' time. I'd heard your last trombonist quit recently, so I thought, 'Maybe they're on the lookout for new players.' And it's a good thing I assumed that, because now I'm sitting where Kyrie would've sat."

Asher's expression soured at the mention of Kyrie's name. *Sore subject,* I thought. *Understandable. A bit of a blow to lose such great talent.* He sat blankly for an indiscernible amount of time, unable to speak his mind.

Finally, he responded, "You're better than Kyrie ever was."

A surprise, but a welcome one.

"You're joking, right?" I asked. "He was one of the best trombonists I'd ever heard. I'm just a dude straight out of college with no degree."

"So was he." He didn't look at me while saying anything involving Kyrie. Instead, he stared at the far wall, contemplating something I couldn't figure out. "But let's get off that subject," Asher said. "You do anything for fun?"

"Practice, mostly."

"That isn't fun."

"It can be if you make it."

"I find that extremely hard to believe."

"To each his own."

"You must be going out sometimes, right? You obviously went to a bar or two, but did you ever hang out with friends, go home to see family? Anything other than music?"

I seemed to have caught Asher's attention by coming off as boring as humanly possible. If there was a cinderblock wall encased around him, I was the pickaxe beginning to tear it down chunk by chunk. I was as interested in him as he seemed to be with me. I trudged onward, digging the tip into that impenetrable wall. "I didn't exactly have that many friends, and I barely go home to my family because…" (*don't tell him about Mom and Dad*) "…because they just live so far away from Massachusetts. In Chicago, actually."

"Did you pick Sanduhr University for any particular reason?" he asked.

"Not really, but they *did* have a very good psych program. It only looked good on paper when I was dead set on going the psychology route, though."

It's difficult to discern whether you should lie to someone you can't read. If you're unable to reach into their head and know what they think and how they think it, there comes a point where you resort to lying profusely, without care. Because if there's one thing about lying, it's an art form of which I am extremely familiar with.

"Was their music school good, though?" he asked.

"I'll be honest with you," I started, not being honest with him at all, "it was a lot better than I expected. I feel like I learned a lot about performing and technique and all that. Even in the short time I was involved in it all."

I had to ham up my skills as a musician in front of him to be sure I was safe to stay in the band. After what Jess mentioned before I moved out, I had been on edge ever since I set foot on the Scyphozoa tour bus. There was no room for disclosing how shitty and awful my musical education was; I needed to stay with them. For my own sake.

"What about you?" I asked.

He clearly wasn't fond of that question. Another man of mystery, it seemed. "What do you want to know?" he asked.

"Well," I began, "why did you start the band in the first place?"

Asher took no time to explain the origins of Scyphozoa to me. It was as if the answer had been on the tip of his tongue before the conversation started. "I'd always thought about starting a band. It always seemed like the right thing to do, like that was what I was put on this Earth for. One night, when I was still in college, I woke up in a cold sweat. I felt as if there was something watching me, but I couldn't lift my head to see it. I was paralyzed there, under the warmth of my sheets and soaking in my own sweat. I tried and tried and tried to move, even so much as a finger. But I couldn't.

"Whatever was standing there at the edge of my bed crept through the darkness and made its way over to me. It got so close I could feel its breath on my neck. I wanted to scream at the top of my lungs, get my roommate's attention, something. But it was no use. All I could do was move my eyes and hope whatever was there didn't want to hurt me.

"Then it leaned closer; I felt its lips on my ear. And it whispered one word: 'Scyphozoa.' And then, like someone turned on the sun like you'd flick a light switch, it was morning. My alarm went off and I could move again. No sweat, no paralysis. Just a clear mind. I knew what I had to do."

The snowfall was starting to pick up, which was quite strange for a city in North Carolina. I was always under the impression that the further south you went, the less snow would fall. But you can always count on climate change to subvert your expectations.

"How did you get the idea to start a band just from some sleep paralysis?" I asked.

"Why did you *actually* want to join said band?" Asher retorted.

I was stumped, dumbfounded. I looked at Asher, who was then staring directly at me. Those blazing oceans in his eyes crashed their waves into my own. Then he softened his gaze, asking, "You want a smoke?"

After touring with Scyphozoa for almost a month, you would think I would at least have the gall to pass on such an offer, but I didn't. I simply nodded, to which he pulled a cigarette pack and lighter from his pants pocket. He removed one from the pack and handed it to me. I feigned gratitude, took the second offering of a dark green lighter, and lit up.

It was another laced cigarette; I was sure of it. Nicotine never turned my brain to absolute mush like these special Asher cigarettes did. It felt good, no doubt, but there was something ominous in the citrusy taste, the overall feeling. I released a gust of smoke as Asher lit his own cigarette aflame. The end lit a bright orange and waned as he relieved the pressure from his lips. He returned his arms to the back of the couch, one arm rested behind me.

"So, tell me," he said through a cloud of smog. "Why did you join the band?"

Something was wrong; very wrong. I didn't feel the need to lie, even the tiniest bit. Everything was sunshine and lollipops in that brain of mine, and lying wasn't nice like those two things, so I didn't dare do it. "I'd recently gone through a tough breakup, contemplated suicide a few times," I said. "My roommate is a really big fan of Scyphozoa, probably a bigger fan than I am, if that's possible. We went to a pub, one of your songs played on the speakers, and he said I should try my hand at persuading you guys to take me in. We both knew the band was coming to town in a few weeks, so the idea seemed more feasible than it would've been any other time. Even when I played for Evelyn and Adam, I was still unsure about whether I should keep going along with it. Like, I wanted to do it, sure. But there was this scratching feeling in the back of my mind telling me, 'No, you need to stay in school. You'll never be successful if you throw everything away and join this random band.' But I pushed on. You offered me that cigarette, I went out on stage, and then I saw my roommate in the audience. When you finished the show with 'Frictional Fiction,' I saw him and my new ex making out, almost like they *wanted* me to see them. And it was right then and there, in the mist and sweat and loud music, that I decided to join. Not because I loved the music, but because I needed to get out of that town. I needed to forget all the pain so I wouldn't literally throw my life away and kill myself the moment I walked off that stage. I don't want to end up like my dad."

4

The words spilled from my mouth in a sloshy mess. It was incomprehensible to me, but Asher looked completely entranced, if not concerned. Tears had flowed from my eyes; I choked a bit on some phlegm as I made my unwanted speech, sobbing some of the sentences out. I never understood how much the weeks leading to my time in Scyphozoa affected me mentally, and the proof was all there now. Hanging, sprawled on the table like the heroin addict's body in the alley four floors below.

My head dropped into my hands, and I began to weep. A few dry coughs passed my lips. Salty tears poured into my mouth, coating my tastebuds with an enormous sadness. I felt a hand rubbing my back, the fingers caressing each vertebra in a soothing motion.

"How close were you two?" Asher asked.

"My dad and I?" I sobbed, bewildered.

"No. You and your ex."

I wiped my dripping nose with the back of my hand and slowly sat back up. "We were pretty close," I sniffled, not wishing to talk about Roselle. But I couldn't fight the urge to lie any further, through the haze of whatever was in that cigarette. "There was always something off about us, though. We would go on dates and cuddle and kiss and all that, and we'd been together for quite a while. But she would never want to have sex, like, *ever*. I would pester her in those last few months we had together, but she wouldn't budge. Always denying, making me think I did something wrong. That's usually how I think, anyway: That I'm in the wrong and everyone else is in the right.

"It wasn't even a religious thing. No metaphorical chastity belt put there by some god or whatever. She just… didn't want to take it that far. And I still respect her for that to a degree, but it was just a shame that we couldn't get that intimate no matter how much I wanted to. Sometimes I think that was the reason she broke up with me, but once I dive below the surface—think about it more and more—it doesn't make any sense. Why would *she* break up with *me*? Really, I should've been the one to cut the rope if that was the case. It annoyed me, sure, but I still loved her. I think I still do, in a weird way, even with what her and Todd did to me."

My mind and my mouth were not connected when I said that anecdote, when I poured my deepest, darkest thoughts onto the floor. But Asher seemed to be sipping on that puddle like a child gorging themselves on cake during their birthday party. Enough cake to spell disaster in the restroom a few hours down the line, but also enough to satisfy in the moment.

"No sex?" Asher asked. "Must've been awful."

"It's not as bad as you'd think. I mean, there was always that aching feeling that I wasn't good enough, but all the other good times outweighed that awkwardness, I feel."

"Interesting. So, you still love her?"

"I don't know."

Asher released his hand from my back, releasing the oddly loving pressure as his palm left my sweatshirt. I felt a subtle prick on the nape of my neck but ignored it. "Love is a weird thing," he said. "We say we need it to survive, but what we all need is that intimate aspect. To feel skin touching skin, lips touching lips."

"I don't think that's completely true."

"I've seen more people suffer from being in love than people suffer from starvation or disease. You can eat more food, take some medicine, but there's nothing that can heal a broken heart. That wound stays until the day you die."

But he had smoked the same cigarette that I had. Was there a sort of truth serum added in the mix of toxins? If so, I had no idea how he could say those things. The only possible explanation, as much as I didn't want to believe, was that he was telling the truth. Love was a construct, and we were the test subjects. A little love here, a little love there. But at the end of the day, there would only be heartbreak. Holes in our hearts that slowly bleed until we either die or do the deed prematurely.

"You should go get changed," Asher said. "The show's in an hour."

I nodded, rose from the couch, and left his room.

As the door closed behind me, I leaned on a wall, tilted my head up, and finally breathed.

5

Evelyn slipped me a tab of acid about ten minutes before the concert. I placed it on my tongue and swallowed, tasting the slightly bitter twang of the tab. "Enjoy the show," she said backstage with a wink.

She nudged my shoulder and waltzed away, skipping into the backstage void like a young prairie girl frolicking through a field of newly blossomed wildflowers. A DJ beyond the curtain hyped the crowd, prepping them for the final course of the night.

I unloaded my trombone from its case, locking each piece together. I greased the inner lining of the slide with oil and checked the tuning with an F and a B flat. I was running a bit sharp, probably due to nerves, but I adjusted the tuning slide accordingly to be safe. The nervous feeling stemmed from the LSD coursing through my body, getting ready to take hold over me when the time was right. It could've been within a quarter of an hour; it could've been right at as the downbeat of the final song rang through the venue.

The dim mirror lights in the small backstage room reflected off my trombone's bell, emphasizing a dirty spot I missed when I polished the horn a few hours before. It was small enough to disregard, so I did.

I stared at myself in the mirror, studying the person I had become since joining the band. My usually mid-length curly dirty-blond hair was cut short on the sides, longer on the top and back. I didn't think I'd look good in a mullet, but the one perk of having curls is being able to pull that bygone hairstyle off with grace. My glasses gleamed in the mirror lights, dotting out the eyes underneath. I was proud of myself for bulking up a little bit; up thirty pounds from the beginning of my freshman year at Sanduhr. My shoulders were broader, filling out my red and yellow sweatshirt better than skinny freshman Joel could have. The outline of modest chest muscles pumped from the top of the sweatshirt, putting a rare smile on my face. Despite the depressing pit I had been hurled into, I still managed to *look* somewhat healthy, and looks were everything in the world of indie rock.

"What are you doing?"

I turned from the mirror and looked down at Marty, a scowl making his usually horrid features even worse.

"Getting ready," I responded.

"Well, good for you. But the concert starts in two minutes. Get out there... Now!"

"Fine, man."

He scuttled off like a hermit crab as I collected myself, took some deep breaths. In and out, in and out. This was to be my fifth show with Scyphozoa, but the anxiety didn't die with every subsequent show before then, and it wouldn't die with every show after.

6

The Lucy, up there in the Sky with Diamonds, didn't take hold of my psyche until halfway through the setlist.

The spotlights danced with white flames, the straws in the crowd's well drinks whipped and wriggled like worms burrowing into the earth. The music wasn't *just* music; it was air. Wafting through every crevice of the bar, crawling under every chair, every table and reaching up into the light fixtures and rafters. Its fingers caressed the audience, holding them in a firm grasp, keeping them alive. The night was young, and the people were basking in its youthful glow.

I wasn't playing trombone; I was speaking. Talking through tubes of shining brass. They were all listening, intrigued with what I had to say, and I played. I blinked and saw whole notes, sixteenth notes, everything in between. I wondered if this was the world we couldn't see; the metaphysical realm in which *everything* could be seen. The molecules in the air, the music fluttering through it.

The crowd bounced to the heavy beat of our song, seeming to float with every jump, causing earthquakes when they landed. Some of them hovered. They stayed in the open air as if standing on invisible stilts. I smiled with the trombone mouthpiece pressed against my face. I was stretching the slide, not simply moving it. I was strong; I could bend metal.

Give me a steel beam and I could take a bite from it, swallowing it whole.

But in the crowd, I noticed something odd. Everyone was feeling the music, dancing without a care in the world, except one person. A dark blob, vaguely human shaped, stood right in the middle of the room, unmoving. It wasn't feeling the music, letting it take over. It stood motionless in the rippling sea of people.

There were no features I could pinpoint in this figure, except for blinding white eyes like two lighthouses standing side by side on the Cape shore. My heart sank, my arm stopped moving the trombone slide. I released my lips from the mouthpiece, becoming all too aware of my rapidly dehydrated mouth. My lips were chapped beyond belief, and my tongue shriveled up. I lowered the horn to my side, keeping watch on the dark figure in the crowd. I should have kept playing, but I couldn't. Whatever was out there wasn't human. I thought maybe it could be a statue in the middle of the area, but it wasn't there a moment before. Do statues have a habit of moving? Are intricate statues a staple of the North Carolinian bar scene?

That pitch-black blob with two glowing dots where eyes should be stared directly into my soul while I tripped on acid while performing for an audience that disregarded its existence entirely.

Everyone on stage looked back at me, confused eyebrows glaring.

"What are you doing?" Jess mouthed while continuing to strum on her guitar.

I caught myself looking away from the dark figure for a second too long. I shifted my focus back over, and it was gone.

Vanished.

The tempo of "Potter's Denial" didn't waver despite every other member of Scyphozoa focusing on me instead of the crowd. My vision blurred; a faint ringing chimed in my ears. Soon enough, the sounds of the world faded out, replaced by a low hum, like the ambient white noise on a quiet commercial airline.

But through the painful silence, I heard one thing in the soundless abyss:

"Fate."

I screamed and fell over, tripping on loose wires. I scrambled to sit upright, seeing the dark figure hovering above me, eyes glowing with malicious intent. No light in the world could illuminate that creature's face. It was a walking black hole, consuming everything in its wake.

But deep down, I knew, it was smiling.

CHAPTER VII

1

I watched shaky smartphone footage of the concert for the entirety of the next day.

I studied the fateful moment from multiple angles: The back of the room, right at Asher's feet, even footage from the bar. I watched as my eyes widened, my trombone fell to my side, my chest rose and fell rapidly, I fell over, I screamed. The song cut the moment my body fell to the ground. Everything was exactly how I remembered, save for one thing. Whatever was out there in the audience—whatever climbed up to the stage and shouted into my ear—wasn't there. In any of the footage. I checked Twitter, Instagram, TikTok. Hell, I even went into full detective mode and browsed Facebook videos. Nothing. Only me acting like a damn fool, embarrassing myself not just in front of the audience in Charlotte, but anyone with access to the Internet.

But it *was* there. There was no denying it. Sure, all the footage said otherwise, but I know what I saw. It was sinister, and it would come back for more.

"You've done acid before, right?" Adam asked.

"Yeah, of course. I'm a college dropout," I said.

We were sitting in the living area of the tour bus, the last room before the toilet and sleeping quarters. Well, only Adam was sitting, lounged on the leather sofa with a blunt jutting from his mouth, sending a steady stream of smoke into the ceiling. I stood in the middle of the foyer, arms crossed.

"I don't know what you think you saw," he said, "but it obviously wasn't there. You were just having a bad trip, that's all."

"But it felt so real."

"Tripping balls'll do that. Evelyn shouldn't have given you that tab in the first place. She knew you were depressed; erratic, even. Especially after that stunt you pulled before we got you out of... what was the place again?"

"Sanduhr."

"Sanduhr! That's right. Weird ass town."

"Right."

"Anyway, I'm sorry that all happened to you, and during a performance, too. I'm sure the videos will die down in a few days' time."

"That's not even what I'm concerned about," I defended. "I'm more concerned about what the fuck I saw. There was something so... *real* about it. Like, when the acid finally kicked in, I saw the air and the music and all that. I saw the straw in some guy's rum and Coke dancing to the rhythm of whatever we were playing. People were legit floating around in that bar. But all that stuff had that mask of heightened reality, you know? It seemed real in the moment, but I look back on it now knowing it wasn't. But that thing I saw? The thing that sent me crashing to the ground and yelling like a meth addict one day without Adderall? I, for the life of me, cannot picture it being anything but real. It was there. I saw it. I *felt* it."

"Every word that comes out your mouth makes you sound more and more crazy."

"I don't care if I sound crazy!" My face grew hot; molten anger flushed my cheeks. "I know what I saw! The videos might say otherwise, but it was there. It was towering over me, darker than anything I'd ever seen. And the eyes! Oh my God, the eyes!"

Adam winced, likely from the ring of fire on his blunt finally reaching and singeing his lips. However, he kept the burnt ash in his mouth and said, "Joel, I love you, man. But you need to let it go. It was a bad trip. Nothing more, nothing less."

2

It couldn't have been your ordinary bad trip, and all the proof I needed was the story Asher told me hours before the show.

He had mentioned a figure lurking in the dark, luring him into a state of paralysis. Cold in his own pool of sweat, motionless against his better judgement, that figure crept up to him and whispered the name of the band he would soon leave the world of academia to create. The idea of that and my later experience being a mere coincidence was baffling to me. Those eyes, like two large coins reflecting the harshest of summer suns, haunted me.

The dark figure, who I began to deem the Man in Black, was imprinted on the insides of my eyelids as if it were the afterimage of a bright light. It stuck there for days, no, weeks after the incident, like a tattoo inked on my eyeballs.

I slept through Christmas Eve, only waking when the bus hit a bump on the highway or braked suddenly in a downtown area. The thought of leaving the enclosed safety of the sleeping quarters was millions of miles away, playing hopscotch with an alien on one of Saturn's moons. I woke up on Christmas morning with a raging headache as violent as a wildfire. My bladder was ready to burst from a whole twenty-four hours without pissing.

I rolled from the cot, my joints cracking from lack of use, and took a blanket with me. I looked like a kid in a makeshift ghost costume as I left the room to use the bathroom. Everyone else mellowed out in the living area. I peered out the window, watching the world go by one mile marker at a time.

"Good morning, sunshine," Evelyn remarked, snickering.

"Morning," I croaked.

I shifted my weight into the tiny excuse for a bathroom and did my business. Despite the weight of the world on my shoulders, that was the best piss of my life. I could actually feel my bladder draining from inside me as the bowl filled with a pale yellow. I washed my hands, left the restroom, and was met by everyone's stares once more.

"What?" I asked.

"Are you alright?" Jess asked, a smoldering cigarette burning at her fingertips.

"Yeah, I'm fine."

The air was thick with smoke. I dryly coughed into the blanket, ejecting the secondhand toxins from my already sore throat.

"Hey, man," Adam said. "I'm sorry for what I said yesterday. I didn't mean to come off like such an ass."

"It's okay," I said. "I'm not mad, but you have to believe me."

"If that makes you happy, I'll believe whatever you say, even if you say you've taken a shit on the moon."

Marty glowered at that comment, to which Adam lightly punched his shoulder. "Lighten up, Marty," said Adam. "You're traveling with a band, for crying out loud. What's one poop joke gonna do?"

"It is simply not professional," Marty huffed.

"Don't be such a prude," Evelyn chimed in, sticking a finger in her mouth, shoving it into Marty's ear. He yelped and scurried off past me into the restroom, slamming the door behind him and locking the latch.

Evelyn laughed into her cupped hands, as did Adam in the same motion. Those twins were so in sync sometimes that it was uncanny, surreal. "Good riddance," she chuckled.

3

The members of Scyphozoa didn't realize it was Christmas until I offhandedly mentioned it.

"Oh, I guess you're right," Asher said. "I didn't realize we were that far into December already."

"How do you just forget it's Christmas?" I asked.

"Not very religious," everyone said with slight variations on the phrase.

"I'm not either, but I like the holiday spirit."

"Santa doesn't have a chimney to squeeze his fat ass through, hate to break it to you," Adam said.

"I guess I don't need Santa if I have a steady paycheck," I said.

"*That's* true holiday spirit right there," Evelyn remarked.

The bus finally stopped for something other than a quick gas tank filling in Dallas, Texas. One of the least likely places in America to get snowfall and we were to spend Christmas Day there. I unloaded my belongings into my hotel room, flicked on the TV, browsed for no more than a minute, saw nothing but the local news and reruns of *9-1-1*, shut it off, and flopped into the way-too-comfy bed.

My stomach grumbled, begging for a morsel of sustenance. I rose from the bed, slipped on my shoes and winter coat, and left the room, remembering to grab my keycard before the door slammed behind me. The sun had already set over the horizon despite it not being close to six o'clock yet. Seasonal depression with a side of actual depression, a dash of dread, and an appetizer of nighttime before the thought of being tired crossed my mind for the day. Yum, my favorite.

I dug my hands into my pockets, to which rain greeted me. A far cry from that pillowy winter frost of my childhood. I threw my hood over my head and rushed from the lobby and toward the bus. I knocked on the door, and Lenny opened up. The Scyphozoa bus driver towered over me, even without the help of the extra step he currently stood upon. "What do you want?" he asked in his terrifyingly deep voice.

"Would you like to grab some food with me?" I asked, unperturbed.

"Ain't you old enough to get food yourself?"

"It's Christmas, man. And all the others probably don't want to bother. Please."

Lenny rubbed his eyes, wiping the sleepiness from his vision. He smirked and said, "Sure, Joel. Where we going?"

4

Waffle House… We spent the rest of Christmas Day in a Waffle House.

I don't want to sound like I'm complaining, because that's far from the truth. This also isn't an advertisement for Waffle House. The words on these pages are neither sponsored nor endorsed by that beautiful breakfast food establishment, truth to God. But I wouldn't mind a little money slipped under the table for my troubles, Walt Ehmer. Ring up my line when you have the chance.

No turkey, no stuffing, bread rolls, mashed potatoes, macaroni and cheese. No sweet potatoes, no gravy, no beans, carrots, or pie. Only me and Lenny chowing down on waffles, hash browns, eggs, and toast. I even over-indulged and ordered myself a Texas Bacon Patty Melt. It seemed right, given the rather unfortunate Dallas location for our tour date the day after Christmas. Lenny ordered his hash browns with the works; bits of ham, slices of cheese, diced onions and tomatoes, some jalapeños here and there, mushrooms, gravy, and chili all doused and mixed over a triple order of that greasy potato goodness.

We ate in relative silence, save for the outside clamoring of cars whooshing by and the low drawl of Christmas carols over the restaurant speakers. When he was done with his potatoes and every other American breakfast food under the sun, Lenny wiped his mouth with a thin napkin. There wasn't a crumb of waffle or puddle of grease to be seen. He had wiped his plate clean. I, on the other hand, still had half my melt to finish, with a few shoestrings of potatoes left to eat. He commented on this, asking, "What do I gotta do to get you to eat like a normal motherfucker?"

"Just let me eat at my own pace, that's all. Everyone's different."

"You eat so slow it's getting on my nerves."

"Do you have to be so angry all the time?"

The irony of me telling someone else that wasn't lost on me.

Lenny responded, "Because I'm not paid enough to do any of this shit. I just spent an hours' worth of driving you hippies on this damn food."

"But you liked it, I hope. The food, I mean; not the hippies."

"Well, shit. Of course I did! But it's the principle of the thing that gets to me."

"I don't know if I like them, either," I said.

"Who? The band?"

I nodded as I took a small bite from the uneaten half of my patty melt. Ketchup and mayonnaise oozed from the back and onto my oily fingers.

"Really? I thought you were some ultra-mega-fan of those folks," Lenny said.

"I thought so, too. But I'm not so sure anymore. 'Never meet your heroes' and all that."

Lenny set his elbows on the table and clasped his ginormous, dark-skinned hands together, forming a makeshift rest area for his chin. "I wanna tell you something, then," he said, his low voice barely able to form a whisper.

"What's that?" I asked.

"I drive them around the country every few months or so. They call me back personally every time. They never want a different driver. Just me. I like to imagine they just like me *that* much that they wanna see my gorgeous face every tour cycle or whatever. I know the truth, though." He took a large gulp of his fourth sweet tea of the night. "They hire me back every time because I don't ask questions, and I accept their generous offer all the same. Sometimes you need a bit of alone time. Me? I've been married before; it didn't work out. She left me, took the kids. Haven't seen her or them since. I use groups like Scypho-whatever-the-fuck to take my mind off shit like that. Watching the country go by for months at a time on the open road. I've seen more cities than I could've ever imagined when I was a kid. More skyscrapers and farmland and taxis and tractors. They afford me that opportunity. But remember what I say when I say this: They're bad news, man."

My eyebrows furrowed. I completely forgot to continue eating my sandwich as the conversation pushed onward.

"Bad news?" I asked.

"Worse."

"Why do you say that?"

"I heard you and… Adam? I think… talking a few days back. How you were talking 'bout some *creature* or something, and he was saying you were just tripping."

"Right." I lit up with intrigue.

Another gulp of tea from Lenny, then he said, "He was lying to you."

"About?"

"What you saw during your little gig in Charlotte. I've seen it too."

I leaned over the table as if the two of us were being spied on, but in truth it was just us and the two employees on staff in that Waffle House. The workers both had earplugs in, though, so leaking classified Scyphozoa information probably wasn't on their radar.

"The Man in Black? With the eyes?" I asked in a soft but harsh murmur.

"Oh, that's what we're calling it now?"

"What am I supposed to call that thing? *It?* I think that's already under copyright."

"Don't be a jackass."

"Sorry."

"As I was saying: Yes, I've seen it," Lenny said. "That 'Man in Black' you're talking about."

"Where? When?"

"All the time, and always when I least expect it. I've seen doctors about it, as much as I hate doctors. Thought I was coming down with a cold case of dementia or that schizo shit. But every doctor, every psychiatrist I seen all say the same thing." He strained his vocal cords and put on one of the most accurate suburban white voices I'd ever heard. "'You're completely fine, sir. You might have anxiety and depression, but nothing alarming.' But I called bullshit; I *still* call bullshit."

"Where do you usually see it?"

"Everywhere. Inside gas stations when I'm filling up, at home when there's a corner that's a little *too* dimly lit, on the news station off in the background. Most of the time, I spot it on the side of the road on those late-night drives. I can never see the full dude, but I can see those goddamn eyes staring at me as we fly by. Like a deer ready to jump in front of the bus, but that thing never does. I feel like it never will. And if it did, it would do more damage to us than the bus would do to it."

"You boys have a good night," said the waitress, appearing out of thin air, as she slipped our bills onto the table. "And have a merry Christmas."

"You as well, ma'am," Lenny said.

She forced a smile; one she definitely didn't want to make due to her working a job on Christmas Day. When she left the vicinity and returned to the cooking station, Lenny leaned back toward me and pushed the conversation onward: "It's not the Man in Black I'm concerned with the most, though. It's this band; every single one of them. There's something so... *off* about this group. Especially that Asher guy; the lead one. He acts all stoic and proud, but there's something underneath it all that I can't put my finger on. If I were you, I'd stay clear of him. There's something in his eyes that send me back to my childhood; that feeling I got when my daddy got mad at me and Momma. Slamming bottles one after another, sometimes smashing them over the counter and threatening her with a shiv. Asher always looks on the verge of snapping like my daddy did. All that rage under the surface, just ready to jump out and kill anyone who just so happens to be in the way."

"I don't think he'd *kill* anyone. Seems like a bit of a stretch."

"Joel, look." Lenny unclamped his hand and took mine in his. His palms were rough like sandpaper, clammy like an eel that's been out of the water a little too long. "You seem like a good kid, despite the rough start."

A fleeting image of the glass shard in my hand, slicing into my palm, as I contemplated bringing it down into Todd's neck. A moment in the haze, a memory as clear as day through the fog.

"But I want to make this very clear," Lenny resumed. "Don't get too attached to them; any of them. They may hire me back every tour because I don't say a lick of anything they do behind closed doors, but I got ears like a goddamn wolf. I don't know what they've told you about that Kyrie dude, but it's not true. I guarantee that. My advice? Get that paycheck and get the hell outta here."

5

The Dallas show came and went like a warm front in winter. I played when I needed to, using the rest of my energy to scout the crowd for the Man in Black.

I saw nothing except the typical rustling of bar patrons. Someone managed to knock down a coatrack by the front entrance, garnering angered shouts from a bartender and a few other drunken individuals. We performed the last song, there were rapturous applause and cheers, and we shouted our thanks into the sea of noise, unheard by the patrons, but the message remained. We were grateful, or at least I was.

We celebrated another successful concert with a round of drinks at a different bar on the other side of the city; a retro bar rather unfortunately called Lee Harvey's. I ordered a burger, Jess ordered a basket of fries, and the other three opted for beers and cigarettes; a dinner of drug-addicted champions. Asher, Adam, and Evelyn sat at a high round table, conversing on stools through a cloud of smoke. Jess and I sat at the main bar. She meekly nibbled on her fries. I ignored her resistance to eating and scarfed down my burger, enjoying every morsel of its cheesy glory. After I asked for a simple Moscow mule on my tab, I asked Jess, "You gonna finish those?" through a mouthful of my last bite of burger.

"Nope," Jess said, sliding the red plastic basket toward me, "all yours."

"Thanks."

I ate the fries one handful at a time, dipping the clumps of fried potatoes into an untouched blob of ketchup to mitigate how unseasoned they were.

"How'd you think we did tonight?" Jess asked. She sipped from her glass of water with shaky contempt.

"Pretty well, I think," I said.

"That's all you have to say?"

"Yeah."

"That's a little disappointing. Weren't you *the* Scyphozoa fan? Busting a nut over us like some Reddit incel?"

"I wouldn't say it was *that* intense, but yeah, I would say I was a fan."

"Was?"

"It's complicated."

"Is it something I did?"

I pondered on the idea, searching the catacombs of my mind with full clarity before I took a sip of my mule. In truth, I felt disdain toward all members of the band for one reason or another. Adam's denial of my issues, Evelyn's rambunctiousness, and insistence that I try all the drugs she wants me to try, and Asher's overall creepiness. Jess, on the other hand, had no flaws that I could think of, unless we were to count the crippling cigarette addiction. But in all honesty, I couldn't knock her for that. The half-empty disposable vape in my pocket refuted my case.

"No, not you. Just the others."

"Cheers to that," she said.

We clicked glasses; me with my mule and her with a beer that she didn't seem to enjoy, but still sipped on anyway.

"Why do you stick with them, then?" I asked. "You obviously don't like them."

"Stockholm Syndrome, probably. I've been with them since the beginning, and I honestly don't remember a life without them. I don't want to call them family, but there really isn't any other word for it."

"Shouldn't you love your family, though?"

Jess took a hearty swig of her beer, finishing it off as her face cringed from the taste of soggy bread water flushing down her throat.

"That's the funny thing about family, I think," Jess said. "You really don't have to love them. You didn't sign some bullshit contract with your parents when you were born, because how could you? You were just a stupid baby who didn't know what anything was, let alone a pen to sign your initials with. Your parents' jobs are to take care of you and make sure you fit the mold of adulthood before they ship you off to the workforce. That's the thing with being human, maybe. That we immediately assume we should love our family because we've been with them so long. We form that attachment because we don't see an alternative. It's basically sacrilege to say you love someone more than your parents because of that. Everything we do is based on the idea of love, but there's love, and then there's loving to a fault. Loving out of spite. I don't love them, but I feel like I owe it to them; to stick around despite all my qualms."

"Did you love Kyrie?"

Her face sank with unbridled sorrow. I knew that look anywhere, because I had seen it staring back at me in the mirror for most of my life. The sunken eyes, the skin-splitting frown. That overall sense of longing only noticed under the skin, within the soul.

"Yes," said Jess. "I loved him."

"Loved?"

"Like I said, and like I'll keep saying, it's complicated."

I glanced back at the table Asher, Adam, and Evelyn occupied. I locked eyes with Marty, who happened to be staring back at me. I hadn't noticed him at the table, likely due to him not even having a seat to sit in. He idled next to Asher like a white van on a neighborhood curb. They were all deep in their own conversation, despite completely ignoring Marty's existence. But he was there, eerily still, looking at me with those bug eyes of his.

"You can be honest with me, Jess," I whispered, head hung low. "What happened to Kyrie? Because if what you said a month ago was true, I need to know if something similar will happen to me. I'm new to all this. You can trust me. Just tell me, please."

"You wouldn't believe me if I told you."

"Look, I've seen things recently that I would have never thought possible. Not drug-induced hallucinations or whatever the fuck Adam was gaslighting me with. Real, tangible things so otherworldly that they couldn't have been anything but real. Please, Jess. I'm terrified, and I don't even know what I'm scared of. Please."

Jess didn't respond at first, waiting for the correct response to cross her mind.

But the thought never came to her, not in time anyway.

Through the sound of music echoing off the walls of Lee Harvey's, I heard a loud crash and the unmistakable cocking of a pump shotgun. Off in the distance, behind one of the masked assailants, I spotted the bar's bouncer dead on the ground. Half his skull split open from the blast. Brains were splattered across the pavement outside, blood spewing in a fountain from the deep wound.

CHAPTER VIII

1

An older woman, maybe in her mid-sixties, screamed with a shrillness the best scream queens of Hollywood would be jealous of. It tore through the night air like a torpedo, sending shockwaves to the other bar patrons, causing a tsunami of screams. People hid under tables and chairs, cowering for their lives. Marty fled to the restroom, slamming the door behind him with so much force a picture frame fell from the nail in the wall it hung on. Glass shattered and scattered upon the floor like sleet.

I looked to my side and noticed Jess was nowhere to be seen. She must have jumped the counter and hid behind the bar, which I also wanted to do, but I couldn't. I tried to move, but felt glued to the seat. I swiveled my view back toward the entrance, where the masked assailants stood, shouting at the dispersing patrons.

"Stay right where you are!" the shortest one sporting a clown mask yelled, pointing a pistol at the older woman from before.

"Empty your pockets! I know y'all got cash on you," said another one clad in a wolf mask, brandishing a switchblade like an oily-haired bully from an eighties movie.

"Sit down!" the shotgun wielding one, wearing a simple black ski mask, shouted at a younger couple.

The blood on the shotgun barrel glistened in the light, like deep red plastic jewels bedazzling a pair of women's jeans. As the masked assailants pocketed as much loose cash as possible, the whines and screams began to drown out, as if someone had superglued cotton swabs into my ears. I tried to shout, to say anything, but nothing came out. I had a mouth, yet I still couldn't scream. I was completely mute, stuck to that stool in Lee Harvey's. My arms were locked to my sides, bound with invisible zip ties. My heels refused to move, buckled to the bottom rung of the stool.

Silently, I watched as the man in the clown mask fought with a blonde woman wearing a large flannel and shorts. She gripped her purse with all her might as he pulled it in a morbid game of tug-of-rope. It ended, the masked man the victor, when he slammed the butt of his pistol into her skull, creating a gruesome dent. That didn't finish her off, it seemed. To be sure, the clown masked man aimed the gun and blasted a hole through her forehead. He snatched the purse off the floor as a stream of blood pooled from the exit wound.

The wolf-masked man slashed a man across the throat in a singular motion, retrieving his wallet as he slumped lifelessly to the ground. The clown-masked man was nowhere to be seen for way too long. I could only move my eyes, and what they saw was nothing in my direct vicinity. But he was out there, I was sure. I felt the warm, wet end of a shotgun barrel pressed against the back of my head.

"Turn around, kid," he said in a gruff voice that pierced through the silence.

"I can't," I mouthed, tears dripping down my cheeks.

The barrel's weight on my skull subsided as a pair of hands grasped my shoulders, pivoting me in the ski masked man's direction. I investigated the holes in the mask where his eyes should've been, but there was nothing. Complete darkness.

"What do you want?" I said, hearing nothing but a low hum where my voice should've been.

"You know what we want... You've always known."

That voice. I recognized that voice but couldn't put a pin on where I'd heard it before. It filled me with dread regardless. The hairs on my back stood on their ends; a chill ran down my spine. I felt sick to my stomach but couldn't get anything to come up. I was stuck in the agonizing purgatory of nausea without the sweet relief of vomiting.

"Give us what we want."

The dark voids where eyes would be started to glow, first with pinpoints of white, then widened into those familiar spotlights of blinding light. The ski mask, as well as the rest of the man's black attire, sunk into the abyss; that black hole only the Man in Black could occupy.

"Now."

Everything went as white as a sudden camera flash, and the screams from inside Lee Harvey's filled my ears once again. They were excruciating, hellish, intense. If that were Hell, I wanted to leave immediately. The shouts sounded tortured, in eternal pain. Those weren't the screams I remembered from inside the bar. The yells were harrowing, perforating through my eardrums. Pain and anguish. That's all I could think to feel.

And then the light faded, and I was home.

Mom was setting the table.

2

"Nice of you to come and help, Joel."

Julie Auguste wore her usual jeans and sweater, adorned with thin-rimmed glasses and a beige Scrunchie holding her hair in place, away from the soup simmering over the stove.

"Sorry," I said, "I didn't hear you."

Everything felt like a dream—the kitchen, the mom, the sights, the smells—but it looked so goddamn real. If I stretched my hand and swept it across the table, I'd be able to feel the intricate grooves of the lacquered wood, to feel the fine layer of dust accumulating from a day of no one being home.

"That's a terrible excuse," she said, "even for you."

"I'm sorry."

I wasn't there, but I was. I felt present in the scene, but in the way a ghost feels seen during Thanksgiving dinner in a haunted house.

"It's a small apartment," my mother said. "There's no excuse for you to not answer when your mother's talking to you from one room over."

All I could muster to do was apologize for something I didn't know I should've been apologizing for. I felt like I started watching a movie half-way through its runtime. The characters had already been established, their arcs set in stone, but I missed out on all of it. It was as if I had traveled through time to that exact moment and had to pretend to by myself from a different timeline.

"Well, the table's already set. Get your food."

There was a plate of multiple grilled cheese sandwiches by the stove, situated next to the steaming pot of tomato soup. It boiled red, reminding me of the bloodshed in Lee Harvey's. As terrible as it sounds, I wished to go back to that gruesome crime scene. The room may have been full of death and violence, but my mother wasn't there, and that was enough.

This place wasn't real, I was sure. The room was real, as were the table, the chairs, the towel hung over the oven handle, the busy Chicago streets many floors below. But this never happened. I couldn't recall the last time my mother cooked for me, let alone used a microwave. She was basically never home in the months leading up to my freshman year at Sanduhr.

She had already made her meal—a plate with a grilled cheese sliced once diagonally and a piping bowl of soup—and sat down, the familiar creak of the chair sending me back to days I wished I had forgotten. I looked down and observed my clothing; clothing I hadn't been wearing just a moment before. My yellow hoodie and black jeans had been replaced with plaid pajama bottoms and a gray Sanduhr University crewneck. The room, I noticed, had the bygone glow of Christmas lights, a plush Santa doll sitting above the spice cupboard, and four little stockings hanging in a row above the refrigerator that had begun to yellow with age and cigarette residue.

"Don't just stand there, Joel. You're scaring me."

My legs moved without my brain giving input beforehand. I was a re-mote-controlled toy robot, and something otherworldly was the snot-nosed kid on Christmas morning playing with the remote. I, or something else, lifted my arms, secured a plate, placed two sandwiches on it, poured a bowl of tomato soup with a large plastic ladle, and brought my food to the table. I sat across from my mother, scooting the chair forward with a screech across the hardwood.

"Eat."

"What is this?" I asked, not referring to the food.

"It's grilled cheese and soup. What else would it be?"

"I shouldn't be here."

"You're never here. Wouldn't make much of a difference." She slurped her soup with venomous intent. "Where else would you rather be?" she continued.

"I don't even know anymore," I said.

"Sounds like you. Always so indecisive about everything."

"You're the one who made me this way."

"Don't blame me for your father's mistakes. Your food's getting cold. Eat."

"You had the choice to fix me. To repair any of the damage he did to me for all those years. But instead of doing the right thing, you became just like him. That crash didn't kill him... he's sitting across the table from me."

"Eat your goddamn food," she scolded.

As if out of thin air, a bottle of whiskey appeared to her left. My mother grabbed the neck, unscrewed the cork, and began pouring the contents into her empty bowl. It sloshed in a caramel wave, mixing disgustingly with the globs of leftover tomato soup. The smell was pungent, filling the room with that distinct inky smell only whiskey could provide.

Her hands became a cloud of nothing, shifting between different forms. I saw wrinkles form and disappear, veins move across bone, fingernails blossom and fold. I shifted my focus to her face, which took on that same ambiguous form of nothing, yet everything all at once. There were faces I recognized from years gone by and faces completely unfamiliar. For a moment, I saw my father. Some more faces, then I saw him again in that slideshow of horrors; his face caved in from the pole he slammed his car into. A huge dent where his mouth and nose should have been. And then it was gone, lost in the sea of everyone.

The bottle continued to pour into the bowl, held by an ever-changing hand that refused to waver. The brown liquid overflowed, spilling onto the table in intoxicating waterfalls. I blinked, and the bottle was gone, the bowl was gone, my mother was gone. I was alone on my side of the kitchen table. I sensed a chill, maybe from a draft, maybe from my nerves. I heard footsteps approach from behind but refused to check my flank. I wanted it to stop. I wanted to go back. To see a doctor, like Lenny said. He didn't have schizophrenia, but maybe I did? That would explain the violent outbursts, the visions of the Man in Black, the general disdain for living.

Then the footsteps stopped, everything went quiet. The bustling Chicago streets outside the apartment window ceased, paused, froze in time. I heard nothing but the breath on my tongue, breathing in and out in slow, methodical beats. The temperature dropped, my breath manifesting into a dim steam from my lips. As I slowly turned, I heard the clinking of silverware. Then a chewing noise, one reminiscent of chomping through tender brisket at a Nashville restaurant. The clinking intensified, growing louder and more painful to the ears like nails to a chalkboard. Shocked with fear, and seeing no one behind me, I turned back toward where my mother had sat moments before, and there she was. Slicing through raw meat on her plate, void of anything resembling grilled cheese.

It was bloody. The plate, the fork, the knife, her fingers, her face; all a mess of gore, smearing across every surface like a kindergartener's finger-painting project. She was ravenous, slurping and chomping down on the meat and guts laid before her.

"Mom?" I whimpered. "Mom, stop."

She disregarded me and continued to feast. She bit into an intestine, its contents spewing and oozing with gunk and spittle. Her eyes glowed, illuminating the room as it darkened in a rapid sunset. My mother, or whatever the thing passing as my mother was, threw the fork and knife to her side and resumed eating with her hands. Flesh slithered through her fingers like snakes.

"Mom, please stop! I'm sorry! I'm sorry!"

She stopped, not in response to me, however. My mother lifted her head as if she were a wild coyote ready to pounce from one meal to the next. "Sorry?" she growled. "When have you ever been sorry for anything?"

"All the time. More than I probably should."

"You haven't been sorry since you were born. Always whining and complaining whenever things don't go your way. It's tiresome. *I'm* tired, Joel."

"I'm sor—"

"NO! YOU'RE NOT! THAT'S THE POINT!"

She stuck a finger in her mouth. Not her own finger, but one she dug from the plate, that heaping mass of bloody death. She bit down on it, crunching with the force of someone biting into a carrot from a veggie tray. "You're so weak, Joel. Every day I ask, 'How is *he* my son, of all people? Why am *I* the one burdened with him?' Do you know how hard it was to raise you, how hard it *still* is?"

I sat in silence, knowing that another word from my mouth would result in more emotional damage. It already hit like a runaway car, but anything else would decimate me like a freight train.

"I'm glad that Roselle bitch dumped you," she snarled. "She was too good for you. Now, her and your little roommate? That's a match made in heaven. You should be proud."

I could barely look at her, and not just because of the glowing eyes, like staring into two bright suns. My face grew hot, more tears in my eyes. "You don't mean that," I argued, choking on my words.

My mother huffed wordlessly, and continued to eat the gory mess that began to spill onto the table with how violently she sifted through the meat and bones. When she was done—and I mean Done with a capital D—she licked the remnants of flesh from some of the bones, sharpened one with her teeth into a makeshift shiv, and jammed the pointed end into the back of my hand, pinning me to the table.

I screamed in pain, seething at the wound in my hand. It oozed blood in a ring-shaped pool. I tried to pull my hand away, but it only made the hole grow, sloshing with more deep crimson.

Her skin darkened, dimming into the stark darkness of the Man in Black. Her clothes disappeared, leaving nothing but shadow. I didn't fight back as the Man in Black pried my mouth open, unhinged my jaw, and inserted one foot into me. Then another. Then his arms, then his torso, and soon he was gone. I screamed as loud as I could, squinting my eyes in anguish.

When I opened them, I was back in Lee Harvey's.

3

The bouncer, who I last saw with only half his head intact, was perfectly fine, standing outside the entrance in all black, his hands hiding from the outside chill in the depths of his warm pants pockets.

I was wide-eyed, in a cold sweat that stuck my skin to the insides of my clothes. I moved my fingers, feeling the sensation of limbs that I had full control over. My body was mine, there were no strings on me.

"Why don't we go to my room at the hotel?" Jess asked.

She saw my face, noticing the fear buried under my features. The dread and terror seeped into my pores like the mountainous ranges of pimples on a teen's face. "Are you okay?" Jess asked. "You look like you saw a ghost."

"I think I did," I said.

Jess took the last fry sitting at the bottom of the basket and crunched down on it, that fluffy crunch only fries could provide, not the bone splitting crunch of severed fingers. We left the bar, leaving the others behind to chat away, caught a taxi, and went back to the hotel.

4

"What do you want to know?"

"Everything," I said. "Anything you can tell me. I know you have things to say, because you've mentioned how you can only tell me so much. You have to skirt around the fine details for some reason, and I wanna know why you feel like you have to do that, too. I've been in this group for over a month now and I feel like I know nothing."

I sat at the desk chair; she sat on the edge of her queen-sized bed. The dim lamplight in the hotel room illuminated our figures in a tan glow. The sounds of downtown Dallas filled the room with an urban aura, in a far-off country away from the highway motels of old.

Jess reached into the bedside drawer and grabbed her pack of cigarettes, pushing the complimentary copies of the Bible and the Book of Mormon to the side. I rose from the chair and moved toward her, snatching the pack from her hands as she rummaged her pockets for a lighter.

"No," I demanded. "No cigarettes. We're going to keep this as sober as we can make it. I need you to be as sound of mind as possible if the things you're going to say are as serious as I think they are."

"Joel," she said, "I need them. They keep my mind off things, you understand. That vape in your pocket tells me everything I need to know. Nicotine's a powerful thing, yet so limiting. Doesn't give the same buzz as drinking or pot or anything harder than those, but the feeling of breathing it all in is what keeps me going, even in times like these. Times like… right now, actually. And the times you're asking for; times that are going to happen in the next hour or so, I think. Please. Give that pack back."

"No."

"Please."

"No, Jess. I don't know what's in these, but it's not just nicotine and tobacco and all the works. If you've been getting these from Asher or whoever else, there's absolutely no way that's all that's in these." I waved the pack in front of her face like a matador waving a red banner in front of a charging bull. "So, let's start with this. What the hell is in these?'"

She looked absolutely defeated. Her eyes dropped to the floor, reminiscent of Roselle staring at the carpet to avoid the situation she put the two of us in, or Todd doing the same for that same reason. I pocketed the cigarettes and walked back to the desk chair, plopping myself down in the faux leather seat with a short and succinct groan.

"Look at me, Jess," I said.

Jess hesitated but decided to shift her regard to me after a moment's thought. She breathed in, holding the air in her system, swishing it around like mouthwash, and exhaled in an ambivalent sigh.

"Alright then," she said. "Yes, it's not nicotine in those cigarettes. Well, actually there *is* nicotine in there somewhere, but there's more to it than that. It's like biting into something you think is a milk chocolate bar, but there's a weird almondy taste to it. And the almonds just so happen to be laced with something you don't want, even though you didn't want the actual almonds themselves in the first place. But you can't bring yourself to be mad at the almonds, not even at the herbs and spices and all that shit laced on their nutty surfaces. That's what those cigarettes are: Normal looking on the outside, but a pleasant, unwelcome surprise once you indulge."

"You're doing it again," I said.

"Doing what?"

"Skirting around the topic. Saying nothing at all with as many words as you can so I get bored and move on to the next question. We'll just go through the cycle until I run out of questions, and you escape the situation scot-free. Just *tell* me."

"I don't know what exactly is in those cigarettes; all I know is that there's some special mix of herbs. Some hippie shit that calms the nerves, opens your mind. Could be some special type of mushroom, or some forbidden fruit, or some weird plant from an old farmer in the Himalayas. I don't know. But it works, and that's all I need it to do."

"Do you all smoke the same cigarettes?" I asked.

"Yes… except Marty, obviously. That thing doesn't like anything."

"All with the same stuff inside."

"As far as I know. Asher doesn't let us buy our own cigarettes."

"Asher?"

"Well, duh. He's the lead of the group. The ringmaster that herded us all together at the beginning."

"But Kyrie wasn't there in the beginning. He was brought on a few years after the band was founded, right?"

Jess became filled with a sorrowful look at my mention of Kyrie Castillo, something I was growing very used to as his name seemed to pop up in every conversation we had with each other. She sifted her smooth fingers through her blazing hair, her nails disappearing into her scalp as she pondered what to say next. "You wanted to know about him… right, of course. Yeah," she contemplated.

"And? I'm all ears."

"You need to understand something before I tell you this. This might not apply to you; maybe Asher and all the others don't want to lead you down the same path they led Kyrie down. You understand, right?"

"Not at all."

"Right."

There was a knock at the door, to which I rolled my eyes. I knew the answers were just within arm's reach, yet still so goddamn far away. Jess rose from the bed and shuffled over to the source of the knocking, throwing a lock of hair from her eyes. She unlatched the chain lock, unlocked the cylinder on the deadbolt, and cracked the door open slightly ajar; enough to see who was knocking without granting them the opportunity to enter.

"Yeah?" Jess said.

"You gonna let me in?" Evelyn asked.

"Depends on what you want."

"I don't think that should be important."

"How'd you get back here so fast? You guys were chatting it up when Joel and I left."

"We just got *so* bored without you two around," Evelyn whined.

Jess huffed and obliged to Evelyn's initial request, opening the door the rest of the way. Jess bolted straight for her spot on the edge of the bed. Evelyn stayed behind in the doorway, observing the hinges as they clamped shut. She locked the deadbolt and latched the chain lock.

5

I wished to not be asked to put myself in the conversation that soon unfolded, but that shooting star in the night sky heard my mental request and flipped me the bird instead, giving a cosmic *Fuck you!* to crush my soul.

The air conditioner rumbled under the window, shrouded by thick beige curtains. Now that I think about it, that entire room—Jess's and mine while staying in Dallas, for that matter—was shrouded in the neutral hues of beige. Nothing interesting stood out about those rooms, which in itself was interesting. The mundanity of life really gets to you when you've seen nothing but the extraordinary for so long. That oversaturation of excitement sends you into withdrawal once the party's over.

The two girls talked about surface-level girl stuff that I'm finding extremely difficult to describe right now. I might get back to you later on that (I won't). Eventually, Evelyn shifted her focus to me, sitting awkwardly in the desk chair wondering whether it would be a good idea to get up and leave. "So, what are you doing up here?" she asked. "You two weren't doing anything naughty, right?"

I blushed, unsure why.

"Uh," I blurted. "No. As far as I know."

"Perfect," she said, a weirdly sinister grin adorning her face.

Jess sat in silence, taking a chance to breathe easy now that she wasn't the focal point of the conversation.

"I've been worried about you, Joel," Evelyn said. "You've been super off lately. Is everything alright? It wasn't something I did, right?"

Again with the worry; again with the wishing well. It had been over a month since my life was a landslide of people worrying on my behalf, and that chance of escaping with Scyphozoa seemed impossible to reach now, like the cookie jar on top of the fridge when I was six years old. Too stubby and sensitive and weak to reach the top and reward myself with an M&M carnival cookie.

"No, it wasn't anything you did," I lied.

My situation with the Man in Black started the night she offered me an LSD tab, something that could've been laced with literally anything. I'd already been put off by my pre-concert chat with Asher, with his ominous tone that seemed to come naturally with the cadence of his voice, but the acid escalated that anxiety to its breaking point. I would've believed the Man in Black was simply a byproduct of a bad trip, like Adam had said, but it kept coming back, torturing me with its blinding eyes, its visions of things that may have been or may not have been. A fleeting image of my mother slurping on fresh human remains flashed in my mind. I shook my head to shake off that memory. Evelyn noticed and said, "I'm not too sure you're telling the truth, Joel."

"You're right, but I'm also not too sure about what the truth even is anymore," I said.

"Explain. In detail."

"No."

"No?"

I grumbled, "Mhm," and stood from the chair. I patted down my pants even though there was nothing to pat down. "Goodnight, guys," I said.

"Goodnight," Jess said without regarding me.

"See you in the morning," Evelyn said. "Bright and early to get back on the Lenny Express."

I nodded and left, unfastening both the door's locks. I wondered why Evelyn had taken the time to lock the doors behind her. She planned to be in Jess's room for a lot longer than I allowed her to. Was she there for her? For me?

Had she heard what Jess and I were talking about?

What had *yet* to be said?

6

The bus tossed the turned as I begged and pleaded for some much-needed shuteye. The one place where the Man in Black couldn't find me was in my dreams, but the incessant bumps and cracks in the highway leading westward out of Dallas wouldn't let me slip away into sleep.

My cot smelled of fresh linen, not that the bedsheets had been washed. The bottle of Febreze—aptly named Linen & Sky—in the restroom cabinet said otherwise. A little spray from the nozzle did the trick well enough, I supposed, despite the slight grime my pillowcase had sustained from repeated nights of crashing without washing my face.

One last jolt of the bus sent me over the edge, angry as hell. If I couldn't sleep, I would force myself to sleep. I wandered from the sleeping quarters into the restroom, flung open the cabinet beneath the sink, and fished out a bottle of melatonin gummies. I popped one into my mouth like a potato chip, gnashed the gooey pill between my molars, and swallowed in a large gulp. I entirely ignored Asher and the rest in the common area as they said, "Hey." I shuffled back into the sleeping quarters and shut the door behind me. The window blinds were tightly shut. I tucked a blanket in the cracks around the door to block the light coming from outside. I locked the door with a soft click and flopped blindly onto my cot like a dead fish. I wrapped the blanket around my body as skintight as physically possible, morphing into a human-filled burrito. I stuck my head under my pillow and pressed the ends against my ears. Any excess sounds drained from my awareness instantly. It was the perfect vacuum of nothingness, the quintessential escape from being alive and present while still happening to be alive and present.

But, for the life of me, I still couldn't fall asleep. The melatonin was certainly putting in the work, slowing my heart rate and bestowing upon me an overall sense of drowsiness. I was so tired, I didn't have the energy to sleep, but it was all I wanted. More than air, more than food, water, shelter. Just the shelter the realm of my dreams could provide; that brick house some big, bad, dumbass wolf couldn't blow down.

I closed my eyelids with enough force to stop a moving train. Bright flashes of colors clouded the fleshy walls encasing my pupils, filling the darkness with major annoyances. I ceased the tension after what felt like hours, letting my eyes rest in a way they felt most comfortable with. My breathing slowed; my heart thumped softly beneath my chest. The colors dissipated, leaving nothing but blackness. There are supposed to be seven minutes between when you shut your eyes for a good night's rest and when you actually drift off into the abyss of your dreams. Someone, or something, put an indefinite extension on that assignment's due date. And I obviously knew what that something was. Because in that dark purgatory between shuteye and deep rest, I saw two glowing orbs shining from miles away. They grew; their diameters increased maliciously, taunting me in my most vulnerable state.

Soon, everything was pure white like staring directly into a laser pointer despite the warning label telling you otherwise. I just… let it in, that Man in Black.

7

I expected a blood-soaked kitchen, but got a bridge instead.

The light surrounding me seemed to get sucked into the sun above, illuminating the calm waters below. Its rays shimmered in the river's ripples, undulating those dazzling beams all around. Calling this river I stood upon a *river* was a bit of a stretch; it was more of a stream. A babbling brook where frogs wouldn't feel too out of place. It was peaceful there. The breeze of early autumn kissed my skin as it wafted by.

I smoothed my open palm over the bridge's railing, feeling the rough wood, toughened from years of wear and tear. My finger examined a hole in that wood, assessing the rings outlining it. All that life, all those years of standing tall in some forest miles away, etched into the railing of that old bridge. There was a story there for that tree an axeman fell to help create that bridge, one filled with the unfairness of untimely death and the sorrow of one's corpse being used after the soul departed from its husk. I thought of my father then. A rare thought, sure, but a profound one, nevertheless.

I remembered one of the few days he smiled, one of the few where there wasn't a bottle within arm's reach. We had gone to a carnival out the outskirts of Chicago, somewhere around Joliet or one of the other suburbs. There were rides and games and funnel cakes and laughing children. I was one of those kids; me, in that pudgy, little body only a whimsical seven-year-old could fill.

Bethany had won a stuffed animal from a water gun game. She had been different that day, too. She usually looked down on me with disdain, but on that day at the carnival, she wore a smile and handed the stuffed animal to me. We were never close, her and I, but being brother and sister comes with an unsaid contract. We live for each other; we die for each other. The sibling code never wavered, even in the dark times we both faced before she was old enough to move out, and I the same.

We perused over toward the Ferris wheel. It was small; obviously, there was no way to ship something as big as the London Eye into a suburban park area. It was humble, though; standing tall enough on its rusted beams.

My mother handed the teenager managing the ride our tickets, inflation taking its toll on the price of admission. Four tickets *per* rider. Grand highway robberies were becoming commonplace at fairs, it seemed.

The car gave as we added the weight of four people to the equation. It rocked back and forth, the world around us swaying on a pivot. I sat on one side next to our father, Beth sat on the other with our mother. Regardless of whether my father had been drinking that day, there was an undeniable tension between the two parents. So much so that they couldn't enjoy their day together, doing the simple things couples should do like touch, sit next to each other on a Ferris wheel, watching the world go by and come back again. They had two children together, brought life into the world *twice* yet still couldn't see eye to eye. Love was out of the question; the necessity to stay with each other was the answer.

I could sense the tension. I was scared to rest my head on my father's shoulder, scared to look my mother in the eye. She hadn't dived headfirst into the same fate of alcoholism my father had at that point, but a grumbling brewed beneath the surface, one that tried to warn me before my father met his fate with a pole at a hundred miles an hour.

The sun set over the horizon, the Willis Tower piercing its surface as it submerged the world into another night at a largo. The blues in the sky splotched with orange, pink, and yellow. Golden hour graced that troubled family in the slow-moving Ferris wheel car, granting one last moment of comfort before the hard times reared their ugly heads.

Off in the distance, as I snuggled with the stuffed animal instead of my father, I heard something thunderous. The car shook. We were at the top: the cusp of the wheel. I peered over the edge of the car, through the grate we were encased in, and saw smoke billowing into the atmosphere. I squinted, studying the surrounding area. Then another boom, another cloud of gray smoke. The echo of screams, of pain, of fear.

"This isn't what happened," I said.

Now they were all looking out, the Ferris wheel halting at the most inopportune time imaginable. Another explosion, more shrill cries for help, pleading through the fumes and smog.

"None of this happened."

My father snapped toward me and shushed harshly, spit flying from his pursed lips. "Don't talk," he said. "Watch the fireworks. It's the Fourth of July."

Boom, boom, boom. The explosives went off one after another in short succession. A thick blanket of panic enshrouded me. I squeezed the stuffed animal to my chest, its elephant head bulging at the trunk, tickling my cheek with its felt touch. My fat fingers held on tight, bracing for the next explosion, then the next, then the next.

Boom.

Closer now, I felt. I dared not look. I buried my head in the stuffed elephant, breathing heavily, beginning to cry.

Boom.

The car rattled, but my family didn't scream in terror. They simply looked on and watched the fireworks, like my father had said. It must have been beautiful to witness, all that destruction. All that death. Limbs were surely flying, people scrambling leglessly across the grass, leaving trails of gore behind them, attempting to find the limbs they lost. I imagined a man without a face, blown off in one of the blasts. Then that man was my father, good old Joel Auguste the First, with a face so mangled and destroyed there was nothing human left. But in that mess of broken bone and torn flesh, I saw a grin. A toothless grin so intense it could burn forests down in one gust.

I lifted my head from the stuffed elephant as another bomb went off. The shockwave sent me sliding across the bench to the corner farthest from my father. They were all watching, as I knew. There was a look of awe in all their faces as they stared at the macabre scene unfolding down below. The screams were faint from down there, growing louder as our Ferris wheel car made its arduous, slow descent. *Boom.*

"This isn't real. You're not real. You're *all* not real. This NEVER happened!" I shouted, squealing with the vocal cords of a kid barely out of kindergarten.

"Hush, now," my mother said from the other side of the car. "It's almost time for the finale."

"Beth," I sobbed. "Please."

"No, Joel. Look."

Bethany pointed off into the distance. My eyes followed her finger, spotting something in the sky. A large black dot hung in the orange sky, inching downward like a fruit fly crawling across the Mona Lisa. It was a beautiful sight, for sure, but one of malevolent undertones. The dot grew larger, as a nuclear warhead plummeted to the earth, heading directly for us.

"No!" I screamed. "Not real! None of this!"

"Isn't this what you want, Joel?" the thing that looked like my late father asked. "Don't you wish it would all end? The pain? The suffering?"

"No... I don't."

"That's not what our friend tells me," he said with a wink.

"Who?"

A finger pressed against his lips.

"Just enjoy the show," he said. "It's what you do best."

Another bomb went off, this time at the Ferris wheel's base. As the wheel caved in, we began to float, to hover in the air, our bodies not wishing to stay within gravity's pull. But we fell, and we fell for a while. The warhead whined in the air above. Before I hit the ground, possibly fracturing every bone in my body, the warhead made contact, sending me back into that glowing white abyss.

I was on the bridge again, in my twenty-one year-old body. The calm air of autumn hugged me close; I didn't want her to let go. Then it wasn't the air, it was someone. A person, I hoped. And it was. It was Roselle, beautiful as ever. I recognized the scar on the knuckle of her middle finger, one that she sustained in a freak tricycle accident many years before. If this were real, I didn't want to leave. If it was fake, I still didn't want to leave. I could've stayed in that moment forever, standing on a bridge in the middle of an unknown forest in some unknown country, over a stream with no name.

But I *did* remember that moment, and it was real. We had travelled into the forests of New England, trying to find our next adventure. This was the bridge we stuck a padlock on months ago. Where was it? Every support on the bridge's railing was barren. No lock. None with *J&R* etched on its brassy surface.

"Are you real?" I asked Roselle.

"I'm as real as you need me to be."

"Was *this* real?"

"No. The experience was, but you remember it differently."

"How so?"

"This was where everything changed for us," she explained. "You thought I was the only one you could spend the rest of your life with, and I thought the exact opposite. When we crossed this bridge, I hesitated to put that padlock here. It seemed… so official. Like I wasn't just locking it to the bridge, but also locking myself to you. Forever."

"I loved you."

"I loved you, too. But people change. You need to let me go."

"People don't change the way you did. One day, it was like someone flicked a switch in you, and you became someone different. Someone else wearing a Roselle skin suit. What happened?"

"That's the thing with breakups," she said. "Sometimes it's best to not ask the questions with answers that'll destroy you. There's a whole world out there; find someone else. Someone better. You need to let me go."

She continued to hug me from behind, hiding herself from my sight. I couldn't bear to see her still, and this figment of her understood that. "I need to let you go," I whispered.

"Now leave. Before it comes back."

I blinked and she was gone, her arms disappeared from around my waist. Leaves rustled playfully in the breeze across the stream. Some fell into the water, floating dreamily down the water with the current, dotting the stream with hues of red, orange, and yellow.

I blinked again, turned around, and there stood Jessica Fitzgerald. The sunset did wonders for her freckles, emphasizing them with beautiful care and precision. She smiled, as did I.

"Hey," I said.

"Hey," she responded.

"Let's get out of here."

"We can't."

"Why?"

The sun set faster than nature would allow. Shadows rolled over the landscape at insane speeds. Darkness blanketed the world; not even the moon hung above.

I was frozen in place, unable to do so much as move a finger. I had grown used to that paralysis throughout the first week of the Man in Black's wrath. As Jess's eye began to glow, I accepted my fate and shut my own.

The bus ran over a large rock on the highway, jerking me awake. No Man in Black, only the darkness I created for myself with closed blinds and blankets shoved under the door.

CHAPTER IX

1

As if the Man in Black went on sabbatical, I hadn't seen it for a few days after the simultaneous bridge and Ferris wheel incidents, but it was still out there. Lurking in the shadows it created in its wake.

New Year's Eve came and went, this time being a holiday the other band members seemed to remember existing, unlike Christmas. Asher rented out a ballroom in some extravagant hotel in San Francisco, inviting random Scyphozoa fans to the event. We drank and partied as the large screen TV showed footage of the glowing ball hung high above onlookers in New York City.

The bitter tinge of one-night romance loomed in the air. I could already smell the odors of sex even before Adam or whoever else took a fan back to their room and fucked them dry. I peered toward Adam, wondering who the face he slobbered on belonged to. Jet black hair, bangs that went over their eyebrows. Winged mascara began to drip with their perspiration. He held her at the waist with both hands, the other with their arms wrapped around his neck at the elbows. They swayed and jived with the music booming over a set of speakers.

Then there was Evelyn, whose back was pressed against the chest of another woman. They moved to the beat, turning to kiss one another once the song crescendoed to its climax. It was sloppy and wet, a web of spit joined between their lips as they separated afterward, twinkling in the light of the giant TV.

Marty was off in a corner, legs and arms crossed like a tiny pretzel someone threw on the ground and forgot about. He was a wallflower in every sense of the word, though it felt as if he deserved to be alone at that New Year's party. That hateful aura surrounding him deserved such a fate; to miss out on the fun of ringing in the next year. He stared through the dim light of the corner at Asher, obviously, because who else would he be looking at?

Asher sat at the makeshift bar, which was basically a folding table with a tablecloth over it, set with an arrangement of drink dispensers filled with an assortment of cocktails in each jug. I shuffled over to him, maneuvering through the sea of dancing bodies. Someone spilled their drink on my tropical button-up. The red liquid stained pink on the white bits of fabric and didn't do much to the blacks and browns, much to my confused state of both anger and relief. I apologized on the assailant's behalf, not wanting to escalate a situation that didn't need to be escalated. I continued my trek toward Asher.

He stared blankly through the barrier of full containers of cocktails. Everything was on his mind, and nothing at all. I knew that look anywhere, since it reminded me so much of myself. ADHD was a hell of a drug. Zoning out being one of the many side effects. His right eye went lazy, pivoting away from the center the closer I approached him. I sat in a folding chair beside him and attempted to find whatever he was staring at in the mass of people but saw nothing. Dancing, clapping, cheering, kissing. But nothing of interest, especially for someone as mysterious as Asher.

"Is everything alright?" I asked.

He continued to gaze into the void. I thought about snapping my fingers in front of his eyes, but stopped myself even as my hand was ready to do so. My arm was halfway between myself and him, fingers positioned to snap erratically, when he responded, "Yeah, I'm fine."

His right eye locked back into place, his focus restored.

"Just a little tired, is all," he added.

"Makes sense," I said. "After playing for three nights in a row in California, I'd think you would be."

"I'm glad it makes sense."

Even though he had said he was fine, he clearly wasn't. In the few days prior, leading up to that New Year's Eve party, Asher seemed to grow gaunter as each hour passed. I didn't know if he had caught some illness in Dallas and it had just then caught up to him, or if he was trying some new drug that had nasty ramifications on his physical appearance, or if he had sprained something in the gym, or if he simply hadn't been eating for a while. What I *did* know, however, was that Asher was losing his youthful glow, that attractiveness that made all music lovers fawn over him, either in person at concerts or online through streaming apps.

His stomach grumbled loud enough for me to hear, to which I asked, "Do you want me to order some food off DoorDash or Grubhub or, hell, even Postmates? You're not looking too hot, Asher."

"Thanks." He smirked, not with amusement, but with annoyance. That fine grimace only seen in people who want nothing to do with you.

"Seriously. I'll even use my own money to pay for it. It's your call."

"Joel, I'm fine," he said sternly.

"Okay, I believe you." I didn't. "But you don't… *look* fine."

"Appearances aren't everything, you know."

"I'm aware. I just want to help."

"You just want to help, huh?"

"Yes. That's why I'm even here in the first place. I heard you guys lost your trombonist, so I wanted to help."

"That's not the full truth, Joel. And you know it."

Almost like a ghost, I saw Roselle out in the crowd, but she vanished into thin air before I could comprehend her being there. All the way across the country from Massachusetts. Like a blissful silence in a welding factory, she was never there.

"I know," I said. "I'm sorry."

"And quit the apologizing. You've said your sorries too many times already."

"When have I ever told you I was sorry?"

This gave him pause. Asher's back straightened in his chair, the arch in his back disappearing as he gained his posture. The room's lighting highlighted the concave structure of his cheeks that hadn't been there a week prior. He began wearing long-sleeved clothing in that week, covering the hulking mass of muscle encasing his arms. I imagined them being a lot bonier than usual under all that fabric. Skin on bone, nothing else. A starving, homeless child hiding behind the curtain of insecurity and vast secrets. The typical bulge of trap muscles connecting his back to his neck was smaller, less bulky. A vertebra made a divot just below the nape of his neck above his sweatshirt's collar.

"Never, I guess," he said, correcting himself. "Why don't you bring some drinks out to our guests?"

"Why can't you help with that?" I asked.

"Don't feel like it. Come on, now. Look at me, I'm obviously not doing well. Help a brother out."

You're not my brother, I thought. *I don't even know who you are.*

"Alright," I said, unenthusiastic.

As I got up from my seat, Asher grabbed my arm in a swift motion and added, "Make sure everyone gets a cup. These are all the same drink, by the way. Just different food dyes in each container."

"Okay."

"And I mean *everyone*. Let's ring in the New Year with a bang."

2

A smile crept onto his face at that last word. *Bang.* I remembered the vision of years before, of the Ferris wheel, of the bombs, the bombs that were never there. Bombs that were planted in that memory like a virus. Crawling through my neurons until I didn't know what to believe anymore. He let go of my arm, a knuckle or two cracking as the pressure released.

I picked up a tray.

"Use the plastic shot glasses," Asher said. "Only a little bit will do the trick. And tell them to *only* take their shot when the ball drops. That's the most important thing."

I nodded, unsure of what I had gotten myself into. I faked a grin and placed numerous shot glasses on the tray, one after another, setting them down delicately as to not spill their contents. I chauffeured the tray around the ballroom with the carefulness of an underpaid waitress desperate for a good tip. I snaked through the gyrating bodies, passing one shot glass to her, one to him, another to whoever else. I made it to the other side of the room, surveying the crowd, empty tray in hand, hoping I managed to give everyone a glass. They seemed to be accounted for.

Well, everyone except myself, obviously.

"What about me?" Marty asked.

I jumped, startled. I hadn't expected him to be standing right behind me. But truthfully, when is anyone expecting such a creepy, little man-boy-thing to seemingly teleport behind them?

"Oh, I'm so sorry, Marty," I apologized. "I'll go grab another for you." I gestured to the tray, miraculously still in my hands after my embarrassing jolt of fear. "You wait right there."

He rolled his eyes as I moved through the crowd once more. I glimpsed transient images of Jess in the crowd, moving to the rhythm, feeling the music in her bones, in her soul. Against the pop and clap of strobe lights in that ballroom, I could make out her bright orange hair. Swaying on the dance floor. Beautiful as a wildfire touching the sky, nipping the stars with flame. Roselle appeared then, an afterimage of light. I may have told her I would let her go, and I so miserably wanted to do so. But she was still there, in my mind, in my world. Across the country, but still in the same room as me. The undeniable scent of her perfume graced my nose. My eyes watered at the strong smell; I began to weep.

Alone on the dance floor.

Alone in the world, surrounded by nothing but bodies. Husks of humans moving to the rhythm of life, never experiencing me.

Never perceiving me.

Always deceiving me.

"Joel?"

I wiped tears from my eyes, the world ceasing its blurriness. Everything focused on Jessica Fitzgerald, whose hand was placed upon my shoulder, the other hand gripping a plastic shot glass full of who knows what. One I gave her. *Don't drink that. For the love of everything: Don't drink that*, I silently pleaded, blocked from speaking against the barricade of my mind.

She didn't ask if I was alright. Didn't tell me she was worried about me. Didn't pout and feign sympathy as I wallowed and wept. She did something more.

She wrapped her arms around me, laid her head on my shoulder, and squeezed tight.

Hugs lived in a separate universe than my own; I couldn't remember the last time I had felt one. But there, in that random San Francisco hotel's ballroom, with pop music blaring on the speakers, the ball ready to drop on Times Square at a moment's notice, I felt seen.

I hugged her in return.

And wept.

3

It was a minute until midnight. Marty, pissed as ever, took it upon himself to get a shot without my help, as I was busy sobbing into Jessica's shoulder.

She rubbed my back with a loving tenderness. Smooth fingers edged with calluses at her fingertips from years of guitar strumming. They caressed each individual ripple of muscle on my back, slid over my shoulder blades as they passed slowly side to side. The song on the speakers abruptly switched to a rendition of Auld Lang Syne.

Should auld acquaintance be forgot,

I never wanted to leave this moment. Why couldn't the Man in Black send me here? I wouldn't have cared if it wasn't real. This felt right, it felt good. The tears streaming from my eyes weren't those of sadness, but those of relief. I held her tighter, leaving no room for her to escape. She didn't want to leave either, it seemed.

And never brought to mind?

The countdown had begun, starting in the fifties, then the forties. The crowd surrounding us added their voices to the mix, crescendoing to as loud a volume as a group of drunk twenty-somethings could muster.

Should auld acquaintance be forgot,

Thirty seconds on the clock, Asher rose from his seat and limped over to the middle of the room. The crowd formed a pathway for his saunter. In the center of the ballroom, Asher raised his own glass.

And days o' lang syne!

"Happy New Year, you dumb motherfuckers!" he shouted.

Twenty seconds. The crowd raised their glasses. Out of each other's hold, Jess began to raise her glass as well, to which I placed a hand on her arm, lowering it. I shook my head; she raised an eyebrow. But she knew. She knew there was something in the hooch. That cocktail of mystery Asher was so adamant I passed out to everyone in the room. *10... 9... 8... 7...*

The shining ball, glowing in an amalgam of LED lights, was so close to the pavement of Times Square. So close that anyone so unfortunate as to be under it would end up like a jelly donut under a hydraulic press. The TV cameras captured the scene, swapping between angles at a rapid pace. A family of five or ten leaning against the barricade, the hosts staring in awe of the glass ball before them, thousands of New Yorkers enjoying themselves as best they could in the bitter cold. *6... 5... 4...*

We two have run about the hills, and pulled the daisies fine;

Evelyn and the woman she shared saliva with raised their glasses over their heads, their arms intertwined behind one another's backs. Adam cheered, spilling the contents of his glass all over the carpet. Yes, carpet. There was a New Year's rave occurring in a *carpeted* hotel ballroom. God save the poor underpaid housekeepers who were assigned to clean the mess left by an indie rock group. Marty stood inches from Asher, raising his glass as well, barely getting it high enough to go over Asher's head.

But we've wander'd many a weary foot,

The strobe lights intensified.

3...

Plastic shot glasses tilted toward many an open mouth.

2...

Someone took their gulp before the clock passed one.

1...

The young man, wearing a cropped tank top and baggy jeans with moccasins, fell to the ground instantly.

Since auld lang syne.

4

No one other than Jess and I noticed. As 2024 made its grand entrance, everyone took their special shot, cringing at the hard liquor, falling to the floor mere milliseconds afterward.

It was swift in its efficiency, all those people—only moments before, as invigorated as the night was young—plummeting to the ballroom floor with the limpness of a Raggedy Anne being thrown from a third story window. The place looked like the aftermath of a gruesome battle; soldiers piled on top of each other with a severe lack of life.

I felt a sharp pain in my chest, crushing my heart under the weight of instant anxiety. Jess held onto me as I wobbled toward the floor. I gripped my chest, feeling my heart meteorically thump, beating against my ribs like a mallet to a marimba. My lungs acted at half capacity. Shallow breaths passed in and out between gritted teeth. I planted a hand on the ground, keeping myself from flopping on my stomach like the rest of the partygoers strewn before me. I felt something boiling in my throat. Bile trickled from my mouth, coming out in a burst of opaque yellow with a single cough. I couldn't remember the last time I'd eaten. Nothing looked appetizing in those past few days, and it culminated in me never wanting to eat anything except for Club crackers and maybe a bowl of soup occasionally. All that was left to vomit was bile, that burning internal fluid that humbles anyone who's been starving themselves.

Jess pounded my back like a mother burping her infant. Not violently, but with enough force to snap me out of my nausea. I looked up, saw the aftermath of 2023, Asher Gaumont standing over them and his shot glass brimming with the enigmatic brew.

I got to my feet, the music continuing to clamor around me, and stumbled to the nearest fallen Scyphozoa fan. I put two fingers to their neck, praying that they were alive. Nothing at first, but then a negligible pulse put my worries to rest. They were all still alive, and I wasn't a witness at the crime scene. Or… well, it was definitely a crime scene, but not as severe a crime scene as mass murder would've been.

Asher surveyed the area, smiling at his work. A job well done, it seemed. He grunted in amusement, Marty copying the emotions beat for beat. Not a single original thought swam in that tiny brain of his. Adam was nowhere to be seen, likely another body among the mass of sleeping ravers. Evelyn, however, stood off in a corner, a blank look stricken across her face. No thoughts, no feelings. Not even a hint of contemplation on what had just happened. Nothing. She crossed her arms, tapped her foot to an uncertain beat. Certainly not the rhythm of the pop song that had started playing.

I looked back at Jess, her face flashing into my vision every few seconds with the timing afforded by the still-operating strobe lights. She was terrified, eyes wide, as was I. Sweat pooled on the undersides of her breasts, turning those patches on her light blue tank top a darker indigo.

"Run," she mouthed.

I didn't want to leave without her, but my mind was foggy, and I was in survival mode. Fight or flight, and all that. I didn't think to nod in agreement, I simply ran. I hid in the shadows, stopping when a flash of light stamped my figure in anyone's sight. I stepped on someone's hand, but they were sleeping. Surely, they didn't feel it. I squinted to find the exit, noticing the bright red exit sign hung above a set of double doors. I snuck toward the red light at the end of the tunnel, taking extra care not to step on anyone else's limbs.

I was so close. Oh, so close. My hands were outstretched, ready to push on the double doors. I was almost out, but I was too slow. The exit sign went dark, as did the entire room. Originally hot with sweat, the air chilled instantly. Even in the pitch-black gloom, I saw my breath release in a mist. Goosebumps crept across my skin. My hair stood on end. I had no idea where I was. If I were in the hotel ballroom, I would know. Object permanence, as novel a concept as it is, was one of my strong suits, being older than a literal toddler. I wasn't in the hotel, but wherever I was, it was unfamiliar, unnerving.

The sound shot out of the space like a vacuum. Nothing could be heard, not even the ringing in my ears. Everything was silent, and I shivered.

A bright flash of light put an end to the confusion.

I was back in my Chicago apartment, the smell of tomato soup permeating in the air.

My mother sat at the table with bleeding holes for eyes.

5

"Aren't you going to make yourself a plate? It's grilled cheese. Your favorite."

"What the hell is this?"

"Oh, hush now. Do you want me to make your plate for you? I don't mind."

My mother bent over the table, a droplet of red dripping from her eye and onto the toasted bread on her plate. I made a move toward the kitchen counter, to which she shot up a stern hand and insisted, "No, let me do it, hun."

"My mom would never be this nice."

"Sure, she would. She *is* me, after all."

She took a paper plate from a drawer and began hovering over the tray of sandwiches. "Would you like one or two?" she asked.

"What's happening?"

"You don't look well, hun. Gotta fatten you up, put some meat on those bones." I don't know how she did it, but she winked. Her eyelid glossed over her hollow socket. I wanted to vomit again. "Don't worry, I know you want two. Soup?"

"Let me leave."

"It's perfectly simmered, just the way your father liked it. He should be home soon."

"He's dead, Mom."

"Dead doesn't mean gone. Would you mind grabbing a mug from the cabinet? I want to fill it to the brim, just for you."

I hesitated, realizing I probably wouldn't be leaving that waking nightmare anytime soon. So, I obliged and opened the cabinet above the microwave. I plucked a soup mug from the shelf and felt a tickling sensation on the back of my hand. Fingers wrapped around the mug handle, I checked for the source of the itching.

I yelped and dropped the mug. It shattered into chunks of porcelain and grains of dust. A cockroach as large as my thumb skittered across my palm. I shook my hand, but the damn roach wouldn't budge. I then opted to swat at it with my other hand, which seemed to do the trick. The roach scuttled on the hardwood floor and toward my mother. It crawled onto her shoe, up her leg, through her pants and shirt, and up onto her neck. She nipped the roach by its skinny leg, lifted it over her open mouth, and dropped it in, a disgusting crunch following soon after.

She licked her lips and said, "Oh! What a mess! Let me clean that up."

My mother trotted out of the kitchen like a mid-twentieth century nanny: Hands hanging limply as she strutted toward the broom closet in the living room. I took the opportunity of being thankfully alone to explore the apartment on my own, without a pair of eyes—or lack thereof—watching my every move.

I wandered to my bedroom carefully, calling upon my muscle memory to avoid every creaky floorboard on my journey. The pictures hanging on the walls in the apartment were all the same as I remembered. Family photos plastered with faked smiles, a few pictures of the older family cat, Marlow. An orange cat, dumb as hell, as those breeds usually are. I entered my room.

What lay beyond the door was something unspeakable.

The bile I'd been holding burst out in a vomited spew onto my bedroom carpet, mixing with the entrails twisted at my feet.

6

It was horrific, to say the least. Intestines hung like drapes from the ceiling, brain matter stuck to the walls like gum under a school desk, and in the center of it all, on my blood-soaked mattress, there was something vaguely resembling a human body, though the way its skin was gone put that assumption into doubt.

"Not hungry tonight?"

I shouted, squealing like a cat not wanting to be rubbed. And at this point, I felt for that fear-stricken feline, except I wouldn't have minded being pet. Getting a gentle caress on the shoulder would have been preferable to being brutally murdered by the creature wearing a Julie Auguste costume.

"What's wrong?"

I refused to turn around. No amount of courage could force me to pivot in her direction. When in that delirium, there was no telling what would be around the next corner. She knew this, could see it right through my feigned stubbornness. So, she did exactly what I wished she wouldn't and walked around me, granting me the luxury of not having to face her myself.

To my morbid sense of relief, nothing had changed about my eyeless mother. Sure, there were still rivers of blood pouring from her sockets, but at least… I don't know. There were so many different possibilities for the horrors the Man in Black would show me, and this specific vision felt like mercy in comparison. Besides, the usual gray of my bedroom walls was dripping in dark red, illuminated by a circle of candles around a skinned body on my bed. I had *slept* there before. My skin crawled. I checked my arm to be sure it wasn't just another fucking cockroach. Nothing there except goosebumps and a general case of the chills.

"Are you coming down with a fever?"

She put the back of her hand to my forehead. I flinched, but that didn't matter to her. She followed the sudden movement with precision, impressively keeping her skin pressed upon mine. Then, my mother pulled back, pretending she had slapped her hand on a hot stovetop. "Oh, dear," she said, "you're burning up. Let me fetch you some ginger ale and crackers. That'll whip you back into shape."

My mother left the room, brushing my shoulder with hers. What I felt underneath her shirt fabric wasn't the usual warmth of human skin, but that of cold nothingness. She reflected her real-life counterpart, a hollow shell of an already hollow woman.

I watched in horror, noticing the finest details in the gore caking every corner of my bedroom. Some of them—the hearts, the lungs, the livers— quivered as if they were still inside a living person. They squelched and churned revoltingly with the gift of life, yet they had none. It was all a nightmare that I couldn't escape from. All I could do was wait for the light to take me back to reality, unless this *was* reality?

I took a step forward, my foot crushing a bit of intestine, expelling filth and fluid across the floor, into the carpet. Another step carried me closer to the bed. I had to know who was lying there, skinned but still breathing. Their chest rose and fell; their exposed muscles expanding and contracting with each calm breath. I wondered if they knew they were a bleeding mass on a bed they didn't belong to, in some apartment in a city where they didn't live. My feet squished more entrails, creating a path of lighter red in that pool of pinks and maroons and browns with each step. I reached the bed, my hands shaking with nervous tremors. I stared into the person's face. There was a hole where a nose should have been, a concave triangle that continued to inhale and exhale oxygen even with its lack of nostrils. The only skin left on the body was on the eyelids, which were shut in sleep. Some areas were cut so deep I could see white bone peaking from underneath the tangles of nerves and meat. Their cheeks were caved in. All of that, with a heaping of lost blood. I poked the person's face, my thought process being: *None of this is real, so why not branch out a bit? You won't have any blood to clean off your fingers once you wake up.* The muscles around their jaw were tighter strung than I anticipated, but it still catalyzed enough of an overwhelming feeling to make me gag on some spit I forgot to swallow.

My hand retracted, fingertips covered in scarlet.

"Don't wake him."

I jolted, turned around, saw my mother, eyeless as ever, standing in the doorway. A mere silhouette standing under the doorframe, backlit by the sunset in the kitchen windows, holding a plastic cup of ginger ale and a box of unopened crackers.

"You mustn't wake him."

Good to know it was a man, hence the skinned penis I neglected to notice during my intense research.

"You wanna give me good reason not to?" I asked.

"It isn't in your best interest."

"My best interest? I think it would be in my 'best interest' to get the fuck out of here."

Her smile, illuminated sparsely in the candlelight, faded. "That's right," she said. "It was *always* in your best interest to 'get the fuck out of here.' That's why you left me to be alone here. I cannot leave, I cannot live. I have no one to care for, and no one to care for me. What's going to happen when I'm sick on my deathbed in some nursing home? Will you come back? I know Beth will, but will you?"

"Of course, I would."

"Don't lie to your mother."

"You aren't my mother. I don't know *what* you are, but it isn't human."

She dropped the ginger ale. It fizzed on the floor, mixing with the organs and blood in a soupy blob. Her other hand crushed the cracker box.

"How *dare* you?" she snarled.

"Where are your eyes, then? Last I remember, you had eyes where those two holes are."

"Maybe I *don't* have eyes. You wouldn't know that, would you? You haven't called a single time since you joined that fucking stupid band. What kind of rock band has a trombone player of all things? Seems like you just wanted yet another excuse to ignore me: Your own mother. If moving miles and miles away just to spite me wasn't enough, going farther away—being in a different city every day—would surely do the trick, right?"

Her voice quivered as blood-tinged tears fell from her eye sockets. She resumed her tirade: "I could be sick. I could be dying. You simply *wouldn't* know. You didn't even tell me about you and Roselle."

I found myself a bit teary eyed at the mention of her name. "You don't get to say her name. You don't even know her," I said through gritted teeth.

"Because you never brought her home."

"No!" I shouted, kicked something that looked like a kidney. "Because you aren't my mother! You don't know me; you'll never know me. I don't even know *you*. Who… *are* you?"

"You shouldn't ask something like that before asking yourself the same question."

"What?"

She beckoned to the bed behind me, to the body strewn on the bed sheets.

"Take a look," she said with a smirk.

I looked, as she commanded. I didn't wish to look, but it was like looking at a car crash. Horrific on the surface, but oddly beautiful in its intricacies. The muscle fibers laced over one another; the nerves tied tight over them like piano wires. The rise and fall of this nearly-dead man's chest; the beating of his heart underneath everything. I surveyed the bloody mass, seeing what she was trying to get me to see. I turned back and said, "There's nothing."

"Look closer," she responded, motionless.

I did as she said, and then I saw it. The eyelids weren't the only pieces of skin left on this poor man. On the man's left forearm, right near the inside of his elbow, there was a patch of skin crudely left there; a patch of skin coated in tattoo ink.

My tattoo.

Breathing became difficult. Oh, so difficult. Like I had just ran a marathon on the hottest day of the year without a drop of water in my system.

"This is who you are," she said. "A sack of meat."

The body was me, and I was him. He opened his eyes and instantly screamed in pain, a hoarseness in his throat more unearthly and guttural than I had ever heard. He thrashed and kicked, sending squirts of blood all around. Some hit my face, seeping into my eye, coating my vision red. I didn't bother to wipe it away, only watched in terror.

"Help!" the body screamed. "I'm burning! Fuck, it hurts! Help!"

"You are just food," the mother creature said. "A pig being raised for slaughter. A fitting end for a son who doesn't have the balls to visit his own, poor mother."

She scurried to the bed like a rat on meth, stuck her hands arms-deep into the body's abdomen, and pulled out something resembling a stomach; gooey, slimy, soaked in fluids. She bit into it, laughing as she ate. Once she finished her appetizer, she dug into the main entrée. Spleen, liver, intestines, kidneys, no appendix, though, since I had that removed after a brief stint with appendicitis in middle school. She ripped and tore through the body, pushing meat out of the way as he screamed and pled for mercy. But it wasn't enough. She was harvesting, eating as if she hadn't eaten in decades. Guts flew everywhere, splattering on the walls and ceilings, some getting on my clothes and sliding off, leaving trails of bodily fluids in their wake. I gagged again, but nothing came up. I was running on empty.

"Won't you join us?"

That voice, that cosmic terror of a voice.

The Man in Black twisted me around and grabbed me by the neck, lifting me two feet off the ground with only one hand. Its head, a mere void, almost touched the ceiling with how tall it was. Those bright eyes stared into my very being. I squirmed, pounding its arm with clenched fists as the air in my lungs turned to ice in my throat. Nothing but a few grunts passed through my lips as my eyes went bloodshot.

"Soon enough, you will."

With no apparent effort, as my vision began to fade from asphyxiation, the Man in Black threw me across the room. I crashed through my bedroom window and plummeted hundreds of feet to the downtown Chicago pavement. A bright light consumed me before I made contact, and I was back in darkness, the only light guiding my way being a red exit sign in a hotel ballroom.

7

I was reluctant to push the handles on the double doors leading to my freedom. If I knew my push handles like I thought I did, I knew they would make a harsh click as the latch released, something that would gain the attention of Scyphozoa.

An ancient song played low on the speakers. "Midnight, the Stars and You" sung by an uncredited Al Bowlly, popularized in the zeitgeist with Kubrick's *The Shining*. Fitting, in a macabre way, as we were in a hotel during the winter, and I was metaphorically snowbound in the building with a bunch of insane freaks. No axe wielding Jack Nicholson, however; just a lead singer armed with a jug of laced alcohol.

My fingers wrapped around the cold metal bars. I tensed, my knuckles tightening with the force of indecision. Before I managed to garner the courage to push the doors open, I heard hushed voices.

"Great job, Ash," Evelyn said.

"Another successful New Year's," Adam said.

"Night to remember, I say," Marty chimed in, probably ignored.

"Keep your voices down," Asher commanded in a whisper. "Where's Joel?"

Better yet, where was Jess? She had told me to run, and I was sorely failing in that regard. Why hadn't they asked for her? Was she standing in their group at the center of the ballroom? So many questions, so few answers.

"Find him… NOW!" Asher yelled.

My heart sank in my chest, and I pushed on the door handles without a second thought. The hotel lobby's light shone into the ballroom, casting light upon the congregation of drugged partygoers. I slipped through the door as I heard the band members stepping over all those people. I had time, I was sure.

I needed to run, so I ran.

8

Fuck, fuck, fuck, I huffed as I ran through the lobby. A group of elderly couples huddled around a flat screen TV snapped their heads to stare at the crazed young adult sprinting through the room, whispering expletives under his breath. "Hey, stop!" the man at the front desk shouted, startling the oldest of that crowd, who was probably hard of hearing as it was.

I ignored him, pushed myself through the revolving doors, and was met with the cool chill of San Franciscan midnight. I had the city at my disposal, so where would I go? I chose to jet to my left, running down the driveway toward the main road leading up to the hotel.

My legs were ablaze with lactic acid. There were splints in my shins, pains in my ribs, aches in my thighs, but I kept running. Nothing else mattered. I passed the Scyphozoa tour bus in all its red and yellow glory. A split-second thought of my personal belongings crossed my mind, but they could keep everything they wanted.

"Joel?"

I stopped hesitantly, recognizing the voice but unable to discern who it belonged to in my tiredness. In the dark, the shadow of a large person lurked toward me.

"Is that you?"

A rough voice, rich as black coffee on a Sunday morning. The figure stepped from the shadows. Through a string of tired gasps, I managed to twitch a smile.

"Oh Lord," Lenny said, jogging toward me. "Are you alright, man? What happened."

Everything spewed from my mouth in that moment, the party, the lights, the drinks, the countdown, the ball drop, the bodies dropping, the next installment in my struggle with the Man in Black. Everything laid on the table like a deck of cards in a casino.

Lenny said nothing; he simply nodded and nudged me toward the bus. "Let's talk before they get here. Knowing them, they already know where your ass headed."

9

Lenny kept the bus's engine off, instead opting to chat in the glow of a nearby lamppost. I appreciated the thought and care he put into keeping me hidden from the rest of them. He sat in the driver's seat, I in the passenger's. He pulled out a camping radio, cranked it a few times to charge the battery, and adjusted the dial until it hit a jazz station, setting the volume to low.

"Wanna eddy?" Lenny asked.

He pulled a small container of gummy edibles from his pants pocket, to which I politely declined. "More for me, I guess," he said, popping an entire gummy into his mouth without chewing.

Lenny swallowed and said, "I wanna let you know something, aight?"

"Sure."

"These guys and gals… They're crazy. Buncha crazy white fuckers, no offense."

"None taken," I said. Lenny looked genuinely worried he might have offended me.

"Good. So, anyway, they're crazy. Scary, even. I've learned to live with that fact since I've been hauling their asses around for years, but it doesn't change the fact they're so goddamn scary. And I'm a big dude, too! Just look at me!"

He raised his arms and pointed at himself as if I hadn't noticed how large of a man he was. "Someone as big as me shouldn't be scared by a load of skinny white kids," he said, "but big doesn't always mean tough. And I am one *soft* motherfucker. But that's beside the point."

"Does this have anything to do with the Man in Black?"

He chuckled with the jollity of Santa Claus.

"You still calling it that?" Lenny asked.

"You got any better ideas?"

"You know, I been thinking about that recently. What do you even call something like that? Shit, I don't even know if that thing's a 'man' at all."

A Miles Davis chart played on the radio. John Coltrane soothed the rhythm with a beautiful saxophone solo. *Gotta be "Round Midnight,"* I thought, sensing the irony of the song with the situation at hand.

"I see shit online about skinwalkers and wendigos and shit like that," Lenny said. "Those shapeshifting things that lure you in by looking like a deer or a bunny or something and murder your ass when you get too close.

To me, though, that white-eyed demon never looks like something it ain't. It's always confident enough to just show itself as it is. Just a pair of eyes on the shape of a man."

"It's turned into people. At least, from what I've seen."

"Well, ain't that great? He likes you!"

"Shut up, man."

I playfully punched his shoulder.

"What does it turn into?" Lenny asked.

"It's more that it is *already* posing as someone else when I see it. There was a hallucination at a bar where I saw people being slaughtered by a bunch of dudes in Halloween masks. One of them was the Man in Black. Another time, it was my mother. Sometimes it isn't anything at all. It's as real as the air we breathe, but nowhere to be found. But it's always out there, watching. Waiting to strike like one of those skinwalkers you were talking about."

"Now you're getting it."

"And it sends me to different places from my past, like it's in my mind and playing around with it. Squishing it like putty between his fingers. It feels *so* real, but I know it never is. There's always something off at first, and then everything turns to shit. Actually, 'shit' seems like a tame word for it. Just *terrible* shit. Gruesome, even. And sometimes it speaks to me."

"It... talks?"

I nodded and said, "It's always some ominous shit. It started with 'Fate.' Subtle, I know. But now it's turned into 'you know what we want' and 'join us.'"

"Shit, man. What do you think it means?"

I whipped out my strawberry banana vape, asked if it was alright to smoke inside the bus, and took a drag, blowing vapor in a gust from my nostrils. "I have no idea," I said, "but I'm at the center of it all. The Man in Black showed me that."

"You seriously gotta stop calling it that."

"Okay! Give me your suggestions for a name change. I'm sure it won't mind getting a new ID," I snarked.

"I got nothing."

I pondered for a bit, taking another drag from the disposable. I searched the deepest catalogs of my mind, sat there in silence for a long while. Then, an idea struck.

"The Great King Rat," I blurted.

"Excuse me?"

"Great King Rat. There's this song off Queen's first album called that. I think it's fitting, considering that thing must be the king of something, and he's a dirty rat. A name as stupid as that takes the edge off it."

"King Rat it is."

So it was ordained; that the Man in Black would be henceforth known by the title of the Great King Rat, so help us God.

10

"My granny had this saying," Lenny reminisced. "She probably stole it from someone, but it went something like: 'If you're wearing rose-tinted glasses, red flags just look like regular ass flags.' She also told my sisters to never tell a man shit, 'cause he'll take your purse and run off with another woman, so who knows if she was right?"

"Seems pretty spot-on to me," I said.

"What I mean to say is: Don't trust Scyphozoa. I've told you that before and I'll tell you again. *Don't*, under any circumstances, trust them, even though you've been a fan of them for a while. They aren't good people. I know good people, and they are *not* them."

"Right."

"I'm serious." He contemplated what he would say next. "Did they tell you about what would happen tonight?"

"I mean, yeah. I was there."

"No, I don't mean the party in general. I'm talking about what they were gonna do to those poor people they invited."

"I guess they didn't mention that." I knew full and damn well they didn't mention it, those fuckers. "Wait, how did *you* know what was gonna happen?"

"They do it every year. It's very lowkey in their media cycle, but they like to call it their 'New Year's Crash.' They dance and dance and dance, then they all drink some weirdo shit and fall asleep for a few hours at the same time. Like crashing a few hours after drinking an energy drink. They all just… fall. And sleep."

"What. So those people knew?"

"Yup. They signed the paperwork and everything."

"If it was safe, why didn't they tell me? And why didn't Asher and all the rest drink that shit with the rest of them?"

"Hell if I know," Lenny said with a grunt.

I peered out the bus door window, scouting the area for Asher and his crew. They were nowhere to be seen in that hotel parking lot. Maybe they'd lost my scent trail.

"It's all so stupid. Why wouldn't they tell me? I'm in their goddamn band, after all," I said.

"I have one more thing to tell you," Lenny said, his voice growing grim.

I looked back at Lenny, ignoring the world outside the window. I leaned in with more intrigue than I ever thought possible.

"I was taking a walk," he continued. "You know, just stretching my legs after days of driving this hunk of shit. I think it was in Charlotte. I was heading back to the bus when I looked down some alley and saw someone slumped by a dumpster."

"I saw that same person, I think."

"You probably did. I think I saw you walking out of there when I was making my way over. But I got curious, 'cause what else am I supposed to do when I'm stuck with a buncha crazies for months? I walked down the alley and knelt by him, noticed how gray and musty he looked. I knew that man was dead the moment I laid eyes on him, but my curiosity still got the better of me. I lifted his head, and you'll never believe whose face I saw."

"Whose?"

"Asher's."

CHAPTER X

1

I wasn't surprised. No one in my situation would be. The laced cigarettes, the laced party favors, the weird tone of voice from every Scyphozoa member, including Jess. I wasn't crazy. They were.

The Great King Rat had appeared in the corner of my eye when Asher and the rest eventually found me sitting in the bus, alone in the dark with Lenny and a cloud of flavored smoke. An edible gummy with a bite mark down the middle rested in my palm. I had indulged when Lenny made his big reveal. There was absolutely no way I could process that information sober.

Asher? Dead? The dead man in the Charlotte alleyway and him were one in the same. But how? Maybe Lenny and I had stumbled upon a corpse who looked oddly like Asher. I wanted to believe that. Believe me, I wanted to. But with all the bullshit happening to me since I joined the band, it seemed as plausible as summer being hot and winter being cold.

As hard as I tried to focus on the Great King Rat, it would always shift perfectly with the movement of my periphery, in the corner of my eye like a fallen eyelash too stubborn to go away. It simply stood there, watching. Those gleaming eyes were pinpricks in my vision. Taunting me in its stillness, torturing me in its lack of action.

But there was Asher Gaumont, alive as ever, entering the tour bus with the others in tow as he commanded Lenny to, "Turn on the lights. It's dark as fuck in here."

"Sure thing, boss," Lenny begrudgingly said.

I kept my focus on Great King Rat, attempting to get it into my direct line of sight, shaking it from my peripheral vision like one shakes loose crumbs from a sandwich bag. It was no use. It wouldn't go away, even as Adam slapped me on the shoulder and asked, "Why'd you run off, man?"

There was a split second where I forgot every word in the English lexicon, from *a* to *zyzzyva*. How do you speak to people you can't trust? There's a lot of thought and care that needs to be put into effect when talking to those kinds of people; the sly and treacherous. Do you smile? Keep it neutral? Are we sad today? Happy? Why did I run? Who is that man over there who was basically skin and bones and hour ago but seems perfectly healthy and muscular now? And what did you do with the real Asher? All these questions flooded my mind in one heaping tidal wave of uncertainty. A tsunami filled every nook and cranny of my brain with doubtful waters.

"I got scared," I mustered.

"Scared?" Adam laughed.

"Yeah," I said, rising from my chair, "because you *dicks* forgot to mention all that shit was planned!"

"Hey, don't get defensive."

"Defensive? Are you fucking kidding me? Of course I'm going to be at least a *little* defensive! I thought I just witnessed mass murder in that goddamn hotel. Wouldn't you be a little defensive if you saw something like that?"

"Don't get mad at us," Evelyn budded in. "Obviously we mentioned it to you. Maybe you weren't listening."

"I'm a musician, Evie," I responded, employing her nickname with the ferocity of a hungry mountain lion spotting a lone deer in the wilderness. "My ears are fine. You all decided not to tell me. Why?"

Silence, interrupted only by the bus engine's low hum.

"Because we never tell our new people," Asher said, his voice less raspy than it had been inside the hotel.

"What?" I asked.

"We like to keep little traditions like that a surprise. It brings a sense of normalcy to the things we indulge in. If we don't tell you beforehand, it'll be more exciting in the moment. Your heart was racing in there, wasn't it?"

"Yes."

"You could feel it about to explode through the cracks between your ribs? There was sweat dripping down your cheeks? Dripping from your forehead? Into your eyebrows? Stinging your eyes every time you blinked?"

"Yes, Asher. What're you getting at?"

I felt the early signs of annoyance. I huffed and puffed like a pouting infant who was on the verge of tears after losing their pacifier.

"You felt alive. Right?"

"Yes," I said.

"And that was the goal. That's the goal of everything involving music, I think. Music is that extra kick everyone needs to simply stay alive. It's better than any drug or plastic surgery, or even sex, for that matter. We live and breathe music in Scyphozoa, and you're part of that. At least, you need to learn to be part of that. Will you learn?"

I didn't say anything. Instead, I examined Asher's face, scrutinizing every detail down to the atom. The strong jaw, high cheekbones, perfect lips, narrow nose, structured nose bridge that strung his threaded eyebrows tightly together. It was all the same, down to the fresh scar printed on his chin. That was most definitely Asher, but I had some doubts. I trusted Lenny more than I trusted my own mother, but what he had said about the body in Charlotte made me iffy about how sane he was as well. Asher was there, looking into my eyes with his blue ones. They were fueled with life, down to the tinges of brown circling his pupils. If that alleyway body, covered in inches of snowfall, had looked like Asher—had *been* Asher—it would be difficult to explain that to my doctor. "Hey, doc," I would say. "Is it possible to die from a heroin overdose and come back?"

To which the doctor would respond, "Why, no, you fucking idiot. Especially if they've been rotting next to a dumpster in the middle of winter for God knows how long."

To which I would say, "But, doc. It was him, I'm sure of it."

And the doctor would say, "I'm not even your doctor. How did you get in my house?"

2

We left San Francisco the morning after, heading toward Portland for another show, then Seattle the day after, and Vancouver the day after that.

I didn't have a passport to present to border patrol once we hit that divide between America and Canada, but I had a crude picture of my birth certificate in my phone's camera roll, to which one officer lifted an eyebrow. "There's something you don't see every day," she said.

"Am I good to travel?" I asked.

She rolled her eyes, the top half of her face shaded in the shadow from her hat.

"Let me see a driver's license or something. A screenshot of some random birth certificate isn't going to cut it."

"Here," I said, opening my wallet and fetching my license.

The officer plucked the card from my grasp and studied both it and the picture of my birth certificate under a microscope. Her eyes were laser beams, burning holes in both my license and my phone. She flipped my license as if there was anything of importance on the other side of the card and presented it to me between two callused fingers.

"You're good to go," she said.

"Thank you," I obliged.

She nodded, the sunlight seeping into her eyes. I saw the Great King Rat in her pupils as the light reflected into mine. That brightness, that gleaming, that burning. My face dropped from an awkward smile to one of fear. The officer noticed this but thought nothing of it. Just another weirdo American crossing the border into a much better country where they don't belong. Par for the course.

I felt the chilled Canadian breeze prick my face as I turned and hopped back onto the tour bus. We played in Vancouver, I played my horn, unfeeling, unaware. There may have been a crowd full of cheers and laughs and smoke and tears. There may have been sound, music. There may have been a band on the makeshift stage in that beautiful Canadian venue. There may not have been a stage at all. Maybe we stood on the same level as the crowd who may or may not have been there. There may have been beer and liquor, water and spotlights, glitz and glamour. Was I even there? I think so. All I could muster to focus on was whether the Great King Rat was in the shadows, the dark corners of that dark room. Its eyes burned holes into my psyche.

I may have played the right notes, the rhythms and articulations. I was in a vacuum, trapped in my own mind. There were two versions of me: The one performing with Scyphozoa, and the one trapped within that performer. A scared little boy encased in the body of a grown man absolutely tearing on a trombone.

The abyss that was the Great King Rat never showed, and I don't feel like I did either. I was a musical ghost haunting that venue with the *whomp whomps* only a trombone could provide.

3

The back of my neck throbbed to the tempo of a Mötley Crüe song blasting in my earbuds. Even with the volume set to the max, I could still hear Evelyn and Adam bicker to each other on the couch across from me.

"There's no way you think bagels are better than donuts," Evelyn said. "You can't be human if you think that."

"What if I'm not, huh? What if I'm Satan himself? Do I seriously not have a soul because I just like bagels more?" Adam asked.

"Yes! I know you already lost your soul years ago, so it *does* make sense."

"You lost yours, too. Don't even."

"I didn't *lose* it, dumbass. I know damn well where it is."

"Oh, do indulge me, great Evelyn Stone."

Evelyn unclipped an earring from her left ear, brushing locks of flowing blonde as she went. She put it to the light, Adam stared intently.

"Here it is," she said. "My soul."

"That's just a cheap earring Mom got you for your birthday. Wasn't that the year you got mono from… who was it? … Oh yeah! Eighth grade. You and that high school sophomore were in that little scandal. I remember now," Adam said.

"Wasn't that the same year you had a hernia in your right nut?"

"You promised to never talk about that again."

"You're the one who brought up Thomas."

"You *still* remember his name?"

"I remember everything, numb nuts," Evelyn said, waving the earring in front of Adam's eyes at every syllable like a crazed pendulum. "But anyway, here. My soul."

"That's just an earring."

"And *you're* just a little shit, but no one's saying anything."

"Go on," Adam huffed, crossing his arms, and slouching further into the couch cushion behind him.

"This is my soul. My soul is this earring. The one Mom got me the same year I got mono from Tom Ferguson. Didn't you pick something to stick your soul into when you gave yours away?"

Adam snuck a look at me, to which I darted my eyes back to the floor and bobbed my head as Vince Neil shouted into my ears.

"Of course I did. If I'm getting what you mean," Adam said to Evelyn, pulling a blunt from his jacket pocket. "What some?"

"You know me so well," Evelyn said, taking the blunt, clamping it between her lips and leaning it to allow Adam's lighter to light the end aflame. Through a puff of smoke, Adam coughed and wafted the air, saying, "I guess mine would be in a grinder."

"You're such an addict. Why couldn't it be something sentimental?" Evelyn asked.

"You can't get addicted to weed."

"Keep telling yourself that."

The bus hit a bump in the highway, lifting me and inch or two in the air and plopping me back down in the couch. An earbud fell from my ear and tugged on the wire on its way down, pulling the other earbud from my other ear, taking Mötley Crüe with it as they both clacked onto the floor. I scrambled to pick them back up, to escape being out in the open to their conversation without the shield of loud music to save me.

"What about you, Joel?" Evelyn asked.

Hunched over with both earbuds dangling from my hand, I paused for a moment and straightened up slowly. "What about what?" I asked, pretending I hadn't heard everything they said.

"Your soul. You sold your soul to drop out of school and play in a band… We all did. Where did you put yours?"

"I don't understand."

She took another drag, blew more smoke. It hung in the air like an opaque tapestry. "You know those Horcrux things from Harry Potter?" Evelyn asked.

"I've never watched Harry Potter," I responded, feeling rather proud about that fact.

"Oh. Well, anyway. The bad guy in those movies split his soul into six or seven chunks and put the pieces into different objects. He could only die once all those pieces were destroyed. I think about that a lot, and I liken it to being in the music industry, no matter how small your role. You sell your soul to put your art out there. Every new art piece you create, the weaker your soul gets. As more and more people critique and slander your work, that's just what happens. So, I find it best to keep my soul close to my chest, or in this case, right under my ear." She looped the earring, a small jewel glinting with hints of translucent pink, back through her earlobe. "It's outside my body, but it stays close. It stays healthy and fruitful and all that. And the more music I put out there, the less diminished my soul becomes."

"Interesting," I said.

This is just gibberish, I thought, but continued to indulge her ramblings.

She frowned as if she heard what I had thought. Realizing she had given me a glare, Evelyn tightened her cheeks back into a sly smile. "So, what is yours locked away in?" she asked.

"I don't know," I pondered. "Maybe my copy of *The Stand*."

"What's that?"

"It's a book."

"I know it's a goddamn book. Explain why you would stick something so precious inside something so flimsy."

Adam was shrouded in a veil of his own smoke. He leaned back and blew another gust from his pursed lips, a slight cough permeating from his lungs toward the end as the smoke dissipated. Another bump in the road, but I kept my grip on the couch cushions to keep myself from flying into the ceiling.

"It's my favorite book, so I wouldn't mind sticking myself in there."

"Yes, but it's all paper." Evelyn took the lighter from Adam's lap and struck it. A low flame wafted from the nozzle, crackling with sparks. "One stint with a little bit of fire and it's up in smoke. The pages, and words, and your soul with it."

"You can lose an earring just as easily," I rebutted. "Kim Kardashian did that just by getting thrown into the ocean."

"I'm not Kim Kardashian."

"Yeah, but I've seen people lose earrings more often than they burn books. In pools, in Lake Michigan, in sewer grates. Hell, even down their kitchen sink. When has anyone had a book burned other than in a house fire or during World War II?"

"During the Qin Dynasty," Adam interjected.

Evelyn nodded, pointing a finger with surprise as if there was an elephant sitting next to her instead of her twin brother. "See? It's common," she said.

"The Qin Dynasty was before Jesus," I said, diving into the depths of my sparse history knowledge. "And a *grinder*? Why would you use that? It would cake your soul with pot."

"I mean," Adam said, "it's already like that."

It was my turn to roll my eyes. If Adam mentioned weed one more time, I was going to hop from my seat and strangle him. It's okay to take a puff or two occasionally but making it your entire personality is where I draw the line.

"Don't be like that, Joel," Evelyn said. "I know you don't trust us after the whole New Year's thing, but that doesn't give you the right to start being smart with us."

"You sound like my mother," I huffed.

"Well, maybe you need a bit of a mother figure. Something you're sorely lacking, it seems."

"What is *that* supposed to mean?" I asked. "Who told you about my mother?"

She didn't utter another word. Evelyn kept her mouth agape for a moment, then shut it and whipped her phone from her pants pocket. She began to type something, the taps and thuds of fingertips against the glass screen beating into the musty bus air.

The conversation was over, it seemed. I unclenched the fists I didn't know were clenched, letting the earbuds within my grip tumble onto my knee and fall to the floor. I ground my teeth, picked myself up, and locked myself in the restroom, where I stayed for hours on end until we arrived in Denver, Colorado.

4

I called my mother and let the phone ring ten times until it went to voicemail. Her custom voicemail message said, "Hello! This is Julianna Auguste! I'm currently not at the phone right now, so leave a message and I'll call you back as soon as I can. Goodbye!"

There was a cheeriness to her tone that I hadn't heard since I was young. That tone she used at the carnival sans the bombing and falling Ferris wheel. That tone she used when making me grilled cheese and tomato soup after a long day at school, without the blood and guts I'd been so familiar with recently. I found myself longing for those times where the weight of responsibility didn't crush me. When the weight of my father, the weight of my mother, didn't squeeze me to a measly pulp.

I tried to call her again. Ten rings. Voicemail. "Goodbye!" *Beep.* I ended the call before I could leave a message.

I swiped through my phone and called for an Uber. After paying, I walked out of the hotel lobby toward the tour bus. I knocked, Lenny opened, and I asked, "Wanna go into the mountains?"

He smiled, a rarity for him, and said, "Sure thing, man. Can I ask why, though?"

"I just need some time to think."

"About what?"

I contemplated the question, answering after a minute:

"Maybe I just need an excuse to *not* think."

5

The Uber driver, a Latino man with the most glorious beard I'd ever seen, pulled into the rest area parking lot, the gravel path, caked with snow, churning under his car's tires. He'd kept the conversation inside the car as natural as possible, avoiding the pitfalls of awkward talks people usually get involved in when using a rideshare service.

He'd recognized me, as a matter of fact. He told me his son, Silvestre, was a huge fan of the band. In fact, he had one of his son's belongings in the car, to which he asked me to sign. I never saw the appeal of autographed paraphernalia, but I obliged and took the book and the pen the driver had fished from the cup holder above the center console. The book in question was a near-pristine copy of Murakami's *The Wind-Up Bird Chronicle*, a novel I had been meaning to get to if it weren't for the taxing nature of college courses, dropping all said courses, and joining a band on a whim.

"I didn't write this book, you know," I said from the back seat.

"I don't have a printed photo of you, so that'll have to do," he said. "Name's Jorge, by the way."

Jorge had kept his eyes planted on the winding road as he bent to reach a hand back. Before I could sign the copy of a book I most certainly didn't write, I took his hand in mine and gave it a firm shake. "I'm Joel. It's nice to meet you, man," I said.

"You're paying me to drive you," Jorge said, "so I'd hope it'd be nice to meet me."

I couldn't stop looking at his beard through the rearview mirror. I wondered what my facial hair would look like if I didn't shave my face every

158

day. Surely not as long and full as the man driving Lenny and me, but maybe something modest enough to be viable. I signed my name on the title page as neatly as possible in the shaky car, making sure to cross my *J* and put emphasis on the *A* of my last name with finesse. I tapped Jorge's shoulder with the book. He grabbed it and settled it in the empty passenger seat. "Thank you so much, Joel," he said.

"It's no problem."

"I know it's not much, but he'll be so thrilled."

"I'm sure he will."

I smiled a bit brighter as each word passed my lips. I may have been at one of the lowest points of my life, but at least I could help someone else smile. To have someone else—Silvestre, it seemed—be the conduit for my own happiness.

"How old's your son?" I asked, noting the Bad Bunny song playing low on the radio. "Después de la Playa," I think it was. Absolute heater of a song. Cultural barriers be damned, I could get behind some hype-ass Latin music.

"He just turned eighteen," Jorge said with a chuckle. "About to graduate high school and leave the nest by August."

"I hope he does well."

"He's got his heart set on a degree in Music Education. I told him, 'No, Silvestre. How will you get any money from that? These Americans hate paying their teachers anything.' But he wants to get a doctorate in that. They pay big money up in those ranks, apparently. Directing college-level bands and even professional ones. He said, 'If all goes well, I can conduct for the Berlin Philharmonic.' Those goddamn Germans know their shit about music, pardon my tongue. And they would pay him well. I just hope he knows what he truly wants."

"It sounds like he does," I said.

"You think so?"

We stopped at a red light before veering off toward the path leading to the hiking rest area. He turned to me, the stoplight glowing through the window in red swatches under the mist of snowfall. His expression warranted a swift response, and I gave him one without much thought behind it, saying exactly what my heart knew, not what my brain wanted.

"I know so," I said.

"You didn't go to college, did you?"

"You're looking at a dropout, Jorge."

"Aw, shit." He clucked a *tsk tsk tsk.* "Why'd you go and do that?"

"Just…" I considered the reasons I had so flippantly dropped out of school. It had to have been a case of college simply not being the right fit for me. Or maybe it was the broken heart, or the stake Todd drove into my chest while I performed at Toss & RUMble. I was locked in a padded room, screaming for a way to get out. Pounding on the walls just to feel something, but the padding dampened the blows one by one, leaving me unsatisfied. Scyphozoa was the key I needed to escape, and I did. But at what cost? I didn't know, and I was unsure of whether I wanted to know. "…yeah, it wasn't the best fit for me personally. I started as a psychology major, then switched to music performance, and now I'm here, sitting in the back seat of your car with this guy."

"So, I'm just 'this guy' to you?" Lenny asked, genuinely annoyed.

"That's not what I meant, Lenny. Live a little," I said nudging his shoulder. He didn't move an inch.

"Well," Jorge said, "I'm glad you went down the path you chose. That's all I want for my son, you know. I want him to be happy. If he wants to teach people about notes and instruments or whatever, *I* want him to do it. If he wants to travel the world with an orchestra, I hope he does. Because the world needs more music, anyway. And it would mean everything to me if Silvestre were the one to add more to it."

We pulled into the parking lot, a small lot in comparison to the three Walmarts we passed on the journey from the hotel to the hiking trail. I opened my wallet, picked out a ten, and slipped it to Jorge. I didn't trust Uber's tipping system, but I believed in the singular power of paper money. "Here you go, man," I said. "Thanks for the ride."

"Don't sweat it, kid," he said, taking the bill. "And here."

He reached into his glovebox and pulled out a notepad. He wrote something on the thin yellow sheet, tore it from the binding, and handed it to me folded. "That's my number," he said. "If you don't want some random guy driving you off this mountain, give me a call. Business is slow with the snow coming down the way it is."

"Thanks, man," I said. "And tell Silvestre I said, 'Hi.'"

"Will do, sir."

I slipped my light blue beanie over my head, squishing my curls under the tight wool. I thanked Jorge again, as did Lenny, and we left the car. I waved as he drove away, back down the path we entered from.

"Now what?" Lenny grunted.

6

Lenny and I walked for hours, watching the sun slowly dip behind the mountains as we trekked through the wilderness. The sky was clear in the distance, allowing for pinks and oranges to seep through the silhouettes of trees. Bathed in golden light, tickled by snowflakes.

"You feeling any better?" Lenny asked, trailing behind me. "I mean since New Year's. In San Fran."

"I'll be honest with you, Lenny," I said. "No."

"Gonna explain yourself, or you gonna leave me hanging?"

"It's been so hard, man. To function, I mean. I can barely leave the bus or the hotel room without fearing for my life. I know King Rat is out there, watching. Waiting for me to leave my guard down."

"I feel you, Joel."

"And it isn't even me being afraid of dying," I added, kicking a branch from my feet. "I could care less if I died today or tomorrow or whenever that thing wants me to die. I'm just afraid of what he's going to show me next."

"It can be hard to reckon with your past."

"It's not that."

"Then what is it?"

Lenny had me stumped there. I stopped walking, dead leaves crunching beneath my shoes. The snowfall slowed, the frigid breeze in the trees halted. The shadows, like harsh tiger stripes on the terrain, faded as the sun disappeared from the horizon, inviting nightfall with open arms.

I didn't want to admit to Lenny that he was right. That may have been the reason the Great King Rat consistently brought moments from my past to my attention, since thinking about such things came as torture to me. My heart ached with every thought of my mother, of Roselle, of my father that crossed my mind. They were the catalysts that opened the floodgates to all the other painful memories permeating in my mind. A chemical reaction so deadly it set my heart ablaze in glorious flame, exploding inside my chest like an atomic bomb.

"I guess you're right," I said through gritted teeth, slowly marching ahead as I pulled my phone from my pocket, flicking the flashlight on.

"I know I'm right," Lenny said. "I was just waiting for you to see that."

We found a clearing; a rocky ledge overlooking the dimming horizon. I set my phone onto the ground, flashlight up, glowing toward the sky, illuminating the surrounding area. I sat on the cold earth, knees curled to my chest, arms wrapped around them. Lenny slumped next to me, his bones creaking with the onset of early aging. As I stuck my vape between my lips, Lenny asked, "I mentioned my ex-wife to you before, right?"

"In passing, I think," I said.

"I don't think about her much anymore. She's kinda like this mole on my neck. Always there, always… what's the word… persistent. She's in the back of my mind all the time but tucked away in a corner that's all dusty and full of cobwebs. The memory of her, I mean. She was a looker, from what I can remember, at least. 'Total bombshell' as you crackers like to say."

"No one says 'total bombshell' anymore, Len."

"We went out, I took her to the best restaurants I could find in Pittsburgh, we married, had two kids. Phyllis and Leonard. Named after me, obviously." He chuckled, hot breath fuming from his nose and mouth. "Can never be too many Lennys running around. I miss those bastards, I really do. Sometimes, and don't tell the others, I whip out my phone while we're on the road and swipe through my photos, just to get a glimpse of them. I don't have any pictures of them recently, though. Just the last pictures we had together before the divorce took her and them away from me. I miss them… so much."

Lenny whimpered those last few syllables, his voice wavering with deep sorrow. He wiped his eyes and continued, "I don't know what you've been through to get you here, but everyone has a story for why they got involved with this goddamn band. Evelyn and Adam ran away from home, Jess ran away from some foster care shit, Marty... well, I don't know why Marty's here. Barely anyone does, maybe Asher. But Asher; he's the sore spot in all this. I have no idea why he started the damn group."

"I might," I said. "He told me some vague story about waking up one night and seeing someone in his dorm room. Not human, from the way he described it. I've been thinking about that a lot recently. I think that same... creature... he saw in his dorm is the same one you've been seeing during these long drives. The same one that's been terrorizing me for the past few weeks."

"The Rat," he nodded.

"Great King Rat."

"You know that name isn't much better than 'Man in Black' was."

"Any improvement, no matter how small, is progress. My developmental psychology professor said that once."

"How profound."

"Big word for you, big man."

"Don't be a dick. I'll whack the fuck outta you."

"Sorry," I playfully replied, chuckling as I stuck my hands in the air like I was surrendering to the police.

"You wanna know something crazy, Joel?"

"What's that?"

"When's the last time you felt... I don't know. Scared?"

I pondered that question for a few brief seconds. I sat in the Coloradan wilderness, on the ledge of some plateau, in the dark, with only Lenny to keep me safe. But I felt fine. I was reminiscing on my past; the good, the bad, the worse. The thought of the Great King Rat didn't even spark a bonfire of fear in my mind. My bones didn't grow cold with terror at the mere thought. Everything was still in that mountainous forest, the trees sung low tunes as their branches swayed in the cold night breeze.

"Not since we left the hotel, I guess," I murmured.

"It's weird, right? 'Cause I feel the same way. I was sitting in the bus thinking about nothing but what bad shit could happen. The worst possible things that could and *would* happen, like I was some sorta... Uh... what's the word?"

"Skeptic?"

"Yeah, that. But out here? Nothing. It's like my brain was about to explode out of my head, but the moment Jorge took that turn toward the hiking trail? Nothing at all. Just calm. Like someone poked a hole in my skull to relieve all that damn pressure."

"I've felt the same way, actually."

"It's crazy, right?" Lenny asked.

"Very much so," I said.

"I think it has to do something with Asher, if I'm being completely honest with you."

"How so?"

"I mean, I don't *know*, but I have a gut feeling he's the sorta ringleader of all this. Every time you all go perform a few miles away from where I parked the bus, I feel the same way. Complete bliss. I don't know how to describe it well enough, but it seems like the further away from him I am, the less crazy shit happens. Have you seen the King Rat guy since we got up here?"

"No."

"Not even the feeling that someone's watching you?"

"Don't think so."

"So, there it is." He maneuvered his huge frame into a crisscross position, slapping his knees with the revelation. "If it ain't Asher causing this shit, it's gotta be one of them. And I *know* for damn sure it ain't you, since I've been stuck with you for the past hour or so and nothing spooky's gone on."

"I have a different question for you," I said. "Not to veer this conversation off course."

"Shoot," he said, a smile raising his cheekbones into jolly nubs under his eyes.

"It's about your wife. Sorry; *ex*-wife."

"Don't be sorry. I make the same mistake from time to time."

"But anyway, how did you get over her? Like, what did you do to stop feeling so shitty about everything?"

"You never get over the people you love, Joel," Lenny said. "Not really, anyway. As I said: I never stop remembering her, or the kids. I keep trying to blame her parents for turning her and the kids against me, those sick fucks. But I know that's childish as shit, and I'm no baby. I just take a deep breath, eat a gummy, and continue with my day. Speaking of which…"

Lenny pulled a small plastic tube from his coat pocket, untwisted the cap, and poured a singular edible gummy into his palm. It was light blue, like the color of antifreeze, and speckled with shining bits of sugar like the stars in the winter sky above. He ripped it in equal halves, popped one half into his mouth, and held the other toward me. "Come on, man," he pleaded, smacking on the last remaining bits of gummy between his teeth. "Live a little. Not for me, though. For you."

I nodded, held my hand open, and let the edible drop into my palm. I studied it in the dim glow of my phone's flashlight and the last gleam of sunlight on the setting day, and ate it without chewing more than twice. As it slid mostly intact down my throat, I said, "Thanks."

"Don't mention it, bud," he said.

"I think I just need to come to terms with things."

"How so?"

"Maybe I just need to accept that things are the way they are," I said, choking up with each passing word. "I need to accept that I can't go back and change them. As much as I wish I could fix all the mistakes I made, I should just accept that shit happens. Because this world's a goddamn mess and I'm just a small part of it. I don't believe in reincarnation, but it I did, I'd wanna come back as a jellyfish after I die."

"What?"

"A jellyfish," I emphasized. "They don't do anything; just eat, shit, sleep, and die. The only things they have to worry about are sea predators, but that's naturally gonna happen no matter what you come back as. Food chain and all that. But I want to have the grace of the carefree attitude of a jellyfish, swimming through the ocean without a care in the world. No reason to graduate college, to pay taxes, to fall in love. I want that."

"That sounds awful, Joel," Lenny said, rather pissed. "That's exactly the opposite of what I'm getting at."

"But doesn't that sound amazing? No responsibility, no reason to be stressed? Just the animalistic urge to vibe underwater and live day to day without a single fuck to give? Wouldn't you want that, too?"

"No. I don't think anyone wants that."

"What do *you* want, then?" I asked.

"I wanna live, man. That's what everyone wants."

"That *is* living, though. In its purest, simplest form."

"Not really," Lenny said. "Living is seeing the world, falling in love, writing a memoir, or an album, or some Netflix show. Living is doing mundane shit day after day while being excited for a new movie to release on Friday, or a concert date slowly approaching. Living is driving across the country month after month, seeing how God crafted the landscape in His image. Living is appreciating the world you were born into, and doing the best you can with the short amount of time you're afforded. Living isn't just eating, sleeping, and dying. There's so much in between that matters. You seem like a cool kid, Joel. But you need to see that there's more to life than running away from your problems. Like I've said, I don't know why you're here, but I know it was heartbreaking in some way. I've felt the same way, too, so I get it. I didn't run from *my* problems; I live with them. They swim in my heart, and I take them with me everywhere I go. I don't let my divorce define me. I let it shape me. I'm more than the pain I've gone through, and so are you. So is everyone. It just depends on how strong you believe you are. Are you strong, Joel?"

I was speechless. The complete antithesis of my way of life, coming so sincere and heartfelt from a man who resented me only a month and a half before. I couldn't help but blink some tears, my eyelashes soggy and damp with sorrow. Sorrow for the life I was wasting, sorrow for the memories I had stuck in a lockbox in the deepest, darkest corner of my heart. Sorrow for the life I needed to mend back together. One seam, one knot, one hem at a time.

"I am," I answered.

"Prove it to me. Prove it to yourself. You got this, man," Lenny said, placing a large hand on my shoulder. It comforted me, that gentle yet firm pat only an experienced father could muster. Despite the hardship placed upon me by my own father, I couldn't help but miss him in that moment. Old Joel Auguste, with the smell of rye in his breath.

"Thank you."

"Now, don't get all sappy with me," Lenny said. "Why don't you call up Jorge and get us off this mountain?"

I called Jorge, he arrived half an hour after, we got in the car, and I received a phone call from Jess.

I answered, saying, "Hello?"

"Where the hell are you?" Jess said, panicked.

"Out for a walk with Lenny," I lied. "Why? What's up?"

"Asher's pissed that you didn't tell him where you were going."

"Why should he know where I'm at? We aren't performing for another couple days. And, as a matter of fact, I happen to be a fully grown adult man. He can't just baby me around like that."

"Just…" Jess sighed, a digital huff of air emitting from my phone's speaker. "Just get back sooner rather than later. Personally, I don't care what you do with your free time, but Asher. You know how he is."

"Well, just tell him to call me himself if it's so important I'm on his leash. Thanks, Jess," I said, hanging up.

I regretted ending the call before she had a chance to respond. I'd been gradually growing fond of her voice since I joined the band. As the thought crossed my mind, another memory of Roselle reached out through the haze.

I ignored it.

CHAPTER XI

1

In a cruel twist of fate, Asher made the terrible decision to move everyone from the Denver hotel to an Airbnb in the Colorado countryside. The cabin was closer to the concert venue—a concert not happening for another whole day—but was only accessible by a winding dirt path that Lenny struggled to drive the tour bus down. Or up, in this case. The cabin was situated on the edge of the tree line on something resembling a mountain, but more of a hill height-wise.

The wooden siding was covered in moss, so meticulously placed on the edges as if the decorations were manmade. It was a quaint little cottage, if not foreboding in its cuteness. One floor, maybe with a loft acting as a second, and a chimney whose girth was proportional with the fireplace it stemmed from. I couldn't deny that cabin looked straight out of a fairy tale, but there was something so eerie about the location, the surroundings, the wall of trees encasing us within the property from all sides. The branches grinned with gnarled teeth, inviting me to stay awhile, maybe even forever.

As I unloaded my suitcase and four backpacks from the bus's underside, I brushed a curl of hair from my eye. My hair was getting rather long in the front, but I dug it. It suited the rock persona I needed to fill; what, with the messy mullet and slowly growing stubble on my chin and cheeks. Still needed to work on the mustache, as I was looking like a regular sex offender with how patchy it was.

I dragged my luggage through the front door, tugging with all my strength. My back to the interior of the cabin, I felt the weight disappear as I squinted my eyes from all the effort. I turned and saw Jess, two of my bags in hand, smiling and waltzing off toward one of the bedrooms. Down a dark hallway, dim with the lack of lights switched on. I couldn't help but grin. A subtle yet loving smirk painted my face. Intrusively, like a gnat that simply won't quit swarming your face, I saw Roselle once again. I blinked, and she was gone.

The night greeted us with a malicious cold, freezing our bones in the absence of heating or a lit fireplace. I took it into my own hands to light the flame. It took a few tries, but eventually the lighter tickled the logs enough to warrant a large blaze. I handed the lighter back to Adam, keeping a straight face as to show him I didn't want to talk. He didn't take the hint, unfortunately, babbling on about the Roman Empire in a way only someone high out of their mind could. Intricate details, no substance. Words strung together to form something resembling sentences. No coherent thought, just vibes.

I simply nodded my head in agreement with whatever he was going on about. Caesar, Augustus, maybe a bit of Brutus and Antony in there. *He must've watched a video essay about* Julius Caesar *on the bus ride over here,* I thought, and I was proven correct seconds later when he mentioned, "I watched this video where they were talking about Caesar and all that. It was so interesting, but they didn't mention how he invented the salad, so I was kind of disappointed."

"Right," I said, pretending I had heard the most highly intellectual statement of my entire life. I crossed my arms and sat myself on the sofa. It was soft, but cold. The fireplace had yet to grace the cushions with its warmth.

Adam continued, I ignored most of it by escaping to the world inside my phone. I scrolled through Twitter, liked some Instagram posts, even attempted to use Facebook. I saw one post in support of genocide and promptly closed the app and turned off my phone, just in time for the rest of the band to appear in the living room.

Marty held a large red bag labeled "DoorDash" on the front, steam emitting from the contents within. "Dig in," he said, to which no one responded.

"It's Asian buffet food," Asher said with a wink.

Then, like starving rats to a stray wedge of cheese, we dug in. Marty pouted as if he were a toddler being told not to stick his grimy fingers in the cookie jar.

2

I hadn't seen Lenny since we parked the bus in the gravel ditch that acted as a makeshift driveway. It wasn't much out of the ordinary; he preferred to keep to himself in the bus while Scyphozoa went about their own business. If I were in his position, trying to wrangle those freaks up and bus them around America, I would want all that alone time, too.

As I crunched on a chicken eggroll, I thought of my eyeless mother crunching on my skinned body's finger. The grinding sound of teeth against exposed bone. The way it sounded like millions of Jolly Ranchers being run over by a semi-truck. I swallowed the bite I took and put the eggroll remnants in its wax paper bag. That was enough food to fuel me through that cold winter night. I thought of the calories in that single bite; maybe fifty if I was lucky. Just enough to get my ass to bed and fuck off for the rest of the night. That sounded like a wonderful plan, and I raced to action immediately.

Everyone else had kindly fucked off to their own rooms. Everyone except Jess, who sat across the antique table slurping some shrimp lo mein. An image of bloody, pulpy intestines graced my mind. I gagged a little as I stood up from my chair, its legs screeching against the hardwood floor.

"What's the matter?" Jess asked, her words muffled through a mouthful of noodles and shellfish.

"Oh, nothing," I lied. "Just a bit tired. Think I'm gonna go to bed."

"Now?"

"Uh… yeah? Why? Can a man not sleep?"

"It's just…" Jess looked a bit flustered. Her hand inched toward her pants pocket, presumably where her pack of cigarettes à la Gaumont were. "Why don't you stay out here a while? I feel like we haven't talked in a while. Not since, you know."

I feigned a yawn, a trick I picked up in my childhood to avoid interacting with my parents past eight o'clock every night. She didn't yawn back, curiously. "I really wanna chat. I do!" I said. "But I *really* need to head to bed. Big concert coming up. You know how it is."

My words spewed out like a faucet with too much water pressure. It was all a lie, but I needed to get the point across.

"Please?" Jess pleaded. "Stay a little longer."

Maybe I was more tired than I assumed, because I found myself sat in a chair closer to her. Nothing but the corner of the old wooden table separated us. I felt my knee brush against hers, but she didn't pull hers back.

"What's going on?" I asked.

"Can't we just talk?"

"About what?"

"Literally anything."

"Okay," I said. "You start, then."

Her face, washed with a grimness all too familiar, brightened slightly, if only a little. She asked, "What's your favorite color?"

"Starting with the tough questions, I see."

"Mine's turquoise."

"Razzmatazz."

"What the hell even is that?"

"It's some shade of pink, I think. I don't know. I just really like the name."

"You don't like the color *because* of the color?" Jess asked.

"I guess I haven't seen that shade enough to have a solid opinion on it. The name's cool, though."

"Wow, you're *so* insightful."

"And *you're* a dick," I retorted.

Jess released that subtle snort through her nose that has slowly replaced real laughter over the years. "And you might be right," she said, her speech accented with a smile. She took her hand from her pocket with nothing in her grasp. Give it to Joel Auguste for stopping nicotine addiction dead in its tracks with just a little charisma and some minor insults.

"I was just joking," I said.

"No," she disagreed, "I can be a bit of a dick sometimes."

"Out of everyone here—Asher, Evelyn, Adam, even Marty—you're the least dick-ish of the bunch."

"You've got such a way with words," she snarked.

"Can't have a career in music without clever wordplay."

Jess lifted her beer bottle in a sort of toast. Beer was a rather unusual drink to have with Chinese noodles, and she seemed to think so as well. But as most college students will tell you: *It doesn't matter what you drink. If there's alcohol in it, it's doing its job.* I remembered sitting with her at the bar in Lee Harvey's in Dallas. Before the Great King Rat decided to put on another one of its horror picture shows. Her scrunched face as she took pained sips of beer, one bubbly gulp at a time. Letting the carbonated bread water fizzle and pop down her throat, knowing full well she hated it. She did the same thing now, beginning to slouch in the old creaking chair, forgetting about her lo mein, letting it cool in the frosty cabin air, its steam diminishing with every passing second.

Jess let another gulp pass her lips before clunking the half empty bottle on the table. Her plate shook with the tremor, the force in which she slammed the bottle down. I was surprised it didn't shatter into shards, scraping and slicing at her bare palm.

"Jess," I said. "Seriously, what's wrong?"

"Hm?" She stared blankly at the dark hallway behind me, her pupils rimmed with the glow of the doorframe at the end of it.

"You seem, like, really tense. Is something going on that I should know about?"

"No, it's nothing. I'm just... I'm just tired, is all."

"Jess," I said, noticing her lapse in thinking. From someone with experience in the field of lying, this was a standard case of making shit up on the fly. "That's not completely true, and you know that."

"Joel, it's really nothing. I've been like this since we've met. You know, all anxious and worrying about nothing all the time. That's why you'll basically never catch me without a cigarette, except for now, I guess. Oh, which reminds me."

She reached toward her pants pocket again. Its rectangular bulge moved slowly as she slipped the pack of cigarettes from it. An unlabeled package, its original marketing worn off from years of rubbing against denim-lined jeans pockets. No one kept cigarettes for that long. Asher's specialty cigarettes were about to make another appearance, and I wasn't having it. I leaned over and swatted the pack from her hand. It flew across the room and slammed into a far wall with a soft thud. As it landed on the ground, its flap opened and a dozen cigarettes slid onto the floor. One fell between the cracks of a floor vent.

"What the hell?" Jess shouted.

"When's the last time you lit up one of those?"

"Why does that matter?"

"Jess, please."

"Three days ago, I finished a pack. Last night, Asher handed me a new one."

"What the fuck is in those?" I asked, demanding *anything* from her.

"Probably the same shit he usually puts in them. Joel, why're you doing this?"

"I'm so sick and tired of the goddamn secrets around here!" I shouted, hoping the others would hear me. "Why can't I know about the cigarettes? What's Marty's deal? And Evelyn, too! Why does it feel like she can read my fucking thoughts? It's like she knows exactly what I'm gonna say before I even know what *I'm* gonna say. And Adam? What the *fuck* is his goddamn deal? He hasn't said a coherent thought since I started seeing shit. And don't me started on Asher. That's a whole different can of worms."

I didn't realize it at first, but I was standing. The chair I had sat in before was now toppled over onto the carpet of the living space behind me. I panted like a dog after chasing the local squirrel for an hour or two. Rage filled every nook and cranny of my body, leaving room for nothing expect a strange feeling of confusion. Everything was questions. Questions left unanswered, that terrifying fact of life.

"Joel, I don't know what to tell you. Where would I begin?"

"You better start talking," I demanded, pointing a twisted finger. "Because I will quit if you don't."

"You wouldn't. This is all you ever wanted, right?"

"I used to think that. Now I'm not too sure, Jess."

She slumped further into the chair, looking painfully defeated. Her red hair drooped over her face, sheltering those deep freckles of hers. A surprising feature, for sure, considering freckles usually fade in the winter months. But there they were; out and proud. Peeking through each strand of orange like hundreds of tiny eyes, or the seeds inside a dragonfruit once you cut it open. She didn't speak though. I gave her time, knowing whatever was brewing in her head would take its toll on her. But still, she refused to speak.

The cabin was silent except for the wintery howling wind outside, blowing gusts of dusty snow past the windows like powdered sugar falling onto a funnel cake. *Watch the fireworks. It's the Fourth of July*, my father had said. In a carnival on the brink of doom and despair, only a few hundred bombs away from turning the Chicago suburbs into a crater big enough to rival the moon's. I didn't want to watch the fireworks, or ride the Ferris wheel, or eat some funnel cake. I wanted the truth. Nothing less than the truth, but Jess wouldn't fess up.

I rolled my eyes and stormed off toward my assigned bedroom, the first door on the right as I entered the hallway. Seemingly out of her distraught stupor, Jess shot her head back up with nothing but fear in her eyes. Unblinking, she rose from her chair like a stray pistol bullet with every intention to gun me down. To stop me from… doing what? Going to bed? Packing my things and leaving as early as possible tomorrow morning? Tearing up my Scyphozoa contract and getting the hell outta there?

But she didn't move. She only stared awash with terror. There was a universe's worth of possibilities for what she could've been afraid of, but nothing I imagined could've prepared me for whatever crashed to the floor in the room down the hall.

3

"Everything good?" I shouted from the safety of my doorway.

Everything certainly wasn't good. No one responded. The air was still, only moving with the draft whipping under the cabin's front door. I looked back at Jessica, who hadn't moved from her spot at the end of the kitchen table. "Jess," I said, wanting to say more, but nothing came out. She was stone cold, stiff as a statue, a frightful look frozen on her. Not a sign of movement to her except her trembling fingers.

I set my focus back toward the source of the clatter. The door at the end of the hall, rimmed with an ominous glow, beckoned me. That golden rectangle, in all its hazy glory, seemed to reach out to me, pulling me into its embrace, promising good fortune if I followed its commands.

Another crash, this one fainter than the first, piqued my interest.

I inched toward the door, leaving the comfort of my room. I felt Jess pull at me, almost telepathically, telling me to not move any closer. To go back to her, chat for a little while longer, and let whatever was in that room stay a mystery. She pulled that invisible string that bound us together in that vital moment; that moment tinged with fate, destiny, and inevitability.

But the pull wasn't enough. The cord snapped as I took another step, and another, and another. I didn't hear footsteps. Jess never came to my rescue. At least, not until it was too late.

Before I knew it, my hand grasped the doorknob, clasped over the cold metal. My warm skin stuck to it, whether through science or the supernatural, even if there may be no difference between the two.

I heard another thump, like a bowling ball falling a few feet onto an air mattress. A singular heartbeat emanated from the room, its origin only one push of the door away.

I opened the door and was greeted by candlelight. The rays flickered and dimmed across the painted cabin walls like a movie projector with its film reel inserted all wrong. It shook the surroundings, giving me nausea. Stomach acid bubbled and churned in an internal earthquake.

The room was decorated with the typical Airbnb affairs: framed stock photos of the Denver landscape, a chalkboard hastily erased of the previous tenants' work, and white linen curtains frayed at the edges, as if they were recently bought from a flea market instead of an IKEA. My eyes scanned the ornamentations, as if my mind was avoiding whatever was near the candles' flame. When I looked over at the bed, I knew that to be true.

There was Lenny, sprawled on the bed in a naked heap of flesh. His chest, hairy as I had assumed, didn't rise and fall with breath. His stomach was mangled, carved with a symbol I wasn't familiar with. It dripped with blood, pooling onto the sheets, staining the white with dark red splotches.

Laid at the foot of the bed with eyes as dead as the leaves outside the cabin was Asher, a needle jutting from his inner elbow joint. He was completely naked, his penis limp with death. Evelyn, Adam, and Marty sat kneeled at the sides of the bed. They hadn't noticed me. I held my breath, unable to discern whether any of this was real.

The Great King Rat wasn't there.

Only, something far worse.

I could move; I had free will to do whatever I pleased. And what did I do with that free will? I decided to breathe sharply, the air sucking through my teeth in a gasp.

Every alive person in that room immediately spun their heads toward me as if I were watching that same movie with a few frames cut from the incorrectly placed reel. Their movements were so sudden I jumped back. I yelped in terror. They smiled with teeth coated in pink, caked with coagulated blood.

I couldn't count Asher as the second corpse I'd ever seen. I saw him in Charlotte, just as Lenny had.

I saw my second dead body in Denver, and it was Leonard Vuala.

INTERMISSION

So it is written... So it shall remain...

Kyrie entered the bedroom, a chill seeping down his spine like ice cold water. On the bed sat Marty, slouched over with his greasy head in his stumpy hands, eyes covered. "Hey, Marty," Kyrie said. "Did you happen to see Asher come by?"

Marty lifted his head, letting his arms rest on his thighs. He wiped them on his pants as if he had stuck those grubby, little extremities into a mud pit. "No, Kyrie," he said, his voice cracking with sorrow. "He must've left."

"No, I saw him come up here. Where is he, Marty?"

Marty's back was turned toward Kyrie, and he maintained a strict lack of eye contact as he spoke. "Not here," Marty said plainly, struggling to purge the sadness from his tone.

There was a single candle in the bedroom; the only thing illuminating the surroundings despite a perfectly functional lamp sitting on the nightstand. No signs of distress hung in the air for Kyrie to grasp at. The only glimmer of uneasiness emitted from Marty's insistence that Asher wasn't in the room. From Kyrie's line of sight, Marty was correct in that sentiment. Absolutely nothing in that room hinted at Asher's presence.

Everything except the shoe neatly hidden—but not well enough—behind the bed, on the side Marty dangled his short legs from. Nothing peculiar in the slightest at first. It was just a stray shoe; forgotten and left to sit on the floor without being packed into a suitcase.

But a sense of clarity overcame Kyrie like someone had adjusted the frequency of the radio antenna in his mind. Not only was it a shoe on the floor, but there was a sock protruding from it, attached to a leg. Its ankle-bone jutted above the divide between the shoe and the white sock, forming a subtle bump beneath the cloth. Object permanence be damned, Kyrie knew there had to be a person attached to that shoe.

He walked forward, prompting Marty to spring from his position on the bed and scamper over to him like a rabid dog. "Stop!" Marty barked in the same essence of that rabid dog, spitting the word with enough energy to halt Kyrie in his tracks.

"Why?" Kyrie asked. "Who is that down there?"

"He doesn't want you to see him like this."

"Who? *Asher?*"

This sent Kyrie past the brink of curiosity, plunging him straight into the depths of overwhelming worry and rapturous concern. His distress flooded from his pores as he shoved Marty out of the way, an easy feat. The tiny man child flew to the floor with the flaccidity of a rag doll despite the lack of effort Kyrie put into the initial push. "Asher, are you alri—"

Asher wasn't alright. His limbs were bent in strange ways, his arms twisting across his torso like tree branches with nowhere left to grow. The first leg Kyrie had seen was completely straight as if someone had stuck a split in his pants. The other leg, however, was warped beyond belief. His shin was under his thigh at an alarming angle. His chest was motionless, even as his pectorals and ribs bent up to the ceiling in a grotesque arch. His eyes; oh God, his eyes. Blank as freshly fallen snow, dead as a cemetery.

Kyrie yelped and kneeled over the body, telling himself over and over that this wasn't a corpse laid before him. This was the man he made love to just an hour before, naked under the lake water, skin against skin. This was the man he fawned over for years, falling in love with him when he first lay his eyes upon him. This was the man who showed him what living meant.

And there he was, lifeless on the floor, his mouth agape with the stench of death.

Kyrie couldn't believe it.

He refused to believe it.

Believing it would make it real, and this wasn't real.

None of it was real.

Kyrie must've slipped on the stairs and hit his head on the corner of one of the steps. He must've knocked himself out, launching him into a nightmarish coma in which he would occupy for years while on life support. He must've dreamt this, because *this* wasn't bearable enough to be real.

But the air was the same inside the bedroom as it was on the first floor, on the cabin porch, in the surrounding forest. The candle burned on the nightstand next to the unused lamp. Wax dripped from the wick, disappearing or reappearing in that mysterious way only candle wax can. Marty groaned in pain from his fallen position at the doorway, sounding like a castrated coyote.

With tears swimming in his eyes, Kyrie whimpered. He didn't know whether this was the result of natural causes, suicide, or something else. Could Evelyn had said something so cruel it forced Asher, that strong and proud man, to march into the cabin and down a full bottle of pills? Did Marty slip him something suspicious at the bedside? Something a bit too strong to be ingested by one person alone?

Kyrie's stomach dropped into a pit of nausea. He slapped Asher's face, and his head fell to the side. He slapped again, gave up after that second impact, and decided to check his pulse. The usual *thump thump* in Asher's neck was gone, abandoned by any blood flow. Abandoned by the land of the living.

Kyrie's own heart began to race, beating at the bars of its rib cage prison. His eyes went glassy, a thin film of tears wiping across his irises. He breathed, no, gasped short inhales and sharp exhales. Kyrie wiped a lock of hair from his eyes, still slightly damp from their escapade in the lake. He heard footsteps as his ears began to ring.

"Get away from him!" Marty shouted.

"No! We need to help—"

His words were cut off mid-sentence, bludgeoned with something hard that hit the back of his head with a loud crack. Kyrie's world went dark.

And seemingly in the same instant he went unconscious, Kyrie woke up, unable to move his arms and legs.

He opened his eyes to the harsh glow of fluorescent lights. His ears continued to ring from the stress of... the stress of something? What was it? *Had* he been dreaming? Where was he? Where was Asher?

Questions packed his brain to its ultimate limit like the Black Friday shoppers of years gone by. They clamored at the inside of his skull, thumping and begging to leave. Kyrie attempted to lift his head but couldn't. As he clenched his neck muscles, he felt something tugging back at him; something was tied around his neck. If he had lifted his head any further, the tight restraints would have choked him. Something tight hugged his cheeks. One of those burning questions managed to escape his mind and find its exodus through his vocal cords and mouth. Nothing resembling words came out, only muffled gibberish.

With a new feeling in his jaw, he clenched, but to no avail. He felt a rubbery object with his tongue; an object smooth and hard in the cavern of his mouth fought back against it. Kyrie could still breathe through his nose in shallow breaths, but whatever was in his mouth, secured in there with straps around his cheeks, blocked both air and words from entering or exiting.

While he couldn't lift his head, he could certainly turn it, and that is what he did. He turned to the right and saw the shadows of gardening tools adorning the wooden walls. *I'm in the cabin's shed*, he thought. *I'm in the fucking garden shed?*

There were hoes, trowels, shovels, and rakes. Over in the far corner, closest to what looked like the only way in or out of the shed, was a snow blower. A large machete hung above it, swaying in the wind seeping through the wall's cracks. Its metallic blade gleamed as it swiveled on the single string it dangled from.

Kyrie thought of his mother, his father. It was that primal urge to scream for your parents when you're in a dire situation. Like a criminal on death row crying for his momma mere seconds before the floor swings out from under him and his neck snaps. But Kyrie was no criminal. He was sure of it.

He pushed the thoughts of grisly death from his mind, but they came back to him like a car crashing into a highway divider at top speed, sending shards of glass and human bone everywhere like meteors in the night sky. He couldn't stop thinking of death, the finality of it. He wondered why. He examined the thoughts under a mental microscope, checking for the intricacies in why he couldn't stop thinking about it. He looked under the bed, checked the piles of clothes in the closet, and did a clean sweep of his dresser drawers. Under a pair of denim pants marred with holes, he found the answer.

ASHER IS DEAD, it shouted.

It pounded against his psyche, making him relive the shock and terror all over again. When had it happened? Five minutes ago? An hour? Yesterday? Last year? Kyrie couldn't remember, but he surmised it to be true. Asher Gaumont, lead singer of the indie rock band Scyphozoa, was dead. He stormed off into a secluded cabin in the woods after not appreciating something Evelyn Stone had said, went up the stairs, went to his assigned bedroom, and died; collapsed because of... *something*.

The wind howled outside, whistling a foreboding tune. It knocked the hanging machete against the wall a consistent tempo. *Clack... clack... clack...* like a snare drum playing a simple fill under the whistled melody. Kyrie's skin flared up in goosebumps. The fluorescent bar above, a long strip of light swaying in the draft, buzzed with electricity; a diminished hum that grated his ears.

He was cold all over, even in places that shouldn't have been cold. Kyrie attempted to lift his head up from the restraints. He strained his eyes as far down as they would go, the intricate wiring connecting them to his brain on the verge of snapping. He caught a glimpse of his naked body, hairs standing on end, scratch marks adorning his light brown skin. One scratch was so deep it dripped blood: red hot liquid slowly spewing from an inflamed, fleshy mountain range. As if the scratches weren't there until he noticed they were, pain shot through his nerves, pins and needles stabbing at him in an agonizing fury.

Kyrie tried to scream. Those screams built up in his throat and remained there, blocked by the gag strapped across his mouth. He wriggled on the cold, flat surface of the metal table he laid upon. It reminded him of the tables they used to cut veggies on during his meaningless restaurant job back in college. God, how he wished he could go back to that place now; what, with the smells of fruits and vegetables and cooked meat and...

Meat?

Thoughts—those dangerous little rats that burrow deep in your mind when you least expect it—swarmed every fiber of his awareness. Gruesome, terrible thoughts from the deepest, darkest abyss of his mind. Was he being treated for slaughter? Had a group of traveling cannibals stumbled upon their cabin, seeing nothing but a fresh meal roaming the halls inside? Was Kyrie next on their menu? A living entrée of raw meat and flesh ripe for slaughter? Like a pig being fattened up before becoming a Christmas ham?

He looked to his right, pivoting his neck, skin against rough leather. Kyrie blinked, unsure of what he was seeing. He blinked again, smudging hot tears from his eyes, exposing them to the frigidity inside the garden shed. As his vision cleared, he saw a brutal sight. One he couldn't and wouldn't believe.

There, on a metal table similar to his own, laid Asher. He was dead, maybe comically so. Pale skin, gaunt eye sockets, hollow cheeks, mouth wide open as if muttering a soundless moan. He was stripped of all his clothing, his abdominals protruding from his stomach like a platter of stale Hawaiian rolls. Kyrie was too cold to get anxious. All he could think of was sleep, its warm embrace beckoning him into unconsciousness. He studied the body with fluttering eyelids. It was essentially the same as the naked figure in the lake, chiseled and rough with thin layers of hair. The skin, though. Pale as teeth, with the yellowish tinge of years of drinking sweet tea.

As Kyrie lowered his gaze to Asher's hauntingly limp penis, the sound of jangling keys sliced through the fluorescent light's painful ambience. He stiffened, jolting back into the position he woke up in. He closed his eyes, letting the tiniest bit of light climb through.

A lock clicked, chains slid from the handles, and the door slammed open. The machete clanked against the shed wall with enough force to em-bed itself half an inch into the wood. Footsteps, heels against concrete, echoed through the shed. They approached louder and louder, stepping to the tempo of Kyrie's increasing heartbeat. Despite the cold, sweat pooled on his skin. He felt colder than before, as if death incarnate had entered the room and eradicated all heat from the shed.

"You have everything prepped?"

Adam? Kyrie thought.

"Well, obviously not. Look, we haven't stitched the connection, yet."

That was the condescending tone Kyrie only associated with Evelyn Stone. *What the hell is going on?*

The sound of a zipper rang through the air. A backpack thudded to the floor, its contents crashing and clamoring together in a jumbled hodgepodge. Kyrie opened his eyes a little further, making sure to not let the assailants see his pupils. He was sleeping, because that was what they obviously wanted: For him to be knocked out for whatever was in store. In that moment—where he saw the glint of light reflecting off a pocketknife retrieved from a backpack on the floor—he wished he was really asleep. But fear works in morbidly mysterious ways, and Kyrie couldn't shut off his brain. The amygdala worked overtime, keeping him aware.

"Found the knife," Adam said.

"Worried you wouldn't find it?" Evelyn asked.

"You already knew the answer to that."

"What about the candles?"

"They're…" He rummaged through the bag. "…right here," Adam said, holding multiple sticks of wax.

"And the texts?" Evelyn asked with crossed arms and a perched eyebrow.

"Right here, fucker," Adam responded, throwing a maroon leather-bound book straight at Evelyn's chest. It knocked the wind out of her. She let out a pained wheeze as the book fell. Its pages flipped open, but Kyrie couldn't see what was written on them.

"Shut the hell up!" Evelyn huffed in a loud whisper. "You might wake him up. He can already hear us as is!"

"Marty sedated him, and you know how strong that shit is."

"I'm aware," she said, a staccato cough punctuating her response.

"Have you two prepared for the delivery?" a shrill voice asked from far off.

"No, Marty. Does it look like we have? You and Adam are two peas in a goddamn pod with how blind you are."

Marty? Kyrie thought at first, then backtracked with, *I'm actually not that surprised he's got something to do with this, now that I think about it. Slimy fuck.*

Evelyn turned to him. He made sure to not tighten his eyes. Any wrinkles on his face would give him away. The jig would be up. The whole shebang would dissolve like sand through open fingers. He kept the illusion of sleep; Evelyn turned away.

"What's up?" Adam asked.

"Nothing," she said, waving an open hand.

"Get those candles lit," Marty said. "Overhead lights off. You two know the drill."

"No Jessica?" Adam asked.

"She refuses to leave her bedroom. Jessica ran up the stairs and locked her door right after I bashed this kid's skull in."

"Wait," Evelyn stopped Marty's villainous tirade. "You sedated him, correct?"

"Of course! He's fast asleep, right? He won't feel anything; he couldn't even feel a sewing needle poking at his foot. He's out cold."

"Alright, we get it," the twins said in unison.

Marty huffed, squeaking like a kazoo.

On Kyrie's right, Adam placed three candles, lighting each as he went. Evelyn did the same to the corpse's left: Three candles, all alight with yellow flame. The fire danced a cruel tango, tickling the atmosphere with ominous pirouettes and pliés.

Evelyn walked between the two tables, reaching up to click the fluorescent light off. As the light died, so did the electric buzz. All that remained was the faint flicker of candlelight and the moonlight sneaking in from the open shed door. Marty noticed this and proceeded to close it, snuffing the night breeze. The air went dead, as dead as Asher on the table next to Kyrie. Motionless, lifeless, without drive or purpose. An empty husk, once full of energy, mitigated to simply wasting space on an overpopulated planet.

It was growing more difficult for Kyrie to make out anything in the dim glow of the room. He released his squint slightly, slowly moving his eyelids. He could feel skin against corneas, the juicy underside of his lids sliding against those liquid sacs that grant us vision. Kyrie spotted the pocketknife's glint, its blade clean and spotless as a hospital room. Adam lifted Asher's cold, dead right hand. The blade punctured the pad of his ring finger. No blood was drawn, only creating a deep hole that split his fingerprints with suspect elegance.

Satisfied, Adam grabbed Kyrie's wrist and prepared to do the same to his ring finger. Kyrie wanted to pull away, to give up the act, but his thoughts bore no fruit. He simply allowed Adam to sink the knife's tip into his finger. The metal slid effortlessly into his skin, sifting past the epidermis and into the meat before scraping against the bone beneath. The pain was searing. Vibrations of metal against bone scratched his nerves, sending shockwaves of pain to his temples. Adam twisted the blade, widening the hole. He slipped the knife out, it dripped with blood. Kyrie felt the pulsing ache throbbing at his finger. It burned, stung like a fresh bee sting. He gnawed on the gag in his mouth, his jaw clenched. Teeth against rubber, squishing like a macabre stress ball. The chewing wasn't enough, as Kyrie couldn't help but groan at the small punctures that followed. A needle slipped through his skin, stitching his finger to that of Asher's. He tried. Oh, he tried to hide the fact he was awake. They needed him asleep for whatever was about to happen. But there was no use. Once the stitching was done, Kyrie's finger attached to Asher's at the pads in the hollow between both tables, Evelyn grabbed the knife from Adam's pocket, its tip still soaked in blood, and began carving into Kyrie's stomach.

That was the breaking point. As the knife split his skin, turning the wound white, then pink, then oozing red with blood, Kyrie screamed at the top of his lungs. The air he had held for so long bounded from his core, wafting in gusts of agony.

Evelyn stopped the incisions, jumped back, and immediately started throwing blame onto someone, as she always managed to do. She shouted, "What the fuck, Marty? I thought you sedated him!"

"He was sedated with something less medical, but sedated nonetheless," he responded.

"*Less medical?!* What did you do to him instead?"

"Knocked him out with a brick."

"You lazy fuck!" Adam chimed in. "Where was the chloroform?"

"We used the last of it on that harlot from Charleston."

"And you didn't *tell* us?" Evelyn bellowed.

"I didn't think we would need to do this so soon, not after the last one," Marty implored. "But what Asher does is sacred, and we need to do what is necessary. You both know the Laws of Scyph. Besides, I put the restraints on him for this very reason. He was bound to wake up. And it seems he has."

Kyrie couldn't comprehend any of the nonsense spewing from the three of them. All his focus was on the gaping wound in his stomach. His eyes were wide open now, frantically searching the room for ways to escape. He pulls at the restraints on his arms and legs. They wouldn't budge. *P-eas*, he begged through the ball gag. *P-eas weh ee go!*

"We gotta make this quick, then," Evelyn said.

She jammed the blade back to where she had stopped, continuing to carve an archaic rune of sorts up and around Kyrie's abdomen. "We didn't wanna do this so soon, Kyrie," she lied as the knife cut a line straight through his naval. "I hope you understand. It's for the greater good."

Kyrie screamed louder than before. Enough force pushed against the ball gag to dislodge it from his jaw. He shouted, "Fuck you!" before the gag placed itself back into its original position with a squeak.

"I wish you would've, pretty boy," she responded with a grin and a turn of the blade. It twisted nerves in its catch like a fork winding up spaghetti noodles.

She raised the knife and planted it again in a different spot, turning it once more. Then again…

and again…

again…

and one final time. The last time, against Kyrie's better wishes, was the most painful. White-hot agony bled from the final twisting point, as if Evelyn decided to lodge it deeper than the five stabs before. He felt the blade's tip apply an unbearable amount of pressure on his hip bone. He writhed and seethed in this torment, wading in every pang and spasm that beat him like a sledgehammer to his skull.

Kyrie begged again for her to stop, or as best he could with the gag still lodged in his mouth. The pleading fell on deaf ears, as she finished the gruesome design on his chest and stepped away as he began to scream for help.

"Will you do the honors?" Adam asked Marty, nodding toward the book on the ground.

"Of course," he said.

With a grin so inhuman and ghastly, Marty fetched the book and flipped to the dog-eared page. After scanning the room to be sure everything was to his liking, he began to recite a passage.

Each passing word brought its own set of horrors. The first line ended with the flickering of candle flames, with one dying out in the process.

The second line sent a shock through Kyrie's stitched finger. A second candle burned out.

The third line shot blood from Asher's finger through the hole of Kyrie's. The stitches dripped red as Kyrie felt Asher's essence race into his body. One vein at a time. Another candle dimmed.

The fourth line produced an aching feeling in Kyrie's stomach. Not the pain wrought by Evelyn's brutal slices and stabs. Something more subtle. Something brewing from within. A hunger spawned there, one that Kyrie couldn't explain. The fourth candle died.

The fifth line brought pain like hellfire. Kyrie, bathed in pools of sweat, leaned his head as far forward as the restraints allowed. His stomach, a garbled mess of blood and torn flaps of skin, began to bubble like water in a pot over a hot stove. The fifth candle ceased its light.

The sixth line—that single word, *Devinco*—sealed Kyrie's fate. There was no turning back, no getting out of this. What was done was done. All he had to do was suffer the consequences. And he did. Oh, how he suffered. The last candle burned out, leaving him one last glimpse of his gurgling abdomen before the inevitable.

It was pitch black. The air was sucked from the room in a vacuum. Kyrie could barely see anymore; tears muddled his sight. He wanted nothing more than to turned back the clock, to forget everything about Scyphozoa, about Asher Gaumont, about the college he attended and subsequently left. If he could've gone back, he'd apply to higher tier schools.

Maybe he would've gotten into one. A place where indie rock was disgraced in favor of the older music every rich donor liked, and in turn, what their bratty student children liked. He regretted falling so madly in love with Asher. He regretted being so head over heels for someone he barely knew, even after traveling and recording with him for so long. Asher was an impenetrable brick wall, and Kyrie a plastic spork instead of the jackhammer required to tear him down. Kyrie wanted to hug his parents, pet his dog, talk to friends of years passed. He wanted to go out on the town, to drive into the countryside with a boy who was honest with him. Who was emotional in all the best ways. Who would care for him as deeply as he would care for him in return. He wanted everything and everyone to not be so one-sided. He didn't want to be a ray of sunshine reflecting and bouncing off every mirror-person in the world. He wanted love, to be loved, to be held.

He would never be afforded such luxuries again.

In the darkness, he spotted two dim dots of light. They looked like distant stars in the night sky; like Orion's Belt if one of the stars decided to have a night off. But these stars were growing into supernovas, and they lit the surroundings in a white burst of searing illuminance. Kyrie squinted as the light consumed him, but when he opened his eyes, the lights were gone.

Then the fluorescents flickered to life, the buzzing returned, and a hand clawed through Kyrie's stomach from the inside. He screamed staring at the bloody appendage jutting from where his bellybutton had been not moments before. It was a brutal, grisly mess. Bits of Kyrie's flesh and bone rose, exploding like an active volcano, spewing gore like clouds of ash blanketing the world in blistering heat.

Another arm like the first crept from the giant wound. Both arms bent at their respective elbows and proceeded to claw their way out of the stomach cavity. The fluorescent beam above flickered, causing a strobe effect in the room. Kyrie only saw glimpses of the horrors exiting his body, like snapshots in an old image carousel. One picture, darkness, the next picture, darkness, and so on.

The arms pushed a torso from the wound, then the lower half of said body. It slithered out of Kyrie, taking bits of muscle and tissue with it. It squelched in its moistness, being born from something dark and horrifically unnatural. Its face was turned away from him, staring out into the open space of the garden shed. Blood painted the walls in a grotesque solid crimson. It dripped from shelves, from garden tools. The machete, still lodged an inch deep into the wall, was splattered with the stuff.

The pain was too much to bear, but Kyrie, in an unfortunate case, insisted on surviving this nightmare. As the creature climbed out of his body and fell out of view onto the floor, Kyrie pulled as hard as he could on his right arm. Freedom was the only thing in his mind, and freedom was what he deserved. His fate wouldn't be sealed in the middle of the woods in some freezing shed surrounded by a bunch of sick cultists he considered his friends. He tugged and pulled. He pulled some more. And more…

There was a tearing sound; a sound so unholy it cut through the congratulatory cheers of the band members at the far side of the shed. The skin connecting Kyrie's hand to his wrist tore like printer paper. Underneath the flesh was bone, then blood. Lots of blood. He pulled harder, exerting the most force he could muster in his state of shock. The skin peeled off like a glove over wet hands and fell with a *plop*.

He was free.

Kyrie ignored the watermelon-sized hole in his abdomen as he lifted his degloved hand and fiddled with the restraints around his neck. He picked at the leather, sifting through the rough surface for anything resembling a latch. Every bit of pressure, no matter how minuscule, felt like hot coals on his exposed nerves and tendons. He persisted because that was all he had left to do.

Marty noticed, raising a finger and shouting, "He's still alive!"

Kyrie quit on the neck restraint and fumbled for the ball gag as Evelyn sat the creature lovingly on a folding chair and reached into the backpack that had contained all the demonic paraphernalia. He managed to pull the gag from his mouth—strap around his neck and all—and said his final words with tear ducts that had emptied long ago:

"Why me?"

Evelyn pulled a pistol from the bag, pointed the barrel at Kyrie, and smiled. "We chose you for a reason," she sneered.

Before a bullet ended the life of Kyrie Castillo, he caught a glimpse of the creature's face. It was Asher, living and breathing on the metal folding chair. Soaked in Kyrie's blood, from head to toe. Completely healthy, otherwise.

Kyrie lifted his bloodied hand to shield himself from the fatal shot. He shouldn't have feared. Really, death was mercy.

MOVEMENT III

THE PROPHET'S SONG

CHAPTER XII

1

I sprinted from the cabin as fast as I could through the damnable cold of Colorado nightfall. Jess trailed behind me. I didn't stop to grab my belongings on the way out. The only things on my person were whatever happened to be jangling around in my pant's pockets: my phone, earbuds, and wallet. My feet slapped against hard earth, the rhythm matching that of my racing heart. Trees zipped by; a loud *whoosh* of air pounded my ears as each one passed.

My mind was mush. Nothing seemed coherent. My worst anxieties had been realized. Lenny hadn't been blowing smoke out his ass about the whole *Asher died in Charlotte* thing. There *was* something suspicious hiding underneath the veil of Scyphozoa, and I had just witnessed it firsthand. Some sort of cultist bullshit involving a ritual that required a sacrifice of sorts. To do what?

To bring someone back from the dead?

A soul for a soul?

Had I been next on the list?

Lenny was dead. His eyes were wide open, frozen in a lifelike picture capturing the final seconds of his life. He had been so jovial; a tough nut to crack. But once I cracked the shell, he was the most lovable teddy bear of a man I had ever met. That warmth he provided, all gone. Dust in the wind.

I didn't have the energy to cry, but the feeling was there all the same. It ate at my insides like a tapeworm sucking the life out of my stomach. It felt cavernous, empty inside. I was as hollow as the Great King Rat, that vicious little shit. Everything had to be that thing's doing, I decreed silently while running faster than Usain Bolt on a good day. No one could be that evil; to take a human life for the benefit of oneself.

I saw Todd's face, all bloodied and broken. The shard of glass tight in my grip, hung over my head with malicious intent. I tripped over a rock and face-planted onto the icy forest floor. My body skidded on the ground like a thin stick of chalk scraping an old chalkboard.

Jess ran up to me, knelt, and grabbed me by the shoulders. *She got me,* I thought. *She captured me and I'm next on death row. She'll just bring me back to the cabin. I won't see a sunrise ever again.*

But to my surprise, she shook me and shouted, "Get up, Joel! We gotta get to the city before they do. Get up!"

"I think I re-broke my nose," I muttered, inhaling the dusty earth.

"Doesn't matter. Would you rather have a broken nose, or have a broken nose and *also* be their next vessel on top of that?"

She brought up a great point, to which I swatted her arms away and insisted I propped myself back up on my own. Snow kissed the blood gushing from my nose. All warmth went to die in the frigidity of Denver; even my blood, the substance providing my body all warmth, seemed to freeze in the dead air.

We continued on.

Blood dripped from my nostrils in small, red puddles with every step I took.

2

I fell onto my ass when I saw two bright lights in the distance, too close to be anything other than that dark void stalking me.

My eyes were frozen over; my vision blurred like someone installed stained glass in front of my pupils. I blinked with the last bit of warmth left in my body. The ice cleared, opaque turned transparent, and I saw a lamppost. A tall, skinny metal pole with two lights at the top situated like drooped bunny ears. I breathed a sigh of relief, articulated with a brief chuckle that materialized into mist from my mouth. It billowed into the night sky, illuminated only by that lamppost.

Jess nudged my shoulder with her knee, begging me to keep going. There was a road in front of us, lit by the two lights up above, which meant there would be cars, but we couldn't stop moving. Jess didn't seem to be in much danger when it came to the other members of Scyphozoa, but I certainly was. I was fresh meat to them, it seemed. Just another pawn in their twisted chess game of life and death.

We walked side by side along the shoulder of the road. I kicked a chunk of loose asphalt into a ditch. It clunked onto a drainpipe's gaping entrance like a church bell on Sunday morning. It was eerily quiet outside; much more silent than it had seemed in the minutes before. When running, nothing is quiet. There's the thumping of feet against ground, the driving heave of sharp breaths, the rattling in your ears with every leap and bound you take, the wind rushing through your hair. But in that moment, with the looming presence of doom hanging over my head, I heard nothing. A void of silence so inescapable, so dreary.

A car finally rolled by, slowly coming to a halt as the driver saw my thumb jutting toward the sky. As the passenger-side window slid down, the woman behind that wheel asked, "Are you two alright?"

I didn't feel the need to answer. The blood enveloping the top of my lip seemed to answer enough of her question. The woman couldn't possibly know the fine details that led me and Jess to the side of this deserted Rocky Mountain path, but she saw there was trouble, and that seemed to be enough. She unlocked the doors, the locks bolted up with a loud crunch, and we let ourselves into the backseat.

"Close the door, it's absolutely freezing out," the driver said. "I can't believe you aren't wearing a coat, young man. You from out of town?"

"Yep," I said, noticing the dried blood covering my lips like lipstick. It tasted metallic, like licking a penny. "Just visiting from Massachusetts."

"And what about you, young lady?" she immediately asked, sounding more interested in whatever Jess was about to say than I had already answered.

"Visiting," Jess lied. "Same as him."

The driver scowled. The strong smell of perfume stung my tender nostrils. They burned with the scent of lavender. "Tough crowd, huh?" she jived. "Where are you two heading, then?"

"Downtown," I said. "Our car skidded on the ice a ways back, flew off the road, and crashed into a tree. We just need to get back to our hotel."

"Oh! You poor things!" she said with a dramatic gasp. "That certainly explains that bloody nose."

I hadn't even thought about my broken nose when the lies poured out of me. I had been surrounded by so many untruths in the past weeks that it felt natural for me to lie so effortlessly. I was a baby picking up traits from my parents during my developmental stages; some good, most terrible.

"Yeah," I said, "but I'm glad we found someone as kind as you to help us back to Denver." I resisted the urge to lovingly flutter my eyes like an aroused cartoon character. That definitely would've been too much. Best to keep it lowkey and blatantly simple when garnering the goodwill of the local cat lady you desperately need a ride from. Jess stared at me while I plotted my next move, gazing longingly into my eyes like there was something beyond me that I couldn't sense. Despite the dim glow of the lamplight through the car window, her hair still glowed ablaze like orange fire. How I wanted to run my fingers through that hair, to feel the smooth scalp under it all. I could have kissed her right then and there, but there was that nagging feeling scraping the back of my mind. The sensible thought that she was a boiling sea of betrayal. Maybe they had sent her with me as a backup in case I strayed too far from the cabin. A last resort in the event that I soiled their deranged plans by going public with everything. But who would have believed me? "A crazed lead singer and his goons killed my bus driver! I may be next! Please, for the love of Bernstein, help me!" That would raise more than one eyebrow for sure, but not enough to warrant any real concern. Just another outrageous story in the cesspool of the modern zeitgeist where anything from a streaker stabbing Barack Obama on the streets to another mass shooting is just any other Tuesday.

But Jessica Fitzgerald was so beautiful. The freckles that refused to grow faint, the button nose that scrunched at every other syllable, the eyes that burned deep into your soul like the living fire adorning her head.

You need to let me go.

A flare of Roselle's memory attacked me like a sudden camera flash in a dark room. I winced, an abrupt pang of downhearted sorrow washing over me. The twists of wrinkles on my face became apparent to Jess, who shared a sympathetic glance.

"Well," the driver said, applying a glossy coat of lipgloss, "luckily for you, I'm heading down that way, as well. Which hotel were you staying at?"

"Comfort Suites," I said, my face buried in my phone as I searched local Denver hotels, saying the first name that popped up. I scrolled through the surrounding area on the digital map and continued. "The one a few blocks south of the Broncos' stadium. On Federal Boulevard, I think." I didn't think; I fully knew, since the answers to my lies presented themselves before me. The driver, deep into a severe case of mid-life crisis, ate the falsehoods up like leftover book club casserole. "Oh! Perfect," she said, her hands shooting up and hitting the cat-shaped air freshener hanging from the rearview mirror. "Let's get moving, then. I have a midnight book club to get to. I was already going to be late as is."

Figures, I thought.

3

She dropped us off at the Comfort Suites in a breezy twenty minutes. The only part of the ride that was relatively smooth was the time of arrival itself. Everything else was torturous. What, from the incessant small talk, to the reapplications of lipgloss on already heavily coated lips, the swerving, the phone calls. If I hadn't been traumatized by the cultish activity back in that remote cabin, I would've feared for my life in the hands of that crazy lady behind the wheel.

The lady opened her glovebox, retrieved a loose tissue, and scribbled something on it with a red ballpoint pen. As I left the backseat, my legs shaking and aching from excessive sprinting in the woods, she rolled down the passenger-side window and flicked the tissue toward me. It billowed in the cool air with the grace of a ballerina during the Swan Lake finale. I caught it before a gust could blow it away, unfolded it, and read the note. It was her phone number, and under it was a note, reading: *I would've seen your car if you really crashed up in those mountains. Take care, and take better care of the girl. She needs it. Tell her to call if you aren't enough.*

She waved, her once genuine smile feeling a bit more sinister, rolled up the window, and sped off, screeching through a red light as she went.

4

Since we naturally weren't guests at Comfort Suite in downtown Denver, Jess and I trekked through the biting cold to a Denny's a block or so away. It was no Waffle House, but it would have to do.

I sifted through my wallet to make sure everything was accounted for. Some twenties and fives and ones sifted past my fingers, flapping like music cassettes in an old jukebox. My debit card and an ancient Subway gift card (one advertising five-dollar footlongs if you could believe it) aligned the leathery pockets inside. I felt safety knowing everything was there, but something clawed at the back of my mind imploring me to check... just check.

Check for what?

Sitting in the booth with Jess across the table, I fiddled with my wallet, poking at the flap under my license holder. When that wasn't enough, I resorted to flipping it upside down and shaking it over the table. After a few disgruntled jerks jangled some loose coins inside the wallet, something fell out of the hidden flap: a key.

Silver, pristine as the day my mother handed it to me.

"What is that for?" Jess asked.

"Apartment key," I answered. I placed the key back in its place and shook the wallet a bit to slip it back into the leather crease.

"Chicago, right?"

"Yeah," I said, sliding the wallet back into my pocket. "Chicago."

"That's where you lived before college, right?"

"Yep."

"I've always wanted to go to Chicago." She took a sip of water from a cup that looked like it hadn't been cleaned in centuries. "For some reason we never managed to tour up there. I always found that weird."

Jess stirred the ice cubes with a plastic straw. They clinked against the glass with the sound of someone whacking the highest notes on a glockenspiel. "I heard winters are beautiful up there," she said.

I didn't have much to say about the apparent beauty of Chicago. I had lived there for so long that anything someone would consider "beautiful" seemed utterly mundane to me. Jess could have told me the green toxins they poured in the river every Saint Patrick's Day were a sight to behold, but I would ignore it entirely. Once you live in a place for long enough, you become complacent to the oddities outsiders see. Pigeons are completely normal to a Manhattanite, a minor nuisance in the hustle and bustle of city life. But place a rural tomboy in Times Square and they'll regard pigeons as the greatest zoological feat since the dodos' extinction.

I decided to play into her childlike wonder, even if only for a brief second. "They can be… sometimes."

"Why 'sometimes?'" asked Jess.

"The Christmas decorations can be pretty, sure. But once December ends, the lights come down and all you have left are busy streets, crackheads asking for cash, and piles of snow sludge on every curb."

"But isn't that the same in every big city that gets snow?"

"I guess so, but every other big city is better than Chicago."

"Really?"

"I don't know. I guess you'd have to see for yourself."

Despite all the trauma her and I endured—her more so than me—Jess managed to crack a smile as she sipped from her water again. "Maybe I might," she said.

Her smile reminded me of someone; someone who was like a ghost haunting my mind. I saw a round face, featureless, but a silhouette I could faintly recognize. There was sadness in her cheer, and the same oxymoronic look adorned this mystery of a person floating in the recesses of my memory. I zoned out; my eyes shifted out of focus. Everything became a blur as I put every fiber of myself into figuring out who I was thinking of. It hadn't been *that* long since I'd seen this person, right?

"What're you thinking about?" Jess asked, visibly perplexed.

If I manage to join this band, and have to drop out, promise me you *will be okay.*

I had said that, I was sure of it. But who had I said it to? Their image flickered and dimmed like candlelight.

Yeah. I'll be okay. For you.

Cameron Wright.

That shy fine arts student. One of the only people left at Sanduhr that I would consider an acquaintance, especially after Jasmine had shown her fangs. He lived in Aurora. It was winter break still if I had my days right. He would be back home for at least a few more days before the spring semester reared its ugly head. Aurora was west of downtown Denver, a far enough drive that it would be inconvenient, but not inconvenient enough for a certain someone.

"I have a plan. Temporary, but a plan nonetheless," I said.

I pulled out my phone and dialed Cameron's number.

Jessica remained silent as I waited with bated breath as the first dial tone rang in my ear. Then the second *boooooop*. A third one. By the time the fourth one began to chime, I was beginning to lose hope, already formulating new survival plans in my head. But fourth time seemed to be the charm when it came to Cameron, because the tone ended abruptly and I heard him tiredly moan, "Joel?"

"Cameron?" I couldn't contain my excitement. I was like a caveman discovering how to use a bone as a weapon. "Cam! It's so good to hear you. How're you?"

"How am I?" he asked sarcastically, that sleepiness slowly dying from his voice. "How are *you*, man? You're in a freaking band! It's been ages since you left. How have things been?"

He seemed to have a lot more words to say when the barrier of in-person contact was lifted, even with words that stung like a thousand hornets in a sandpit. I had forgotten how exciting it should have been that I was in a touring rock band; especially one I hadn't auditioned for. A wondering of how everyone back at Sanduhr perceived me after the whole debacle tickled my mind. Sure, some people would be impressed, but most others would view it through a more cynical lens. Local nobody becomes a college dropout on a whim, go figure.

It shocked me in an unsurprising way whenever someone mentioned my being in a band. I felt appalled at the thought considering the horrors I'd witnessed, but then I remembered how big of a deal it was on the surface. I couldn't fault Cameron for being excited about something like that.

"I'll be honest with you, Cam," I said. "Things haven't been great. Or, I guess, not as great as I hoped."

Jess silently glared at me, raising an eyebrow. *Not as great as I hoped* was certainly the understatement of the century.

"Oh, I'm sorry to hear that, man," Cameron said. "What's up, though? It's out of character for you to call, like, ever. Is something up?"

"Yeah, actually. I'm in downtown Denver right now, and the hotel we were staying at kicked us out. Are you still on winter break?"

"I'm still here for a few days, yeah. I think I know what you're implying, but—"

"We need a place to stay, and all the Airbnbs and other hotels in the area are booked out the ass. If you wouldn't mind, could we stay at your house for just a little while?" I needed to ham it up a little further. "If that's too much to ask, I understand. I'm just super desperate right now."

Cameron went silent on the other end, the warbled static of dead-end conversation whispering in his place. This lasted so long I lifted the phone from my ear and checked to see if he was still there. The screen said he was, what with his name plastered at the top and a timer progressing forward in time right under it. I squished the phone back onto my cheek, its glass eerily warm to the touch.

"You still there?" Cameron asked after a click and a scuffle over the line.

"Yep."

"I just had to ask my mom, but she said it was okay. Just as long as there's no drugs and it isn't *all* of you. She doesn't like that Evelyn girl very much."

"Perfect."

"Do you need a ride, too?"

"No, I think I have that covered. I'll be over there as soon as I can."

"Can't wait. We need to catch up."

"For sure. See ya, man."

"See ya."

I hung up and set the phone down on the table.

"'As soon as I can?'" Jess repeated.

"Well, yeah," I reasoned. "We gotta get out of the downtown area, at least. Like, as soon as possible."

"You know that old saying about Chinese food? About how the more you eat the hungrier you get?"

I nodded.

"Can we at least order some pancakes before we head out?" Jess asked, begging like poor little Oliver Twist requesting the tiniest morsel of stale bread. "I'm starving, and I left my cigarettes at the cabin. Please."

5

I was worried Jorge would deny my late-night request for a ride. He was a family man, after all. His son, Silvestre, was home for the holidays, getting one last break before his final semester of high school. I assumed Jorge had a wife or husband to crawl into bed with every night, one who shielded him from the Denver cold under the warmth of love and duvet coverings.

Jorge was a saint, and I shouldn't have doubted him for a second. Undeterred by the fact it was almost midnight, Jorge picked up on the second ring. "Joel!" he shouted, his voice digitally crackling.

I imagined his partner telling him to shut the hell up and go back to bed. I imagined Jorge sitting in his underwear on the edge of the bed, his phone nestled in his marvelous beard like baby birds waiting for a supper of worms.

"If it's about a ride, I'd be more than happy to," he continued.

"It was a long shot calling you, anyway," I said. "You sound like you were asleep. I can just call an Uber if it's too much trouble."

"Too much trouble? I haven't been this popular with my son since I took him to Chuck E. Cheese when he was six. I *know* people in his favorite band, which means he basically knows you, too."

"You don't need to chauffeur me around just to keep goodwill with me," I implored. "You're a good enough guy that that isn't necessary."

"But…" I heard his phone slip and fall to the floor. The rustling of clothes being put on danced in my ears. I had been right on one count, at least. He picked his phone up and said, "But I insist. Besides, I couldn't sleep anyway."

"We're at the Denny's near the Comfort Suites downtown. I need to get to Aurora. Would that be too much trouble?"

"Of course not. And 'we?' Is Leonard tagging along again?"

"No," I muttered with unbridled sadness.

"Alright. I'll be there as soon as traffic allows me. You remember the car?"

"Yep. I'll see you then."

Jorge hung up; I slipped the phone into my pocket and held my head in my hands.

"I miss Lenny, too. Don't get it twisted, Joel," Jess said.

"Get what twisted?"

"I'm not a monster like the rest of them."

"I want to believe that."

"Please do," she said, reaching across the table and holding my forearms in each hand. Jess tugged them, to which I placed them longways on the table, one on top of the other. She moved her hands over my arms, and rubbed them with her thumb, slow and calm. The calmest I'd ever seen her. "There's so much you don't know. But when we get far away from them, I can tell you."

"Why can't you tell me now?"

"Evelyn will hear me."

6

Jorge pulled into the Denny's parking lot smoothly as the hot butter sliding atop the steamy buttermilk pancakes Jess carried from the restaurant in a to-go box. I had gone into the restroom to take a few drags off my vape so as to not make her ravenous for the cigarettes she left in a secluded cabin miles away. It was just as grimy and horrifying as you'd expect from a downtown Denny's restroom. Dirt clogged in the floor tile lining, specks of dried piss dotting the toilet bowl, paper towel dispensers as barren as the aftermath of an atomic blast; no discernible way to dry my hands in sight, save for my seductively dry pants legs.

I wiped my hands as if to scrub crumbs from my thighs as I spotted Jorge parking in the lot outside the window. I sauntered by our table and signaled Jess to get up. The waiter must have come by with the food while I was doing my business. She snatched the box with firm hands and slid from the booth's bench seat. "Everything to your liking?" I mocked, referring to the pancakes, whose smell wafted through the thin cardboard box. The aroma was sweet, salty, and pungent. That combination of maple and buttermilk bombarded my nose and made my mouth water.

"Oh, of course," she said as we walked out the door. "But don't even think about eating them. I don't remember you pitching in."

"Wouldn't dream of it."

I was dreaming of it. My stomach felt like a hollow pit with how hungry I was. Thankfully, the interior of Jorge's car masked the pancake smell immediately. The air freshener, blessedly fragrant of sandalwood as opposed to the cat lady's tyrannical lavender odor, merely complimented the maple syrup smell, distracting me from wanting to stick my face into Jess's to-go box and absolutely devour her flapjacks.

I sat in the passenger seat; Jess sat in the back. I gave Jorge the exact address of Cameron's home, reading it succinctly from the hasty text message I received after Cam and I's phone call ended. Jorge bellowed, "Oh! I've been around those parts before. I was worried you two were wanting to go to… the worse part of Aurora."

"Good neighborhood, then?" Jess asked, eyeing her food.

"By Aurora standards, the best."

"That's not very reassuring," I said.

"Trust me," Jorge said. "You won't have nothin' to worry about in that neighborhood. All nice people for the most part."

"The most part?"

"Can't trust white folk," Jorge said, looking bashful, as if he didn't mean to say that. "No offense. There are some good ones out there. Hopefully you two are, I mean."

"I try," I said, playing into it.

He laughed a hearty chuckle befitting a mall Santa after his smoke break. "You're too funny, Joel," he said. "You should quit the band and do stand-up. Don't tell Silvestre I told you that, though. He loves you."

I refrained from mentioning I was in the midst of running away from Scyphozoa, and that he was about to be my accomplice in the act as soon as the engine purred onto the freeway. Once we bumped out of the Denny's parking lot, the glovebox flew open, snapping from its worn hinges.

"Could you close that for me?" Jorge asked. "I need to get that sucker fixed."

I nodded, went to slam the glovebox as hard as I could, but stopped. The usual glovebox stuff—tissues, registration papers, small toolkit—wasn't in there. Instead, there were books. A few more Murakami novels sans *Bird Chronicle*, some Grisham, Koontz, King. All pocketbooks, compact in nature and perfect to shove under your car's dashboard. But laced within the bindings and big author names was something shiny; something that caught my eye like the Holy Grail to King Arthur.

A revolver, loaded with six rounds. I leaned forward and checked to see if Jorge was concentrated on the road ahead. He was, and I shouldn't have doubted he'd do anything different. He was the best ride-sharer I'd ever ridden with. As he maneuvered onto the turnpike, I snatched the revolver and shoved it into my pants, feeling the cold metal against my inner thigh.

I slammed the glovebox shut.

7

Once we neared the end of the midnight downtown Denver traffic, there wasn't much in terms of conversation to be had. I appreciated Jorge for understanding when it was the right time to talk to someone. Sometimes people aren't in the right state of mind to indulge in social chatter, and sometimes there are people who don't respect those people's boundaries. Jorge was not one of those people. Instead, he raised the radio's volume and set the interior heating to high. After a mere minute, I almost forgot I was in one of the coldest places in America with how warm it got in that car.

The radio station was in the middle of playing The Police's "Every Breath You Take." The lyrics were haunting as ever, describing someone always watching no matter how many steps you make or how many breaths you take. What had Jess meant by "Evelyn will hear me?" Was there some sort of telepathy that came gift-wrapped with joining a cult? An inherent ability to hear people's thoughts? I was still unsure if demons or ghosts or whatever were involved, but I was sure of one thing: The Great King Rat was the king in the castle, the dragon protecting its cave of gold, the chess master waiting for all the pieces to fall into place. I wondered if everyone in Scyphozoa could read minds, but Asher was too stubborn to be able to, Adam was too high to, and Marty… well, I still wasn't sure about Marty. But honestly, could anyone? Getting to know him was like trying to have sex with a statue. You can ask for consent as much as you wish, but there's still nowhere to stick your dick.

Regardless of the congested highway's worth of thoughts brewing up in my noggin, there was a memory fermenting in the brew. It bubbled to the surface; millions of air pockets attracted to the thumping bass of The Police over the radio. They burst in little *pops*, blasting bits of memory into my consciousness. I thought of a time when I heard that song for the first time, sitting in the bed of a pickup truck at a family reunion.

There was a crude speaker lying on the grass. The sun beat down on my face. I was seven or eight; years before my first pimple decided to make its grand entrance. I had escaped to the comfort of the driveway, away from the commotion in the backyard. It was all too much, having to see the people who had a hand in creating my father, as it was a reunion for his side of the family. They were all sitting around on lawn chairs, watching the other kids flail around with a beach ball while they drank beers and talked sports. The women of the family weren't included in those conversations, being delegated to staying inside and doing all the cooking for the dinner that wouldn't happen for another hour or so.

One of those women was my mother, dressed in an apron she wasn't particularly fond of.

"It makes me look fat," she had gossiped with my father's sister, Aunt Wendy. "Like I'm about to have *another* kid. Could you imagine?"

"Junior's such a sweetie, though," Aunt Wendy had said, referring to me with the only name I was allowed during those get-togethers. Such was the woe of sharing the same name as your alcoholic father. "I don't think any of us would mind seeing another one of you running around during these reunions."

"I would sure mind."

"Don't be so crass, Julie. You love your son."

"Sometimes I wish we'd stopped after Bethany," my mother whispered, surveying the kitchen to make sure I wasn't around to hear.

Unluckily for her, I managed to hear everything. I had just left the bathroom after taking the longest piss of my known childhood. My hands were dripping wet from the lack of dry towels in the bathroom, and I hung my head around the corner, listening to every word. I was rather good at eavesdropping, much to my own detriment, as in cases like this.

I didn't cry in that pickup truck, one that I wasn't sure of the owner of. I was full of enough hate to stop the tears dead in their tracks. The most devastating thing a child can know is that their mother never wanted them. What makes it more devastating, an earthquake to one's heart, is knowing their mother wanted one child, seemingly birthing you in a lapse of judgement rather than a want for another child. I listened to The Police, bass heavy and rattling on the dirty speaker sat under the large tree, shielded from the Texas heat. The dark truck bed burned at my arms and legs, baking me like a panini under a sandwich grill. I didn't think about my father, for him I could care less, even then. All my synapses fired at my mother; someone I should've looked up to. That nurturing figure of legend, the love of so many little boys' lives as they were growing and developing in this dark and dreary world. I heard hooting and hollering from the backyard; one of my cousins probably hit another one square in the face with the beach ball. I smelled the pungent aroma of grilling hot dogs, charring burgers, and the sweet stench of macaroni salad. Pasta and mayo and olives and hard-boiled eggs and celery and peppers and paprika. I didn't want to eat; I didn't want to socialize. Why would I? There was no reason. I was the black sheep of the group, someone totally unwanted in the grand scheme of things. I didn't stir in that pickup truck, only listened to the song, letting the music swallow me whole.

The song faded out of earshot, soon replaced by "Those Lazy, Hazy, Crazy Days of Summer" sung by an ominously joyous Nat King Cole. That must've been a song request from my grandfather, or one of his many siblings. As the first key change rolled about, I felt the truck buckle and sway under newly applied pressure. I opened eyes I didn't realize were closed and looked toward the source of the subtle ruckus.

Bethany climbed into the truck bed and said, "Scooch over."

I wordlessly moved to the side. Beth sat beside me, taking in the summer rays that had been baking me to a crisp for half an hour before. She took one glance at me, which was all she needed to understand the situation at hand. I was upset, enough so that I was angry enough to *not* cry about it. Beth had that unique quality to her that most other people didn't, that innate ability to feel sympathy and empathy and everything in between. She didn't know the specifics, but she knew I was in pain. Torturous, seething mental anguish. She didn't say anything; just ruffled my hair and laid down, her bare shoulders touching mine, shrouded in a baby blue tee.

We stared at the leaves in the large tree, watching them sway and dance as Nat King Cole gave way Billy Joel on "Zanzibar." The blinding blue sky peaked through the branches, not a cloud in sight for miles on that sweltering summer day. A few more songs came and went before Bethany propped herself on an elbow and asked, "What's up?"

"Nothing," I lied stubbornly.

"I don't believe it."

"Nothing. Stop bugging me."

I turned on my side, my back to Beth. She sighed, started to get up, second-guessed herself, and rested back into her elbow-propped position. "You gotta tell me, Joel," she said. "I'm your sister. We're supposed to tell each other everything."

"I don't wanna talk."

"Can you at least tell me the general idea?"

"What's a general idea?" I asked. That combination of words wasn't in my vocabulary.

"Like, the reason. I don't know, just tell me," Beth begged.

We went back and forth, me denying her access to my thoughts, her taking a jackhammer to that bank vault. Eventually, I caved. The vault door exploded from its hinges, and Beth saw all the secrets within. At least, the ones I had locked in that specific bank.

The tears finally came, as unexpected and unwanted as I apparently was to my mother. I poured my heart to Bethany, her childlike wonder fading from her face the further I went. Her smile dissipated like a fog during a thunderstorm. There was rage in there, marred with sorrow. That empathy of hers spread as a virus spreads through one's immune system, destroying white blood cells in the battlefield of sickness.

I felt nothing but sadness, entrenched in the depths of a childhood wasted. Who can a child be if their parents don't care for them? If they never wanted him around in the first place? You become a black hole, like the Great King Rat. A hole in reality that sucks all joy and light into its core, never to be seen again. Depression incarnate, dejection inevitable.

I choked on tears and phlegm, unable to get any more words out. I wanted to say so much more, but there comes a threshold in which cannot overcome. One that is so burdened by sadness that even the most skillful climber couldn't conquer that mountain.

"That isn't true, Joel," Bethany consoled, pulling me into a seated hug. "It just isn't. Mom loves you just as much as she loves everyone else."

"How do you know?" I managed to ask through a wall of tears.

"Because she's your mom... She's my mom. She's *our* mom. Moms aren't supposed to not love their kids. Dads... well, dads are different. But Mom loves you so much. She probably drank too much wine. She might not know what she's saying, but she definitely didn't mean it. Trust me."

I buried my face in her arms, soaking her shirt with warm despair.

"Besides, there's a way out of it."

What? I lifted my head in confusion, wiping my snot-ridden nose with my hand. "Way out of what?" I asked.

"Her thinking that way."

A cool breeze tickled my skin, bringing goosebumps out of their summer hibernation.

"You could always just run away," she continued. "Leave everything behind, like you're doing now. Like you've always done. Running away from your problems instead of facing them."

She hadn't said that. There was a sternness to her tone that hadn't adorned her during those years of blissful childhood. A tone more adult, more sinister. She hadn't said that, and this wasn't a memory as much as it was real. Sure, I had reminisced on a traumatic day on my own with the help of The Police, but there was something wrong. A paranormal darkness shrouded that midsummer day of years past.

"You can just kill yourself."

"What?"

"Kill yourself, Joel," she repeated. Her eyes, which had reflected sunlight moments before, glowed a boundless white. As unnecessary as a spotlight during the day, as ethereal as snow in the summer. "Kill yourself and you'll never have to run away again."

Bethany rummaged into her pocket, pulling out a water pistol. It gleamed with those early-2000s neon greens and yellows and oranges. There was water in the chamber, locked and loaded for shooting. There was no possible way that water gun had fit in her pocket, but nevertheless it was there, pliable in the space between us like putty in a child's fingers.

My child's fingers.

No, I'm not a child.

My name is Joel Auguste, I'm twenty-one years old, I'm a trombonist, and I've had a hell of a winter. This was all a memory, one that was real to a point, becoming tainted with something otherworldly, something evil.

I stared down, the barrel of the water gun pointed between my eyes. It shook in my hands, little tremors of nervousness. Bethany, or whoever she was, told me to end my life repeatedly like choir boys singing Hallelujah. She slammed her fists into her knees with every syllable, pounding each word into my head. Pounding like a hammer to the final nail in a coffin.

I didn't blink. I feared the void waiting for me behind my eyelids, that inescapable dark. The pistol wavered; I felt the trigger's weight under my fingertips.

Then I blinked.

The summer heat, the bright sun above, the people chatting in the backyard; all these disappeared as my eyes opened again. I was met with the dark interior of Jorge's car, the radio tuned to the local rock station, and Jess gazing out the back window as miles of trees zoomed by.

I stared down the barrel of the revolver, my finger curled around the trigger. I quietly clicked the hammer back into place and slipped the gun into my pants.

CHAPTER XIII

1

Jorge twisted and turned the car through a long, winding driveway. As Cameron's home came into view—a strangely standard suburban house tucked away in the outskirts of that Aurora neighborhood—a light frosting of snow began to fall. Intricate flakes floated onto the windshield, melting instantaneously from the heat inside the car through the glass.

I paid Jorge handsomely; we said our goodbyes. I never saw him again. Not that he died or anything. I miss that man, though. Him and his charm and glorious black beard. I hope his son is doing well. Truly. He departed from the timeline of my life forever, fading into the crowd made up of billions of others. Some may even share his face in the great human salad bowl occupying this planet.

As his car bumped over gravel into the night, Jess and I rang Cameron's doorbell. I lifted my finger from the button. Jess asked, "What's the plan, even? Are we staying the night? Throwing a little slumber party while the others are out hunting us? We can't just stay in one spot forever. We need to keep moving."

"There's no way they can find us up here," I said. "Like Jorge said:

Aurora isn't that great of a place. They'll probably search other places around Denver. They won't come here."

"You don't know them like I do."

The front door opened as Jess concluded her statement.

"Joel!" Cameron shouted, going in for a hug I wasn't expecting, but deeply appreciated. "It's so good to see you. You must be freezing. Come in!"

I nodded and took a step into his pleasantly warm home. Jess followed closely behind.

"Oh!" Cameron said before I could move another inch. "Take your shoes off. My mom gets really worked up about boot trails in the house."

"Oh, sorry," Jess and I said.

2

Cameron's mother was an absolute saint. In the thirty minutes Jess and I took between the initial phone call and arriving at their home, Mrs. Wright had baked Pillsbury chocolate chip cookies and neatly set them on a platter for us to enjoy.

"When I heard Cameron was having some school friends over, I just couldn't resist," she said. "We live so far away from Sanduhr that we almost never see people from his school come by. Us being a whole day trip away and all that."

I sat on an armchair in the living room, Jess on the adjacent leather couch. There were still Christmas decorations scattered throughout the home. Tinsels strewn across various mantelpieces, stockings hung above the electric fireplace, a skinny plastic evergreen tree tucked into the corner. I felt warm and fuzzy on the inside, like a warm glass of eggnog while waiting for Santa to squeeze his fat ass down the chimney, or lack thereof considering the fireplace was electric.

"I get it," I said. "I'm from Chicago, so I usually don't see anyone from school during breaks, either."

"Chicago?" she amusedly asked. "It must be gorgeous up there this time of year."

"Not as nice as you'd think."

"Oh, no?" She looked genuinely disappointed to receive that news-flash. "Maybe not so much the actual city, then. Are the neighborhoods around town nice, though?"

"They can be. Some are a bit… uninviting. But most of them are nice. There's a town called Joliet that's a bit further out. I went there a few times with my family when I was a kid because of some carnival thing they threw every year. The area seemed a lot more welcoming than the other suburbs around downtown, but you still gotta drive a bit to get there."

"Would you like something to drink with those?" Mrs. Wright asked, nodding toward the platter of warm cookies on the coffee table. "We have bottled water, milk, apple cider… anything you'd like."

"I'll take a water, if you don't mind," Jess said.

"Oh my God, pardon me," Mrs. Wright said. "I've been ignoring you all this time, young lady. What's your name?"

"Jessica Fitzgerald."

"That's such a beautiful name. You're a friend of Cameron's, I presume?"

"No, I'm actually just a friend of Joel's. I don't go to school anymore."

"Oh, that's too bad. You seem like a bright young woman."

"It just… wasn't for me."

"I understand. I went to this yoga class for years, and I absolutely *loathed* the other women in the class. Always talking about their husbands and their sneaky affairs and their kids getting detention and '*Oh no! Gotta get Johnny out of jail, again!*' I wish I had the confidence to leave that class sooner, like you had to pursue something outside of college. Does that make sense?"

"It does," Jess agreed, but her expression said otherwise.

I felt for Jess at that moment. There was so much pain and suffering beneath her eyes; so much that she wouldn't—couldn't—share for all those weeks touring on the big red and yellow bus. There was nothing I needed more than for her to spill everything involving Scyphozoa to me. Nothing related to how they made "Frictional Fiction" or "Drive" or how the audio equipment manages to make my trombone sound like that. I wanted to know what they did. What they *really* did behind closed doors. When the curtains are lowered and the only thing you can see is Asher and the rest performing some cult shit in a secluded cabin in the mountains near Denver. What they had done to countless others before Lenny.

Was I next?

Surely, I was.

There was a glow in Asher's eyes that hinted such things. A subtle, faint glow that showed his blatant ignoring of me. Maybe truly seeing me as nothing but a sack of meat, juicy and prepped for grilling or deep frying. I thought about Kyrie Castillo and the mystery surrounding him. Jess needed to fess up, because as I chomped down on a chocolate chip cookie fresh from the oven, questions had replaced every cell of brain matter in my skull. I couldn't think about anything other than the horrors I'd witnessed, the horrors yet to come. The Great King Rat in all its wickedness, the visions it showed, the memories it tainted. The rapture in its glowing white eyes, those spotlights of darkness, emptiness. Hollow beams that shot nothing but terror into my mind.

3

I won't bore you with the details of the rest of the night. Cameron came back from the bathroom, dressed in a green and black Sanduhr University tee with matching pajama bottoms that looked so comfortable, as if someone had sewn them with actual clouds. Mrs. Wright let us be, leaving the room and presumably going back to bed. We talked for a little while, Cameron brought up Jasmine, who seemed to be just a fleeting memory to me instead of a tangible human being.

Looking back on it, with another cookie in my mouth, I realized I should have listened to her instead of shrugging off her valid concerns. There was evil in the band, and I was too blind to see it, but she had the foresight I didn't. Maybe I would've winded up dead, like she said, if I hadn't made acquaintances with Lenny. But, yet again, he'd probably still be alive if I hadn't graced him with my presence, if I simply hadn't thrown my college credits away and hastily joined this band. They were cunning, though, but frothing at the mouth for something. Maybe Lenny would've died regardless. Maybe Scyphozoa was starving; they needed to feed.

I lay in the guest room, side by side with Jess on the same bed. We had our backs toward each other, laying a few feet apart. There was an awkwardness embedded under those bedsheets.

I closed my eyes and didn't dream.

4

I woke to an ominously quiet house. The air was still, only wavering with each breath Jess took, shrouded in sleep. I didn't like it: the silence. It reminded me of that fugue state the Great King Rat put me in time and time again, where all the air felt sucked out of the room in a vacuum and the only thing you could focus on was the darkness.

Drenched in a cold sweat, I shook Jess awake. I started with light jostles, moving into violent rattles when those didn't work. She was an extremely heavy sleeper, it seemed. Her hair was a lion's mane of fire, knotted and full, when she finally awoke. Jess muttered something unintelligible under her breath as she propped herself up on her elbows.

"There's something wrong," I said.

"What?" asked Jess, wiping sleep from her eyes.

"Do you feel that, too?"

The drowsiness fell as soon as she noticed the deafening silence.

"It's too quiet," she said.

"What time is it?"

She rolled over and lifted her phone from the carpet, hanging limply over the mattress like an old doll. "Five," she said.

"In the morning?"

"At night."

"We slept for over half a day?"

"Well, when was the last time you slept? Like, truly slept."

I hadn't slept well in weeks. Whenever I had dreams, they were poisoned. Malignant tumors showing in the theater of my sleep-drenched brain. I'd been afraid to drift off unconscious for a while now, as evidenced by the lavender bags sagging under my eyes.

"Not for a while," I responded.

"We should get up. Check on Mrs. Wright and Cameron."

"Way ahead of you."

I grabbed my meager allotment of belongings and shoved them into my pockets. Jess did the same, with the added bonus of combing her hair with clawed fingers in the absence of a brush lying around.

We hurried from the guest room and went upstairs toward the kitchen. No one was there. Glasses were newly washed, some still steaming from recent dishwashing. The ceiling fan in the living room spun moderately, sending light gusts of dusty air into the foyer. I wanted to call out for either of our gracious hosts, to shout to the Aurora hills, but the density of the atmosphere in that house was bearing down on me. No one was in the kitchen except Jessica, but I felt as if millions of eyes were on me. All watching with microscopes, critiquing my every move, researching for their time to strike. To sink their fangs into my flesh and rip me open like some meaty Ziploc bag full of strawberry jam.

I said nothing, only signaled for Jess to follow. She ignored me, instead leading me through meandering hallways lined with family photos and small endtables dotted with decorative plates and teacups and smaller framed photos propped up on flimsy kickstands. Jess opened the back door, we slipped through the doorway, and stood in the cold January weather on Cameron's backyard patio. I had taken the heating inside the home for granted, it seemed, as my skin immediately flared in gooseflesh.

The indoor lights shone through the windows and illuminated the yard in yellow squares. Dead grass, losing the last of their summer green, glistened gold in the rays. But in the distance, beyond the lights from inside, just toward the fence aligning the property line, two white dots glowed. Perfectly aligned, as if they were a pair of eyes. Two bright pinpoints in the expansive nothingness beyond the house light. Like shining a flashlight through a piece of black construction paper that had a staple hole in it. Two eyes seeing us, observing us.

Watching.

Waiting.

Waiting for what? I thought.

Jess grabbed my arm so hard it felt like the skin on my wrist would tear off like a sticky note from its adhesive stack. She pulled with unexpected strength, lurching me toward her as she ran. We sprinted across the house's side, the winter breeze stabbing our faces with frigid pinpricks.

"Why are we running?" I shouted.

My question immediately found its answer. Not from Jess herself, but the four ominous silhouettes standing in Cameron's driveway. One tall, two the same average height, and one short and stumpy.

They found us.

And Cameron laid tossed on the gravel, blood seeping from his temples and stomach.

5

"Thought you could run that easily?" Asher asked.

I was frozen in my spot, feeling as if ice cubes had accumulated around my feet and kept me planted on the cold, winter ground. Jess inched forward, the dead grass crunching beneath her step. I thought of my broken nose, the crunch I heard as the cartilage separated from my skull. Todd had done a number on me that last day in Sanduhr, my fall in the Colorado wilderness just a day before reawakened that sensation, and all I could hear as Jess walked toward Scyphozoa was the sound of broken bones. A death march toward her doom; sauntering back to her captors.

"Seems you didn't run far enough," Asher continued.

Their shadows intimidated me. Jess and I only wore the clothes Cameron had let us borrow: More Sanduhr University merchandise, all tee shirts, and not enough to shield us from the cold. But the remaining four Scyphozoa members wore puffy winter jackets that made me warm just by looking at them. They stood side by side, all in order of height; tallest to hilariously shortest. The harsh lamppost light made them look like card-board cutouts painted black, the only thing hinting that they were alive being the breath wafting from their lips when they spoke.

"Nothing to say?"

I glanced at Cameron's limp body. I studied him with panic in my eyes, terror infecting my soul. I checked from a distance for any sign he was alive. They couldn't have killed him so mercilessly, right? They obviously hadn't given Lenny much of a chance, but Cameron was an even kinder soul, one that melts your heart just in his mere presence.

I saw his back rise and fall under his winter coat; scattered breaths tinged with pain at every gasp, but breathing, nonetheless. Relief would be an understatement. I thanked whatever higher power I could that Asher and the rest had spared him, even for a little while.

"How did you find us?" Jess asked.

The scene was like a standoff in some old spaghetti western movie. The four remaining band members standing guard against Jess, with me off to the side and Cameron between us all.

"How do *you* think?" Marty piped up. "You made it too easy for us. Like Asher said, you should've run further."

One of the figures in the middle of the group grabbed something from their pocket. With the flicker of a lighter, I saw it was Adam. He lit up a blunt and ripped sweet marijuana from the shaft. There was a smoothness to the action that exhibited years of practice. It wasn't addiction at that point; it was a necessity.

With a puff of smoke, he said, "I'm not too sure why you didn't just jump on a flight and get the hell away from here. Was something holding you back, Joel? Was something chained to your foot that you just couldn't shake off? Is it that bitch standing here?" Adam shifted his focus to Jessica. "We should've let you go the moment you didn't wanna join us. You were always a half-member to us, anyway. Someone who was too pussy to truly be a part of the group. Just because you played the keyboard and helped with vocals and songwriting and guitar doesn't mean you were in the fuck-ing band. Not really. You were such a prude all… the damn… time. Why wouldn't you just try it once? Too scared of the rush?"

"You don't need to ask her all that," Evelyn said, fumbling at her pants pocket for something indiscernible under her denim. "I already know. She's scared. She's always been scared. Ever since her poor little mommy and daddy brought her to the park and left without her. Something that *awful* must've had a big effect on such a little girl. Just… traumatizing." There was a hint of mockery in every word. "And she thought she could find a new family in us all those years later, after whoring around with a bunch of scrawny fucks? Apparently so. But we weren't good enough, it seems. Why else would this lost little bitch run away with some mediocre trombone player who's in way over his head?"

Despite the cold, I grew hot with rage. I chose not to speak, but just this once.

"Of course we were gonna find you, Jessica," Evelyn resumed. "You may try to be quiet around everyone, but that mind of yours is so full of thoughts. And they're so… *loud*. I could hear you from miles away, like you were just *begging* for us to come. Getting to Aurora was easy enough, but you were such a dumbass that you decided to read the exact address off someone's phone. I'll hand it to you; You tried your best to forget you saw it, but you were too weak. Too stubborn to forget because that's what your best at."

"And what's that?" Jess asked.

"Fucking everything up."

I moved slowly over toward Cameron, still lying mostly motionless in the driveway. The remaining members of Scyphozoa didn't seem to care, but they surely noticed. Their eyes were daggers stabbing my psyche, keeping me from helping my friend, but I resisted their judgement and trudged ahead. I knelt at Cameron's side and rolled him onto his back. A deep gash in his side gleamed in the dim glow of lamplight, a hole permeating there, writhing in textiles of skin and muscle tissue. The flesh around the wound was pink and puffy in stark contrast to the paleness consuming the rest of him. He was losing a lot of blood, but he was still alive. I had time to take him to a hospital, I was sure of it. A tear fell from my cheek onto the gravel; I wasn't sure when I had started crying.

"Scared to lose another friend, Joel?" Evelyn asked.

"Shut the fuck up."

"She's not asking," Asher said. "She already knows, which I'm sure you're very aware of now. There are no secrets in Scyphozoa; just the things Evelyn decides to not share."

"He will die tonight," Marty said. "One way or another. Could be blood loss, infection in the open wound, or anything else."

"Natural causes, maybe?" Adam sneered, followed by a chuckle. His teeth glinted in the light. I wanted to punch those impossibly white teeth out of his jaw. To watch them clink to the ground and mix seamlessly with the gravel would be a dream come true; a dream I hadn't wished for until that moment, but a good one, nevertheless.

Cameron moaned in agony, blood gushing from his mouth in warm red spurts. I placed my hand on his cheek and moved his head to the side so he wouldn't choke. He lifted an arm and nimbly swatted my hand away. Cameron lifted himself up slowly like a forklift raising a heavy load, a crate full of meat, perhaps. I backed away and got up.

"Cam," I said, "go back inside. Let us handle this."

"They came to my house," he spit. "They hurt my mom. They dragged me from my room, threw me on the driveway, and sliced the fuck outta my stomach. I think I'm the only person ready to handle this."

"Cameron, please."

"They fucked with my family. It's only right."

He hawked some snot in his throat and spat onto the ground. A pink glob splattered on the rocks. His face was bruised and scuffed from the apparent dragging and throwing onto the gravel. An eye was in the early stages of swelling. His hair was matted with blood; it dripped onto the tops of his ears. I couldn't stop staring at the wound on his side, watching as a consistent stream of blood poured from the ravine. It soaked the hem of his pants, dyeing them maroon.

Cameron turned to the four ominous figures. They were all members of a band he was only slightly familiar with; he had no sentimental connection to them or their music. But there was one thing he knew: They were nothing but evil. They had assaulted Mrs. Wright. They had him up for ransom, and I wasn't sure what I was supposed to pay for his rescue.

Before he could say anything, I interrupted, "What do you guys want? If you want me to come back to the band, I will. I'll do anything you want… Just leave him and his mom alone. They don't deserve to be involved in… whatever all this is."

"Oh? Jessica never told you?" Asher asked.

"Told me what? About the cult shit? The way you twisted fucks killed Lenny? He had two kids, you know. He ever tell you that? He was one of the sweetest guys I'd ever met, and I only knew him for, like, two months. And what did you guys do? You killed him. You fucking *murdered* him."

"And you're curious to know why."

Asher stepped out of their formation, sauntering toward me with the stride of a school bully shoving his way through a crowded hallway during passing period. I backed further away. He moved past Cameron, ignoring him completely as if he were a ghost that only I could see. The space between us condensed, squeezing with the tension. The air grew thick; sweat beaded at my temples despite the cold.

"Don't you just want to know *everything?*"

There were only a few feet separating us by then. His breath fogged my vision as he blew it between his grinning teeth. There were lights in his eyes; two white dots, one dead center in the middle of each pupil. No light source could have reflected that light. These were lights that had always been there, like a dreadful birthmark. Birthmarks that had their own thoughts, feelings. In those minuscule white dots, there was malice brewing in the bright depths. I couldn't look away. I was fearful, sure, but it felt like a necessity to stare.

"I don't," I admitted.

Asher looked displeased. He was eager to spill the beans, to lay all the cards on the table, but I wasn't having it. I knew deep in my heart that I needed to know—for my own sake and the sakes of everyone left in my life—but I couldn't give him the satisfaction now.

"That's just too bad," he said. "And to think… I was actually considering letting you off the hook. I was going to find someone else to take the mantle; it's easy as fuck nowadays. Everyone wants a piece of me, but I want everyone. Whole. No pieces, just the entire fucking thing."

Asher lifted a bloodsoaked hand, letting a red strip of flesh fall like a yoyo on a string. He lifted the strip above his head, tilted upward, opened his mouth, and let the meat drop. He closed, chewed, and swallowed. I stared in shock. The piece of flesh was nearly the same size and shape as the wound in Cameron's abdomen.

"You see," Asher said, "there's just no satisfaction in picking at a meal. Sifting through the different courses, looking for the parts you like and the parts you don't. The real fun comes from the flavors of each piece coming together in one big amalgam of taste. Sweets, sours, bitters, savories. Oh… I just love the taste. Fortunately, we don't have to feed very often, but when we do: It's an absolute treat. And getting away with it is the best… god-damn… part!"

He chuckled, as did Evelyn, Adam, and Marty. Ugly, disgusting laughs; ones drenched in malignancy and intent to kill. They had already ripped a chunk out from Cam's side. What else were they willing to do?

I got my answer in the form of a pistol.

Evelyn drew the gun from her oversized pants pocket, held it by the muzzle, and walked it over to Asher, who took it and studied it as if he'd never seen a gun before.

"I don't want things to go the way they're headed," he said. "But if you're not willing to cooperate any further…" He cocked the pistol. A dead ring echoed in the cold air. "…then you leave me no choice but to make some drastic decisions."

"What the actual *fuck* are you talking about?" Cameron blurted.

Asher turned his attention toward him.

"I'm talking about you, of course."

"Excuse me?"

"You're directly involved now. You obviously don't know the finer details, but you're a witness. You harbored both Jessica and Joel, here. And you *obviously* mean a lot to Joel, so I don't see any other option besides the one I'm about to fulfill."

"And what's that?"

Asher responded, not with words, but with a pull of the trigger.

A thunderclap boomed from the barrel. Puffs of gunpowder blew into the night, a millisecond's worth of light blipped from the chamber. In one short *pop*, I screamed as Cameron's head lurched back, a red spray oozing from the back of his skull. A fleshy starfish blossomed where the bullet exited. A blooming flower of swift and immediate death.

Cameron's body tumbled to the ground, not a shrivel of life clinging to his bones.

The blame fell on me, and me alone.

6

There's this thing that happens when someone dies. The people whose lives they affected feel a sort of aftershock in the wake of their death. It harkens back to that adage of one seeing their life flashing before their eyes as their breathing slows and their heart ceases. It's a force so powerful that the others around them can only think of the times in which they were alive. His life flashed and that is all I could do as I watched Cameron Wright's body slump to the gravel driveway.

When I first met Cameron, he was a shy freshman fresh out of the womb of high school. He kept his backpack straps tight around his shoulders, his headphones cranked up to full volume, and he walked with the urgency of someone unwilling to make any small talk in the hallways. I hadn't switched my major from psychology to music at that point, but I saw him sitting in a corner at the dining hall from time to time. I regret not talking to him sooner. The unbearable weight of being a bystander while someone else struggled to adapt to a completely new environment, especially someone like Cameron, was too great. I couldn't resist ignoring him, like everyone else did. I must have seen him sitting alone, chewing on another soggy dining hall cheeseburger, at least fifty times before I finally switched my major and moved myself to his habitat in the Sanduhr Fine Arts Building. Him and Jasmine and all the rest. I watched him grow from a cocooned caterpillar into a freed butterfly. Only I was the reason his wings were clipped; why he couldn't fly into the sunset.

Because there he was, dead as the moths flying into the Wright family porch lamp; a bullet sealing his fate, a lump of lead sizzling in the frosted grass many yards away.

I had screamed so loud my vocal cords gave out. It hurt to swallow, every gulp feeling like a knife to the throat. Jessica was slouched over Cameron's body, crying for someone she barely knew. Her hands were shaking both from the cold and the nerves. Her bottom lip trembled, as did mine. My ears rang with the echoes of the gunshot, a high-pitched tone that grated against the general calmness of that Aurora suburb.

When the shock disappeared, anger replaced it. I stomped over to Asher, unfazed by the pistol being aimed in my direction. I was two feet from him, my warm breath billowing over his cold face. I was drenched in sweat despite the frigidity; Asher was as dry as Death Valley. Not a twinge of anxiety racked him. He was in control; he'd always been in control. I didn't know how, I didn't know why exactly, but I knew he was the puppet master, pulling all the strings from behind the curtain, wreaking havoc on me and countless others. I thought of Lenny, I thought of Kyrie Castillo, I thought of Cameron, who had been living and breathing only moments before. I felt nothing but unwavering sorrow for the lives they could have led, the people they were and the people they could have become. That sorrow fueled my rage, clouding my judgement as I stared into Asher's eyes two inches above mine. My breaths came out in short, aggressive bursts; his came out so calm that there was barely any hint he was using his lungs in the first place.

"What're you gonna do?" Asher asked. "What kind of power do you think you have over me?"

"Enough to put a stop to this bullshit," I said through gritted teeth.

"That's a pretty harsh thing to say while your friend's lying dead with a hole in his head. I'd hardly call that 'bullshit.' Just the price you must pay for thinking you could leave us."

"You're a fucking cunt."

"Not the first time I've been called that. I take it as a badge of honor."

I remembered the revolver jammed in my pants, suddenly feeling the cold metal grazing against my thigh. But Asher had his own piece on him as well, and it would've spelled my doom if I made any sudden movements, especially with the other three Scyphozoans standing guard mere yards away.

"A bit childish to call anyone a cunt when you're losing an argument," Asher said, "but I wouldn't expect anything less from you, seeing as you are who you are. A wildcard, an ungrateful kid, someone who obviously can't be trusted."

"You're not gonna lecture me on trust. You of all people."

"I'm the most trustworthy person you'll ever meet, Joel. You want the truth, and I'm willing to give it to you. All you need to do is say the word. Otherwise, I have no other option but to do something I'd rather not. It's your choice." He glanced at the pistol clung to his hand at his side. "One last choice."

I wasn't going to give into whatever scheme he was pulling. I broke eye contact with him and looked behind me. Jess still hovered over Cameron's body, weeping, and whispering something discernible into his dead ears. The tufts of her red hair slipped into his gaping mouth. Blood oozed from the gunshot wound, pouring in one slow stream into his eye, soaking the whites crimson.

I looked back at Asher, his stoic expression the same as it was the moment I recognized him in the driveway. I couldn't stand seeing him unfazed by the ruthlessness of the situation he directly caused. A little sympathy would've gone a long way. Not long enough, but *something* would've been appreciated. But there was nothing, and I wanted to kill him right then and there. I regret letting him go that night. My fate wouldn't have been sealed under that Colorado moon.

"Asher!" Evelyn shouted. "He doesn't want to know. Let's kill him!"

"No! You goddamn whore," Marty interjected. "We aren't going to kill him. We'll let him fend for himself if he doesn't seek the truth."

"What do you say, Joel?" Asher asked.

I didn't answer with words.

How could I?

I collected some saliva and spat it into his face.

Asher didn't seem to register anything, simply wiped the spit with an open hand and flung it to the ground. He smirked, his infuriatingly perfect face forming wrinkles that didn't show age but showed his unfortunate beauty. No one would believe me if I managed to say everything I witnessed here tonight. Because, as American media has proven time and time again, the pretty one stays on top. They can do no wrong. But Asher *had* done everything wrong, and he had another trick up his sleeve.

He looked to Marty, nodded, to which Marty nodded back. Marty unsheathed a long blade from his shirt sleeve and proceeded to slice down his arm. He started at the wrist, working the blade down to the elbow as he walked toward me on those stubby legs of his. The closer he got, the more I could hear the knife slicing through pale skin like it was a wet sheet of paper. The wound opened like a zipper, the white skin turning to pink then to red as blood squelched from the incision. It dribbled down his forearm in a rich film of crimson before he lifted it to his mouth and sucked the blood. He slurped most of the excess, but it wouldn't be enough to fully stop the bleeding.

The blood stopped, though, because why wouldn't it? Just my luck, honestly, when Marty stopped slurping the blood like Mom's tomato soup and showed the wound once more. This time, it was a dark ravine in his forearm, one with no end and no beginning. All light poured into that crevice, never to be seen by human eyes again. I could see the entirety of space and time in there, yet nothing in the slightest. It meant everything and it meant nothing. God only knew what lied at the bottom of that pit.

Marty smirked a disgusting grin as I soon realized I was frozen in my shoes. I could barely move; not even lift so much as a finger. I couldn't fight back no matter how much I tried. The loaded revolver shoved deep into my pants wouldn't be used to its fullest potential, much to my dismay.

With a flick of his wrist, the same unbearable darkness of the Great King Rat shot from Marty's wound. It manifested under the lamplight as a door, one that opened, revealing some semblance of light. The light bent and twisted with colors I had never seen before. It was mesmerizing, almost enough for me to forget about every terrible thing that happened in my life. All I could think of was the color tickling my eyes, the frequencies bombarding my sight with wonder and awe and sheer terror. Mortal eyes were never meant to see this.

Once the door had the width and height to let people through, Marty ceased building it and flicked his hand toward Jessica, who had begun to stare at the portal in complete and utter horror. She had seen the portal before, and she knew what was on the other side.

Like magic, Jess slid across the gravel away from Cameron. She screamed, pleading no… no… *NO!* as she moved weightlessly toward the cosmic door. She flopped onto her stomach and kicked and shouted. She clawed at the ground, a sea of rocks and pebbles parting under her fingers. With another flick of his wrist, Marty flung Jess into the portal. The doorway made a guttural sound like a bass guitar with the amp turned up way too high. She disappeared in an instant, a hot flash of light being the last of her.

"What did you do to her?" I shouted.

"See for yourself," Marty sneered.

He pointed his outstretched hand to me, and I felt a pulling sensation on my skin like an invisible boa constrictor tightening itself around me. I slid toward the doorway, the colors morphing and shifting the closer I got. My feet skid across the ground. Evelyn and Adam giggled too loud for comfort.

"*What did you do to her?*" Evelyn mocked, wiping away imaginary tears.

I didn't fight the pull toward the doorway. My fate was behind the indiscernible colors, the swatches of nondescript hues swirling in a whirlpool of everything. My last glimpse of Earth before entering the portal was the silhouette of Asher Gaumont.

The dim light faded, leaving nothing by a dark shape.

His eyes burned bright with white light.

CHAPTER XIV

Your usual Christian hell is washed with fire; this hell was bathed in gore.

Bodies writhed. They twisted and turned in pure agony. The suffering was palpable, bursting from their bulging veins, all green under their pale skin, or whatever was left of their flesh.

I hesitated to refer to these things as "bodies." Truly, the word popped into my mind, my fingers hovered over the laptop keyboard, but I couldn't type it out. Because when something is referred to as a "body," there's this standard that word sets. Something that is or was alive, something that could feel love, something that could bear pain. There was a hint of life to those bleeding, fleshy things lining the floor, the things that painted the horizon of that vast hellscape. But past the painful movements, I couldn't bear to call them bodies. They were just set decorations for a world I was never supposed to see. A place I still see when I sleep at night. That pitch black sky and that luminescent horizon. Pounds and pounds of flesh so pale and sickly it glowed neon aqua in the dark night. Organs spewing from the bodies with blood so dark and thick it looked more like tar than bodily fluid. There were eyes in those mounds, mouths with too many teeth, ears and arms and legs and genitals all mangled from centuries of fusion. They mixed into a melting pot of one body, one being. The sight was ghoulish, so grotesque I vomited on the ground; the ground made of blood and bone.

The doorway closed as a small shape pushed its way through. Marty stepped from the portal with relative ease in stark contrast to the way I tumbled through. I had landed with a mouthful of what I thought was a wet tarp. Unfortunately, as you now know, it wasn't a wet tarp. As Marty emerged from the doorway, and as it disappeared behind him, I scraped the remaining bits of liver from my mouth. I only knew the taste because of the time my grandmother decided to cook liver for dinner while she babysat me and Beth. I had been horrified choking down the slimy cooked organ back then, but that horror didn't compare to the hell Marty had thrown me into… and Jess. *Oh God… where was Jess?*

I ignored Marty as he sauntered past. My eyes darted around the immediate surroundings, searching for anything resembling an actual human woman. I called her name. *Jess… Jess?… JESSICA!*

That place was eerily silent except for the curdling flesh making up the ground and hills and mountains. But I heard a faint *squish* that stood out from the rest of the squelching filling my poor ears. I followed the sound, limping on a bad knee. My feet sank half an inch into the slippery floor with every step I took. I stopped and listened for the squishing noise again. I heard it to my left; I limped in that direction.

Around a corner coated with fine hairs and pus-filled blemishes, I found Jess lying on her stomach, her arms outstretched in the same position she must have fallen in. I fell to my knees and grabbed her by the shoulders. "Hey," I pleaded, shaking her. Her hair tumbled over my hands. "Jess… Please… *Come on!*"

She groaned, a spittle of blood splatting from her lips. I hadn't seen any serious injuries on her; I surmised that she must have simply fallen from the doorway too hard. Maybe she had slammed her head onto a ribcage or a femur protruding from the ground.

"Jess, we need to go," I said. "Please, get up!"

"We're fucked," she moaned.

Jess rolled slowly onto her side. Still no signs of damage on her, much to my relief.

"What do you mean?" I asked.

"He's just gonna leave us in here. He's gonna open another portal, walk through, and lock us in. You see all the shit around us? It's a graveyard. Soon enough, we'll be part of this mess. My eyes will be over there and my vagina over there. And we'll still be alive. Everyone here is. We'll be alive and suffering forever. Until the end of time."

2

"Holy fuck," I gasped.

I reached for her hand. Jess was hesitant, seeming to consider an eternal life of perpetual torment as better than whatever was waiting for her back on Earth. But she grabbed my hand, and I hoisted her up. She wiped the remaining bloody dribble from her lips on her shirtsleeve.

"What's the plan, then?" Jess asked. "Where the hell did Marty go?"

I immediately regretted letting Marty slip my mind for even the briefest moment. I was so distracted by Jess's well-being that he ultimately became unimportant in the grand scheme of things. But now he was the name at the top of my Most Wanted list. I remembered him sauntering off while I was busy looking for Jess. Him gliding across the fleshy, disgusting terrain one step at a time without a care in the world. But he *did* have a care; a care so vital to the Scyphozoan scheme that he needed to leave me and Jess in this neon hell of guts and bones to fully realize said scheme.

Nausea began to set in as I gazed across the writhing landscape. Miles and miles of subtly wriggling appendages, blinking eyes, and throbbing phalanges. All those tiny movements coalesced into a burning sickness, curdling my stomach, and rendering me dizzy beyond belief. I fought through the world spinning around me despite feeling vomit bubble in my throat. If I swallowed just once, it would likely open the floodgates and I'd heave toward the ground once again. Through the haze of oncoming sickness, I surveyed the horizon under a microscope. Marty couldn't have been far; he'd been walking at a snail's pace.

But what if he was already gone?

What if he had already opened another cosmic doorway and stepped his happy ass right in?

What if Jess and I were banished to a fate so brutal it would render us painfully immortal? Bound to the fleshy mountains surrounding us?

Sheer willpower couldn't stop the vomit from rising. The floodgates opened, not with a hearty gulp, but with the spiraling thoughts bombarding my mind. I bent over and let bits of food and bile spill upon the ground. A mouth moaned in disgust a few feet away.

I felt a hand caress my arched back; fingers glided over the grooves up and over each vertebra lining my spine. I collected the last chunks of puke and spat it in one gross glob. I stood straight, ready to give up, when I spotted Marty a quarter of a mile away, give or take. He strutted with annoying determination, slow and sure of himself.

I pointed in his direction and said, "There. There he is."

Jess took her hand from my back and chimed in: "We gotta get close. When he opens another portal, we kill him and step through."

I never thought I'd be so down with the idea of committing premeditated murder, but we were no criminals.

We were revenge artists.

3

Jess and I bobbed and weaved around flesh mounds with stark resolution. We were trained snipers perched miles away in the blistering desert, our sights trained on one common enemy. We were wolves on the prowl for an unsuspecting deer in the dead of night, only this deer was the most annoying fuck either of us had ever come across. And he was an accessory to murder. He had a hand in it, likely using this hell dimension as a means of travel between the western mountains of Denver to the suburbs of Aurora.

Evelyn was the recon.

Marty was the getaway driver.

He wouldn't get away this time, though. Thanks to the faint glow of pale skin in that place, bone indentations were made more glaringly apparent. They popped from the ground like molehills by a soybean field. And, best of all, they didn't audibly squish under the pressure of worn sneakers like sweaty flesh and bloody gore did. We hopped from bone to bone with a gazelle's grace, stepping carefully on pointed toes instead of flat feet. The work was meticulous, fast enough to close the distance between us and Marty within five minutes. He was still far ahead, but I could finally make out the slimy sheen of hair grease at the short distance we were from him.

We made our way behind a tall cylinder of meat. It was gargantuan in scale, towering over us like a redwood tree in both height and girth. Branches comprised of arms and legs and penises sprouted the higher the trunk rose, with leaves of toes and finger and all different types of hair adorning those twigs. It was oddly beautiful in its vulgarity. There were other flesh trees just like it dotting the landscape ahead.

"Is this a goddamn forest?" I whispered over my shoulder to Jess.

"I guess so," she responded. "People grow into things they're familiar with in here. And once one tree sprouted, more people copied their homework. We're looking at centuries' worth of plagiarism in the form of a forest."

Between the silhouettes of two trees, Marty walked. Jess bent down and dug her fingernails into the ground. Blood seeped from the wounds of thousands as her fingers wormed deeper into flesh and gore. She grasped something and slowly pulled it from the fresh wound in the earth. Skin and muscle tissue bent and twisted as Jess pulled a long, white tube from the hole. Only it wasn't a tube. It looked to be a femur.

I was horrified for a split second, but that terror subsided rather quickly. I'd seen far worse. "What'd you do that for?" I asked.

"Aren't you gonna get something to beat him with?"

I awkwardly reached into my pants and revealed Jorge's glovebox revolver. It reflected the neon teal hue of that gory hell; its six bullets sat snug in the cylinder.

"And *why* didn't you use that earlier?" Jess asked.

Definitely a fair point, but the shock of the past few days clouded my judgement so profoundly that the thought of using the revolver in

Cameron's driveway was just that: a thought. One that waded in the river of my consciousness. Cruising on by, waving with a short hello, and going on its way.

"You know," I said. "Seeing your friend shot dead by someone you looked up to can really make you lose your cool. I'm sorry if I wasn't thinking clearly during a goddamn traumatic event. I've had a long week."

"You're telling me." She rolled her eyes. "Try being around them for years."

As Jess wiped blood onto the flesh tree from her makeshift femur-club, I felt nothing but pity for her. I only experienced the terror of Scyphozoa for a little under three months; she was trapped with them for multiple years. In comparison, I only had a nibble of the maggot-infested steak that she was forced to eat in its entirety for years before I came into the picture.

"Let's go, then."

I nodded, attempting to hide my sadness for her.

4

Jess hopped to a ribcage; I followed her exact movements. We bounced from bone to jutting bone like frogs leaping from lily pad to lily pad.

Marty stopped in a small clearing. He unsheathed the long blade, ready to slice down his forearm once again. Sweat dripped from my pores. The pits on my shirt were damp with perspiration, but I wasn't bothered. I could be musty all I wanted; my only focus was on waiting for Marty to open another doorway and put a bullet in his puny little skull before the door slammed shut. I hadn't felt bloodlust like this since I almost plunged a shard of glass into my roommate's neck. I was being childish then, I was ready to admit, but now there were real stakes.

I wasn't about to let Marty walk away.

We were close enough to see the tiniest details. From behind another flesh tree, I noticed the dark ravine in Marty's forearm was gone. It had fully healed in the time between throwing us into the doorway and ending up in this spot. There wasn't even a scar. It was like he hadn't healed, but time had reversed on his arm. Like the cells reverted to a past form instead of creating scar tissue in the present. Smooth as a baby's bottom, as much as I hate the saying.

He proceeded to insert the knife into that smooth skin, slicing down from his wrist with jarring precision. The wound bled, the blood evaporated in an instant, and that hollow void appeared where muscle tissue should have been.

As Marty seemingly summoned another portal from thin air, Jess was ready to pounce. She had crouched down and laid in wait like a tiger prowling in tall grass, seeking its prey. The image of that tiger was all too easy to muster. Her unkempt orange hair made it so. She held the femur with malice, gripping it with enough force for her knuckles to run white with intent.

I laid a hand on her arched back, taming the beast before it acted too rashly. Her back muscles flinched upon contact. "Forget I was here?" I whispered.

She turned and rolled her eyes. I thought *I* was drenched in sweat, but nothing compared to the absolute tsunami cascading down Jess's face.

Before I could console her, a loud *whoosh* boomed from beyond the flesh tree. In the clearing, another portal—swirling with those fantastical colors from every edge of every universe—opened.

And Marty already had a foot in the door.

5

I wasn't trained in the art of firearms. I was a psychology major turned performance major, for Christ's sake! Arts and Sciences turned to Fine Arts, but nothing in those two areas of study could've prepared me for the sheer terror that enveloped me when I placed my finger on the trigger.

The six-shooter felt weighty in my hands. I wasn't sure how to properly grip the thing, but I *had* played my fair share of Black Ops 2 back in the day, and I had a bit of a rapid-fire trigger-finger in that game's multiplayer arenas.

Within a fraction of a second, my mind raced; it sped through an entire

NASCAR race before I had time to blink again. If I shot Marty in the leg that was still planted in the flesh world, would he just fall into the portal anyway? If I shot him in the head, would the portal close instantaneously, dooming us to an eternity of torment? If I shot him in the arm, would the same thing happen because of the wound adorning it?

I surmised that the only option was to shoot him in the neck. It wouldn't kill him instantly, but it would stun him for long enough to keep the doorway open, but also fatal enough to let him bleed out in a state of paralysis.

I squinted my left eye, stared down the sight, locked onto Marty's neck as well as I could. There was no time left to wait.

I had to fire. I *needed* to fire.

Nothing else mattered.

I clicked the hammer and pulled the trigger.

BANG!

A hole appeared in Marty's shirtsleeve; I missed. But he reeled back as if I *had* shot him in the neck, grasping at the crater in his shoulder to stop the bleeding. Rivers of red poured from between his locked fingers, inching down the back of his hand as he lost his balance and dropped the blade.

Jess charged at him with the femur in tow, screaming like an Amazonian warrior; a war cry screeched from her lips and rang through the hollowness of that place, echoing off every fleshy rock and stone, every porous tree and blood-soaked hill.

I ran after her. The revolver's barrel released snakes of smoke from the last shot. A trail of gaseous gunpowder followed me like a comet's tail. Jess wound the long bone back and struck Marty in the head with a loud crack. The bone refused to shatter from the impact, but Marty's temple caved in as the club made contact. Blood spurted from the wound as he lost his balance again. Jess was ready to strike once more; the femur came back down, only to be met with an open hand, catching it before it could cause more damage. Marty gripped the bone and smiled through teeth stained scarlet. Jess struggled to remove the femur from his grasp. He hooked her under the jaw with a clenched fist. She fell to the ground, letting go of the bone as she went.

Boiling with anger, I raised the gun, ready to fire. Marty dropped the bone. It clunked to the ground with a soft thump. Still smiling—the blood between his teeth accentuated the animalistic shapes of each tooth—he raised his arm and pointed an open palm to me. In a pinching motion and a sharp flick of his wrist, the revolver slipped from my hands and flew toward him. Before it reached his grasp, I lunged toward him. Tears filled my eyes with how fast I went, like a strong wind had blown dust into my corneas.

Marty held the gun, studied it as if he'd also never seen a fucking gun before, and cocked the hammer. I jumped forward, arms outstretched, and tackled him to the ground as his finger curled around the trigger.

A shot rang out. Dismembered mouths screamed in terror. A bullet hole appeared in a mound of flesh a few yards away. It spewed fluid in a misty stream, like how people bled in that Tarantino western movie. Pained screams encircled us as we tussled on the ground. I punched him square in the cheek and felt something loosen inside his mouth. He spit out a tooth. But there was nothing signaling pain. No scrunched facial features, no tensing muscles under his clothes.

He laughed.

I swear to you, the fucker laughed.

On top of him, I laid another hit in the same spot. His head reeled from the blow, resting back into place as if he were waiting for another punch. So, that's what I gave him: Another punch. And another. His cheek turned bright pink then dark indigo as the bruising process took hold. But nevertheless, he still laughed. A deep, bellowing chuckle you'd expect from an audience member at a stand-up comedy show, not from someone getting the shit beaten out of them in some goddamn body horror hellscape.

"Couldn't even get me down yourself, huh?" Marty spat. "Needed some help from that bitch to bring me to my knees? Typical from you."

I was stunned; not from the profanity that was so unlike the Marty I came to know, but the knee he hit my testicles with. I gasped and fell backward. Marty took the opportunity to lay a few blows of his own on me. A fist, small but powerful, smashed into my nose. Straight-shot hits that stung with the pecks of a million wasps. I immediately felt the swelling. My nasal cavity filled with blood and closed like a spaceship's airlock. I could only breathe through my mouth. I let in short, shallow gulps of air as Marty attempted to cave my nose in. Between punches, he said, "You were too weak for us to use, anyway… Always running away from your problems… Always complaining, always wanting to know everything. Some things are better kept secret from weak little shits like *you*."

The pain in my loins subsided just in time for me to block another punch. I swiped at his gnarled forearm and sent him flying. I propped myself up on my elbow and stood up. Jess lay on the ground poking her jaw. I prayed it wasn't broken. I limped toward her with blood dripping from my nose like water from a broken pipe under the kitchen sink. "Jess are you—" I started to ask before something tugged on the back of my shirt.

With all the strength he could muster, Marty threw me to the ground. Before he could get on top of me, I slapped him across the face. He gripped my arms and pulled me toward him as he fell. We rolled down a hill. He let go halfway down the slope. The world, or whatever that place was, spun around as I tumbled further down. Finally, without warning, I felt something warm and slippery grace my skin.

Then my whole world was enveloped in darkness.

I swam to the surface of whatever we'd fallen into. I broke the barrier and gasped for air.

When I opened my eyes, all I saw was red, like I had somehow fallen into a photographer's dark room. I blinked the soupy stuff from my sight, wiping my face for extra measure. It's not every day you experience what it's like to be submerged up to your chest in a lake filled with nothing but blood. I took in the terrifying sight, using every one of my five senses to *make* sense of it all. Blood in that world, when pooled together in that much abundance, isn't red. It runs black and thick like a ghastly mix of molasses and crude oil. Its metallic taste sat on my tongue while I tried my best to spit everything out. The smell was the worst. The air above that lake was thick with metal. The smell of coins you've held in your hands for too long. It overwhelmed my nose. I coughed after every inhale, tasting the iron.

I waded in the lake, scouring the area for Marty. *Maybe he drowned*, I thought. *His stumpy little arms couldn't keep him up for too long, right?*

Despite the blackness of that lake, I noticed neon ripples. They weren't mine. I was tall enough to touch the squishy bottom of the pool; I was motionless in every aspect except my neck. A fat bubble rose to the surface mere yards away. It sat there for a moment before popping, then another bubble appeared, then another, *pop*, another, *pop*. The bubbles went in a straight line before they ceased entirely. When I expected another blood bubble, out came Marty from the depths gasping for air.

I lifted my feet from the lake's bottom and vigorously swam toward him. My muscles howled in pain. Swimming in regular, chlorinated water was difficult enough, but swimming through a lake full of shit with the consistency of French onion soup was a whole different task.

Marty noticed me and swam toward the shore in a worried frenzy. He was faster than me, sure, but not fast enough. He was so focused on escaping that he neglected to use that dandy telekinesis of his on me. Once he made it to shore, he stumbled from the lake and climbed up the hill. He left maroon footprints in his path. When I made it to shore shortly after him, I began to run uphill. My aching thighs didn't allow me to go as fast as I needed to. My clothes were sopping with blood. I trailed lazily behind him.

I huffed and puffed with every leap and bound. "Get back here, you bitch!" I yelled.

He stopped for a split second and pushed me back with his open palm. I went flying down the hill, tumbling over fingers and bellybuttons and ears.

6

I must've elbowed someone in the jawbone, since when I landed awkwardly on my arm at the bottom a distant mouth yelped in agony.

Marty was in the lead by a long shot. I wondered what he would do once he reached the top. *Is Jess still out for the count?* I hoped not. There was a gun and a knife up there: two very popular tools for murder. My blood ran cold thinking of the many ways Marty could end her life. A bullet in the gut, or maybe right between the eyes. A throat slash, perhaps. He could even hack away at her leg like the doctor at the end of *Saw*. I was sure he had every intent on killing her as brutally as possible despite having the easy job of simply leaving both me and her in this place to rot for eternity.

Suddenly, everything went silent. No wails miles away, no wriggling limbs attempting to separate themselves from the earth. All this as my pulse quickened. My heart thumped violently in my chest, a bass drum of dread pounding away beneath my ribs.

There was a scream, then a gurgling noise as I nearly lost my last sliver of hope. Over the crest of the fleshy hill, Marty flew down, bumping into everything as he fell like a chip in a Plinko machine hitting every peg. He left a curvy trail of tar-like blood as he descended. While he fell, I kept my gaze on the summit.

Jess slid down the hill with elegance despite her very apparent head injury. Her jaw was swollen beyond belief, but her hair did a nice job of covering it up. I rose from my ass and walked toward Marty's strewn body. He was still alive, surely, like how a cockroach refuses to die even when the United States military sends a nuke to its exact location.

Disappointingly, Marty coughed up some bloody spittle. The waves in the lake calmed down. The gallons of liquid held still as Jess found herself on the shore at the bottom of the hill. Jorge's revolver was in her right hand; Marty's blade rested nicely in her left. The edge dripped with black blood, oily and hot from recent slicing. Marty had a rather nasty gash across his eye. The blade had slit his eye open, popping it in one quick slice. It oozed from its socket in a mess of pink jelly. He coughed a bit more, gathering enough spit in his mouth to spit at me. It failed to make any distance, instead rising two inches above his mouth and splatting onto his cheek. "You're… goddamn… cunts," he said. "The both of you."

He rolled onto his back. "Why did you have to mess with things you didn't need to?" he asked. "Why couldn't you just be a normal fucking person and stay in your lane? You could've stayed in college, could've found a job that didn't involve us, could've had a beautiful girlfriend or whatever the fuck you're into back home…" An earthshattering pause, then an unnerving smile. "How's that Roselle doing?"

A chill snaked its way down my spine.

"How the fuck do you know about her?"

"We know everything, Joel. Don't act dumb. You've always known."

You've always known.

Where had I heard that before?

"I'll ask one more time: How… is Roselle doing?"

His skin grew paler by the second. It might have been due to blood loss, but I knew it was something darker than that. He was losing power; whatever that "power" of his was and wherever it decided to come from. They all had some sort of power, some ancient evil broiling in their veins I couldn't begin to imagine. Marty, Asher, Adam, Evelyn…

Jessica.

But how?

"How she's doing is none of your fucking business," I said.

"But it *is*, though," he sneered.

"How?"

"Did you two ever fuck?" I reeled back from the audacity of the question but listened intently. There were answers in those words, no matter how strange and painful. "That's the most important thing. Evelyn always said she was sure you and little Miss Roselle hadn't, but her sight can be a bit… foggy."

"Joel," Jess said. "You don't have to answer. Just let this little shit die."

"No, go on," I said to Marty.

"There's a certain equation that goes into the things we do. It involves dying; it involves coming back. But we come back a little different each time. We needed you, Joel. As much as I was against it, especially after that faggot Kyrie. Couldn't stand him taking Asher's attention away from me. But we needed you. He was starving, and we didn't have any spare meat in the freezer for him."

"What?"

"Are you dense? *You* barged in when we were taking care of that fat fuck Leonard. You saw what we did. It's… *necessary*. And he was so hungry. He needed another hit, and Leonard was the key. As was Kyrie. As were countless others… As was *you*."

"What the hell are you talking about?"

"A sacrifice."

Jess's shoulders went slack, and she dropped the femur with a soft *thump*. She covered her mouth with shaking hands and sat on an elevated skin mound. She looked like that Thinker statue, only a lot more macabre than the French could've imagined when sculpting it.

"A sacrifice is always necessary," Marty continued. "The body and blood of a virgin soul is required for the resurrection."

I remembered the connect-the-dots book I used to carry around when I was in elementary school. Started at the first dot, tracing lines from point to point with my father's work pen; a pen that he would scold me for taking from his desk. I would trace with the pen's tip jammed into the paper, leaving harsh, inky indentations as it glided across the page. Once my work was done, I would see a horse, or a frog, or even a dog playing with a tennis ball.

I connected the dots here, in this hell comprised of nothing but flesh, blood, and bone. They hadn't let me join their band because of sheer musical skill; I wasn't even sure if I was as good as I thought I was two months prior. They let me join them... for what? To be a tool? To be a lamb ready for slaughter when Asher or any of the others found it imperative? The trombone playing was just a little side thing, an extra side of steak fries for the sirloin entrée.

"We die, and we are reborn," he said. "It's as simple as that. And when we rise again, we are granted the Great One's power. Little pieces of strength that make us better than the rest of mankind. We gave up our humanity as a sort of token of gratitude, an exchange in return for the awesome power of the cosmos.

"You could've been one of us. You're so scared." He laughed, launching bits of saliva and blood inches from his face. "The Great One could have healed you; He could have made you better. You wouldn't have to be such a damn pussy and run away from everything like a scared fucking cat. You ran away from home, you ran away from your friends, you ran away from *us*. When will you run from her?"

Jess lifted her head. She was glassy-eyed; a universe's worth of thoughts was ready to burst from her head and form into tears. She got up and walked to me, holding the gun in her hand, reaching out to me. I took it from her and studied the cylinder. Four bullets left.

"We can help you stay," Marty continued, a quivering to his voice bubbling to the surface. "You just have to let Him in."

"No."

I fired.

A hole erupted in his forehead. Waves of black blood and chunks of brain and skull shards shot from the back. It seeped into the blood lake, intertwining his insides with the entrails of millions. A haggard smile was permanently etched onto his greasy face. His eyes, even in death, trailed me like those of the Mona Lisa. Always watching no matter where I was. A single drop of blood snaked down his head. It pooled into his eye socket.

7

I trudged up the hill; Jess followed suit. Not a word shared between us. The potential for conversation hung limp in dead air.

I refused to speak to her. I had too many questions. I got the answers I sought, but with every answer there were thousands of new questions. I was terrified, relieved, angry, distraught, jubilant, filled with unbridled dread.

At the top of the hill, Marty's doorway flickered and dimmed. His power, or the power of the "Great One," waned. The fantastical colors warped and shifted from vibrant to dull, and back to vibrant again. The cacophony of sights seemed to be fighting for life, as if the doorway itself was alive and didn't want to die. It pleaded for mercy as it sank into nothingness. I walked through without checking on Jessica, but I was sure she would continue to follow me. No matter how much of her was shrouded in mystery, I felt an overwhelming sense of certainty she would stick by me. And despite the suspicions I should have degraded her with—all those unanswered questions—I wanted her with me. By my side.

The ominous neon glow of that world ceased.

The blood and guts faded like a bygone memory.

The glimmer of winter snow met me on the other side.

It was late in the evening. The chill of half past midnight froze the sweat to my boiling skin. It steamed as I exited the portal; wisps of fog emanated in translucent white tendrils.

We were in the middle of a road, blockaded by tall buildings on all sides. Icicles hung from the bottoms of parallel-parked cars and window-panes adorning every floor of every building. Snow flurried down like confetti at a music festival. It sauntered from the sky without a care in the world. As if my world hadn't shattered piece by piece in the last few weeks. I suffered both inside and out, but the snow still fell. The world kept spinning.

The snow entranced me. It pulled me from the earth to the heavens, showing me the light in a world of ruthless dark. I could almost taste the clouds that hung above. They smelled of funnel cakes and cotton candy. I was a balloon floating adrift in the sky. My helium would never dissipate. The only thing tying me to the world was the frail string attached to my rear.

Jess tugged at the string and yanked me back down to Earth.

"Joel?"

"Yeah?"

"Isn't that the Willis Tower?"

I turned around and saw the looming black body of the Sears Tower. Any sane person would refuse to call it by its new name. Its two white spires scraped the gray, wintery clouds. Lights illuminated sporadic rooms on random floors. People living their lives; people that I would never meet. There's just too many of us.

"Yeah, it is," I said.

"Why are we in Chicago, Joel?"

A tidal wave of realization bombarded me.

This was Marty's next destination. With that blade in tow, he would go to Chicago and punish me further, even as I lay in eternal torment in that hellish world of gore.

My mother was next on the hit list.

CHAPTER XV

1

I knocked on the door a lot louder than the landlord would have liked, but when you're in a race against time, something as trivial as knocking on a door too loud just didn't matter in the grand scheme of things.

"Would you pipe down?" my mother's next-door neighbor asked. Mr. Marbury looked like he had aged five decades in the span of a few short years. The stink of cigarette smoke wafted from his unit as he slammed his door open and stuck his head into the dimly lit hallway.

"Sorry, Mark," I said, intoning his first name for the first time in my life. I had greater things to worry about. He didn't scare me anymore like the Great King Rat (or "The Great One" as Marty seemed to call him before I splattered his brains eons away).

He didn't seem to recognize me; the last time we interacted, my hair was cut short, and I was much shorter.

"You should clean yourself up, bub," he said. "Best get that blood off of you before I call the cops with a damn noise complaint."

"Anything you say, sir."

He cocked an eyebrow and slipped back into his apartment, slamming the door shut way louder than my knocking was. With that knowledge, I waited a moment and continued to knock on the door. Short staccato notes banged with a grating tempo, rattling the door on its flimsy hinges, accenting each beat with an annoying timbre.

I heard footsteps approaching from inside the apartment. I slipped a finger over the peephole. If Julie Auguste saw her son coated in blood outside her door, there was no way in hell she would open the door. Scratch that; she wouldn't even open the door for me if I had my hair gelled back and wore a proper suit and tie. "Oh, you finally got your life together," she would say. "Congratulations." Then the door would close in my face and break my nose... again. I really broke my nose a lot during my tenure with Scyphozoa, didn't I? I'm surprised it hasn't fallen off yet.

The footsteps grew in volume until they stopped. Two round shadows peered from under the door. She checked the peephole, was met with nothing but darkness, and hesitated to open the door. Then the deadbolt clicked, and the door creaked open.

Left ajar due to an unlatched chain, I saw half my mother's face. A look of minor annoyance from being woken up in the middle of the night turned into a look of complete and utter terror. Her eyes widened, taking in the sight of her son who seemed to have come from the trenches rather than stopping by on tour.

"Joel?"

2

The first thing I noticed upon exiting the shower with a fresh set of clothes was that there weren't any liquor bottles in the kitchen. The walls were a little more barren than I remembered. The typical photos of Bethany and I were there, but none of the rare pictures we all took together as a family. If the memory of my father hadn't seared itself into my head, I would've completely forgotten he had existed. There wasn't a trace of him left inside that unit. No pictures, no belongings, no beer bottles. Julie Auguste had scratched him clean from history.

She let Jessica use the shower without question. Both her and I looked like stray dogs straight from the battlefield, all bloody and aching with tired bones and minds, panting from a hard day's work of slaughter.

"What the hell happened to you two?" my mother asked, seated in the armchair adjacent to the couch Jess and I sat upon.

"It's… a long story," Jess said.

"Oh, I'm so sorry. I don't think I even asked for your name."

"Jessica," she answered with a pained smile.

"*Jessica.*"

My mother seemed to like that name. She studied Jess with raging curiosity. This marked the first time I had come home with an actual human woman. Even Roselle never had the pleasure of taking the trip back from Massachusetts to northern Illinois.

"She's gorgeous, Joel," my mother said.

Jess blushed as I completely ignored the explanation aspect of the conversation and instead asked, "Cleaned up your act?"

"What do you mean?"

"When's the last time you had a drink?"

She looked at the floor in shame. There was something so repeatedly peculiar about people looking down when faced with difficult situations. Roselle had done it, Todd always did it no matter his state of sobriety, even Jess found herself looking away anytime we had spoken in the beginning. But what I saw in my mother was an unbridled amount of shame crushing her from the shoulders like someone had tossed a sack full of cinderblocks onto her back.

"Not since I saw you play," Mom said.

"What?"

"I was scrolling thought Facebook when one of my old girlfriends tagged me in a post. She asked me, 'Why didn't you tell me your son was a rockstar?' I knew you were going to join a band the last time we spoke. I regret pressing 'End Call' that night; I regret talking to you that way. Because when I saw that post—it was a video, actually—I didn't see you as just my son. I saw you as something more. I saw how much you had grown as a person despite your father…" A choked expression washed her features. "Despite me."

"He *is* really good, Ms. Auguste," Jess said.

"Call me Julie, please."

"No problem."

"But regardless," my mother continued, "you looked so… *confident*. You were never that confident when you were young. Anytime something even slightly negative happened to you, you would run. It was like you'd simply disappear whenever you thought you were in danger of being scolded or reprimanded, or something or other. But up on that stage, you looked so happy. It was cathartic for me to see you with a smile on your face; you never smiled around me. Especially after your father passed. And I'm sorry for the way I treated you after that. Sure, I could blame it on Joel slamming that car into a pole." Jess left the room and hid in the kitchen, shielding herself from familial woes unrelated to her. "I could blame it on the snowstorm he decided to drive in. I could blame it on the booze, I could blame it on you, I could blame it on Beth. But I can't blame anyone or anything other than myself." Tears welled in her eyes. "I know you must hate me, but I've been trying to get better.

"I started journaling whenever my thoughts were too dreadful to keep locked in my head. I went to an AA meeting right before Christmas. It was just… awful. Not because of the people pouring their hearts to complete strangers. Not because of the wisdom and healing those proctors offered. It was awful because, as I was sitting there in that circle, I pictured your father sitting across from me. I imagined what would've happened if he had set down the bottle and drove to an AA meeting instead of off the road." The tears flowed like rivers down her cheeks. Each word came out in pained spurts. "Maybe things would've been different. Maybe you wouldn't have been so adamant on going to school so far away. Maybe I wouldn't have gone down the same path he did."

"Why didn't you call?" I asked, feeling the beginnings of sorrow broiling in my throat.

"I wanted to let you live your life without me. I didn't want to bring you down while you were making your way to the top. Was I mad that you threatened to drop out of school? Yes. Was I even *more* mad that you *actually* dropped out? Of course. But I couldn't stop being proud of you, and I didn't want to ruin that for you."

I nodded, neglecting to speak. While I had footslogged through the perpetual torment that was touring with Scyphozoa, my mother was… *proud* of me? The woman who was standoffish with me ever since I could remember. The woman who openly stated she regretted having me. The woman who lost her abusive husband and carried on his legacy of abuse in his absence.

"I don't have to forgive you, you know," I said.

"I don't expect you to."

"Then why did you clean up your act?"

"Because a mother's love is stronger than anything else. You know the statue of Atlas carrying the world on his back? He seems to be struggling to do that. A mother could take over and do slam dunks with that globe."

A slight chuckle passed my lips. When was the last time my mother made me laugh? A lump in my throat manifested. It pushed moisture to my eyes, but I didn't cry. I couldn't.

This was all too good to be true. I took a quick glance around the living room, stared into the kitchen where Jess had hidden away. Everything looked real. Everything felt lived in. The sense of malignant artificiality was nowhere to be felt. The Great King Rat, the Great One, whoever, wasn't here. The air felt calm, like a gentle caress after a bad day at school. Only I didn't have a bad day at school; I had been to hell and back, witnessing some of the worst horrors in the universe, things so terrifying the human mind could barely comprehend them.

No one—not even my mother—didn't deserve to know the gory details.

But I told her.

Every gruesome detail she could take.

3

She examined me with a fine-tooth comb, trying and failing to see find any signs of drug usage in my features, posture, the whole nine yards. Everything I told her was true, so much so that Jess found her way back from her secluded spot in the kitchen to the couch cushion beside me. She nodded in agreement, even with the grisliest and most terrible specifics.

I told my mother about the circumstances leading to my involvement with Scyphozoa; how I was a huge fan of the group, and was coming off a bad breakup, and they were touring, and they would be in Sanduhr for a gig, and the world's brightest light bulb had gone off in my head. I told her about the first few gigs. They were fun; I had the time of my life. But there was something dark brewing under the surface. Evelyn was condescending, Adam was comically high all the time as if he were desperately trying to hide something, Marty was... *Marty*, and Asher was the kingpin of all the queer happenings. I neglected to mention the New Year's incident. I neglected to mention Kyrie Castillo; a lapse in memory that was overshadowed by my sorrow involving both Lenny Vuala and Cameron Wright. And Cameron's poor mother, who was hopefully only knocked out inside that Colorado home instead of brutally murdered. Unlike her son, who had a soul so pure he didn't deserve to meet an end as gruesome as the one he got.

I told her about the Great King Rat; that ruthless pursuer that showed me tainted scenes from my past, using the people in my life as puppets to get what it wants. I told her about the visions of this very apartment, the grilled cheese, the tomato soup, my skinned body lying naked on my bed, the Rat using her as a skin suit as it gutted me like a fish.

I told her about the ritual, or the tiny bits I could surmise from fractured memories and Marty's frankly terrible explanation in his final moments. But once I mentioned the glyphs carved into Lenny's naked stomach, with Asher lying dead at the end of the bed, my mother got up from the armchair and said, "Stop. That's enough, Joel. I believe you."

"Seriously, Mom. You're in big fucking danger! Don't joke about this."

"There's no way in hell you're coming up with all this on the spot. Your father—hell, even your sister—would call bullshit immediately. There's this look in your eyes that's telling me you aren't lying. So, I believe you. Please, for the love of God, don't say anything else."

She beckoned me to stand, so I did. My mother brought me into an embrace far warmer than any other hug she'd given me in my twenty-one years of life. I felt her diaphragm hiccup as she choked down another spell of tears. "I'm just glad you're alright," she finally sobbed.

I lifted my arms and returned the embrace, to which she moved a hand to the back of my head, stroking my curls with the tenderness of a mother's heart.

She had told me I didn't have to forgive her, but in that moment I did. We cried together, mother and son.

4

I slept in the comfort of my childhood bed. I dreamed of nothing, as if someone had stolen my ability to do so. Jess slept in Bethany's vacant bedroom. She needed one night to herself, something I completely understood. It's like the social battery phenomenon in college. You interact with so many people during the day that when you get home you can't stand the thought of seeing another human being for at least twelve hours. Only she had been around the same four people for years. A bystander to their misdeeds. If I were her, I would have slept for centuries, let alone only eight hours.

I woke up to the faint aroma of cigarette smoke. I slid from bed and tiredly stumbled out of the room and toward the balcony. The door was left slightly ajar. Cold air caressed my face. A bead of snot dribbled from my nose. I wiped it with the back of my hand as Jess came into view on the balcony, a cigarette perched between her lips.

She wore Bethany's clothes better than Bethany ever could. Bless her soul, but my sister was hopeless when it came to putting an outfit together that didn't make her look like a complete bum. A cream-colored beanie sat upon Jess's head; a thick, gray winter jacket wrapped itself around her. I walked a little further and noticed she was standing with my mother. She wore a fluffy, green bathrobe and a pair of equally fluffy slippers. A lighter was lodged in her hand, but no cigarette in her mouth to accompany it.

"Thank you, again," Jess said to her. "You know, for the smoke."

"It's no problem, Jessica. I needed to get rid of that pack, anyway. I only had that as a last resort in case things got rough, but relapsing is a whole lot worse than whatever comes my way at work," my mother said with a chuckle.

I decided to not interrupt. I quietly slipped onto the couch and lay facing away from the balcony, listening intently to their conversation.

"So, where are you from? I've seen you in the videos with Joel. Have you been in the band for a while?"

Jess exhaled a sigh of smoke and said: "I... honestly don't know where I come from. My parents never told me where I was born. They never put me in school. We travelled all over the place until one day..." A painful pause. "I'm sorry. I shouldn't trauma-dump on you. We just met last night."

"No, no. It's alright. My daughter's a psychologist. She gets the listening genes from me."

"Well," Jess continued as she pulled from the nearly empty cigarette, "they left me. In a park. I think it was somewhere over in Pennsylvania. Actually... yeah, I *know* it was in Pennsylvania because the first place I went to for help was a cheesesteak place. I just ran in there, my face all wet from crying, asking the manager for their phone. 'Can I use your phone?' 'Is there a payphone?' 'Do you have any quarters?' 'I'm lost, please help me.'

"It was a burly Indian man in there, I remember that much. He wasn't an employee, but he tapped me on the shoulder and handed me his cellphone. But I was so... I was so overwrought with anxiety I just... I just couldn't remember my parents' phone numbers. Neither one of them. I even asked that man, 'Do you know my mom's number?'" Jess laughed in the morbid hilarity of it. A joke with a punchline only she understood. "I left that place and just wandered the city. And to be honest with you, I don't think I ever stopped wandering. Half the time, I don't really know where I am. I just go from place to place, never taking in the life I was granted and the life that was stolen from me when my parents dropped me off at that park and left me forever.

"For the first year, my only goal was to find my parents. It was stupid. Well, I mean I was *obviously* stupid, since I was nine going on ten. I still clung to the hope that they had simply misplaced me like a sock in a laundromat. Because what else was I supposed to think? I was so little. Sure, I wouldn't say I had much of a childhood leading up to that, but it's not like I *wasn't* a lost little girl, you know?"

"I understand."

"If this gets to be too much, I'm sorry. I just, haven't been able to vent in so long."

"You can stop whenever you need to."

"Thank you." The click of a lighter echoed into the living room as Jess lit up another and inhaled deeply. "I got thrown into foster care when I was eleven. I guess being a nomadic preteen wasn't *technically* legal. My first foster family was a bunch of cunts, pardon my French, but the second one was a big improvement. They actually gave me a bed instead of some stiff cot in the basement; they weren't in it for the money like that first family, I guess. While they were great for a time, they were still kinda strict. Mrs. Wenders, the foster mom, forced me to take piano *and* guitar lessons. She said, 'I'm going to make a prodigy out of you.' I was a bit apprehensive at first, but honestly, I think that was just the early onset puberty talking. I grew to love it, I think. Playing piano made me feel so just… expressive in a way that I couldn't be through plain words or conversation or whatever. Moved from Mozart to Bach to Joplin. And the guitar lessons. Oh, those guitar lessons! My teacher was an absolute sweetheart. I think he was fresh out of college with a guitar performance degree, but was falling on hard times. But you could never tell with him. He was always smiling and encouraging me to push forward even when my fingers slipped to the wrong chord."

"What's your favorite song to play?"

"'Love of My Life.' That Queen song."

My mother laughed, saying, "One time, I came home late from work, and Joel was already home from school. When I tell you he was *screaming* the lyrics to that song, oh my God. He had his headphones in and couldn't hear that I was home, so I opened his door and sat and listened for a bit. It was almost like Freddie Mercury himself was in my home. But he eventually noticed I was home and yelled, 'Get out! Get out, Mom!'"

Jess erupted in a cacophonous mix of laughter and coughing.

"Didn't know he could sing, too," Jessica joked.

"Should've known from that moment he'd be in a band someday."

"I just wish it could've been a different one. Scyphozoa isn't the best group for someone with goals and dreams like his. They're… so *suffocating*. They reel you in and leave you out to dry. Even without all the cult stuff."

"How'd *you* get in that band, though?"

"Well, I eventually got kicked out of the foster system. Being eighteen and all didn't help my chances in staying with that family. I got kicked from the system; they didn't want to adopt me. Simple as that. I eventually had my GED by the time they threw me back onto the street, but I had no way of applying to colleges or anything like that. I couldn't find jobs any-where…" An ominous pause. "So, I found other means to pay for myself. I'm not gonna get into it. But eventually my life coincided with Scyphozoa. In a bar, of all places. I'd found a poster on some lamppost saying that there was a band in need of a keyboard player. I hadn't played in such a long goddamn time, but the money was decent enough so I look my chances and called the number. Two nights later, I was in that musty bar playing simple chords underneath some frat guy's terrible singing. Asher Gaumont was there in the crowd."

"Asher's the lead singer, right?"

"Yeah," Jess agreed with another cigarette pull. "And he was off from the moment I laid eyes on him. But back then, he didn't look the way he does now. He was all skinny and malformed like some mutant beanpole. His hair was long and greasy, and he looked like a single gust of wind could pick him up and blow him to Saturn. But his voice. God, his voice. So soothing and persuasive. That's how he got me. He convinced me to throw my nothing of a life away to play keyboard for his indie band that had just started. As the months passed, though, he started to look healthier. His muscles ballooned and his jawline popped out. But I never saw him go to a gym. Never caught him doing pushups in his room. It just… happened. As naturally as the leaves will shrivel up and die in autumn.

"Him and I were close. I told him nearly everything about my shithole life, and he told me things about his, even if he obviously skirted around some vital things. It even got so intimate that we fucked a few times. Sorry for saying fuck, but that's what it was. We *fucked*. After the last time, he wanted nothing to do with me, but he kept me around. In all honesty, I barely talked to anyone in Scyphozoa until Kyrie came around. He was our new replacement for our trombone player, after our first one died of an overdose. I loved Kyrie so much; he was so pure and sweet it was intoxicating. He was basically the brother I always wanted but never had. I should've done more for him. I should've told him to quit while he was ahead. But Asher had a grip on him so strong he couldn't. Kyrie was in love with him; anyone could see that. And at this point, I knew what Asher and the others were involving themselves in. Something so terrible that I can't even call it demonic shit. It's more than that, something cosmic. Like those Lovecraft stories. You know the ones?"

"I think so."

"And that's what I felt for your son when he showed up. I was absolutely terrified for him because I knew Asher's endgame. But there's this power they have over me that wouldn't let me help Joel. I couldn't do *anything* until it was too late. I'm sorry I couldn't get him out sooner, Julie."

"That's alright, Jessica," my mother said. "I'm just glad he found his way home."

5

Mom went to work an hour later. She made Jess and I scrambled eggs and bacon before she headed out into the icy Chicago winter. As we ate in silence, a thought bombarded my mind. It was early January in the Windy City, and said wind howled through the rooftops of hundreds of neighboring buildings.

"Have you felt it?" I said, sipping a glass of iced tea.

"Felt what?" Jess asked after swallowing a mouthful of eggs.

"Like, a presence."

"You mean *the Great One?*" she mocked.

"Yeah, that."

"Nope. Not since we got dumped here."

"It feels… good. Like, *really* good. It's like I've been holding my breath since November and just now let it out."

255

"Try holding in your breath for three years."

"Let's not make this a competition. I'm trying to make a point."

"And that is?"

I paused, hesitating to say what I felt was true.

"We're free," I said.

"But they'll find us."

"Free *for now*. What are the odds they find us right now? In an hour? A day? A *week* from now?"

"I guess you're right," Jess said.

"Let's go have some fun."

CHAPTER XVI

1

My idea of "fun" involved heading down the street to the Loop area to sit my ass down and listen to the Chicago Symphony Orchestra play whatever they had planned for the night.

Jess and I walked through the halls before the show started. I immediately showed her the concessions stand with a bar shaped like a gigantic cello on its side. She beamed with a sense of astonishment I hadn't seen on her usually stoic face. She ordered a cheap plastic cup of wine, neglecting to realize she left her money in Colorado. I paid for the overpriced drink, buying myself a gin and tonic.

We sat down in seats that felt miles away from the stage. The concert hall was spacious in its enormity. Intricate designs carved the walls, harkening back to an era long gone. The walls were white, the seats a deep red. An arch of those same red seats encircled the main stage where an orchestra would soon make its appearance. The performers' seats were perfectly symmetrical with the conductor's stand in the center, closest to the drop-off where the stage became audience seats.

Jess sat with her arms tucked in her lap. She hadn't removed either Bethany's coat or beanie since we arrived. "Aren't you warm?" I asked as a sea of elderly people poured into the hall.

"Do you even know what we're gonna be watching?" she asked, ignoring my question.

"Yeah, but I'm not telling you."

"Why?"

"Why should I tell you?"

"Because I wanna look up how long it is so I know when we're gonna leave."

"Come on, now. It's not gonna kill you to sit for… however long we're gonna be sitting here."

"I just don't feel safe. I know we're far away from them for now, and that *thing* isn't gonna be prowling around without them to tether itself to. But you must understand, Joel. I haven't really been out since I joined that damn band. Sure, we'd go to a bar occasionally after shows, and I'd get to see the outside world when we got off the bus and walked a few feet to a hotel or Airbnb house. I've been trapped in a cage with them that just so happens to move across the country constantly."

"You're safe," I assured.

"How can you be sure?"

"I'm not, but I'm here with you. That should be enough."

The ensemble filed onto the stage, they tuned, and the conductor made her grand entrance to rapturous applause. She was clad in a sleek black suit; her blond hair was tightly bound in a ponytail. The conductor bowed, motioned toward the ensemble, and continued her trek toward her position at the middle of the stage.

To my relief, she didn't make some grandiose speech before the show started, describing the piece in a way that allows for no individuals in the audience to interpret the work on their own. Jess continued to keep her hands clasped in her lap. Luckily, we were the only people in our section of the hall. We were so high up you could almost touch the clouds.

The conductor lifted her baton; the ensemble readied themselves in one swift motion. The hall grew silent with anticipation. The air was thick with suspense. Everyone was eager for the baton to drop and the music to begin.

And then it started.

Sweeping string lines, bits of brass flourishes, beautiful woodwind phrases. All these mixed in the stew that was Mahler's second symphony.

Over the course of the panoramic piece, Jess loosened her grip. Her hands slowly maneuvered toward her seat's armrests. By the time the fifth movement roared into the hall, any semblance of stress evaporated from her like a puddle on a hot summer day in Arizona. She was completely and utterly enamored with Mahler's masterpiece; one I had seen performed once before at Sanduhr University's concert hall. The melody, the harmonies, the chords all possessed her with a deep sense of belonging in a world she seemed shunned from all her life.

The trombones toward the back of the ensemble boomed with a wall of sound as their main feature in the piece made its appearance. The melody was damning, angry. There was a rage behind every note that felt like a torpedo of unrestrained fury. Despite the ferocity of that section, Jess poked at my hand with her pinky. I looked down at both our hands; her eyes were locked on the ensemble. I twitched; her pinky curled and led the rest of her fingers into the hollows between mine.

We held each other as the music crescendoed to the symphony's conclusion. The choir, who had been sitting in silence for the entire performance thus far, finally came into the scene with voices as angelic as Mahler intended. It was his "Resurrection" symphony, after all. The conductor waved her arms with controlled barbarity. The violins, violas and cellos all looked as if their arms would fall off if the tempo increased even one more beat per minute. Music captured the hall. Nothing could escape the rhythm, the beauty of it all.

In an instant, the ensemble hushed. A faint hum of tones echoed throughout the hall, but the orchestra played on. In the final moments of Mahler's second, the music calmed yet kept that same fierce quality from minutes before. As the harmonies swelled, I vaguely heard Jess's seat creak next to mine. She leaned to lean, cupped a hand on my cheek, and drew me in for a kiss.

For a brief time, I forgot I was human.

I became nothing in the back row of the Chicago Symphony Orchestra's concert hall. I had taken up space in the universe with my useless atoms, but they were no more. Nothing else mattered except for that kiss. My ties to life and the people around me disintegrated; my shackles became unbound.

Roselle was just a name.

Jessica Fitzgerald was real.

2

It looked like a tornado had materialized solely within the apartment and tore everything to shreds. The door was barely on its hinges when we got back to the complex. Papers and various shattered glassware were strewn across the floor.

I shouted for my mother, pleading for her to come out of hiding. Because if there was one thing all of us Augustes had in common: we were good at hiding from our problems. But this problem looked to be way too severe for Julie to scamper away from.

My shoes crunched over bits of broken plates and picture frames as I frantically searched the apartment room by room. When my searching bore no fruit, I rang her up on my phone. She went straight to voicemail the first time. I checked my bars. A full four with 5G. I called her again. No answer. Just the voicemail. And I called again… and again… and again.

"Hello! This is Julianna Auguste! I'm currently not at the phone right now, so leave a message and I'll call you back as soon as I can. Goodbye!"

"At the tone, please record your message—"

I hung up. My eyes were ready to burst from their sockets. Jess sifted through the remnants of the living room. *What the hell happened?* I wondered. *What the actual* fuck *happened?*

My mind raced with the possibilities. Maybe a group of burglars were having a tough day and decided to raid a single mother's Chicago apartment? But none of the other units had been ransacked, and surely not to *this* degree. It was all too targeted. Too calculated. There was a meticulousness in the carnage. The perpetrators hadn't caused all this damage. Everything could have remained untouched if my mother hadn't fought back.

But against *who?*

I knew the answer; I'm sure you do, too.

I didn't want to believe it, even when Jess lifted a crumpled piece of notebook paper from the relatively untarnished armchair. "Joel?" she said. "There's blood on this. It hasn't even dried yet."

I swerved around the toppled couch and grabbed the note. Wet blood stamped onto my fingers as I unwrapped that dreadful wad of paper. Printed in the cleanest handwriting I had ever seen, there was a note hidden inside.

> *Hope you enjoyed the orchestra!*
> *They really sounded __amazing__ tonight.*
> *Wish we could've stayed for the finale.*
> *Guess you can tell your mother all about it*
> *when you get back to Sanduhr.*
> *You'll know where to find us.*
>
> *Sincerely,*
> *Ash*

"What're we supposed to do?" Jess asked.

"We call the police," I said bluntly.

"The police? Those fucks will never believe us. They'll lock us up before they even consider going after them."

"I guess… there's nothing else to do but do what Asher wants."

"Him and the rest will kill us both if we follow them."

I peered at the individual framed photos of my mother, Bethany, and myself, all shattered from the violence that ensued mere minutes before we arrived.

"They'll kill my mom regardless," I said. "We might as well try to save her from whatever the hell they have planned for her back in Sanduhr."

Jess nodded.

We trudged through the debris and out the broken door.

Before the sun had a chance to rise, we were on a flight from O'Hare to Boston.

MOVEMENT IV
GREAT KING RAT

CHAPTER XVII

1

Years before, my family visited my grandparents on my mother's side. We didn't really do too much during that little vacation. I was relieved to be away from the trials and tribulations middle school presented. All the judgmental stares, the various cliques, the teachers who wanted to teach at universities, but couldn't, instead taking their anger out on the students.

Their house was a quaint little cottage erected in some ancient suburb. White and gray stone outlined the structure, adorned with pink shingles that lined the wood-framed windows. The roof was a similar pink, only a bit duller and browner from years of age and rainfall.

My father had knocked himself out with half a bottle of whiskey, my mother was in the kitchen arguing with her parents, Bethany was in the guest bedroom chatting with her school friend on her Blackberry. I sat on the couch and perched over the back cushions, staring out the front window, gazing out to the dimly lit street in the dead of night.

There was a car out there. A black SUV that you could barely see if it weren't for the lamppost reflecting light off its sheen. Exhaust fumed from the tailpipe, but the headlights were off. I wondered if anyone else in the neighborhood could see the minivan. And if they could, I wondered if they were seeing the same minivan I saw. Because, to an adult, it might have been completely normal for a black SUV to be parked outside with its lights off and smoke billowing from its exhaust pipe. But to me, a band kid blossoming into his terrible teens, that SUV was the most terrifying thing I had ever seen. The unknown was darker than the known. There may have been someone behind the wheel. They could've been staring directly at me through the tint of night. For some odd reason, though, I couldn't look away. The unknown—no matter how petrifying; no matter the depths to which it can take your psyche—is the most intriguing aspect of life. Like a car crash, we can never look away, even if we have no idea *what* we're looking at.

Eventually, still with the headlights off, the minivan slowly crept down the road and out of sight. It came back around, plodding along at a snail's pace as if the driver were taunting me. It came again, once more, another time. The minivan's route was hypnotic, unpleasant. I knew that if the driver's side window rolled down, I wouldn't see anyone behind the wheel.

Just a pair of glowing white dots where eyes should be.

2

Jess navigated the airport rental car around the streets of Sanduhr, Massachusetts with that same hypnotic cadence.

Every pothole felt like a monstrous abyss with the deliberate speed she drove the Honda Civic at. The Sanduhr suburbs were quite like the one my grandparents lived in. The roads were chipped and cracked from years of water and ice damage, the foliage was dense despite the lack of leaves in the winter, and the homes were picturesque in their stature. Through the wooden claws of tree branches, you could see the faint outline of Sanduhr's downtown area. A dark spot in the hollow of brightly lit buildings pinpointed the university's location.

"There was a power outage at the university," I said, recalling something I had read online once the plane had landed in Boston. "And the roads are so icy that maintenance can't get out to the breakers to fix anything."

"You're telling me," Jess joked. "I've been trying to *not* hydroplane since we got into city limits. I can't believe you *chose* to go to school here."

"I can't believe it, either."

We were the only ones on the roads due to the weather. While Sanduhr could never claim to be a busy town, especially when compared to the Boston behemoth a few miles west, I'd never seen the streets as empty as they were that day. The silence was deafening, the lack of life eerie in its deficiency. I thought of the bustling streets teeming with college life. People traveling from their dorms and apartments to their classes, students riding bikes and electric scooters when they're late for wherever they are needed, cars honking at other drivers who made multiple traffic violations within the span of a short few seconds. Those were all memories, though. Everyone was shut in; doors locked; windows shuttered. Not a single moving car dotted the roads. The vehicles parked outside were caked in thick sheets of ice like melted glass. And those trees; those damn trees. Their branches twisted at jarring angles, pointing at us and laughing with the voices of the wind.

You're gonna die here.

Welcome home, Joel.

You're gonna burn in hell, fuckface!

Jess drove slowly around a sharp turn onto the main road that sliced Sanduhr in two. The back tires skidded as the turn reached its end, rattling the sedan's cabin. "Why couldn't the airport have four-wheel drives?" she asked. We slid down Main Street like kids sledding down a slick, snowy hill. Traffic lights were out of the question; the sedan slid through red light after red light.

We made it to Sanduhr University's campus a whole hour later. The sun had set within that time. The glow of dusk basked in teardrop icicles hanging from the trees and gutters. The car rolled around the campus's main library; a daunting building too large to be stationed at a New England college. In the glow of the setting sun, the building towered over the horizon, blocking out the world. The lights were out, the windows dark with the lack of power surging through the university. *Guess no one thought to invest in backup generators*, I thought.

"What's the plan now?" Jess asked. "What did the note say again?"

I fumbled around in my pocket and pulled out the bloodied note Asher had written.

"Other than him saying my mom will be waiting for us in Sanduhr," I said, "the only other hint is 'You'll know where to find us.' What the hell is that supposed to mean? This isn't some National Treasure bullshit; they kidnapped my fucking mom and brought her here. It's not some sort of riddle or anything."

"He didn't say, '*you* know.' He said, 'you *will* know.'"

"And?"

"Asher's a songwriter. He likes to plant little references and clues in his lyrics, no matter how stupid I think most of them are. '*You hated me and my bottle of Jack, So why'd you keep coming back?*' Like, come on. That's so stupid. A middle schooler could write something deeper than that."

"You know, I actually thought 'Frictional Fiction' was good before you said the lyrics instead of singing them."

"No one gives instrumentals enough credit," she scoffed. "Good music will always make up for shit lyrics. That's the one constant in the music industry. Taylor Swift would be out of business if people could hear her over the instrumentals."

The car crushed the ice lying over a pothole and violently hitched. Jess continued: "He said, 'you *will*' because he knows we will eventually know where to find them. Like how we guessed the power outage that's only affecting the campus has something to do with them. Great! Awesome! Step one complete! But then there's the next step to worry about. And the next. And wherever they take us, promise me something."

"What's that?" I asked. Her eyes stayed locked on the road as if the street would disappear if she looked away.

"No matter what happens, survive. Let those bastards know who they're fucking with."

3

A modest flurry of snow descended from the dark heavens as the sun fully disappeared. The only light at Sanduhr University came from the bright headlights of our rented Civic, shooting beams of yellow glow into that cold, damning night.

In the headlights, there was a dark spot like a dead pixel on a flatscreen TV. Something so minuscule, yet so noticeable all the same. As Jess slowly approached the spot, it grew and took the shape of a person, only it wasn't a person.

It was the Great One.

That Great King Rat.

"We're close," Jess said. "It only stays close to where Asher is."

The car inched further and further toward him. The wheels bumped over blocks of ice and crunched over the road's newly laid layer of snow. Jess didn't hover her foot over the brake; she let the Civic coast forward. I breathed heavily, as if I were laying on the ground and someone sat on my chest, not allowing air to flow through my lungs as my ribs compressed them.

Jess didn't falter. She approached the Great King Rat with the normalcy of two roommates seeing each other after a grueling day of classes. She'd been living under the looming threat of the King Rat for so long that fear was out of the question. She was coming home, in a way. Into the loving embrace of the epitome of evil. A cosmic terror so profound and otherworldly it couldn't take a completely physical form in our mundane world. He could only take the shape of a man, but with some caveats. It was a pale imitation, something copied from years (centuries? millennia?) of observing us, watching us, mimicking us. And he stood mere inches from the hood of the rental car, taking in the light emitting from the headlights and offering nothing in return. A black hole with arms and legs and white, glowing eyes.

"My children," it said. Its guttural voice boomed throughout the car as if it were in the back seat with us. "Scyphozoa awaits."

"Fantastic," Jess remarked, continuing forward.

The car glided through the Great King Rat's figure. The creature evaporated into a billowing cloud of black smoke. Its eyes remained seared into my corneas like a tattoo etched into my vision. I blinked and I could still see them on the backs of my eyelids.

Always watching.

"They're at the School of Music," I said, not knowing where the thought came from. But I was sure they were there. Something inside me told me so, whispering the answer as if it were sacred and true.

"Take a right here."

4

There we were, standing outside the front door of the building I swore off two months before. The place I spent countless hours in preparing from an impromptu audition for an indie band I adored. The place where I wore rose-tinted glasses as I played and practiced and poured my soul into the art of trombone, the art of music, the art of that universal language. I remembered sitting in practice room 218 with the lights off and my earbuds in, listening to music from all genres and backgrounds as I calmed myself down from another stressful day of being a Fine Arts student at a research university.

Jess and I carefully walked to the front door, making certain not to slip on the ice. I intoned a Hail Mary and tugged on the door handle. It was frigid to the touch, but the glass door creaked open instead of buckling against a locking mechanism.

Inside, the cold didn't let up. The heating system was down, as were the lights. I pulled out my phone and shone the flashlight; Jess did the same. "Where do you think they are?" I asked.

"I don't know," she replied. "*You're* the one who used to go here. It doesn't look like that big of a building, so we'll find them eventually. We got all the time in the world."

"Not really," I said.

"Where should we start?"

"We can go around the offices on the first floor. If no one's in the room, close it tight and lock the door. We check them off the list one by one until there's none left to check. Then we'll move upstairs to the practice rooms, and then downstairs to the rehearsal rooms."

"Sounds good."

I took one side of the administrative hallway, and Jess took the other. We searched room after room, each bathed in darkness; the only hint of life inside being whatever my flashlight caught in its beam. Empty coffee mugs, graded final exams from the previous semester, some instruments tucked away in cases or propped up on stands. Halfway down the hall, I entered my trombone professor's office. An assortment of instruments was neatly displayed in the corner by a shelf filled to the brim with lead sheets and other scores. But no Asher… or his little henchmen… or the demon who had them all under its thumb.

I shut the door and moved onto the next. The French horn professor's office was next, but before I could open her door, I heard a loud clatter from a few doors back. It came from Jess's side of the hallway.

I raced down to the source of the noise and slid into the doorframe, knocking the wind out of myself. I fumbled for my phone; shone the light into the office. Among a wreck of cellos toppled over like musical dominos—in the rubble caused by so much violence in such a short period of time—stood Evelyn Stone. She had Jess in a chokehold. Her hair was matted against Evelyn's body, sopping wet. The pungent odor of gasoline filled the air. Jess wriggled around, kicking her legs like a wild animal caught in a trap. She grunted, the only noise she could muster was a horrific choking noise.

Evelyn looked sick. Her cheekbones were more pronounced than ever. Her eye sockets were clear as day in the glow of my flashlight. The harsh light accentuated every bone that jutted from her frame. She was clad in some disgustingly unclean undergarments. A bra and panties crisp with dried mud. "Just crawl out of a ditch to get here?" I asked, still catching my breath.

"I wouldn't make any more smartass comments if I were you," she said. Even her voice sounded sick. A shrill rasp coated every syllable. "Not out loud, and not in that fucking awful head of yours. I can't stand to listen to you anymore."

"Let her go, Evie. She didn't do anything wrong."

"SHE HELPED YOU KILL MARTY!"

Evelyn jerked Jess violently when she attempted to kick her way out of the chokehold again. "I didn't like the fucker, to be fair," Evelyn continued. "But we *needed* him. Don't you see that now? I know she's been feeding you all these lies about us. Tell him, Jess. Did you lie to him?"

Jess coughed up a morsel of blood. It dribbled down her chin like fruit punch mixed with gelatin and molasses.

"Right, I forgot," Evelyn said. "You were never one for words."

"Quit it!" I shouted.

I took a step forward, to which she pulled out an old flip lighter.

"I wouldn't do that if I were you," she grinned. "You've already done enough damage. Surely you don't wanna be the reason this cuntass bitch turns into a fucking fireball." Evelyn laughed, coughed from the force, and laughed some more. "You always thought her hair looked like fire, didn't you? You were *constantly* thinking that. Every time you two were in the room together, it was always: 'Her red hair looks like a beautiful flame... Oh my! What a gorgeous head of fire on that girl!'"

"Stop," I said.

"And now your wish will be granted, you bastard. All you have to do is take another step forward. Come on... do it."

She flicked the lighter open. A small flame burst from the exhaust and settled a moment or two later.

"Come on, lover boy," she taunted. "I fucking dare you."

I looked into Jess's eyes. They bulged, bursting with untamed fear and rage. The theatrical nature of Evelyn's murder attempt was admirably twisted. I honestly didn't know what to do. I was unarmed, save for the phone in my hand.

"What else can I to do?" I asked.

"Leave us be," she said. "I have some business to attend to with Miss Jessica here. But don't worry..." Evelyn rubbed her gaunt cheek against

Jess's head like a child snuggling with a stuffed animal. "I'll take *good* care of her. Just have some kinks to sort out. Then she'll be good as new. Ash is in some band room downstairs. Don't mind my brother, though. He's lurking around upstairs trying to get the jump on you."

She winked, her wrinkly eyelid sliding over a bloodshot eye. "Don't tell him I said that. Only if you see him, though. Have fun!"

"Is my mom down there with Asher?"

She smiled a wretched grin. Her teeth, usually white, were stained yellow like she'd drank thousands of gallons of sweet tea and smoked a million cigarettes since I saw her last. "I guess you'll just have to check for yourself."

"I guess I will."

The lighter flickered, dancing its macabre flamenco in that dire moment. I felt drawn to the flame like a swarm of moths flying into a bonfire. There was nothing else in the world except that little fire and Jessica. I kept completely still, only allowing my chest to move with the rise and fall of my shallow yet succinct breaths.

"Don't think about it now," Evelyn said. "I can hear that brain of yours. Just walk away and leave us alone."

The hand holding the lighter quivered. The flame bobbed and weaved with the motions. *I'm gonna walk away*, I thought. *I'm gonna walk away and never come back. I'll* run *away if you want. I'll be your lapdog, bitch. Just don't hurt her. I'll walk away.*

"That's the spirit," she responded. "Go on, now."

I'm leaving now. Don't worry about me.

"It's not that serious, Joel. Get the fuck out."

I hadn't moved yet, despite thinking I would. I poured those thoughts into Evelyn's ears, deafening her demonic power with repeated phrases and incessant lies. But they weren't lies. They were facts, the truth. Sure, I would leave and find Asher. I would find my mother, who didn't deserve to be involved in whatever the hell any of this was. I would leave the room with its tiles drenched in petrol.

I'll see you around.

Evelyn cocked an eyebrow. "I'll... see you arou—"

I charged at her like a police squad with a battering ram. She didn't scream or attempt to move out of the way. She stood completely still, Jess wriggling beneath her tight grip. Thinking she had the upper hand, Evelyn dropped the silver lighter. Time seemed to slow to a grinding halt. The lighter plummeted, swimming down through the air like someone wading through lava solidifying into obsidian.

I swatted at the lighter before it could make contact with the gas puddle. It snapped shut as it flew into a dry corner and became enshrouded in the darkness residing there.

"You fucker!" Evelyn roared.

She released Jess, letting her fall to the ground, but not before Jess hit her head on the corner of the office desk. She went limp on the floor. A few drops of blood beaded from the newly open wound in her forehead.

Evelyn reached into her pocket and pulled out something dark and metallic. Before she could raise her arm any further, I grabbed her wrist. She used her other arm to slug one across my face. The pain blossomed on my cheek like a wildflower. It surged through me like fungi on a felled tree deep in the woods. I kept my grip on her hand. It was half-submerged in her pocket, yet I saw the glint of a pistol. A small peashooter. Small enough to fit in her pocket, packing enough punch to blow a hole between my eyes.

She laid onto me again. I heard a bone crack. It could've been her knuckle; it could've been my jaw. I was running on nothing but adrenaline and a childlike sense of hope. I squeezed her wrist as another punch collided. She was screaming. One continuous note raspy and throaty and filled with gravel. The gravel that lined Cameron's driveway back in Aurora. The gravel his blood soaked, filling each uneven crevice with red liquid. I squeezed her wrist harder and harder, putting the rest of my waning strength into crushing every intricate, tiny bone connecting her hand to her arm.

I wanted to rip her to pieces.

A wet crunch sounded as every muscle in my body reached the point of overexertion.

"FUCKING SHIT!" she yelped.

I finally released my grip as she stumbled away and into a bookshelf.

She dropped the pistol from her hand. The hand hung from mere threads of nerves and tissues, the bones in her wrist snapped beyond comprehension. She cradled her mangled appendage as printed musical scores toppled over her. I held the gun, felt the weight. For such a small firearm, it had some serious heft.

As she continued to writhe in pain, I slipped the pistol into my pocket and caught the glint of the fallen lighter. I rose from the floor, grabbed the lighter, and went over to Jess. She was out for the count. I wrapped my hands around her shoulders and dragged her from the office. I propped her up on a wall outside the room, examining her head wound. I brushed a lock of hair from her eyes and planted a kiss on her forehead. Drops of blood smeared onto my lips, but there were worse things to worry about.

I stood in the doorway. My flashlight beamed into the room. Harsh angles lit up in the gloom.

I flicked the lighter open. It spewed a few sparks yet released no flame. I clasped it shut and reopened it. Second time was the charm, as a small fire glowed orange to my strange delight.

"Bitch," I said.

Evelyn Stone didn't have any final words, only horrified shrieks. As I dropped the lighter into the pool of gasoline, it ignited into a great sea of fire. The rings of flame encompassed every corner of the puddle before contacting her. When it did, a brilliant light consumed her. She screamed, bursting a few blood vessels the louder her powerful wails became. Those blood vessels fused to her slowly melting skin. Evelyn bubbled and dripped like an ice cream cone by the beach, revealing nothing but red underneath her usual paleness. Her painful tears evaporated in the heat.

The fire tickled the ceiling before I found it necessary to use a fire extinguisher.

I wanted her to feel true pain.

No one knew exactly where she came from, what she did with her life before entering the gates of Scyphozoa. But I know exactly where she went when her clock ran out:

Straight to hell.

5

I extinguished the fire before the entire room became nothing more than a pile of ash and rubble. In the aftermath, there was nothing but crispy, blackened paper and the charred body that used to carry the soul of that goddamn percussionist.

Her eyes had burst and melted down her ashen face, leaving a trail of viscous jelly in their wake. That blond hair of hers was all gone. Between the cracks of flaking skin, chasms of congealed blood peered through. She was the surface of Death Valley grafted onto a somewhat human form. A Pompeii victim in the 21st century; the volcano localized entirely within a Sanduhr University office.

I couldn't stomach the slight, let alone the smell. I covered my nose and turned into the hallway. Vomit erupted in a short burst of previously eaten airline pretzels.

Jess wasn't where I left her.

I wiped my mouth and exploded into hysterics.

"Jess?" I yelled. "Jess! Where are you?"

Silence.

I heard footsteps above my head. The slow *clomp* of snow boots.

The brother Stone was on the prowl.

CHAPTER XVIII

1

With the pistol in my right hand and my phone in the left, I silently climbed the staircase to the second floor. The wind whistled and howled; someone must've left a window open. The air chilled. Hot breath fogged my sight like a windshield before hitting the defrost button. Either the cold caused my trigger finger to tremble, or the overwhelming nerves brought on the frigid shiver.

I clenched my jaw to negate my chattering teeth. I took my breaths slowly and in increments. I recalled my time in high school marching band. You can't stomp around the football field when moving from one set to the next, forming indecipherable shapes against the green turf. You must roll your step; start on the heel, roll over the arch, and end on the ball of your foot. I rolled each step walking down the hallway, shining my flashlight through each door's window.

The numbers passed. Room 201… 202… 203. My face throbbed with pain, the last living remnant of Evelyn Stone haunting my nerves. An ominous aura filled the hallway with every room I checked. Empty spaces; abandoned places. Not a hint of life. Even Adam's footsteps had ceased. A hollow pit of silence bombarded my senses. I picked my chapped lips and discarded the flaking skin. A pang twinged there, ebbing with the droplet of blood seeping from the newly opened wound.

I made it to practice room 218. There was no time for reminiscing, but the urge was too great. I thought of the countless hours I spent perfecting my craft. Memorizing partials and slide positions and entire songs; maybe this note should be a little sharper or flatter. Screaming profanities whenever I fucked up the solo in "Drive." Neglecting the few people I had to talk to when school was in session. Becoming a truant. Refusing to go to classes I didn't care for. Scyphozoa was everything I needed.

Nothing of note inside that room, much to my relief. I didn't need any more trauma tied to room 218. I turned around and faced the dreaded room 217: the largest practice room in the building, almost comically so. I pushed down on the handle, felt the door jamb click, and opened it slow and steady, shining my light into the dark with the peashooter in tow.

I heard the plucking of piano keys.

"How're you doing, Joel?"

2

"Hey, Adam," I said.

"You're not going to answer my question?"

He sat at the piano with his back turned to me. He played a somber melody, tickling the ivories to the tune of Beethoven.

"I'm…" I choked on my words. "I'm doing fine, Adam."

"That's wonderful."

"You know why I'm here," I said, sifting past the bullshit.

"I know."

"And you know I have a gun."

"I know. I just want to talk."

"What if *I* don't want to talk?" I asked.

"Then that's your choice," he said as *Moonlight Sonata* continued. "But I think you want some answers, and I'm willing to give them to you before your time is up."

There was a finality to those last few words. A sureness in his tone that was unwavering. It shook me to my core. I lowered the pistol.

He continued to play as he said, "Asher calls it Scyphozoa, Marty called it The Great One, you called it The Man in Black, but now you call it The Great King Rat. That one must be my favorite. Like, I understand why Asher calls it what he calls it; I *don't* understand Marty's lazy term for it. But your name is so full of hate, so much creativity. I've always liked that about you, ever since you popped into that alleyway. I knew your name already, sure, but I didn't know *you*. That night, you were so full of disdain and drive: two things that are essential for this line of work. The Great King Rat isn't real, Joel. At least, not to our human minds. There needs to be a sort of catalyst present to be able to perceive it. It lives inside all of us, even you. Its children."

"What the fuck are you talking about?"

"We carry its children. That's what gives us eyes. There's a fully formed offspring in my system, wriggling around in there. There's one inside you, too. Right there in the nape of your neck."

I held the pistol and my phone in one hand, felt the back of my neck with the other. There was a bump there. I thought it was a groove in my spine, peeking through my skin. But then it squirmed. I screamed into the cold. Now that I was aware of something living inside my skin, I couldn't stop feeling it.

"What the *hell* is that?" I yelled.

"Its children, Joel. We carry its babies."

"Oh my God." I stepped back, reeling from the knowledge that there was something inside me, squirming and wriggling with life. "You're lying," I said. "You're fucking lying."

"There's no other explanation, Joel. But even with the vast knowledge the Great King Rat has bestowed upon me, the *one* thing I don't know is where *it* came from. I'm cursed with the burden of knowing, but I'm more cursed with the one piece of knowledge that slipped away. And for that, I'm sorry. Some things are better left forgotten, I suppose."

An academic sort of tone seasoned Adam's words, something I never expected from him.

"Is that why you're always high out of your mind?" I asked. "So you don't have to know everything?"

"Precisely."

Explains a lot, I thought.

"Why is it that you all have these weird… *powers*?" I asked, hating every word I said. "Does it have to do with the killing?"

Adam completed the first movement, but instead of moving to the second, he started the first from the beginning again. It was hypnotic.

"There's a certain ritual that needs to take place, yes. The result is resurrection, in a sense, but more of a literal rebirth. For those who undergo the rebirth more than once, they come back a little different every time. It involves the connection between a virgin vessel, the offspring of your King Rat and the original host. Without the virgin birth, there can be no resurrection."

"But Lenny had children."

"Yes, he did," Adam agreed. "But they were adopted. Leonard was sterile. Eventually, his wife got so fed up with the lack of sex that she packed herself and kids up and left him. A truly sad story."

Gears started to turn as I remembered Roselle's insistence that we never fucked.

"He didn't deserve that," I said.

"Oh, I agree. He must have been a wonderful father."

"No!" I shouted. My voice, tinged with hate and biting sadness, echoed in the exposed piano wires. "He didn't deserve to *die*! Not for any reason, and especially not for whatever sick fucking game you're all playing."

"Just like Evelyn didn't deserve to die."

He stopped playing in the middle of a phrase, keeping his foot on the damper pedal. The notes of seconds past rung until they diminished. The air felt sucked from the room like a vacuum. My breath turned to mist from my lips. I remembered the cold. My fingers tightened around the pistol grip.

"You think you're all high and mighty," Adam continued, rising from the bench, finally turning to me. He persisted in mocking me, saying, "'*Oh! These people around me are so fucking evil! Oh, save me, Rose. Save me, Mom! Jessica, please free me from this place; these people are trying to murder me!*' Yes, Joel. We *were* trying to murder you, but we would've liked you to stick around for a *little* longer, so your disappearance would've been a little more believable in the press. But, NO! You had to be *curious*; you had to stick your fingers into things you had *no* business touching." He started to cry as he slowly walked toward me. I saw the same gaunt face that haunted Evelyn's before I torched her. "And now my sister is burnt to a crisp downstairs! Isn't that just *hilarious* to you, Joel? With any luck, she's still got some blood left in her, but WHO KNOWS?"

He shrugged his shoulders maniacally. "Oh, that's right! I *do* know. It's all unusable because you fucking *boiled* it all! Anything that's left is probably congealed beyond belief. She's gone forever, and all thanks to you."

"She was covered in gas before I even set foot in that room," I reasoned. "She was going to torch herself and Jessica regardless. I just did her the favor of lighting the match, so she didn't have to."

Anger brewed underneath his paper-thin skin. I was sure he would lunge at me, take the gun, and paint the floor red with my brains. He could've wrapped his hands around my neck and slowly choked me to death. But all that rage cascaded back into the sea of torment after a moment. A new sense of purpose filled his complexion. His eyes relaxed; his cheeks flushed.

"Save those bullets for Asher," Adam said calmly. "He's got Jessica and your mother on the ground floor. He's waiting."

"What's he gonna do?" I asked.

"I don't know," he said. A disgusting smirk crawled across his face like a centipede.

He turned and walked back to the piano. He leaned into the instrument's body and began tugging at something. After a few seconds of struggle, he managed to pluck out a piano wire with a sharp *thwip*.

Adam twined the ends around both hands, tightening the middle portion with enough effort to slice into his knuckles. The wire sunk into his bony hands like a hot knife through butter. Thin red lines protruded from the paleness of his skin. With unblinking eyes, he stared with that same ferocious smile from the Toss & RUMble alleyway. The dawning cold of an approaching winter pinched my memory. The twins passing a bong between themselves, their blonde hair shining in the moonlight of downtown Sanduhr.

He pressed the exposed wire to his neck, held it there for a short while, and with one last breath he said, "I've accepted my fate, Joel. I hope you do, as well."

He sharply flicked the wire to one side, then moved to the other. The sawing was slow at first, an andante tempo accented with sharp staccatos of wire slicing flesh. The tempo soon accelerated into a lively, gory concerto. With every quick swipe, a spurt of blood splattered to the floor. Adam sawed faster and faster. The rhythm was haunting. He became drenched in a fountain of red. A crunchy pop rang through the practice room as the wire cut through his throat.

Scarlet polka dots adorned the floor beneath his feet. The dots grew larger with each drop of blood spilt. His white dress shirt was completely drenched in the stuff. But even through all the horror—all the pain he inflicted upon himself—he never blinked, never faltered. He stood completely still as the wire contacted his spine. As Adam made one final slice into his spinal cord, his arms went limp, his knees buckled, and he tumbled to the floor. His head ripped from the small amount of meat left in his neck. It rolled in the blood pool like a bowling ball down a slick lane.

His eyes were still open.

Even in brutal death, those eyes were haunted with knowledge. With all the facts the universe had to offer, save for one dead zone. Scyphozoa, the Great One, Great King Rat. That eternal mystery.

A cockroach skittered from the open piano and burrowed into his gaping, dead mouth.

From the stump where his neck used to be, a slimy, black slug slipped out and scampered away into a dark corner.

3

I was out of vomit to spew. The one perk of someone leaving a window open inside was that I could get fresh air in the hallway. I hunched over and coughed profusely. Dry heaves emanated through the hall, grating against rough tiles and paint peeling with age.

A bout of emptiness filled my being. A hollowness that consumed my mind and rendered me without rational thought. I was truly and utterly lost in all this. I had answers—maybe too many—but those answers gave way to more questions. The "why" of it all. *Why* had this happened? *Why* was it allowed to continue? *Why* did I throw myself into this whole mess?

As I walked down the stairwell, more questions than stars in the night sky filled my head to the point of nausea. My shoes clacked with every step. I didn't care for sneaking around the damn building anymore. Evelyn was a charred, bloody marshmallow. Adam was nothing but a torso and a severed head full of roaches. Marty had his brains blown out on the shore of some distant hell.

There was no one left but Asher Gaumont.

He knew I was here. How couldn't he?

I took a fateful step onto the ground floor. A red glow radiated from the ensemble rehearsal room at the end of the hallway, toned with the flickering gold of candlelight.

"Fate."

I followed the voice bathed in crimson.

CHAPTER XIX

1

In the band room door's window, a horrific sight awaited me.

Shades of red enveloped everything. Through the small window's mesh, faint outlines of darker figures danced in the light. Something hung in the air, another moving across the floor. The shine of percussion equipment and other various instruments left out over the winter break. Through the thick wood of the door, a vague hum graced my ears. A melody beautiful in its despair.

I breathed in. Oxygen calmed my ratting nerves, but only to a point. It was now or never.

This was where I needed to be.

The roads of fate led me here, and here I remained.

I opened the door slowly. Warm air caressed my face with the softness of a mother's hug after a tough day at school. The hinges creaked; the door scraped the floor below. The hum turned into discernible vocals. Still soft but sung at a powerful pianissimo. Asher sat in the middle of the room, surrounded by a circle of candles, cast in the red light of a portable heater. It hummed with a drone that complimented his song, purring underneath with a consistent tone. He faced me, sitting crisscross in that circle of flame and melting wax. Behind him, crudely hung from the ceiling by extension cords by her wrists, my mother squirmed. Still alive, thank God, but only just. Streaks of black poured and dried on her face, running like a stagnant stream over her eyes and lips. Lips that were so unlike mine. So distant, yet so familiar.

Jess lay in the corner toward the emergency exit. She was out cold; her chest rose and fell with hints of life. Her limbs contorted horrendously like someone had thrown her into that corner.

"Welcome back," Asher said, ceasing his quiet song.

The door slammed behind me. I hadn't even realized I'd walked far enough into the room for that to be possible. I turned to look at who had shut the door. In the red light, I saw a ghost.

Cameron Wright.

2

"You son of a bitch," I said to Asher.

"Let's talk this out, Joel," he said.

"I think I've had enough talk to last a lifetime."

I lifted the pistol and aimed, lining the sights between his eyes.

"I know," he said. "And I'm sorry. I didn't mean for things to get so out of hand."

"Out of hand?" I asked. "You've been *killing* people. Seems like things were 'out of hand' before I even showed up."

"I wouldn't say so. Just look at your friend back there."

Asher sneered and lifted a pointed finger. I turned to look at Cameron. It wasn't some illusion conjured up by Scyphozoa or whatever I should call it. It was real; it was the same Cameron I remembered letting me into his home. The home where his goddess of a mother cared for Jess and I without really knowing us. Such a pure soul he was, but he was tainted with resurrection, standing before me in the dim red light of the band room. His usually calm eyes jittered with fright, scratch marks ran down his arms; whispers crawled from his throat. He was a wreck, to say the least, looking more like your local crack dealer than a Sanduhr honors student. He was alive, but at the cost of another's life.

"It's not right," I said.

"Not a lot of things are," Asher said.

I turned to Asher once again, training the pistol's barrel to his forehead.

"That concert you went to?" he continued. "Do you know how much electricity that wasted? Or what about the trombone you started on? Do you know how many starving Asian kids had a hand in making it for a few cents an hour? Everything comes at a price. While you sat in college and pursued an education, there were kids across the ocean who couldn't, let alone get a drop of water to drink. *Everything* has its price."

"That's... so one-sided."

"Explain yourself, Joel."

"I'm not the one who caused people to suffer thousands of miles away," I said. "And I certainly don't murder people like you and everyone else in this fucking band did."

"'Did?' Interesting use of past tense."

"Yeah... 'Did.'"

"You're aware I can just bring them back, right?" Asher asked.

He seemed to be enjoying himself. A chuckle even slipped through, the bastard.

"Good luck with that," I said. "Marty's millions of miles away, Adam sawed his head off, and Evelyn's nothing but charcoal."

His laughter turned to raging hysterics. Asher's singing voice, one I used to admire fondly, emitted from the bursts of giggling. I thought of him singing "Frictional Fiction" to a crowd of adoring fans. Fans who had no idea of the darkness lying beneath his, admittedly, beautiful exterior. Yet, fans who knowingly got drugged on New Years. But it was tradition, right? Nothing wrong with that, of course.

"I'm going to miss you," Asher said. "You're so weirdly confident about everything. That's what I liked most about you. That even despite your skittishness and violent tendencies, you try to feign confidence regardless of the situation. It's admirable, truly."

Footsteps. Then the pistol wasn't in my hands, but in Cameron's. He had plucked it from my grip and brought it over to Asher. The moment I thought about charging both of them, something held me back. The heater's buzz diminished into a nearly inaudible hum.

I felt a presence so damning it kept me in place. My muscles were paused like someone had used a TV remote on me. The Great King Rat—the true Scyphozoa—stood under my mother, seemingly appearing out of nowhere. It had a grip on me, holding me in place from across the room with an immense strength unknown to mere human thought.

Cameron presented the gun to Asher. He smiled, but as he reached for it, he jolted back.

"Give me the gun, kid," Asher calmly demanded.

"No," Cameron whispered.

"What?"

"No." Cam said it louder that time.

"And why is that? Give me the fucking gun."

"I can't."

Cameron examined the pistol. His frantic eyes calmed as he slipped his finger onto the trigger. Soon enough, though, he whipped his head around and yelped like a dog getting its tail stepped on. He stared at an empty corner, his eyes trailing something I couldn't see.

"There's nothing there," Asher said.

"You don't see him?" Cameron asked.

"No."

"There's a man over there."

"It's nothing. You're just seeing things."

"Yes!" Cameron shouted. "I *am* seeing things. Ever since you brought me back, I keep seeing things. And they see me. And they *speak* to me. Even when I tried to sleep, they keep... *talking* to me! They never quit. They want to be freed; they keep telling me. 'Please save me!' 'Can't you help me?'" He squinted into the corner again. The ghost must've disappeared as suddenly as it appeared. "They're everywhere; the dead. Spirits that are stuck on Earth because they died without purpose. They want to go to Heaven."

"There is no Heaven," Asher corrected. "You've seen it."

"And I keep telling them they're lucky to be here instead of there! But they just… don't… listen. I can see them, they can see me, but they can't *hear* me. Why won't they just shut the hell up?" Cameron pointed the gun at Asher. "Why did *you* do this to me? Why couldn't you just let me stay dead?"

"Because we needed you."

"Yeah, to get to *Joel*."

I wanted to say something, but Scyphozoa had my tongue.

"And look!" Asher said. "We got to him. There's your purpose. And now that you know our secret, why don't you stay with us? You can live long. Eat well. Never fear death."

"No."

Cameron lowered the gun, contemplating. Tears welled in my eyes, but I couldn't blink them away. My vision focused on him, and him alone. A dark tunnel vignetted my sight. I watched as he lifted the pistol once more, his mind made up. "Joel," Cameron said. "I forgive you."

He shoved the barrel into his mouth and fired.

3

Not a speck of shock on Asher's face. Nothing registered that he witnessed the suicide. Instead, he shrugged and rose from his sitting position.

"It was worth a shot," he said. "Could always use some fresh meat."

The dark figure released its grip on me. My muscles relaxed and became useful again. I tripped on thin air as my thighs twitched. The pistol lay in a pool of blood and chunks of bone and brain. It lay under my mother, behind Asher. It was too close to him to consider booking it, grabbing it from the floor, and filling him with hot lead.

Jess continued to lay in the corner, stirring subconsciously, telling me she was alive.

"But *why*?" I asked.

Asher stepped over a few candles, inching toward me.

"Why not?" he responded. "I was given purpose, and it's my job to fulfill that purpose."

"And what would that 'purpose' be?"

"To feed the children. To grant the gift of life to those so unfortunate to pass before they've served their own purposes."

"And what's in it for you?"

He stopped and stared at the floor, thinking. He then lifted his head and flashed a grin. "Have you ever thought about where you go when you die?"

"No," I said. I did, though. All the time.

"Well, you've seen it. It's not a great place to be. All those people sacrificing their flesh to form a planet God knows where. But the *feeling* you get as the light leaves your eyes is unlike anything you can imagine. It's beautiful." He chuckled, continued. "I've killed myself dozens of times, overdosing on heroin. Not only do I get to feel that rush—that high—but I get to experience ascension. Pure bliss in the subtle embrace of death. Wouldn't you like to be a part of that process? That's why we brought you on, anyway."

I wanted to wrap my hands around his neck and squeeze until I felt the crunch of his Adam's apple under my thumbs. I wanted to stick those thumbs in his eyes and feel the sockets burst. I wanted to take that pistol and lay the barrel on his cock, pull the trigger, and watch the shaft explode in a geyser of gore.

"You didn't think we hired you for your *talent*, right?" Asher asked. "I surely hope you didn't think that."

"Why wouldn't it be talent?"

"Scyphozoa needed you."

"Yeah, because the band was down a trombonist—"

"No!" he shouted. The room seemed to shake. "Not the fucking *band*, you idiot. Him! The god of all cosmoses. The mediator of life and death. Scyphozoa!"

Flashes of white in the darkness. The room didn't just *seem* to shake; it rumbled with the intensity of a mild earthquake.

"Another offspring was born," he continued. "We needed a new host. You fit the damn bill, with the added benefit of being a potential virgin sacrifice! It was a two-for-one deal! We couldn't pass it up. *He* couldn't pass it up."

Asher's voice began to fade as the low blare like a thousand tubas welcomed itself in. A bright light consumed everything: The floor, the instruments, the candles, the Asher, the Jess, the mom, the me. Even the dark bloodstains on the floor brightened into a sharp pink before being engulfed in blinding, cosmic light.

4

"Why did you have to fuck *everything* up?"

It was me against him. Him against me. Out in the vast neon expanse of a world made of flesh and blood, thumping veins like animated tree roots, a waterfall of blood in the distance churning with iron and the cells of infinite lost souls.

Nothing followed us into the realm of the damned except us two. No one else in the room, none of the various abandoned instruments, and—most important of all—no pistol. That punctuation that would've ended Asher's life sentence with a single bullet.

"We had a good thing going!" he shouted. "We trusted you! Why couldn't you give us the same trust? We could've done great things."

"You call this shit *great?*" I said.

"We were given a gift from God!"

His eyes glowed white. He charged at me with the fierceness of an agitated bull. I rolled out of the way; a jolt of sharp pain in my shoulder as I landed. Asher skid across the terrain like a sports car flooring the brakes. His shoes scraped against the ground, leaving trails of blood where his feet had been. The cries of millions rang out for miles around. It was deafening hearing all those people feeling the same pain. No words, just moans and groans. Haunting in their abundance.

I held my shoulder, squeezing tight to mitigate the pain. I swore Asher growled at me, angry as all hell that I was still alive.

"You are nothing," he said, but it wasn't his voice. "You are a mere speck in the cosmos. A small, insignificant mote of dust."

I was done talking.

I knew what I had to do. The only thing stopping me was my own inadequacy. I needed to take charge, be my own man. Not just for me, but for the people I grew to love. He came at me again, his eyes growing brighter with every step. I couldn't help feeling like a deer in headlights, waiting for the inevitable crash. He screamed with an ancient raspiness, a guttural tone that sounded like the growling of a thousand coyotes. I braced myself for another dodge out of the way, but as I began to tumble, I felt a strong grip wrap around my ankle.

I slid onto my back. The thing wearing Asher lifted me by my foot and smiled a strangely toothless grin. The Great King Rat never needed to smile, and it was obvious it was its first time. The wrinkles were all wrong; the skin suit wasn't fitting correctly. Asher's muscles tightened; his veins bulged in those fibrous arms.

"No more running, boy," Scyphozoa said.

It used Asher's free hand to grip my femur. Both hands clenched with otherworldly strength. As it kept my thigh bone in place, I felt a sharp *crunch* in my foot. Before I knew it, I was flying like a tree branch primed for fetching. I screamed as I plummeted to the ground, all to stop the pain. But nothing could be enough. You can't just *forget* you're in pain, as helpful as that would be. I landed on my injured shoulder again. The pain was agonizing, like an older sister pinching you and never letting go.

I watched the pure rage in his face, his cheeks scrunching together as if pulled by strings. He was approaching uncanny valley levels of discomfort. Not quite human, but close enough. I rolled up my pants leg and examined the damage. My ankle—or where it should've been—was swollen and purple, throbbing to the increased beating of my heart. A solid white island underneath the skin desperately wanted to peek out. A shard of bone was broken, trapped inside my body's prison.

Before I was fully aware of myself, I was kneeling before Asher Gaumont. He held me up by my hair with one hand; raised the other high above his head. I whimpered, feeling each individual thread of hair pop from their follicles as he pulled my head back. "Why can't you see?" the demon asked.

"How many did you kill before me?" I spat.

"They were reborn. Given new purpose… I only wish it were more."

"If they were reborn, they'd still be alive."

"Oh, child. You *still* don't see." It lowered Asher's free hand, and his fingers curled into a menacing claw. It gripped the side of my head with four fingers, leaving Asher's thumb over my left eye. "Let me help you," it sneered.

The thumb plunged into my socket with horrifying ease. A blistering *pop* rang inside my skull. I screamed as many expletives as I could muster. The new hole in my head dripped instantly, pouring a monstrous concoction of blood and viscous eye gunk. I screamed and screamed and screamed as Scyphozoa kept its thumb lodged in my socket, twisting the appendage here and there to maximize the torment. The nail scraped the intricate lining of flesh and bone. I felt nothing but a sense of my bones being scratched with sandpaper. It tore nerves, ripped skin.

It was laughing through Asher, using him as a puppet. The laugh was primordial, low, unnatural. A stark mimicry, as if from someone who only observed humans yet wasn't human themselves.

With only half my vision, the primal urge to defend myself kicked in. The demon's thumb, stuck mere millimeters from my brain, hooked and curled. I felt every movement, every distinct twitch and curl, as I flung my arms around like a mouse with its head caught in a cheese trap. I shouted *fuck* and *shit* and *cocksucker* and everything in between as something cold and long graced my fingertips. It was so out of place in that humid, barren wasteland. My fingers wrapped around the shaft; I pulled and strained my muscles with all my remaining strength.

Through the maniacal laughter and the beating of my own heart through my hollow eye socket, I lifted the object. It seemed to slide seamlessly from some sort of outer shell. Underneath, there was the ticket. The final seal.

I wrapped my free hand around Asher's torso and plunged the rod into his chest.

5

I blinked once with my good eye and felt the cold wash back over me like an early morning shower. Upon opening that eye, the Sanduhr rehearsal room greeted me with frigid, bared teeth. The gloomy windows, the strewn instruments, my mother strung up to the ceiling, a reborn Cameron missing half his head, Jess knocked out in the corner.

The pressure in my hair follicles ceased. Asher slumped before me, falling to his knees. The inner tubing of a trombone slide impaled him straight through his abdomen. It exited through his spine, its silver sheen coated in glistening red. He coughed, spitting blood in a fine spray. His shirt grew dark with the stuff, like a time lapse of mold growing in a murky public shower.

Losing his balance, he fell forward. The force sent the slide slowly further through his torso. A slimy, squelching sound filled the room.

The room fell into deep silence. Nothing but the *drip, drip* of blood seeping from Asher's mouth and the rasping breaths that seemed to come from not his mouth, but the two identical holes in his stomach.

"What good will this do?" he croaked, hanging his head low.

I refused to speak.

Asher lifted his head and turned to look at Jess. An idea, something horrible forming in his brain as the last of his dying neurons fired away, popped into that head, curling his lips—moist with blood—into a devastating grimace. "Yes, lord," he said to the whispering dark. "Do what you must."

Asher's eyes glowed white. His expression went slack after a single tear fell from his eye, replaced by the contorting face of Scyphozoa. Ripples formed underneath his clothing like a million maggots squirming on a rotten slab of steak. He, or Scyphozoa for that matter, stood up on his feet, seeming to completely forget the mortal wound in his chest.

Scyphozoa pulled the slide from Asher's stomach in one sickening jerk. The squelching intensified to unbearable proportions. The puckering and sucking of flesh and bone tightening up as the metal slid from Asher's torso.

When it was out, Scyphozoa threw it to the floor. It fell with an acute clank. From inside the tubing, bits of muscle tissue and body fat spilled out onto the tile in a grotesque sludge of chunked filth. From the hole in Asher's body, blood gushed out like a midtown fountain. Scyphozoa made no effort to show pain; it wasn't its pain to feel.

The ocean waves underneath Asher's shirt intensified. A roaring storm over the sea of torment, escalating into a horrific swarm of festering worms underneath that crawled to every square inch of his body. His face contorted and rippled until I could barely recognize anything human, save for those white eyes. His nose snapped; blood poured from every orifice. Whatever was underneath his skin was struggling to surface. Asher's skin began to tear liked taffy being pulled from both ends. I thought I heard painful screams, not from Scyphozoa, but the remnants of Asher. His soul cried out for forgiveness, sensing the mistakes and sins he made.

For the people he murdered out of a sick need to get high, feel that rush, and peer into the heavens repeatedly.

For the people he indoctrinated into his twisted beliefs.

For the people he held captive as they were forced to witness the awesome power of Scyphozoa.

Asher Gaumont died for the last time in the Sanduhr University band rehearsal room. From the shriveled carcass, the Great King Rat emerged, tearing free from Asher's skin like a caterpillar emerging from its cocoon.

His guts spilled onto the floor, a mishmash of entrails and yellowing bones. There was nothing left of Asher once Scyphozoa climbed from him; nothing but a mortifying pile of human spaghetti and marinara on the tiles below. I hadn't realized I had fallen to the floor during the process, but I was there, panting, gasping for any semblance of clean air. But the air was thick with death. A pungent, citrusy smell filled the room, mixed with the metallic stench of Asher's blood. The throbbing pain in my empty eye socket, bumping and pumping red-hot torment throughout my skull, was secondary to what I witnessed.

The entity stood proud over Asher's disgusting remains, eyes beaming. Its pitch-black skin glistened with blood like an oil slick; it rippled as its children squirmed underneath. It seemed more tangible than the shadowy form it usually inhabited, but nonetheless ghastly. There was the idea of a mouth under its eyes. A grin was planted there, revealing razor sharp fangs coated in a deep maroon.

"I persevere," it said.

It pointed a gnarled finger my way. My muscles went stiff. Paralyzed, I watched as Scyphozoa sauntered toward Jess. My eye widened in horror as it took slow, methodical steps across the band room floor. Jess stirred in her corner, in the process of waking up from whatever forced slumber she endured.

I wanted to shout, to get up and rush at Scyphozoa. To warn Jess that she was next in the unknown, long line of possessed people. People under the control of something their minds couldn't comprehend. A being so alien—so elevated above humanity—that it uses us for benefits we cannot see. Maybe there were no benefits; maybe it did what it did because it found the cruelty hilarious. Evil that pure and refined knows no bounds.

Scyphozoa held Jess by her chin, lifted her head. Her eyes crept open. She didn't have time to understand what was happening. She was awake, but her brain wasn't. She could see, but the details were hazy. Like a stray ice cube on hot pavement, Scyphozoa melted into a black sludge and poured itself into her mouth. Her eyes glowed white, and once all the sludge was gone, there was a loud pop like firecrackers. Jess's eyes dimmed, and she fell over coughing a storm.

6

I limped over to her, feeling my fractured ankle scraping inside me with every step.

"Jess!" I said. "Jess? Are you alright?"

She was hunched over, her back arched and shaking with every dry heave. She stuck two fingers in her mouth and gagged profusely, but nothing came out.

The lights flickered on, casting harsh shadows through the room. It was a goddamn mess in that rehearsal room. Blood coated the floor and walls in fine splatters. Flies awoke from their winter hibernation to swarm around Cameron's second corpse and whatever was left of Asher. The candles burned into waxen puddles.

As Jess continued to try and vomit Scyphozoa from her system, I scoured the room for any means to get my mother down from her makeshift shackles tied to the ceiling. I grabbed a piano bench and positioned it under her. Carefully, I stepped up and fiddled with the extension cords. I managed to untie one of them. It left an indigo indent around her wrist. "Sorry, Mom," I said. I didn't know exactly what I was apologizing for: either for her dangling from one arm or for the entire situation. The gruesomeness of it all. She tried to change, to fix herself for me. And this was the thanks she got.

Once I untied the second cord, I caught her before she could crack her skull on the tile.

"Joel?" she asked, dazed.

"Are you okay, Mom? They left the apartment a complete mess."

"No, Joel. I'm not okay." That classic Julie Auguste sternness crept to the surface as she found her footing. Her smirk faded as her vision cleared. "Oh my God! Your eye! Where the *fuck* is your eye?"

"It's gonna be alright, Mom."

"Asking me if *I* was okay when your goddamn *eye* is gone?" She grew hysterical, her hair flying in wet strands as she flailed her arms angrily. "Where the hell are we, anyway? Who did that to you?!"

"Him," I said, pointing to the human Slurpee on the tile.

My mother vomited at the gruesome sight, adding her puke to the Asher soup on the floor. "I'm going to call 911," she said, wiping spit from her mouth. "Don't touch *anything* with that hole in your head. Don't need you getting an infection while I'm distracted."

"I'll be fine, Mom."

I wasn't. It fucking hurt.

She bent over to Cameron's body and rummaged through his pockets for a phone. When she found one, she spammed the power button until the emergency call screen lit her face in blue light.

"Hello? Yes? I need an ambulance," she commanded. With her hand over the microphone, she asked: "Where are we?"

"Sanduhr University School of Music," I said.

"They took me all the way to Massachusetts?"

"Yeah."

She rolled her eyes and resumed her conversation with the dispatcher, stepping over bits of bone and entrails as she left the room.

7

Jess began to cry. First, a tear or two. Then, a stream of sadness. Longing for a life she wished she wasn't born into. Wishing to reverse the clock and be sucked back into her mother's womb. A fresh restart.

I hovered by her, rubbing her back, feeling her lungs sputter with every uncontrollable sob.

"I don't wanna be him," she said.

"You aren't," I consoled. "And you *won't* be."

She writhed, fighting something from within. Her eyes rolled to the back of her head; tears still streamed down her soft, bruised cheeks. I thought of the corpse in the Charlotte alleyway, of the jovial chuckles Lenny made, the drugs, the concerts, the small-town fame of everything. I thought of the cloud of cigarette smoke enshrouding her, that beautiful face with the pointed lips and the razor-sharp eyes. Her red hair falling over her face, shining in its natural gleam. She was still here. Still Jessica. No amount of cosmic power inside her could change that.

Jess came to a few moments later. Her sobs subsided. The hollowness of the room became more apparent in the silence.

"I can keep it down," she said. "I don't know for how long, but I can."

"You will," I said, smiling.

She sat up and wrapped her arms around me. I flinched briefly, hesitating to receive such an embrace from her after all that had happened. But I let her take hold; I hugged her back. She was just as warm as ever, despite the demon crawling inside her. She resumed her tears. I felt her chest heave with every pained sob. Rubbing her back, I felt her sweat-drenched shirt, the vertebra poking smoothly from underneath the fabric.

We sat there for what seemed like hours. Warming each other as the building's heating system finally kicked in. Her shivering dissipated along with her sadness. The pain in my hollow socket waned.

As the sound of ambulance sirens echoed through the windows and into the halls, we shared a short kiss. Lips on lips, mine chapped and hers warm and soft like a perfect pillow on a cold winter night.

Red and blue lights flashed into the room.

We were free.

For a while.

FINALE

Jessica Fitzgerald broke up with me three years later.

I couldn't blame her in the slightest. It had been a long time coming. I'd been wondering for the past year if the spark would finally die out. The flame was tinged in darkness, an inherent evil that encased her soul like the sugar coating a candy apple. That evil was in there; it lived and breathed the same way a barnacle survives on a whale's surface. The flame burned, ignited enough to carry us through the rest of our lives like a phoenix taking flight, rising from the ashes, and soaring into the night with the power of a thousand suns.

I had no questions about why she left; I knew full and well why she did. That cancer thriving inside her finally grew to malignant proportions. It consumed enough of her soul to take control, even for a short moment.

On our last night together, we nestled into bed, taking the gift of waking up next to one another tomorrow morning for granted. We kissed, running our fingers up and down each other's backs. I felt her warmth; she felt mine. I had told Jess I loved her, and she repeated it back to me steadily, her breath steaming my cheeks. Despite knowing she had the chance of not seeing me ever again once she closed her eyes for the night, Jess was confident in her speech. She loved me deeply, completely.

And she knew that I did, too.

That was enough.

I woke up the next morning in a bed colder than usual. Half awake, I fumbled at Jessica's side of the mattress. There was nothing except carefully made bedsheets. I turned, taking some of the covers with me, and saw exactly what I feared; all I had left to fear. She was gone. Nothing but an orange sticky note where her naked body—those graceful curves—should have been.

I rubbed the sleep from my eyes and grabbed the note. It tore from the duvet with a simple *thwip*. I held the note to my face, studying the neat handwriting written in black Sharpie. The words were as elegant and beautiful as she was, tinged with the underlying sadness that articulated her being. I read the words unremittingly, running them through my mind incessantly to the point of memorization.

I didn't cry. During our first year together, or maybe even during our second year, I might have. But three years spent with someone you know will leave you are three years you grow comfortable with. Like warm tomato soup and grilled cheese after a rainy day. Or days spent at a local carnival, surrounded by family that are just as complicated on the inside as you are on the outside. The time for tears had passed like dust in the wind. It was as if she had been gone for years already, not suddenly vanished from the bed we had snuggled into only hours before. When the moon hung high in the night sky and greeted our weary eyes with the blessing of sleep.

I trudged through the streets of Chicago to that weekend's performance of Holst's *The Planets*. In the concert hall, an energy with the timbre of a college town bar and the subtlety of a snoring dog filled every crevice. Every carved structure. Every full seat in the hall, beaming with lives both old and young. All clapping as the conductor entered the stage and presented the ensemble. We stood up, our instruments in tow. Flutes and violins and cellos and French horns.

And there was me and my section. Principal trombonist for the Chicago Symphony Orchestra, something I never thought to be possible.

Losing my eye was a bit of a setback, naturally, but I had been playing trombone for so long that the lack of depth perception wasn't an issue. Muscle memory took its course where my sight couldn't.

After "Neptune" reached its somber conclusion, I was itching to run from my seat and put up my horn. The ensemble stood from their seats, we bowed with the conductor, the audience applauded. A few younger kids toward the back whooped and hollered like it was the best concert of their lives. It might have been. I don't know. Music can be more subjective than comedy sometimes.

My mother greeted me in the main lobby with an assortment of beautiful flowers nestled in a nest of thin plastic. Bright red and yellow tulips beaming at me like the colors on the Scyphozoa tour bus. I ignored the memory and gave her a hug instead, snuffing out the past horrors brewing in my mind.

"Where's Jessica?" she asked.

"She… couldn't make it tonight."

"Oh, that's too bad," she said, pouting. "Was hoping to see her after the show. Is she coming tomorrow?"

"I don't think so, Mom."

My bottom lip quivered slightly. Being a mother of almost thirty years, she noticed. Her eyes softened from her initial excitement into a look of deep sadness. Empathy emanated from her as she brought me in for another hug. The sound of bustling concertgoers went mute as she squeezed me as tight as she could. There was nothing like a mother's hug. Sometimes that love can move mountains, stop the world from spinning. All those impossible things that are seemingly made possible out of sheer loving spite.

I visited her apartment after the performance. We sat in the renovated living room sipping mugs of piping hot peach tea.

"So, Jess is gone?"

"Yeah," I mumbled.

"She didn't… you know… leave anything for you? Nothing to remember her with?"

"No."

"That seems very unlike her."

"Well, she wasn't *like* her anymore. That's the whole point, really. Once she couldn't contain what was inside her, she had to leave. I don't know where she went." I ruminated in that fact for a moment. "*If* she went anywhere, that is."

My mother reached for my hand, resting her palm over my fingers, rubbing my thumb with hers.

"I'm sure she's out there, sweetie," she assured. "She's strong."

"I know," I said, taking another sip of tea.

Over a few glasses of wine, I told my mother about the past three years. I told her how Jess and I hopped between bars, danced until the stars dimmed and the sun rose, and went to a hockey game or two from time to time. Those were her favorites, even though she never struck me as the hockey type. It might not have been the sport itself she enjoyed, but it was the coldness of the arena, and the security she felt as she laid her head upon my warm chest. In the arena, she felt the safest besides when we were in bed, and that was a beautiful thing. I left the apartment a little more buzzed than I wanted, gave my mother another hug, and thanked her for the tulips.

I don't wish to bore you with the details of Jess and I's relationship, because we both know how it ends. No matter how much we wanted to believe the opposite, there would come a day where she would have to go, where she would have to make one final sacrifice.

I keep her sticky note framed above my nightstand. One fleeting reminder of the love we shared, and the love I would never replicate with another. I think about Todd, Roselle, Marty, Evelyn, Adam, and Asher all the time. I think about how Todd and Roselle didn't last. About the landscape of flesh the late members of Scyphozoa are suffering in. Their flesh melting into the stones of bone. I think of where Jess may have gone.

Where Scyphozoa took her.

I read the sticky note every night before I turn off the lamp and curl into bed. Its words—her lyrical words—are as hauntingly beautiful now as they were the morning I first read them.

> *I woke up last night holding a knife to your throat.*
> *The blade was pressed to your skin, but you didn't wake.*

SCYPHOZOA

It's time for me to go.
Don't be sad I'm gone, be glad I happened.

- Jess

Sometimes I wish I could have said one last goodbye. I wish I was awake to give her a final embrace; to get one last look at her before she vanished from my life and lived forever in nothing but my memory.

But that's where all good things go, I suppose.

September 26, 2023
February 29, 2024
Lexington, KY

ACKNOWLEDGMENTS

Here's the part of the book I've been dreading to write since I finished the first draft. No, it wasn't the carnival bombing or the body horror or the gross, icky intimate scenes. Yes, it's the acknowledgments section.

That's not to say I'm ungrateful to anyone; it's very much the opposite. My number one fear isn't being possessed by a cosmic entity. My number one fear–coming from someone who sat down and wrote a horror novel spanning over 100,000 words over five months of incessant typing–is expressing gratitude. Because if I'm truly grateful for someone, I don't know how to act around them. Catch me yapping my damn head off when I'm around close friends and colleagues because *that's* how grateful I am to them. There are so many people in my life who made me the person I am today, and here's a comprehensive (not really) list of most of them. Hold on, sir. It's gonna be a sappy ride.

Firstly, I thank my parents, Kristin and John, for supporting me in all my endeavors. As much as you both wanted me to be a baseball player, I'm glad you two allowed me to play trombone and write silly stories instead. And, thank you for not being as awful as the parents depicted within this novel. Like, seriously… thanks.

Thank you to my extended family members; a group of people so vast that I cannot name all of them here, but shoutout to all the Srours and Geises out there! Love you all, even if it would take another whole novel's worth of words to list all of you.

Thank you to Kevin Endrijaitis, Jacob Phillips, Kira Wrigley, Noah MacMillan, Mason Kearney, and Bryana and Dalton Grove for filling countless nights of my life with hilarity and joy. Wouldn't use Discord without you guys.

Thank you to numerous past and present members of the University of Kentucky's Trombone Studio—led by Bradley Kerns—including but not limited to Kamilo Davila, Keaton Fuller, Sam Gritton, Will Hatten, Zack Huwalt, John Koenig, William Middleton, Kai Miller, Yankier Perez, Vladislav Petrachev, Juan Saldivar, JoJo Verrett, and Zach Wilson. And, that isn't to neglect the trombonists who've made my life so much brighter in UK's Wildcat Marching Band these past four years: Brayden Sosa, Bryanmarc Ray, Carter Baie, Chase Michaels, Daniel Clemons, Dillon Robinson, Ethan Hambleton, Isaac Morrelles, Jake Singleton, Jonathan Schares, Josiah Cadman, Josie Smith, Julia Kollitz, Lillian Penird, Lucas Kinzer, Madison Jones, Mattye Jackson, Nathan Ellis, and Thommy Snow.

This book would also not be possible without the brothers of the Alpha Gamma chapter of Phi Mu Alpha. Long live Sinfonia!

Thank you to every teacher I crossed paths with during my journey from kindergarten to twelfth grade at Mascoutah, Illinois' school district. I wouldn't have fixed all the spelling and grammatical errors in this novel without your boundless wisdom.

Thank you to the staff of the University of Kentucky's Department of Psychology and College of Fine Arts, as well as the various professors at the Lewis Honors College who opened my eyes to a world in desperate need of more stories. Special thanks to Dr. Chelsea Brislin for her work in the humanities and for proctoring two amazing honors courses that I will cherish for a long time.

Thank you to the employees of Joseph-Beth Booksellers in Lexington, Kentucky. Your combined passion for reading and sharing stories inspired me to write this book. I appreciate every single one of you with my whole heart.

Thank you to Eli Ratliff for reading this story before the publication date. Your feedback did wonders during the editing process.

And finally, I am of the firm belief that there is no such thing as originality. How *can* there be when we've had literal centuries to write stories for every passing generation to enjoy? With that said, I've compiled a list of all the books I read and listened to while drafting *Scyphozoa* to give credit to all the works I garnered inspiration from in one way or another:

11/22/63 (2011) by Stephen King
American Gods (2001) by Neil Gaiman
The Ballad of Songbirds and Snakes (2020) by Suzanne Collins
Billy Summers (2021) by Stephen King
Chainsaw Man, Vols. 1-3 (2019) by Tatsuki Fujimoto
Convenience Store Woman (2016) by Sayaka Murata
The Deep (2015) by Nick Cutter
God Emperor of Dune (1981) by Frank Herbert
The Kamogawa Food Detectives (2013) by Hisashi Kashiwai
Lessons in Chemistry (2022) by Bonnie Garmus
Little Heaven (2017) by Nick Cutter
Lovecraft Country (2016) by Matt Ruff
The Love Songs of W. E. B. Du Bois (2021) by Honorée Fanonne Jeffers
Maeve Fly (2023) by CJ Leede
Norwegian Wood (1987) by Haruki Murakami
Pet Sematary (1983) by Stephen King
Revival (2014) by Stephen King
The Shining (1977) by Stephen King
The Troop (2014) by Nick Cutter
The Violin Conspiracy (2022) by Brendan Slocumb

CONTINUE ON FOR A BONUS SHORT STORY...

IN A BED OF WILDFLOWERS

IN A BED OF WILDFLOWERS

I dreamt of a meadow the morning my brother died. Instead of hearing the guards shouting for him to wake up, I frolicked through a field of wildflowers; pink, purple, blue. I sat on a picnic blanket with my wife as they unlocked his cell and discovered the deep gashes running down his arms. My children I'd never see grow up—growing up as a life sentence beckoned me with gnarled hands—danced to nature's tune. Silent, graceful.

Clang… clang… clang…

"Roberts?"

My little girl fell onto the grass and scraped her knee on a rock. Tears welled in her eyes as I bandaged her up and wrapped the boo-boo with my father's plaid handkerchief. "You'll be fine," I soothed, brushing her wavy, golden hair between my fingers. "You're safe now."

Clang… clang…

"Roberts! Wake up!"

My daughter snuggled in my lap; a PB&J sandwich squished between her pudgy fingers with jelly so sweet she forgot about the pain. My son ran circles around the blanket, holding an orange toy plane to the sky, buzzing his lips akin to the sound of a fighter jet's engine. I caught one last glimpse

1

of Joanne before the flowers wilted and the dream faded.

"Wake the fuck up, Roberts!" a guard shouted as my cell door swung open, hinges screaming from a lack of oil.

It took quite a while for the blinding light of the hallway to dissipate. Everything looked like a camera flash refusing to end. Everything except the hulking dark mass standing before me, wielding a baton like some street thug.

He grabbed my arm and tightened his grip so hard my wrist cracked. He flung me from my cot, and I tumbled to the floor with a ragdoll's limpness. Blood dripped from a newly opened wound in my scalp.

"Clean yourself up and follow me," the guard huffed.

"Mr. Roberts," the psychologist said. "Your brother is dead."

The pain in my head kept throbbing in incessant bursts, like a bass drum mallet hammering from inside my skull. I couldn't hear her words underneath all the noise. Her mint green sweater was the cleanest thing I'd seen since my detainment. I was embarrassed, to say the least, her clean clothing in comparison to my orange jacket smudged with droplets of red, hot blood.

"Could you repeat that?" I asked.

She leaned forward in her chair.

"Your brother has died, Mr. Roberts," she repeated. "You aren't obligated to tell me, but did he have a history of... acting out?"

"He was in prison, wasn't he?"

"I guess so, Mr. Roberts."

"You don't have to keep calling me that."

"Would..." she checked her papers. "...William be better for you?"

"Bill," I said, the name feeling wrong on my tongue.

"Okay, Bill. Your brother died, likely by suicide sometime last night. Did he have a history of suicidal tendencies during your formative years together?"

"Not that I was aware of."

"And how are *you* taking this situation?" she asked, flipping through more papers until she found a blank sheet.

God, she looked just like my wife. Flowing, auburn hair that sat just right over her shoulders. That perfect nose that scrunched into a tiny ball as she sniffed the dust from her nostrils. The full lips oozing with lip gloss.

"Bill?" she asked.

But it wasn't her, it was the psychologist. Wearing a green sweater Joanne would never be caught dead in.

"I'm sorry," I said. "What was the question?"

"How are you managing yourself after this morning's events?" "I'm..." My eyes separate as the room grows blurry, trailing off into that realm of thoughtlessness. But I return to the land of the living as the psychologist clicks her pen in anticipation. "I don't know how to feel."

"Did you love your brother?"

Reggie and I lost our freedom on a night that felt like a day. The downtown streets were alive with people, the city's veins pumping with music and joy. Couples locked hands as they left the nightclubs. Cars honked and swerved to a strange tempo. The lampposts and blinding neon lights clashed in a cacophony of color.

Reggie tripped over a crack in the pavement and scuffed his knee. I went to help him up, but he raised a hand and drunkenly insisted, "I got it."

He stumbled into a bar as I walked behind him, ready to catch him if he fell up or down the steps. I was in awe of him, truth be told. I remembered our childhood together; him being as skinny as a human could be, playing kickball on the local little-league baseball fields. The man staggering before me wasn't that kid anymore. Large muscle bodies layered over his bones underneath a tight shirt, leaving nothing to the imagination. Yet, despite all that, he was still the same loving kid I grew up with. My accomplice in stealing from the cookie jar, my kickball team captain, my partner in crime.

The bouncer didn't ask for our IDs. He simply nodded to the both of us and watched as we sauntered by. The weight of humidity bore at us like an aching wind. People danced and rubbed their sweating bodies against each other. They swayed and kissed and shouted into the night, their voices echoing with the music blasting on numerous speakers hanging from the ceiling. Neon lights illuminated the bar patrons, sending everyone's skin into shades of bright blues and purples.

Through the commotion, I kept my focus on Reggie. He bobbed and weaved through the sea of people towards the bar counter. He bumped into a woman. Her hair, unruly yet flowing like fire, whirled as she turned. The woman's anger quickly turned to lust as Reggie effortlessly grasped her hand and twirled her around like a music box ballerina. She smiled as he planted a kiss on her cheek.

He let go of the stranger and disappeared into the crowd.

I followed.

"Yes," I said. "I love him."

"Elaborate," the psychologist said.

"How am I supposed to elaborate? Isn't 'love' just an inherent thing everyone knows about?"

"No, Bill. That's why I'm asking for you to explain."

Fleeting images of a childhood long gone flickered through my mind. I blinked and saw the neon lights. Reggie's back. The woman's hair.

"Let's think of something else, then," the psychologist said. "Is it hard for you to live?"

"Excuse me?"

"Is it hard for you to live? Without him, I mean."

"I wouldn't say I've had a lot of experience as of yet."

She wrote something on her notepad. For the life of me, I couldn't begin to guess what about my smartass reply caused her to scribble *that* much onto the page.

"Straight answers with me, Bill," she said, soothing yet direct. "We have limited time, but I need to fill your report. But, from what you've given me, I don't have much." She glanced over the notepad. "You prefer to be called Bill instead of William. You loved your brother. He didn't have a history of suicidal behavior… What else?"

"That about covers it," I said blankly.

The psychologist huffed and slammed the notepad shut.

"Alright," she said. "Thank you for your time."

She rose from her seat and walked to the door behind me. Her knocks against the metal frame bombarded my ears. I thought of the corner of a table, how someone could easily slip and fall into that corner, poking out an eye or fracturing their skull. *Blood.* Oh, there was so much blood.

I hadn't noticed the guards had already escorted the psychologist from the room before another set of them came in to unchain me from the floor and send me back to my cell.

I lay on my cot wondering about death. Where we go when we die. *If* we go anywhere. I went to the cafeteria during my lunch block with that thought aching in my mind, permeating there like an ever-growing cancer. I picked at my hastily thrown together lasagna with a dull, plastic fork. The pasta squished and moaned as I applied the tiniest amount of pressure, folding in on itself like wet flesh under a blade. The plastic knife sitting off to the side beckoned me. It told me that everything would be okay. *Just snap me in half and use the remains.* So, I did. I studied my makeshift shiv with curious intent. Watched as I dug the sharp plastic into my wrist and drew blood. It beaded and pooled at the botched incision, leaving a pond of red on my pale skin. I was so numb. Oh, so numb. I carved deeper toward my elbow, shocked only by the damage such a childish blade could inflict.

I imagined the wound opening like a door, the patrons inside welcoming me with open arms. My brother would be there, happy as the day we lost our freedom. A hug was all I could ask for. The warmth of it, the tempo of a low heartbeat drumming against mine. Coordinated with the world.

"Bill," the psychologist said a week later. "If you aren't going to cooperate, I can still find ways to help you. Nothing you do will turn me away. The state pays me to visit incarcerated individuals such as yourself. And this time, I have all day. You can refuse to answer my questions all you want, but I *want* to help you."

It hurt to cross my arms, but I did anyway.

The psychologist glanced at my bandaged forearm and quickly looked back to me as if I hadn't noticed.

"I'll be blunt with you," she said. "Cognitive behavioral therapy isn't going to work with you. This isn't a bad thing, truly. There are a *lot* of other avenues we could take."

I grunted.

"So, you're receptive to the idea of trying something different?"

The fluorescent bulbs above us buzzed like a trillion bees sought refuge in my eardrums. Her silence was deafening. It enticed me to speak, but I stood my ground. She jotted something down and shut the notepad noticeably less aggressively than the last time we spoke. Her eyes squinted in thought just as my wife's did when she was stumped on a crossword puzzle.

"What's your opinion on music?" the psychologist asked.

"Why?" I asked, unexpectedly.

She reeled back in her seat in astonishment.

"Finally got a word outta you..." She shook her head, chuckling slightly. "Sorry, that was unprofessional. I received my master's degree in music therapy after getting my bachelor's in general psychology. Do you like music?"

"Who doesn't like music?"

"You'd be surprised."

I nodded, signaling her to continue her ramblings.

"Are you skilled in any particular instrument?" she asked. "That is... if you have played an instrument before."

In fact, I had. I went to college pursuing a business degree, but I found myself participating in the university's guitar studio from time to time, much to my mother's pleasure. The smile on her face whenever I played my grandfather's old acoustic was etched into my mind like someone tattooed it onto my neurons.

"Guitar," I said.

"That's perfect," she said, drafting an entire novel's worth of words into her notepad, it seemed. Keeping her eyes glued to her paper, she continued: "I'll put in an order for a guitar through the prison system. I'll tell them it's for therapeutic purposes, obviously. You won't have to worry about storage for it; it'll be in my possession for safety reasons, as you're aware."

I nodded tiredly. All I wanted was sleep, not the blinding fluorescents hanging above. But if this were the way I could cut my session short for the day, by God, I would do whatever it took. Even if that meant agreeing to everything the psychologist said, as much as I hated the idea. Let her collect money from the state and be on her way.

There were private rooms in the bar. Past the counter and down the hallway, locked doors lined the walls, hiding people behind their deadbolts. Reggie walked down the corridor, tripping on air in his stupor.

"Where are you going?" I asked.

"I need to piss," he slurred, wrestling at a doorknob that wouldn't budge.

"Don't think they have toilets in these rooms, Reg."

"I know that," he said, not knowing that.

He jangled more doorknobs until he felt one click under his grasp. Reggie's face lit up, anticipating the emptying of his bladder just beyond that door. I reached a hand to his shoulder and let it rest there. I said, "That's not a restroom, man. Why don't I show you where they are?"

Reggie swatted at my hand like it was a horsefly.

"No," he demanded.

He turned the knob and let himself in.

I stood back, refusing to be a part of the embarrassment ensuing before me. Someone had to be in there. Maybe two drunk lovers getting frisky in their stupors. Belts unbuckled; bras unlatched. Regardless, I let him make that blunder. Because, if nothing else, people only learn from their mistakes, right?

But I heard something all too familiar waft from the sweaty room as Reggie stepped inside. Dim lamplight engulfed Reggie as I heard my wife scream from inside the room.

I walked over from my leaning point on the wall across the hall and shuffled to the room's doorframe, both hands gripping either side. The air was damp with perspiration, thick with the scent of sex and lavender perfume. Sat on a desk chair was Joanne. On top of her was a man I'd never seen, his member straight as an arrow over the pile of clothing adorning the floor. He wore her lipgloss in more areas than just his lips.

"Bill," Joanne pleaded, covering her bare breasts with a stray T-shirt. "This... this isn't what it... I'm so sorry."

I couldn't say anything. The words simply refused to come out. Shock would've been an understatement, but that shock turned to terror as Reggie stomped toward the mystery man and planted a fist into his nose. I heard the crunch of bone against cartilage. The man plummeted to the ground, yelping and cradling his broken nose in his hands. He kicked his feet like a child throwing a tantrum.

"Reg," I managed to say.

The name hung in the air with uncertainty. I was frozen in time, unable to stop the hands of fate. *Why was she here? Who's watching the kids? Who is this man? Why is she here? Why is she here? Why—*

Reggie raised his knee and planted his shoe into the man's skull. A crack echoed through the small space. He stomped once more, and again... again. The cracking ceased and morphed into pained gurgles. Reggie breathed heavily from all the effort. A night's worth of drinks bubbled in his stomach. His skin grew pale but went straight to a bright pink as he focused on Joanne.

"Why'd you... you make me do this?" he asked her, tripping over his words.

"What?" she responded, her voice wavering with tears.

"You wanted to hurt him," he said. "You wanted to hurt my brother!"

My eyes widened. I rushed at Reggie as he grabbed my wife by her hair. She screamed and fought against his grasp. I wrapped my arms around his waist from behind, tugging at him with all my strength.

"Reggie! STOP!" I yelled.

He responded with an elbow to my eye. I clutched at the throbbing socket and fell backward into the far wall. Joanne shrieked with enough force to shatter glass. Then, the shouts stopped. The world stopped. Reggie lifted her head from the desk and slammed it down again.

Crunch. Crunch... crunch.

I could hear my heartbeat in my chest. The room was so silent you could hear a feather drop to the floor. I glimpsed a look at the mystery man's face—what was left of it—only to taste my dinner from hours before.

I heaved over the old carpet until everything was out, and when I finally looked up, the bouncer stood in the doorway, mouth agape.

A tear with the weight of a thousand suns fell from my eye.

Infinite sorrow in that small amount of water.

I could hardly see the guitar strings through the mist of tears pooling in my ducts. No distinction between where one wire ended and the next began. My left hand caressed the guitar's neck, my right hovering over the sound hole. I blinked moisture from my eyes, and the room came into focus, the psychologist staring with interest from across the table.

She had brought her own guitar, a brilliantly shining acoustic painted baby blue with wildflowers dotting the sheen. "How're you holding up, Bill?" she asked with a mother's soothing voice. "Getting that guitar in here took a lot more paperwork than I intended. How's your week been? Any developments?"

"No," I coughed.

"None at all?"

"Nothing comes to mind."

I expected a disappointed grunt from her but got a C major chord from her guitar instead. Her fingers graced the fret delicately, the chord vibrating through the room and echoing off the cinderblock walls.

"What do you remember?" she asked.

"What do you mean?"

"On the guitar. Do you remember any songs from your childhood? From sometime more recently. Before all this?"

"If you're asking if I know *Wonderwall*, I'm way ahead of you."

She chuckled, stifling the laugh with the sleeve of her sweater.

"If *Wonderwall* is all you know," she said, gesturing to my guitar, "be my guest."

The hint of a smirk brushed my face. I squandered it immediately and checked my fingering. *What chord does it start with?* My back straightened. I searched my memory for the last time I touched a guitar. No, not during my undergrad. It had been during my first summer out of school. We were at the local park, my mother and me. Her pale head adorned with a baseball cap for a team she didn't even know. My fingers searching for the next tune. We sat under the shade of an oak tree, resting upon a picnic blanket as birds chirped and children played. I hadn't played *Wonderwall* that day. I'd played a Queen song, one from their earlier repertoire. *Love of My Life*, it was. That was her favorite. I'd forgotten that. But truly, everything I played was her favorite, as long as I was the one strumming the guitar.

"Play it again," she had said, her voice raspy from the chemo.

"But my *poor* fingers, Mom," I whined sarcastically.

"Could be your last time."

That morbid joke hung in the air like a thick fog on that humid summer day. I didn't know whether to laugh or cry. The tears were stuck in my sockets, but a laugh bubbled in my throat all the same. But there were no tears with my mother. Every day spent with her was a day filled to the brim with joy. She slapped my knee with her frail, withered hand and chuckled, bellowing to the soft breeze.

Between laughs, I strummed the guitar and plucked the beginning of that Queen tune once more, my mother watching with nothing but love in her eyes.

I blinked and was back in the holding room, sitting across the table from the psychologist. My fingertips hummed with that distinct feeling one gets after plucking strings. That subtle vibration that rattles the skin.

"What was that?" the psychologist asked, intrigued.

My cheeks grew hot and red. "It was nothing," I said, my eyes refusing to meet hers.

"It was a good start... not *Wonderwall*, obviously. But anything is a good starting point. Would you mind continuing?"

"I would."

She frowned. "What did that song mean to you?"

"Pardon?"

"The one you just played."

"I told you it was nothing."

"Bill," she said, shifting forward in her seat. "I'm here to help you. If you don't want the help, that's fine. I can leave. But if you do, you *need* to cooperate with the program. We aren't done with day one of your music therapy and you're refusing the treatment. What else do—"

Her voice rose until it abruptly stopped. *What else do you have left?* she would've asked. It was a valid question; even my prisoner's angst couldn't deny that. My mother was gone, my brother was gone, my wife was gone, my children would never see me again. What did I *truly* have left? A life spent in these walls, watching paint dry as a form of rehabilitation? A life spent without a true sense of quiet. With how overcrowded this prison was nowadays, where could one truly find peace?

The day after Reggie was sentenced to life for the second-degree murder of my wife and her one-night stand, I was on trial as an accomplice in their deaths.

The man she cheated on me with was the son of a wealthy donor to the city's football stadium, I later found out. A child of nepotism sucking on the tit of one of the city's most esteemed businessmen. He had more money than I could ever dream of, and he used it to sway the court in his favor from beyond the grave. My lawyer assured me I would only face up to twenty years in prison, if even that. But more evidence came to light; evidence that I—and I alone—knew was fabricated.

What is someone supposed to do in such a situation? I hadn't had a drop of liquor that night. It was Reggie's birthday, and he wanted to spend it with me. Just me. And I wanted to enjoy it with a clear mind free from an alcoholic haze. This was my reward? I was too able-bodied to *not* be an accomplice, it seemed.

I rose from my seat in the courtroom, my hands shackled together. I listened to the judge lay down the verdict. "Life" was the only word I could hear. Nothing else mattered. As guards escorted me from the courtroom, I caught one final glimpse of my children. A son and a daughter. My little girl who had my eyes, and my little boy who had his mother's. Before I left the building, I watched their aunt pull them from their seats and out the adjacent doors.

I wasn't allowed visitation from them until they were legal adults.

They would forget me before then.

Weeks passed. Every few days, I would be forced from my cot and led to the holding room where the psychologist greeted me. The same, "Hello, Bill," each time. The same inflection, the same tone, unwavering in its delivery. Her guitar would be as shiny and bright as ever, and my prison-sanctioned instrument would always be propped against the table.

"Welcome back," she added today.

"Hello," I said.

"How're you holding up?"

"You know," I said, surprised with how much I pondered the question, "I've been doing pretty well."

"Fantastic, Bill. I'm glad to hear it."

Her smile lit the room with the light of a thousand candles. I still saw my wife in that smile, but it was different nowadays. I didn't find myself swallowed by grief, but bathed in joy. The joy of Joanne's memory. Her smiling face in that bed of wildflowers, soothing my heart as I stroked the hair on my daughter's head.

"Is it hard for you to live?"

"Hard?" I asked.

"I asked you the first time we met. Before the music and the healing. Do you feel that it's hard to live?"

I contemplated her words, letting them simmer in my mind. I thought of the steel bars and cinderblock lining my cell. About the guards who didn't care if I lived or died. About my brother who couldn't bear the weight of all this. About my mother who lost her battle when I needed her most. About my wife—who I still loved—who slept with another man. About my children who'd never see me again. About the sun, the stars, the wildflowers blooming in a meadow not far from here.

I sat the guitar on my lap and strummed a note instead, then another, and another.

I lived.

Section title font set to **Rexor Pro** in accordance with FG Studios' licensing guidelines

9 798990 262522